beautiful thorns

BOYS OF BELLEROSE
BOOK 4

JAYMIN EVE

TATE JAMES

Tate James

Jaymin Eve

Beautiful Thorns: Boys Of Bellerose #4
Copyright © Tate James, Jaymin Eve 2023
All rights reserved
First published in 2023
James, Tate
Eve, Jaymin
Beautiful Thorns: Boys of Bellerose #4

Cover design: Emily Wittig
Editing: Jax Garren (line).

For those who can't sing except in the bedroom. That's all you need to bag a rockstar. Or four.

follow us

For book discussions, giveaways, and general shit talking from Tate or Jaymin, please check out their reader groups on Facebook:

Tate James – The Fox Hole
    Jaymin Eve – The Nerd Herd

content warning

Boys of Bellerose is a rock star mafia reverse harem story where the female main character finds her happily ever after with more than one lover. It's a four book series, so cliffhangers should be expected throughout, until they find their happy ending.

This series touches on darker themes and includes both graphic sex and graphic violence.

Some characters have traumatic pasts, and there is mention of miscarriage, drug use, addiction, and murder. Should you have concerns, please apply discretion in deciding if this story is right for you.

- Tate & Jaymin

one

BILLIE

In the moments after shots rang out, and before I could even see who had fired those shots—or if anyone had been hit—Angelo threw himself on top of me, completely covering my body with his own. As I went down under his bulk, my pulse raced to epic levels, and my damn life flashed before my eyes. The fucking cliche of that happening, when I've always thought it was a bullshit line used in books, was infuriating.

Maybe it was that I'd just hallucinated my dead father that brought everything to the forefront—these brief and random glimpses of my life.

Like the first day I met Jace, both of us scrawny, missing teeth, and with more attitude than any fucking child should have. He called me a brat and I called him a butthole and we were soon best frenemies, hanging out and happy one minute, fighting and name-calling the next.

The toxicity of our relationship would be disturbing, if part of me didn't absolutely live for that shit. I couldn't lose him. I couldn't lose us. Not when we were almost back to the happy again.

And then the next memory was the day I met Angelo. My Angel. The next boy to come into my life and turn it on its fucking head. Our first meeting had been similar to mine and Jace's, on the top of the hill where we'd all lived. But we hadn't really talked until our second meeting. That was at the local playground, one of the few times I'd gone there without Jace, and these two bullies were chasing me around trying to push my face into the dirt. My mom had been busy on her phone, not looking in my direction, and I'd been doing a pretty good job evading the assholes, when Angelo stepped out of what felt like thin air and pummeled them both.

He'd been my savior from day one, and even now, in what might be our last moments, he was throwing himself in between danger and me. I couldn't lose him. I couldn't lose my guardian angel when I'd only just gotten him back.

As the shots faded briefly, I heard Grayson's roar, the

sort of roar that spelled out a complete loss of control, and it shook me to my core. Was he okay? My silent, strong, protective Gray.

He was the one who stood in the shadows so the rest of us could exist in the sun, and in truth, I wanted to live in those shadows with him. At least some of the time. The rest of the time I'd pull him into the sun with us because he was equal parts light and dark.

He'd come into my life at a time when I'd had nothing, and now he meant everything. I couldn't lose him. Not when we were repairing our bond and building a stronger foundation.

Or was his roar about Rhett? My knight. My savior. There was no way I could imagine living in a world without his selflessness. Without his kind heart and wicked sense of humor.

I couldn't lose him either.

I couldn't lose any of them and survive with my soul intact.

It was fucking ridiculous that any one woman could have four true loves. Four men that filled her metaphorical life-well with love and music and laughter, but here the fuck I was.

On top of the world.

About to lose it all.

My breathing grew shallower as I remained

motionless under Angelo. My brain was screaming at me to push him off, get up, do fucking something to ensure that my life wasn't over now. But I couldn't make myself move. I was frozen in fear. Not knowing what had happened was scarier than guns pointed in my face as men attempted to kidnap me and cut my head off.

Even worse... was that truly my father out there in the mask? Or did the high-tension situation have me imagining things?

Something to discuss with Dr. Candace. That was if we survived this day, of course.

Angelo's weight was yanked off me quickly, too fast for him to have moved, and that was the moment adrenaline finally did its fucking job and kicked in. The hazy memories of the past faded, and once again I was reacting like someone in the middle of a dangerous situation. Jumping to my feet, I took in the scene.

Holy fuck. The scene was... a lot.

Firstly, Vee was in the room.

She was the first person I saw, dressed all in black, brandishing a gun, and looking all sexy rebel. *Bitch.* The fact that I didn't immediately know if she was on our side or against us cemented how deep the trust damage was between us. If she was on our side, she was going to have a hell of a time explaining her fucking part in all of this.

Because without Vee's betrayal, we wouldn't be in this position right now. Double-crossing bitch.

And if any of my boys were hurt, she would be dead to me. No matter what she said.

There was no evidence of where the earlier shots had come from, and I wondered if maybe it had been Vee on her way in to distract the assholes in the room. To my relief, it looked like everyone was alive at this moment and fighting with various black-clad individuals. The man who'd looked so eerily like my father wasn't in my immediate vision, so I focused on my boys.

Grayson threw punches, still letting out a grunting roar every now and then, his face carved from stone. He never looked around or broke eye contact, and I would say he was a man with a mission as he took down the first gunman and then the second almost as fast. Beside him, Rhett was swinging a guitar case around quite successfully, though he did almost take out Jace, who had chosen to go the same route as Gray and use his fists as weapons.

There was too much close-contact fighting for weapons to come out, but as more of Vee's people poured into the room—at least I hoped they were hers and she was on our side, since she was waving them on—those who'd attacked us earlier started to figure out they were in trouble.

That was when the familiar man reappeared in the corner of my vision—I refused to believe my own delusions that it was my father—carrying Angel over his fucking shoulder. He held a gun and crept along the edge of the room. I had no idea how he'd managed to take down that six-foot-four beast of a man, but I would guess some sort of sedative or stun gun, since Angel was completely motionless.

He couldn't be dead, though. Right?

You wouldn't carry a dead body... unless you needed evidence.

That surge of adrenaline shot higher, followed by panic, and I raced toward the same exit the man was heading for, even as Vee started screaming behind me to stop. "Wait!" I snarled at the man, ignoring Vee completely. He paused as he looked back over his shoulder at me, and I stumbled to a halt with my hands raised. "Is he dead? Did you kill him?"

He pointed the gun straight at me and smiled, and unless my father had a damn twin, a dead man was standing here in this room.

"My little Billie Jean. No words for your dad? Just worry for this punk-ass bastard?"

That voice, so fucking familiar, almost sent me to my knees. The shock... the shock was near debilitating as my brain tried to comprehend that the father I'd thought was dead for nine years was standing here before me.

Apparently alive and well *and a fucking gangster*.

"What did you do to Angelo?" I snapped back, finally finding my voice. "Let him go. Please. For me."

What a stupid line. This man had faked his death and disappeared for nearly half my life. He clearly didn't give a single fuck about me.

"Sorry, kid. I need to make a point to Giovanni, and what better way to do it than with his prized son and heir. After what this bastard did to you, this is the least he deserves."

What he did to me? My father had to be referring to when Angel had left me and married Vee, which meant he'd been keeping an eye on things even from his *grave*.

"Billie!" Vee screamed again, and this time she was close enough that my ears hurt. She reached me in the next moment, and in the split second where I turned to see if she was about to shoot me in the back, my bastard back-from-the-dead father scurried out the door.

"No!"

Sprinting toward the door he'd just exited through, I burst out into the night, only to find a dozen or more men surrounding my father, guns pointed in my direction.

Vee yanked me back into the room, just as shots rang

out once more, and there was no way the cops wouldn't show up sooner or later.

"Let me the fuck go," I screamed as I swung a fist and clipped the side of her face. "Don't fucking touch me, you traitorous bitch."

She backed up a pace, gun still in her hand but pointing toward the ground. Her other hand was pressed to her cheek where a red mark was already forming. "Nice hit, Billie," she said, not sounding mad at all. "But if you go after Wilson, you'll be dead faster than you can scream out Angelo's name. He won't kill him yet. This is a major power play against the Riccis. And there's a reason for everything he does. But... we have time to save him."

The way my brain was swirling made me sick.

"Wilson?" I echoed, dumbfounded.

But there was no chance for her to reply because Grayson upended an entire glass table behind us, smashing it over the bodies of the remaining assholes who had been in here earlier. Vee looked over her shoulder, a pleased smile entering her face when she saw it was only her people left.

"That went better than I'd hoped," she said quickly. "No deaths on our side. Exactly as planned."

The need to smack her in the face once more rode me so hard that I actually had my fist clenched, and it was moving before I managed to stop myself. She'd let me have the first one, but the second might get me shot.

"Angelo got kidnapped," I sharply reminded her. "Fucking. Kidnapped." *You insane bitch.*

"Not the first time and won't be the last," she shot back. "They'll probably keep him here in Europe for a bit until the heat dies off, and then he'll be transported to America to use in this fucking insane war with Giovanni. We'll find him before they can do too much damage."

There was a cold, calculating streak in Vee that, in all fairness, she'd never really hidden, but she also hadn't exactly advertised it. I should have seen it though, especially when Angel told us that Vee was his choice to take control from Giovanni. He wouldn't have suggested someone who wasn't capable of the job.

"Thorn," Rhett rasped, reaching me in a sweaty mess. Some blood was sprinkled across his face, but otherwise he looked uninjured as he threw his arms around me. "You're okay."

Physically, yes. Mentally... so fucking fucked up.

"Are you okay?" I managed to choke out as he wrapped me up in his familiar hug. "Not hurt?"

"Totally fine," he reassured me, before pulling away to press a kiss to my lips. I was still too shocked to even kiss him back. "Billie?"

Blinking rapidly, as if that would help clear the fog in

my head, I whispered, "He took him." I cleared my throat and tried again louder. "He took him."

"Who?" This came from Jace, who had reached us now. Grayson was right behind him. The three of them crowded around me, blocking Vee completely from sight. "Who took who?"

I was trembling. I hadn't even realized until this second, as the adrenaline wore off and the pain crashed, that my entire body shook. "My father. Back from the dead. And he just *took* Angel. He plans to use him to destroy Giovanni."

Grayson rumbled and then took off through the same door I'd used, but it was too late. They were long gone now, all those men and guns and the damn father I'd lost.

Along with the love of my life.

Well, one of four. But that didn't mean I could spare any of them.

We had to get Angelo back, no matter the consequences.

BILLIE

Rhett led me over to the couch, careful of the broken glass and furniture that littered the floor. He was taking such painstaking effort to keep me safe that it eased some of the swirling panic that had been holding me in a near incoherent state.

Jace had followed Grayson and so had Vee, with the rest of her people, and so it was just me and Rhett in the awkward silence.

"Thorn, love, you're starting to scare me."

That knocked more shock from me, oddly, and I managed to suck in a deep breath and turn to face him, to see him clearly, without the fuzziness of vision that I'd been experiencing. To my surprise, some relief crossed his face before I even said anything. "You were nearly hyperventilating," he said softly in explanation. "Your breaths are short and rapid, and I wasn't sure if you were going to pass out or not."

That might explain the fuzziness.

Thankfully, a few more deep breaths added clarity that had been missing a few seconds ago. Clarity and anger.

"Gray and Jace?" I said shortly. "Can we check on them?"

I was pushing up from the couch as I spoke, but it turned out there was no need so sat my butt back down. They were literally walking through the door, safe and uninjured. From what I could see anyway. Everyone was a little beat up and spattered in blood from the fight, but I couldn't detect any life-threatening injuries.

"Prickles," Grayson murmured as he reached the couch. He dropped to his knees before me, uncaring of the debris on the floor, and wrapped his arms around me. "You're okay."

"He lost it when he couldn't see you," Jace said drily. I couldn't see Bellerose's lead singer around Grayson's broad shoulders, but I already knew the expression he'd be wearing: a little smirk but with dead eyes, the kind that hid everything he felt deep down.

"We all lost it," Rhett replied huskily. "They were

trying to take *our Bellerose.* Our little Thorn. Those motherfuckers."

Grayson was still holding me like his life depended on it, and no lie, it was one of the nicest hugs I'd had in a really long time. Full-bodied, holding all the parts of me together. Another sliver of calm followed, and when he pulled away just as Jace dropped down next to me on the couch, I was able to think and breathe almost like normal.

This was also when Vee returned to the room, by herself this time, her weapon out of sight. My glare was joined by three others as she strolled nonchalantly across to us. This fucking bitch had some lady balls on her. Guess you needed them to survive in the male-driven mafia world.

Which was all well and good until she used them against us.

Grayson was on his feet in the next second, and he towered over the couch as he stood protectively between us and Vee. "You have two fucking seconds to explain before I break your neck."

The words weren't shouted like I would have done. Outside of the curse, his tone was akin to having a perfectly pleasant conversation with his grandmother, while threatening to take her life.

"I will explain everything, I promise," Vee said

immediately, and I peeked around Gray to see she was holding both hands up in front of her. "The rest of my people have taken up security around the perimeter, so we're safe to chat for a few minutes and come up with a plan."

"To save Angel, I fucking hope," I snarled, my emotions unable to be hidden as well as Gray hid his.

"Of course," she replied smoothly. "But as I said, we have time. I already have people looking out for his new location, and we'll go from there."

Grayson grunted. "And why should we trust you or your *people?* You set us up. You allowed them to get close to Billie, and that's unforgivable."

Vee's expression fell. "I admit that part took me by surprise. Obviously. I had no idea they were going to try and curry favor with me by attacking Billie. The second I caught word of that, I was here with as many of my people as I could gather in a short time. We set off all those shots on our way in to distract and buy time. I figured you all could work it out for a few minutes until we made it inside."

So it had been Vee shooting up as a distraction. It was a good plan, unless we'd all been killed in those few minutes. "You take too many risks with other people's lives," Rhett said softly, clearly thinking the same as me. "We aren't pawns on the board for you to play with and sacrifice as needed. That's not how a fucking friendship works. You let us think we were friends, Vee."

Some of her bravado fell, and she rubbed a hand across her eyes as weariness descended briefly over her features. "You know... fuck. I'm sorry. I'm really fucking sorry. I've been in this world of cutthroat bastards for too long I honestly forgot how to have friends and not just alliances. But I swear to you all, I never intended for any harm to touch you guys."

"You took the drugs to build up money and resources to take down your father?" I asked, and she nodded briefly.

"Yes. Everything I have is tied to the Altissimos. Angelo's money and resources are tied to the Riccis. We need our own cash and weapons to make a true play for the crown. We need our own people behind us, and what better way than a gang that's already established and powerful in a country that's not controlled by either one of our families."

I should have seen this coming, really. She'd all but told me back at the concert venue when she was so proud of this gang controlled by a woman, a structure that she admired and aspired to. It was the perfect setup for Valentina Altissimo.

"What happened to the woman who was running the gang in Berlin?" I asked shortly.

Her smile grew. "Giana."

I just stared at her before shaking my head. "So much for wanting her *out* of the gang world, safe and sound as a fucking accountant or whatever."

Accountant. Fuck, the irony of that considering what happened to my mother. I really needed to think of another "boring" job to use in these situations.

Vee's expression grew more somber. "In all honesty, if G had asked me my thoughts on it, I would have told her to run kicking and screaming away from this world. I never wanted that for her, not even for a second. But my love is a stubborn, amazing, incredibly intelligent woman. When she returned here for safety, she decided on her own that if we were to stay together and have a true future, she had to step into the darker side of life. She's apparently been finding her feet in this gang ever since, helped along by the ties she already had to them through her cousins." She shrugged. "When I went to see her, I almost fell over at how strong and fucking badass she's grown to be. My fears were holding her back, and now... we're true partners. In crime and life. And we're in a fucking excellent position to take down the assholes who have controlled and hurt and ruined us more times than I can mention."

God, it was actually poetic for her to team up with the girlfriend she was forbidden from being with in a Bonnie and Clyde takedown of her family. If I didn't want to punch her face in right now, I'd be hugging her.

"This is why you wanted to come on this tour so badly," Jace finally spoke up. "To get to Giana."

Vee shrugged again. "Yeah, not going to lie, I was hoping to see her. But mostly, it was to get away from my family long enough to come up with a plan. Then a fucking plan fell into my lap, and if that wasn't a manifestation of my goals in life, I don't know what would be."

Definitely convenient, if it weren't for one tiny little factor. "Where is my father taking Angelo?"

Angelo was still kidnapped, and we were sitting around calm as anything.

"Multiple vehicles took off from here," Grayson said, relaxing his protective stance as he moved from between us, and I could stop craning my neck to see around him. "Whoever took Angelo had plenty of resources behind him to ensure that this snatch was successful." He sat on one of the remaining couches, Vee took the final one, and all of us eyed her.

It was a tense situation, made even worse by the missing Ricci.

"It was my fucking father," I said for what felt like the twentieth time, feeling sick to my stomach. No one had acknowledged the madness of that yet. Like, did they all think I'd had a psychotic episode? Turning in my chair, I gesture to Jace. "Did you see him? He had Angel over his damn shoulder."

"How could it be your father?" Vee answered before Jace could. "He died nine years ago, right?"

"I thought he did," I shot back. "But it was dark and smoky, and I just saw two bodies. Maybe I just assumed it was my father? Maybe my memories are more messed up than I realized."

"There would be forensics," Rhett reminded me gently. "They would have identified the victims with more than just who they assumed was in the house."

"That can be faked though," Grayson said suddenly, reminding all of us that he was just as involved in the underworld. "Someone completed that hit before me, and that shouldn't have happened. Maybe Billie's father had something to do with that."

The ass dropped out of my world with that one statement.

Grayson had all but said that my father'd arranged to have my mother killed, but that couldn't be true, right?

But... how would he know to fake his own death unless he knew she was going to be killed?

Fuck. I couldn't think of that right now.

"We have a big problem, guys," Vee said suddenly, and I didn't like the way she was laser focused on me.

"You mean outside of you being a double-crossing snake whose actions and lies got us all nearly shot and Angelo kidnapped?" Jace replied conversationally.

Vee just nodded. "Yes, outside of that. If Billie is sure that the man who took A is her father, then we're in more than a bit of trouble here."

"How so?" Gray growled, clearly done with Vee today.

Vee cleared her throat, shooting me what looked like an apologetic stare. Not that it mattered; I knew what she was about to say. I hadn't forgotten from before.

"That guy who took Angelo is *Wilson*." There was an extended pause, so Vee continued, "*The* Wilson. The one who started the Wilson cartel and has been making unprecedented moves across the underworld for the past near decade. The Wilsons aren't a family like the Riccis; it's an organization run *by* Wilson. That man who took Angelo."

This got their attention, especially Gray, who shifted forward in his seat with a muttered curse. All I could think about was the timing, though.

Nearly a decade. My father had been out there building an army of criminals for a decade.

Basically, since the fire that let him fake his own death. The same one that covered up my mom's murder and killed my unborn baby. Or maybe even longer?

My father, back from the dead, was the enemy we

suspected to be involved in much of the carnage littering our lives lately.

He'd been closer than we realized the entire time.

And now he had my Angel.

Fucking hell.

JACE

Billie was in shock. Her complexion had paled to a worrying shade of gray, and her hands trembled despite how tight she held onto Rhett's fingers. But otherwise, she was handling this truth bomb of epic proportions admirably. Better than I feel like I would have, in her shoes.

Hell, even I was struggling to swallow the information. The Wilsons weren't a family at all; they were a gang run by _Wilson_. Billie's dad wasn't named Wilson; that would have surely sparked some kind of recognition from Billie, Angelo, or even me. His name was —is—Bruce Bellerose, but I guessed "Bruce" died in that fire nearly nine years ago. He couldn't very well continue using a dead man's name, so he must have created a new identity.

"The Wilsons were around before Billie's parents died, though," Grayson said, his concerned gaze on Billie. My Rose. His Prickles. She didn't deserve this twist.

Vee shrugged. "I don't have an answer for that; I just know *that man* is Wilson himself. He's met with my parents on several occasions, and they introduced him as such."

Billie made a choked sound like she was trying to laugh but couldn't find the humor. "So he was planning this *before* everything happened? Didn't we suspect the hit on my mom came from the Wilsons? That she was cooking their books?"

Gray just frowned, then sighed. "I'll do some digging. My associate will know more."

Billie shook her head, her expression falling further. "And what will that cost you? Last time you did some digging, you came back covered in bruises, Gray. I don't want or need you getting hurt just for my answers."

"She's got a good point," I agreed, fighting the urge to touch Billie. To wrap her the fuck up, sheltered in my arms, as I stole her away from this damn life. "We don't need to risk your safety, Gray. Not now." I shook my head, giving him a pointed look.

He seemed to understand what I meant—that Billie was already holding on by a thread without adding the stress of injuries to the rest of us—and gave a nod.

"I'll see what I can dig up," Vee drawled, already typing on her phone. "I assume you all don't care if I get hurt in the process."

Billie jerked like she'd been slapped, squinting up at Vee in disbelief. "I care," she insisted, her voice firm if hurt. "Just because you were using us, doesn't mean *we* are shitty human beings. Like it or not, I considered you a friend, Vee; so yeah, I'll be upset if you're hurt."

Vee's hard expression softened, and she gave Billie a sad smile. "It might not seem like it right now, Billie, but I *am* your friend. I just show it a little differently."

Billie sank back in her seat, looking exhausted, so I stood to usher Vee out of the room. "You need to leave," I told Angelo's wife quietly. "I know you want to help; I believe you when you say you care about her. But right now she needs to process."

Vee scowled like she wanted to argue, but she was also smart enough to know when to push shit. Now was not one of those times. She shot another worried look over my shoulder at Billie, then sighed.

"Fine. But I'm leaving my people to ensure you're all safe for now. Local law enforcement has already been paid off, so you have some time, but I wouldn't hang around longer than necessary." She paused in the doorway to look back at me. "Jace... be kind to her. She doesn't need your head-fuckery right now."

Irritation burned in my chest, and I sneered. "Like you're one to talk."

Not waiting for her reply, I shut the door firmly in her face, then grimaced when I saw the splintered frame and busted locks. We definitely couldn't stay here. But that begged the question: Where *did* we go?

Back in the living room, Rhett held Billie in his arms, his face buried in her hair as he rocked them both gently. Grayson had a broom out and was sweeping up glass from the marble floor, pausing only to give me a questioning look.

I shrugged, then tipped my head toward the bedrooms. He understood, silently following me along to the room that would have been mine for the week.

"We need somewhere else to go," I told him, folding my arms over my chest. "This place is—"

"Obviously," he muttered. "And we need to address the tour. Call Brenda; she'll need to start working on a strategy to release us from the rest of the concerts now that we've lost Angelo."

Fuck. The tour. That hadn't even crossed my mind.

"The label will probably try to dump a random bass

guitarist on us to finish out the shows." I groaned, sitting heavily on the end of the bed, my elbows resting on my knees. "I can't believe this is even happening."

Gray sighed, then gave me a comforting pat on the shoulder. "You might be surprised. The drugs are gone, the money is gone, and Angelo is in the hands of his enemy. Giovanni might cut his losses and let us cancel. His motivation was never to make our fans happy; it was only about moving drugs. So... hopefully Brenda can figure it out. Want me to call her?"

I gave him a small grin. "No, it's fine. I'll deal with her. You work on finding us somewhere to stay tonight. And maybe for the rest of the week, too. You know Billie won't want to leave the area without Angelo. Not that I blame her."

Grayson huffed an annoyed sound. "She needs to go back to America. You all do. Now that we know how closely tied to this gang war she is..."

I knew what he was saying was true, but it didn't make it any easier to accept. "Angelo is my brother," I said quietly. "I can't just walk away like that... and neither will she. Not now." Not when we'd finally reconnected with *our* Angel.

Gray just grunted and left the room. I suspected that wasn't the last time we would discuss this topic, but I put it aside for now. My phone was still plugged into its charger beside the bed where I'd left it before the break-in, so I grabbed it to call Brenda. Thankfully, it was daytime at home, and she answered on the second ring.

"We're in shit," I told her by way of greeting.

She sucked in a sharp breath, and I could imagine the curses rolling through her mind. "Okay. Police trouble, media trouble, or worse?"

"Worse." Although I imagined this could fall under both police and media trouble too. "Dead bodies and bullet-ridden house kind of worse. And they took Angelo hostage."

Brenda clicked her tongue. "Where's Hannah?"

That startled me. Where *was* Hannah? Had she been involved in the break-in? She'd checked all our security requirements before we arrived, but then I guessed perimeter alarms didn't mean shit once someone had kicked in the front door.

"I have no clue," I replied honestly. "She left us here earlier this afternoon; we haven't seen her since."

"Give me a minute; I'll call you back." Brenda ended the call without waiting for my reply, leaving me sitting there with a silent phone in hand. While I waited for her to return my call, I left the bedroom and went looking for the video surveillance unit. Maybe it'd give us some clues about where they were taking Angelo.

Unsurprisingly, Grayson had already found the control unit near the foyer and was scrolling through the footage.

"Find anything?" I asked when he glanced up.

"License plates," he replied, pausing the video feed from the front gates. "I've already sent them through to my contact here, but Vee might have better connections."

My phone buzzed in my hand, and I accepted Brenda's call.

"She's not answering her phone," Brenda told me in a terse voice. "What time did you say she left the house?"

I frowned, thinking. "Uh, maybe two? Thereabouts. She left after the leasing agent."

"Where is your security team?" she asked, and now I felt really fucking dumb.

"Uh... I don't know." Then an uncomfortable feeling washed over me. "Gray, scroll back to when we arrived this afternoon."

Grayson did as I asked without question, finding the moment we'd all arrived on site, and we watched the black-and-white image without sound. Brenda waited, silent on the line, as we fast forwarded through our entry and then slowed back to real time when the agent left. Switching to the street side camera, we watched as Hannah and the agent woman chatted for a while, then the agent hopped in her car and drove away. Hannah answered a call, then started to walk toward the waiting town car.

Then she got shot in the head by a man with a suppressed pistol and dragged into the bushes.

The driver of the car leapt out, gun in hand, but was shot in the head by a second, unseen, assailant.

"Shit," I breathed. "Hannah's dead. Do whatever you need to do, Brenda, but we will not be continuing the tour. I don't care who sues us over it; we're fucking done with this game."

"You and me both, kid," she replied in a tired voice. "Tell me about Angelo. What's going on? Who took him?"

I rubbed my eyes, feeling the weight of all the violence and tension sitting across my shoulders. Angelo and I had been through so much; this couldn't be how it ended. I couldn't accept that. "We're working on tracking him down, Brenda," I said instead of answering her questions. "Just deal with Big Noise, and we'll keep you posted on where we end up."

She sighed. "I don't like it, but I get it. Plausible deniability. What do I tell the label?"

Grayson and I exchanged a look, and he shrugged.

"Tell them the truth," I said back. "That Angelo was kidnapped by armed assailants and the rest of Bellerose are deeply shaken by the attack. That we request patience and privacy as we work through our trauma. The fans can't argue with that, and neither can the label. Not after everything."

"I agree," Brenda said in a sad voice. "Do you need me to find you somewhere else to stay?"

I dragged my lower lip through my teeth, thinking, then glanced into the living room where Billie still sat in Rhett's lap as he stroked her hair lovingly. "No, we can work it out," I decided. "The fewer people who know, at this point, the better."

"Good. Stick with Grayson; he'll keep the rest of you alive. Good luck, kid." Again, she ended the call without a goodbye, but that was standard Brenda, always too busy for pleasantries.

Slipping my phone back into my pocket, I grimaced at the video screen, then ran a hand over my hair. "So, what now?"

He turned off the monitor and faced me with a blank expression. "Now, we pack our shit and get out of here. I've booked us suites at the Plaza Royal for tonight under aliases; we can figure out a plan in the morning."

I frowned, sensing something... off about his phrasing. "A plan to find Angelo?"

Grayson shrugged. "Sure. To start with. Then I think we start talking about the bigger picture—how to extract us out of this violent conflict. All of us. Ricci included. He's one of us now."

Damn right, he was. I should have known it'd be Billie who brought us back together. We were all hers now, the boys of Bellerose indeed.

four

BILLIE

R elocating from the messed-up house to a ritzy hotel in the middle of Monaco was a whirlwind of activity. Money got exchanged with every handshake, and by ten at night we were secured into the sub-penthouse of the Plaza Royal hotel —the kind of suite that came with its own indoor pool overlooking the water.

I tried to pull myself together enough to ask what the *hell* we were doing about Angelo, but ultimately, we were all too wiped out to get far. I hit the pillow hard, falling into a deep, blissfully dreamless sleep, and woke up the next morning feeling like I'd been hit by a truck. Bruises darkened my left side, adding to the myriad burns and scars I already bore from this life, and I winced as I toweled myself dry after a shower.

"How'd that happen?" Rhett asked with concern, tugging off his boxers to get into the shower himself.

I grimaced. "Angelo dove on top of me. This must be where I hit the floor."

Rhett nodded his understanding, leaving the shower door open while he started to rinse. "Thank fuck for his quick thinking."

"Agreed," I murmured with a sigh. "I'll take bruises over bullet holes any day." I bit my lip, worry curling through me once more. I met Rhett's eyes in the mirror, knowing he saw right through me. "Do you think he's okay? *Wilson* wouldn't hurt him too much, would he? Like... surely, if he wants to bargain with Giovanni, he needs to keep Angelo in one piece. Right?"

Rhett's hesitation told me everything I needed to know. "I hope he's okay, babe. He's been growing on me."

I forced a small smile to my lips. "Like fungus?"

He grinned back. "Just like fungus. I'm sure Gray and Vee already have answers for us." He turned the shower off and accepted the towel I handed him. "It'll be okay, beautiful Thorn. I promise." His kiss on my lips was gentle and full of *love*, nearly making me cry.

"Don't make promises you can't keep, Zeppelin," I whispered with a lump in my throat.

He stroked a thumb over my cheek, his eyes on mine. "Then I'd better keep it. The last thing I'd ever want is to let you down."

From him, I believed it. We dressed and made our way out to the enormous living area, where Jace snored on the couch. There were enough bedrooms for all of us, but he'd muttered something about keeping an eye on the door before we'd all gone to bed. I guess this was what he'd meant.

Grayson sat at the window, reading something on his phone, but stood up when I approached. His strong arms swept around my body, holding me tight as I damn near strangled him with my hug.

"How did you sleep?" he rumbled, tightening his grip as he carried me over to the couch. He sat down, pulling me into his lap, and I snuggled closer.

"Heavily," I replied. "Do you have any news?"

"I do," he confirmed. "Rhett, order us room service?"

Jace snored again, and I extended my foot to nudge him. "Wake up, Adams," I said when he stirred.

He groaned, then focused sleepy eyes on me with a frown. "I had the most fucked up dream that your dad was still alive, Rose."

I cringed. "Not a dream, Jace. More like a living nightmare. He's alive, the head of a cartel, and also holding Angelo hostage. You awake now?"

Jace blinked at me, then scrubbed his hands over his face with a longer groan. "Okay. Yep. That all happened. I'm awake."

"Hungry?" Rhett asked with the hotel tablet in hand.

"Fuck no," Jace replied, sitting up. "But I'll take a pancake stack and coffee."

"Same," I added, my stomach rumbling. We never did get to eat the pasta Angelo was making last night, and now my belly was reminding me. Gray still held me in his lap, and his hand slipped beneath my shirt to stroke my skin under my ribs, sending little butterflies flapping.

Rhett finished the order, then flopped down on the armchair opposite us. "Okay, what's the news?"

"Vee's contacts did some research into Wilson," Gray said. "Or when *this* Wilson took over control. The original Wilson founded the group some twenty-odd years ago in Northern California but ran afoul of the local controlling gang and got chased out of the area. He then set up shop *very* quietly in Siena and spent several years working from the shadows to build his power base without alerting the Riccis."

Confusion rattled through my brain. "The original Wilson *wasn't* my father?"

"No. From what we can see, he worked for the original Wilson, laundering money through his mechanic business. Then around the time of the fire... things

34

changed hands." Grayson's fingers stroked across my belly in a soothing way, and I tried really hard to absorb the information with detachment, like we were talking about strangers... which we kind of were.

Rhett muttered some choice curses, looking up at the ceiling. "That makes more sense as to how he grew so powerful so fast, I guess."

"Definitely," Grayson agreed. "But we still aren't sure what his quarrel is with Giovanni. It seems more personally motivated than just market share. And then there's the question of what happened to..."

"My mom," I croaked. "Here I was, thinking she got killed for her involvement in criminal finances and my dad was collateral damage. Now I don't know what happened or who was to blame and—" I broke off with a hiccupping sob. Fuck, I needed to pull it together.

"We'll work it out, Rose," Jace said softly, reaching out to take my hand in his. It was an intensely comforting gesture from him, and I gratefully squeezed his fingers. He got it. He knew how close I'd been with my parents. Thinking of them as criminals was tearing me up inside.

"So, what now?" Rhett asked, yawning. "What happens to Angelo... and to us? The tour?"

"Canceled," Jace replied, not letting go of my hand. "I told Brenda to sort that side out. I'm fucking done playing nice with Giovanni's bullshit."

Grayson and Rhett rumbled their agreement, and a small measure of relief washed through me. At least that was one thing off our minds, not needing to keep up the pretense of having fun playing concerts without a bass player... again.

"The three of you need to return to Naples," Grayson announced, and I stiffened. He held me tighter, preventing me from climbing out of his lap in outrage, but *damn,* I was about to. "Hear me out, Prickles," he growled in my ear.

"You better have a fucking amazing reason because right now the answer is a resounding *hell no* from me, Grayson." I was already mad. Big mad. How the fuck he could think I'd be okay returning home *without Angelo,* I had no clue. Surely, he knew that was insane.

"I'm with Rose on this one," Jace agreed. It didn't escape my notice that he was calling me Rose more and more or that he still held my hand in his.

Grayson sighed in frustration. "I understand that you all think you can—" He cut off as a knock sounded at the door.

"I'll get it," I said, extracting myself from his grip. "In case you guys forgot, you're all pretty recognizable."

Rhett leapt over the couch, rushing to the door ahead of me. "I'd rather be recognized than risk you getting shot, Thorn baby." Before I could argue, he yanked the door open and let the hotel employee push a cart of food and coffee inside.

Thankfully, no one got shot and the hotel staff didn't make a fuss over the celebrities in the room. Maybe it was a regular occurrence at a place like this. Rhett unloaded the cart onto the coffee table, and Jace grabbed his coffee like an addict. Not that I was much more restrained with my pancake stack.

"Okay, back to Grayson's momentary lapse in sanity," Jace said a few minutes later. "I think we are in agreement that none of us are leaving until we find Angelo. Right?"

I nodded firmly. "Right. I won't just pack up and leave him as my father's captive, and you can't fucking make me."

Gray said nothing, just raised an eyebrow at Rhett, who'd been uncharacteristically quiet.

My blue-haired boy sensed our attention and looked up with a pained expression. "Sorry, Thorn, I'm on Grayson's side with this. It's not safe here, *especially* knowing your dad is Wilson. We can protect you better at home in Naples. Right, Gray?" His opinion was a hard punch to the gut.

The big guy nodded, then shifted his concerned gaze to me. "Prickles, I know you want to help, but surely, you can look at this objectively. You don't have the skills or connections to *actually* help, and if I'm constantly worried about your safety, am I really focused on finding and freeing Angelo?"

My eyes widened at the blunt honesty, and it felt like the air had been knocked out of me for a moment. "Wow. Seriously? I'm a *liability* now?"

Gray was immune to guilt trips. He just held my gaze steadily. "Aren't you?"

Rhett intervened before I could lose my shit. "Okay, okay, I think we're getting a bit... uh... Look, let's just start over. Thorn baby, I don't think Grayson meant you're a liability, he just means that *you* are more important to him than Angelo. So if he was forced to choose who to protect..."

Grayson nodded, unapologetic. "Because I love you, Prickles. You'll always come first, so I'm *asking* you to go back to Naples with Rhett and Jace, so I can focus on finding your mafia prince. Honestly, I'd rather send you to a remote cabin in fucking Iceland or something but I know you wouldn't go, so I'm scaling back to a reasonable request. I have security in Naples."

Fuck. When he put it like that... sure, it made sense, but every cell in my body was screaming at me not to leave. Not to turn my back on Angel. He wouldn't leave me if the roles were reversed. He didn't when I'd been taken by Giovanni's guys. He'd saved me, and now I needed to save him. Didn't I?

"Babe, it's okay to lean on us for help," Rhett said softly, coming to kneel on the carpet to take my hands in his. "You're not in this unconventional relationship alone, remember? We're all in with you, which means we're also in it with Angelo, the big, handsome dickhead. And we all have different strengths. Jace's is to keep us all grounded and humble by always having a bigger ego and more arrogance than the rest of us..."

"Hey, asshole, I do not," Jace muttered, scowling in offense.

Rhett smirked. "And Grayson happens to be a badass ex-murderer who is stupidly well-connected even after eight years out of the criminal world. He is the best person to track Angelo down, with Vee's and Giana's help, most likely. Can you trust him to do this for you? For all of us?"

I chewed my lip, really trying to accept what he was saying. "I guess your strength is being the voice of reason, huh?"

His grin turned wicked. "Thorn baby, I'm clearly here to provide competition in bed because I hold the record for giving you the most back-to-back orgasms."

"You sure?" Grayson purred, and I fought back the urge to laugh. I actually wasn't sure who held that title, but I'd let Rhett claim it for now. Until we got Angelo back.

"As for *you*, Billie Bellerose," Rhett continued, ignoring Grayson. "You're—"

"Our heart," Jace said softly, cutting him off with an intense stare in my direction. "You're the one who reminded us all what it feels like to love... and be loved. You're the sunshine creating a rainbow out of our miserable, wet day."

Well fuck. When did Jace decide to jump all in like that?

"Three days," I whispered, addressing Grayson. "Let us stay for three days while you look for Angelo. We won't leave this suite; we won't risk any danger. If you haven't found him in three days, I'll get on a plane without any resistance... but I need to have hope that you'll find him. And when you do, I want to *be here*." Even if I understood that he'd spoken the truth about me being no help whatsoever.

Grayson nodded slowly. "Three days, and you don't leave this suite. I can accept this on one condition."

"Anything," I agreed quickly.

The corner of his mouth twitched in a sly smile. "You sleep in my bed all three nights. It'll help me focus if I can smell you on my sheets whenever I return to sleep."

The heated look in his eyes told me he had other

things in mind that would help him *focus*, and I was all too willing to oblige. "Deal," I agreed.

Three days... I pinned all my hope on Grayson and Vee's ability to track Angelo down before that time was up because the idea of leaving the country without him made me feel physically sick. I'd just gotten him back; I couldn't fathom losing him for real this time.

five

BILLIE

After we finished breakfast, Grayson left. Jace disappeared to his bedroom, and a few moments later the sound of guitar music trickled out to us to say he was working on new music again. Jace's favorite distraction had always been composing... after sex, of course. But with that off the cards between us, he was going straight to the art of songwriting to deal with his feelings.

Rhett turned on a movie for us to watch, but within about twenty minutes he was fast asleep again. He seemed so peaceful, so I flicked off the TV and pulled a blanket over him so he could rest.

We'd brought all our luggage with us, so I hunted

through my suitcase for a swimsuit. The indoor pool was calling to me, and my restless energy was demanding exercise. I changed, then checked on Rhett again before opening the glass door off the living room to the narrow lap pool. Tossing my towel on one of the sun loungers, I dipped a toe in the water and smiled to find it heated.

I drew a deep breath, then dove right in. The water hugged my body as I started to swim, holding me afloat as I soared the length of the pool, then executed a sloppy tuck turn at the end to return. I used to love swimming in high school, excelling at swim meets. But then I'd become a reckless teenager in love with her two best friends and quickly lost myself in *other* physical activities in my spare time.

Up and down the pool I swam until my head stopped spinning with worst-case scenarios and my limbs ached with exhaustion. Only then did I notice the pair of men's legs dangling in the water near the stairs.

"Hey," I puffed, swiping water from my eyes as I surfaced near Jace. "How long have you been here?"

He gave me a lopsided smile. "A while. Do you feel better?"

I nodded, wordless.

"Can I join you?" he asked, gesturing to the water.

Again, I nodded, and he slid into the water with barely a splash. Graceful bastard. He swam closer to where I floated, deep enough that I couldn't touch the bottom and keep my head above water.

"I guess there're worse places to hide out for a few days," he murmured, his lashes low over his eyes as he glided through the water. He was tall enough that he could keep his feet on the ground, but I quickly ran out of energy and grasped for the edge.

He settled beside me, our elbows brushing as we looked out at the view from the pool edge. It really was a pretty place, just soured by our circumstances.

"Angel will come back to us, Rose," Jace said after a long moment of silence. His voice was soft and sincere, his gaze moving to my face as he rested his cheek on his arms. "I wouldn't even be surprised if he freed himself before Gray got there."

I gave a weak smile back. "Sounds like something he'd do," I agreed.

We lapsed back into silence for a while, then Jace nudged me with his shoulder. "What's on your mind, Billie Bellerose? Talk to me."

I knew what he was asking... not that he had no clue what I was thinking about, but which issue *specifically* was on the front of my mind right now. I wet my lips, resting my wet hair on my forearms so I could look at him properly.

"Can I, though? Talk to you, I mean. Without

sparking another fight or sending you running away to fuck me out of your head with groupies?" It was a low blow, but there were a lot of scabs on our relationship that hadn't yet healed.

Jace, to his credit, didn't flinch away from my accusation. "I don't always deal with my feelings as maturely as my bandmates," he admitted, "and when it comes to you... I fuck up more than ever. But you must know I didn't fuck anyone else that night, don't you?"

I drew a deep breath and blew it out slowly. "Yeah. I do... that time. But what about—"

"No one, not even once, not since that night at the farmhouse... Once we crossed that line, Rose, I was entirely yours. Whether you wanted me or not. Whether *I* wanted to be or not, for that matter." He gave one of those sexy half smiles that made my stomach flip. "I was an idiot for ever believing you'd stopped loving me. Back then I was so hurt, so heartbroken, and my ego was totally crushed. If I'd been older, if I'd had the years of missing you to reflect on, it'd have been so fucking obvious you were lying."

"You're right," I murmured, unable to look away from his deep blue gaze. "But I guess everything happens for a reason... somehow. We were just kids then, Jace. There's no way we could have known what we had without first losing it."

He took a few deep breaths, then hummed a sound of agreement. "You're probably right, though I wish more than anything I could turn back time and do it all differently. Even just a few months. There are so many things I wish I could take back, so many cruel comments that you didn't deserve, Rose."

I smiled, trying to lighten the emotional weight sitting between us. "And some I definitely did deserve."

He grinned back, then sobered up as he gave me a cautious look. "How are you coping with the whole... Bruce Bellerose back from the dead thing?"

I shifted in the water, raking my fingers through my wet hair as I considered his question. How *was* I coping? Not well. Or maybe better than expected? How was one supposed to react when their dad comes back from the dead as a gangster who aims a gun at their head and kidnaps their second-chance lover? Was there a rule book?

"I'm maturely choosing not to really think about it," I finally said, "except when the most annoyingly intrusive thoughts force me to. But I have some questions for Bruce Wilson. Fucker doesn't get the name Bellerose any longer. It's mine."

"Ours," Jace murmured, and I turned fully to face him, keeping just the one hand on the pool wall.

"Ours? As in yours and mine?"

46

"You are mine," he said with a shrug. "So, logically, it stands to reason that what is yours is mine."

This fucker and his logic. Logic that was a painful thud in my heart, making my body feel heated and odd. Floaty.

"I'm scared to let myself fall fully for you, Jace," I whispered. "You were my first love. The first boy to wander into my yard and heart—"

"And panties."

A snort of laughter escaped me. "Shut up, I'm trying to be fucking serious here."

His expression sobered as he moved closer so there was almost no space between us, and the heated water felt near jacuzzi temperature now. "I'm being serious too. I'm all in, Rose. All the fuck in. And I will wait as long as it takes for you to believe me. The love between us never went anywhere, but it was the trust that ended up damaged. And whatever the fuck it takes, I will rebuild the trust between us."

"How?" A choked sob of a word, but every part of me was broken and bleeding. Once again. Still, it didn't feel as fatal as usual. Maybe because I suddenly had so much hope as well.

"By never letting you down again."

He was dead serious, his eyes blazing with sincerity and truth.

"I will be there to celebrate every high in your life, Rose, and when there are lows, I will lay in the ditch with you and protect your soul and heart with my own. No grief or loss will you face alone, and if there's a chance for me to take the burden, I will do so with zero regrets. My heart is yours. My love is yours. I am yours."

This might be the reason I always fell in love with musicians. Their words are poetry, and they are filled with so much passion. When it's focused on you, you feel like you could do any fucking thing. It's just when you lose it that the world turns drab and gray.

A gray that had almost destroyed me multiple times.

"I'm not sure it's going to be as easy as that," I said, choking up. "There are some words that can't be unsaid. Some actions that remain between us, no matter how many times I try to push them aside."

Jace was silent, and I wondered if he'd just run now. Now that I'd made it a touch more difficult for him in this journey he'd started toward healing. But just because he was ready to look to the future, didn't make his recent hateful words hurt any less. Not the shit that went down nearly nine years ago, but the shit he'd said in recent months. That was what I was struggling to move past.

"You're right," he whispered. And fucking hell... I was surprised he'd so readily agreed. "I have said and done some unforgivable things to you, Rose. So along with rebuilding trust and never letting you down, I'm going to start today with something I should have said long ago. I'm sorry."

Two words. Straight to the heart like an arrow from the devil's bow.

He has a bow; it's obvious.

"I'm sorry for not fighting harder for you when we were teenagers," Jace continued, even though I hadn't said a word. I was just staring at him like my mind was temporarily out of commission. It actually kind of was.

"I'm sorry that I spent the next eight years feeling sorry for myself, and instead of growing into a strong man who was worthy of you, I ended up a pathetic mess who thrived in his pain."

As mad as I'd been at Jace over the years, and especially over the last many months together, it bothered me to hear him speak ill of himself. I barely managed to stop myself from defending the man back to himself.

"I'm sorry that when you told me about the baby, my first instinct was to fall into my own pain once more. For that, I will be eternally sorry. Blaming you, when in reality it was me I was mad at, is one of the most fucked up things I've ever done. I should have been there with you, Rose. I should have fucking protected you. And whether we would've lost our little girl anyway because that was her life path, who knows, but I should have been there. Either way, I'll never forgive myself for that. It's why I insisted on therapy because I needed to do anything I could to help you heal, to try and repair the damage I'd caused by not being there when you needed me the most."

At this point I had to interject.

"No, Jace." I shook my head roughly. "That's not yours to carry. It was my choice to lie to you. Mine. And as a result, *I* took away your chance to be there. I understand why you were so angry with me in the forest. If someone took away my choices like I did to you, I'd be mad as well. Big fucking mad. So for that, I'm sorry."

Fault lay on both sides in this fucked up set of circumstances. Both of us had a lot to make up for, and maybe... just fucking maybe, for the first time, we might finally be moving in the right direction.

Jace placed his hand against my face, the heat of his palm burning through me to join the inferno roaring in my chest. "You have always been selfless, Rose," he whispered. "Your lie was for me, and my reaction was for me. There's been too much *me* in this journey so far, and I'm ready for there to be so much more *you*."

"What about an *us*?" I choked out.

His expression softened, and there was so much

emotion in that gaze. So much *love.* My tears slipped free before I could stop them.

"There's always been an us," he told me, his thumb caressing my cheek as he wiped tears away. "And there always will be. We were a forever from the first moment we met."

Deep, painful sobs ripped from my chest as I crumbled forward. Jace wrapped me up so tightly, holding me like I was the most precious person in the world.

"The love never did go anywhere," I told him, letting myself relax against Jace. A salty chlorine scent mixed with the subtle hint of his aftershave, the familiar scent of my first love. It started to calm me, the tears finally subsiding. That had been a cleansing sort of pain, and while we weren't fixed by any means, we had started the healing process. Finally. "Our trust is damaged," I continued softly, "but I have to believe that it can be repaired. That we can find the happiness that we deserve. If there's enough love, it will be worth the fight."

I'd never truly been able to let him go, and for that reason, I was willing to give this a real shot.

His grip firmed to the point it was almost painful, but I didn't make a sound. I'd never make a fucking sound, even if he ended up breaking all my ribs. We needed this more than any other healing in the world, and when the last of the tears seeped from between my lids, I knew I wasn't the only one overwhelmed with grief and pain... and love. So much love and hope.

Jace held me like that for so long that I lost track of time, and my body started to wrinkle into a giant prune. When we eventually pulled apart, I tilted my head back to stare into his beautiful face. A face that, for once, held no anger or pain or resentment. He looked free in a way I hadn't seen in years. Young and free from the burdens of our lives.

One of his arms loosened so he could cup my face once more. "Forever, Rose. That's what I need from you."

I needed the same, but it was going to take time.

"As amazing as it is to hear you say that," I said, clearing my throat, "I'm moving forward cautiously. We have a lot of shit to sort out still, but as long as you're ready to work toward the same end goal, then we are in agreement."

Jace just stared, and I felt the need to continue on in my verbal babble. "What I'm saying is that rebuilding trust is going to take time. I have worries, fears, and reservations. All the love in the world won't change that until... I guess it does change."

I worried about pushing back against him once more, unsure of how he'd react, but all he did was smile. A real, genuine smile. "I've got the rest of my life, Rose. I've got all the fucking time." He kissed me before I could say a word, and then there were no more thoughts. Our lips moved together without the anger and lust that usually drove our kisses, and I got to truly explore his mouth— his taste, his tongue, still dominant as it claimed mine— and it brought back so many memories.

Jace had been my first in all ways. First love, kiss, sex. Angelo had been my second in all things.

In the end it made no difference. I loved them both exactly the same, but there was a poignancy in this moment. A circle of where we'd begun, where we'd been, and now back to the start again.

"I love you, Rose," Jace whispered against my mouth, and despite all the bad shit that had happened in the past twenty-four hours, I found myself smiling. This moment would be actually perfect if Angel were here.

"I love you too," I replied. "Always have, always will."

As we both knew and had agreed on, a lack of love had never been our issue.

His kiss was firmer this time, and as butterflies unfurled in my stomach, my legs moved involuntarily to wrap around his waist. Jace moved us away from the edge, the kiss deepening and the sensitivity of my body increased as his hands stroked up and down my sides.

Part of me was angry that we were making out while Angel was lost to us, hurt or worse... Yeah, not even going there. But I also knew that there was nothing I could do to help him right now. The best people for the job were searching, and he wouldn't begrudge me having this moment with Jace.

I could practically hear his voice in my head shouting out his joy. The three of us back together was such a dream it could be called a fantasy. Jace and I needed to heal so that when we had our Angel back, the three of us could find the same healing.

"Is this okay?" he whispered against my mouth, and I responded with a moan.

His chuckle was more like the old Jace, with just a hint of arrogance. "Oh yes, I know that sound very well."

The water was too deep for me to touch the ground, but he was more than capable of keeping one hand under my ass, holding me up, while the other twisted in my bikini top, shifting the cups so my tits sprang free, nipples hard and aching. Fuck, the water brushing against them was more stimulation than I could handle, so when Jace's hold on me tightened and he lifted me so his mouth could close across the right one, I almost screamed.

Letting myself go, all the worries and pain briefly faded under his mouth. His free hand continued to slide down my body, even as he sucked and scraped his teeth across my nipple. His fingers slid down the seam of my swimsuit, sliding under and brushing across my clit. My moan was louder as I jerked against him.

"My Rose," he growled. "Always so responsive."

Only with the four men who owned my heart. I'd found it difficult to ever find pleasure with any other, like my body went on strike the moment she wasn't with the ones who'd claimed her. Lucky for me there were four of them now.

Jace slid one finger and then a second inside me, and there was no resistance. I was too wet for a little pool water to slow him down. He lifted his head from my nipple to kiss me again as he leisurely thrust his fingers into my pussy, slow and sure in a constant rhythm that had me tightening my legs around him as the swirls in my belly grew stronger.

This was one of the most destructive kisses I'd ever felt, but I had the sense that from the rubble of this destruction, something beautiful could grow.

Something beautiful and real and incredible... if he kept his word and rebuilt the trust between us.

"I love you," he said between the long, drugging kisses. "I love you so fucking much, Rose."

"God," I sobbed—fucking sobbed as I fell apart under his touch. The orgasm was a slow build, but it went on for so damn long that if Jace hadn't been holding me up in the water, I'd have for sure drowned.

"God has nothing on me, baby," he said with a grin, "and I think it's time I proved that."

His fingers slid from me, and then we were naked. Somehow.

His hard length pushed slowly inside me, and it was clear that today, of all days, Jace was in no rush.

He was loving me with every part of himself, and I wondered if I would survive the overwhelming emotion of it all.

Hey, I guess there were worse ways to go than loved to death.

Especially by Jace Adams.

ANGELO

Drip. Drip. Drip. Drip. Infuriated, I shook my head just to break the monotonous rhythm of my own blood dripping into the puddle at my feet. I was hanging by my wrists from a heavy chain, and from what I could make out through one eye—the other was swollen shut—I was in some kind of warehouse. Maybe an old metal shop or something? Either way, I was long gone from Monaco.

I raised my head again, testing how tight my neck had become. *Ouch.* That mother*fucker* who'd stungunned me had a lot to pay for. I hadn't gotten a good look at him, but the asshole who'd beaten the crap out of me yesterday let slip that it was Wilson. Not *a* Wilson, but *the* Wilson. Turns out, my father had been hiding a lot from me, not the least of which being that *Wilson* was one man with an intricate network of paid employees and an axe to grind with the Ricci family.

The whole abduction, torture, imprisonment thing was not new to me. It wasn't my first rodeo and was unlikely to be my last. Sometimes it'd be rival gangs, but sometimes it was my own family... teaching me a lesson or training me to withstand duress. Either way, I wasn't worried. Not about myself, anyway. Fear for what'd happened to Billie nearly choked me, though. Was she okay? All I could remember was guns going off and diving onto Billie to get her out of the line of fire. Then someone grabbed me, and it was lights out.

Footsteps sounded outside my cell, and the heavy metal door squeaked as it opened, admitting one of my guards.

"Good morning, princess," the greasy-haired bastard with heavy fists greeted me. He was missing a tooth and sporting a swollen nose from when I'd headbutted him yesterday, and that made me smile back.

"Oh good. It's you again. I was starting to think I'd hurt your feelings." I forced some snark into my voice despite how much my body was already flinching with anticipation.

Not one to let me down, the guard sneered back, then

slammed his fist into my gut. The air knocked out of me, and I coughed, but the chains prevented me from going far. I just swung back ready to catch the next one.

"Wilson told us not to kill you," the dumb shit said between hits, "but he didn't say to keep you pretty. So long as your daddy knows it's you being executed in front of him, that's all that matters."

Well... that plan was about what I'd expected. What was surprising, though, was that *Wilson* had been the one to snatch me. Implying Wilson was a man, not a family. I'd foolishly assumed otherwise. But now I knew, and I had no doubt I could use that information to my advantage. After all, one man meant he was *paying* for his goons. The Riccis and Altissimos and most other mafia families leveraged the bloodlines and family respect, which held a lot more power than just coin.

Thinking of the Altissimos reminded me of my wife. Fucking Vee had screwed us over and taken the drugs for herself. I would be mad about it, if I couldn't see the strategy behind her actions. She'd *always* wanted more out of her life, but not in the same way I did. Me? I wanted nothing more to do with my family or the crime they were engaged in. I wanted to get out, totally out, and join Bellerose for real. I wanted a future with my Bella.

Vee wanted to become the next biggest, baddest bitch in Siena. She didn't want to get out, she wanted to stay *in.* She wanted to rule and had never hidden that from me. Despite how pissed I was that she'd gone behind our backs... I'd still do everything possible to support her dreams.

That's what a good friend did.

After the dumb-shit guard was satisfied with my beating, he left and I let myself drift into sleep while still hanging from my chains.

With no clue how much time had passed, I awoke once more to the sound of the cell door opening and a guard stepping through. Thankfully, this guard was the *smart* one.

"I'm allowed to let you down today," he advised me in a quiet voice. "But if you try anything, you'll be left to hang there indefinitely. We clear?"

My response was just a grunt. My chest hurt enough that I wouldn't waste words if they weren't necessary. The guard gave me a wary look, then nodded to himself and fished out a set of keys from his pocket.

Short fucker needed to use a stool to reach the cuffs holding my wrists in the air. The second they unlatched, I crumbled to the floor in a painful heap. A low groan rattled out of my bruised chest, but all in all, I wasn't in too rough shape.

"You good?" the guard asked cautiously as I slowly pushed myself to hands and knees. He had his gun in hand, but I knew he wouldn't use it. Not for deadly force, anyway.

I chuckled. "Sure. Good. Where are we?"

The guard shook his head. "I can't tell you that, Ricci, come on. Ask me something easy, like what's for dinner."

"Okay. What's for dinner? I'm starving." I really was, despite the rolling nausea in my gut, probably from the motion of swinging from chains while deprived of food and water.

The guard handed me a plastic water bottle, and I took careful sips so I didn't vomit it all up. "No fucking clue," he replied with a smirk. "But it'll be bad, whatever it is. Settle in and get comfy. You're here for at least another eleven days."

He started to leave, and curiosity sparked inside my fuzzy mind. "Your buddy coming back for another visit any time soon?" The guard who'd roughed me up seemed to be trying to prove a point. This guy, though, recognized *who* I was and had been smart enough to show respect.

"Probably," the guard replied with a shrug. "You can take it, I'm sure."

He wasn't wrong. He left me alone again, leaving me the bottle of water when he locked the heavy door once more. Eleven days, he'd said. Why such a specific amount of time? Was there a meeting planned with my father, maybe?

Fuck, I hoped Bella was okay. If she wasn't... well... this cursed mafia war hadn't yet seen carnage like I would deliver. And I'd enjoy every bloody second of it. Which meant I needed to get out of this goddamn cell. Now. Regardless of whether they were taking me right to Giovanni, I couldn't sit idle for another eleven days wondering what had happened to Bella. Or to Jace. Fuck, even to those other slick fuckers... They were all growing on me, much to my own surprise.

I had a few hours to look around the room and ponder over a reasonable plan, but without knowing where we were or how many guards I'd be facing outside this cell, there wasn't much I *could* plan. So I simply bided my time until the door opened again.

To my satisfaction, it was the asshole guard with heavy fists. I couldn't have picked a better victim if I'd been given the choice.

I waited in the shadow behind the door, making him look around the room in confusion for a moment. Then I crept up behind him with a jagged piece of plastic from the water bottle and slashed him across the eyes. Was it strong enough to do any major damage? No way in hell. But it was enough to scratch his eyeballs, and that gave me the moment of distraction necessary to take possession of his gun.

The idiot shrieked at me, hollering about how *I'd pay* and all that crap, but his warnings held as much water as a fishing net. I didn't shoot him, though. Why go alerting the whole building to my escape so soon? Instead, I knocked him out with the butt of his own gun, donned his steel-toed boots, then caved his head in with my foot.

When I was finished painting the ground red, I divested the guard's remains of all his other weapons and keys, then quietly let myself out of the cell. The corridor was only marginally brighter, lit with ancient halogens that flickered with every step I took. How infuriating. It reinforced the suspicion that I was in an industrial warehouse, though. Maybe in the basement, given the lack of light.

A low rumble of an engine or machines filled the space, but I dismissed the sound as I calmly searched for a way out. A few moments later, I stumbled into a room where a group of guards sat around smoking and playing cards, totally at ease.

Two of them reached for their guns automatically, and those two both ate lead before they could get their fingers on the triggers.

"Anyone else want to be stupid?" I asked in a conversational tone. It was so much more unnerving when the guy holding the gun seemed unaffected by killing, and I really was unaffected.

There was a dramatic pause, then the remaining guys dove for weapons, and I popped off a rapid-fire round of bullets, splattering the walls red as my ears rang.

"I take that as a yes, then," I murmured to the room full of bodies. Whatever they were getting paid, it wasn't enough. I exchanged my gun for one of theirs and checked that it was fully loaded before also taking their spare ammo and a tommy gun.

I sighed as I continued hunting for the way out of this never-ending basement level. If I had to kill every single person I met on my way out, then so be it. Nothing would keep me away from Bella even a moment longer than necessary. Surely, Grayson had kept her safe, though. Or Rhett. Or, shit, even Jace... though he was about as good with a gun as my great aunt Claudia... which still wasn't *bad,* but I'd pin my hopes on the other two first.

It took me a while and several more dead bodies before I found a narrow staircase and made my way up. At the top, the door was also metal and secured with the kind of latch that seemed almost... *nautical.*

Realization and dread rolled through me as I pushed the door open and stepped out with my guns raised.

"Fuck," I spat. Not at the twenty-odd armed guards pointing *their* guns at me—fuck those assholes—but at the view. The very wet, *middle of the damn ocean* view. My stomach hadn't been roiling from my beatings and the swaying on my chains, it was churning because I was on a *goddamn ship*. "Well. I should have seen this one coming."

"Put your weapons down!" One of the guards barked, his face twisted in anger and outrage.

I smiled. "You must be new. Here's how this is going to go. Since clearly none of us are leaving this tub until it docks, you can either kill me now—which we both know you can't—or I can kill all of you. Unless you'd like to investigate option three?" Silence met my offer, and I relaxed. These fuckers were loyal to the dollar, not the man.

"We're listening," someone said, and I quickly located my smart guard.

The angry dude who'd told me to put my weapons down seemed to disagree, though. "Fuck that, we're not making deals with—" *Bang*. Smart guard put a bullet through angry—stupid—guard's head.

"You were saying, Mr. Ricci?"

That was more like it. Why kill them all when I could flip them to my side?

seven

BILLIE

Grayson might have requested my presence in his bed for three days, but he never managed to make it home long enough to reap any benefits. Some mornings I woke up to his scent on the pillow, along with a note to explain where he'd been that day, but his presence was sorely missed.

I couldn't really complain when he was out there tracking down Angelo though.

On the morning of the deadline for my compromise, I woke up resigned to the fact that we'd probably be boarding a plane today, and I still had no fucking clue where Angelo was. The pain was a dull ache now that never went away, no matter how distracted Jace and Rhett attempted to keep me. In the end, all of us were a mess, and there wasn't anything that could fix it except the last two boys of Bellerose being back here. With us.

"Hey baby," Jace said when I stumbled out of the room. He was coming from the stairs that led to the gym, a towel across his shoulders, impressive-as-fuck chest and abs on display. "Sleep okay?"

I nodded, tilting my head back for his kiss. Jace had been making good on his promise to do better, giving me all of his time and attention, but also taking the cues for when I needed a moment alone. That part was the most surprising—younger Jace had never been able to leave me be, even when it was what I needed. This time he was doing things differently.

"Gray called," he added when we pulled apart, just as Rhett stepped out of his room, making his way over to wrap me up in his arms.

Now, I was sandwiched between the two of them, and fuck, the stirring in my stomach was akin to an entire flock of birds taking off.

"What did Gray say?" I rasped.

Jace smiled at the strangled sound of my words. These bastards knew what they did to me, and while he might be on his best behavior, he was still Jace.

"They found out some information on Angelo. They

talked to people who saw him the day after he was taken."

The lustful thoughts faded. "Alive?" I burst out.

Jace nodded. "Yes. Gray is on his way back here now with more information. He didn't want to say too much over the phone in case they were compromised."

Okay, that was fair. "If he was alive two days ago, then maybe our guess that Wilson would wait to enact his plan against Giovanni is right. Right?"

Jace nodded, his voice growing deeper. "Yes. Gray said if they didn't kill him straight away to send the body to Giovanni, then they're waiting for maximum impact. They want him alive so Giovanni can watch them kill the heir."

As terrifying as that concept was, at least we had some time. Maybe. Unless Angel was on a plane right now, and we were wasting our time here in Europe.

That terrifying topic of conversation faded off then as the two spent some time giving me more morning snuggles and kisses, before I reluctantly left to shower and change. I wanted to be ready and waiting when Gray returned.

I emerged in jeans and a sweater, socks on my feet, hair pulled back into a bun, and minimal make up. The scent of food dragged me to the main living area, where four room service trays were being placed on the table.

Jace helped set everything out while Rhett tipped the hotel staff.

When we were alone once more, we sat to eat in a somewhat comfortable silence, all of us waiting for Grayson. Thankfully, we didn't have to wait long; we were still eating when the front door opened. Jace and Rhett reacted like we were about to be ambushed, on their feet and blocking me from view before I could even get up.

As much as I loved the display of love and protectiveness, it also bothered me. A fucking lot. I was no more willing to lose them than they were to lose me. I wouldn't survive it.

They relaxed when Grayson entered the room, and he ignored both of them to lift me off my feet and deposit a long, searing kiss on my lips. "God, I missed you, Prickles," he rumbled, sounding gruff and tired.

"Missed you too," I replied with the truth. "Come and sit; we have food."

He carried me to the chair, seemingly unwilling to let me go yet. When he sat, I remained on his lap and handed him a few of the small egg sandwiches. He wolfed them down in an instant, and I knew that he'd been neglecting both sleep and food over the past few days.

"Coffee? Juice?" I asked as we waited for him to finish

eating. While we were all desperate to hear the rest of Grayson's information on Angelo, his wellbeing was just as important.

"Coffee, please," he said, sounding more relaxed and at ease now that he'd eaten. "And another kiss."

It was a relief to have his demanding side back in play.

After making his coffee as he liked it, black as night with no sugar, I handed it to him with a peck on the lips. I was turning away with a laugh, when he rumbled out a "Fuck no" and captured my face. This time the kiss was *all* Grayson—dominating, his tongue tangling with mine as he controlled the pace. By the time he was done, I was breathless and confused about what the hell just happened. The Gray effect.

Grayson had a way of stealing my sanity and reason, until I forgot everything, including the heartache in my life.

"Tell us what you found out," Jace said, leaning forward in his chair, his coffee mug loosely held in one hand. "We're done waiting around for information. We need to know."

It wasn't just *my Angel* missing. Jace had just as much to lose here.

His brother.

"Right." Grayson was back to business. "So, we

tracked Wilson's path from the house to that first rendezvous spot. That was where he handed Angelo off to some of his associates to be transported to the next drop site."

"Did they do that to make it harder to track him?" I asked, twisting on Grayson's lap so I could see his expression.

"Yep." He nodded. "Change the path frequently to confuse any who are tracking you. That way no one knows the end destination, just the next step. No matter how many of Wilson's people we managed to find and torture, we could never get more than one step farther."

"But he was alive two days ago," I said, confirming what Jace had already told me.

"Alive and well, apparently. There was no evidence of abuse, which is a good sign. It means they have bigger plans for him than a quick and clean death. They want to make it a big spectacle, so they'll be patient."

None of that sounded like a good sign, but I understood what he was saying. It was what I'd been hoping all along: We still had time to save him.

"Do you know where he is now?" I asked. "Did you manage to track down all the different groups who moved him?"

I was expecting a no. I mean, they'd only had three days. How much could they have learned in that time?

To my surprise, he nodded once more. "Yes, we actually did track Angelo down. He's on his way home to Siena."

I jumped out of his lap, spinning to face him as my panic took hold. "If he's already on the way, then we're too late. They're going to arrive long before us, and Angelo will be killed before we can save him." All of the hope I'd been desperately holding onto was dashed in a split second, as panic threatened to send me to my knees. "This can't be happening," I cried.

"Prickles, love, breathe," Grayson said calmly. Too calmly. That calm broke through my panic, reminding me that Grayson wouldn't be casually sitting here eating breakfast if we were in a race to get back to America before Angelo. There had to be more to the story.

"What aren't you telling us," Rhett said, twisting his lip ring around in one of the only nervous tics I ever saw from him. "Is Angelo going to get to America before us?"

"Nope," Grayson replied immediately. "He's on a cargo ship. That route, depending on the weather and such, should take at least ten to fifteen days."

Ten to fifteen—what the actual fuck?

Now I had a new damn worry to add to the plethora consuming me.

"We need to go after him!" I might have stomped my foot like a toddler, but seriously, fifteen days in a cargo ship with god knows what being done to him. This might actually be worse than what I'd been expecting.

Grayson's lips twitched, and despite his fatigue, his eyes were lit up. "Aww, you're so prickly right now. I'd like to throw you over my shoulder and work out all of your anxiety."

Shaking my head, I managed not to roll my eyes.

This time he laughed out loud, and that made me feel a tiny bit better. It didn't happen a lot, but when it did, I loved to hear Grayson's laughter. "They're not going to waste time, money, and resources transporting him secretly into America, unless they want him to arrive in one piece," Gray reassured me. "Angelo will be fine, outside of a little fucked up from spending fifteen days in what can be rough waters."

"There's no way for us to rescue him?" I double-checked.

This time it was Rhett who chuckled. "Do you have a secret pirate ship that we're not aware of, Thorn?"

Yeah, okay, he made a good point. "Look, there's probably a decent chance I have an aunt who's a pirate that could pop into the picture at any time." I had a father who'd returned from the dead, so it wasn't that farfetched. "But for now, I have no known contacts for travel on the open seas."

"I could get us on a cargo ship too," Grayson added,

"but that's not going to help Angelo. If anything, it will be worse for us to arrive after him. Instead, we now have the chance to make a real plan to save his stupid ass."

That had all of my attention, and I sat again, this time in the armchair near Gray. I wanted everyone completely focused on the next part of this conversation. "How do we save him?" I asked.

"Our plane is ready and waiting," Grayson replied. "We should pack our shit and get back home ASAP. Vee and Giana are coming with us; the rest of their people will take commercial flights, if they can easily get into the US, while those with shadier pasts will be on another cargo ship leaving tomorrow. Eventually, Vee will have a veritable army on American soil."

"They're going to help with Angel?" Jace confirmed.

"They are." Gray nodded. "Vee loves our mafia prince and will literally slit throats to save him. Trust me, Wilson has very few members of his organization left in Europe after we got through with them."

For once, I loved that we had bloodthirsty allies with questionable pasts on our side.

Rhett leaned back in his chair, hands resting on his flat stomach. "So, we return home and start building our army to intercept Wilson before they can get to Angelo when he docks."

"Bingo," Grayson said with a nod. "We know the

route this cargo ship is taking; we just have to track it the best we can and wait for its arrival. They won't get Angelo without a fight."

The *without a fight* part was truly terrifying. At this point I had *one* of my loves in danger, but when that ship docked, I'd most probably have four. None of them would stay behind, but they'd definitely try and make me.

There was not a fucking chance.

As I sat in the living room of our swanky hotel, I formed my own secret plan to work on until we rescued Angelo. A plan to ensure I could be at the docks that night.

Which meant I needed to get really good with guns.

Like, yesterday.

eight

BILLIE

The next few hours were decidedly less somber than the last three days had been. We finally had a plan of action. We knew where Angelo was and that he should arrive alive in America.

Alive was the word of the day for me.

After Grayson's return, we spent our time packing and dealing with calls from Brenda. At one point, Jace just put her on speaker.

"Big Noise is spinning this as a crazed vendetta against Bellerose," Brenda said bluntly, "by a disgruntled musician wanting to be part of your fame." She sounded like she was reading from written notes. "They found Hannah's body, along with most of your security, which

76

was included in the press release as an example of the danger you're in. We want your fans to understand that there was no other option but to cancel the remaining tour."

Jace's face was stonelike as he stared off into the distance, the phone held tightly in his right hand as we all listened in.

"Have they mentioned Angelo?" Grayson asked from his spot near the doorway.

Brenda paused, releasing a long breath, and her tone returned to normal. "No. Giovanni made it very clear that there was to be no mention of his missing son. That's, according to him, an internal matter he's dealing with." Another pause. "Is he alive?"

Grayson grunted, so I answered the question. "He's alive."

No way would we give more information over an unsecured line.

"Good." She paused when her baby cried, then added, "Your plane is ready and waiting. I've had three different safety and security companies check it over, but I suggest using your own as well if you can find someone."

"We'll find someone," Jace bit out, and then he hit the hang-up button, clearly done with the conversation.

It wasn't Brenda's fault, but she wasn't part of this inner circle and couldn't truly understand what was happening. All of this business talk when we were in the middle of a mafia war was frustrating.

"We should head to the private airport," Grayson growled, seeming at the end of his patience for the day. "Vee texted to say she's there and that her people are going over the plane. We'll ensure it's as safe as we can possibly make it to fly out of here today."

That was all I needed to know. Getting out of here and on our way to the same destination as Angelo was all I could focus on. That and the plan to save him once we got there.

"I'll call for a car," Jace muttered, and it didn't escape my notice that he was in a fucked up mood, a slightly triggering thing for me, especially since I didn't trust that we were in the place where we could call out bad moods, or even offer casual, public comfort to one another.

But in the vein of healing and moving forward, I decided to give it a shot and see how he reacted.

Our first real test toward the "changed man" attitude he was working on. The first of many tests, no doubt.

Whatever, I had trust issues.

"I'll get our bags," Grayson said before I could confront Jace.

"I'll help," Rhett added, dropping a kiss on my cheek as he walked past. My smile was there before I could stop it; it was nice how genuinely happy Rhett made me. Each of them brought a different facet to my happiness, and Rhett's was pure joy.

When they were out of the main living area, I turned to Jace, who was scrolling through his phone, no doubt looking for the car service's number. "Everything okay?" I asked him.

My tone was blunt but not angry. I wasn't angry. I was terrified we were about to go back ten steps again. It was our usual, after all.

Then, to my surprise, he took a deep breath and the tension that had been holding his features tight relaxed. He stopped scrolling his phone and gave me all of his attention, the full force of his lethal blue eyes and charismatic energy. "Sorry, Rose. I'm in a shitty mood."

Okay, well... we were actually off to a good start.

"Worried about Angel?" I pressed.

He nodded, scrubbing his free hand across his face and through his hair. "Yeah, that's the most pressing fucking worry I have. But also the tour. This is the second time we've had to cancel on fans, and you know... I never wanted to be that sort of musician. A flaky as fuck one. One who let down the very people who gave us fame and fortune. Who supported us when we were nothing, and now they think we're too fucking famous for our own good. I didn't want to be that sort of rock star, and yet here we are, disappointing them once again."

My relief was huge that his mood had nothing to do with us or the regression of our relationship—yeah, probably a little narcissistic of me to think that everything was about me. But with Jace, that was kind of how it went. Instead, I got to do what I'd missed doing with him for years.

Support and comfort him through the hard times.

Stepping forward, I wrapped my arms around him, holding on tightly as I hugged him with everything I had. "I'm so sorry, Jace," I whispered against his chest. "It's not fair, and I promise you, the true fans will understand. They will know your heart and the way you give so much of yourself to the music and, through the music, to them. You've always shared big time with the fans, and when this has been dealt with, we will find a way to make it up to them."

His phone hit the floor with a crack as he closed his arms around me, holding on even tighter than I was. "The fact that you use *we* when referring to the future makes it a lot better," he rasped. "We will deal with it, and I'm just so fucking grateful that I have you. We're heading home to find Angel. To find the last of Bellerose and bring him back to us."

"Fuck yes, we will," Rhett chimed in from nearby, making me jump. "We are Bellerose, and we won't take this shit any longer."

"Therapy is making him way too chirpy," Jace grumbled before he released me slowly, almost as if he was reluctant to let go.

Rhett just laughed. "Dr. Candace might be a genius. I've only had couple of sessions, but it's making such a fucking difference."

"We're so happy about that," I told him, patting Jace on the chest. "Even this asshole."

Jace grunted in the universal language of the man, and I headed for a Rhett hug. He dropped the bags he'd been carrying in time to catch me around the waist and swing me around once, before my feet hit the ground and his lips were on mine. "Love you, Thorn," he said when he pulled away, leaving me a little dazed. "You're the best fucking thing to stumble into my life. Ever."

Damn, being this loved was potent... and addictive.

"I should send Giovanni some flowers," I joked, "since his murderous ways are what sent me running into that alley."

"Save the flowers for his funeral," Grayson said as he dropped about six bags in the pile near Rhett, "'cause that'll be the only time you get anywhere near that bastard."

That was fine by me.

After that, Jace managed to retrieve his phone, which was only a little banged up, and call the driver to pick us up. The hotel staff got all the luggage down, and we just swaggered out like fucking rock stars, dark glasses and all because we were also rock stars in mourning.

When the cars pulled out of the hotel, there was a massive swarm of media and fans outside, and for a brief second, I thought we were going to have to stop.

"They'll run them all over," I gasped, when the driver told us to hold on, speeding up as he maneuvered the car to the left to try and get free of the crowd.

Jace, who was on my right, wrapped an arm around me, pulling me into his side. "They'll get out of the way. The media might be vultures, but they're not stupid vultures."

Rhett, on my other side, snorted out a laugh. "For the story of the century—first glimpse of Bellerose since the second tragedy that canceled a tour—they might take a few extra risks."

Thankfully, no one did get run over, most of them diving out of the way of the speeding SUV. I glimpsed a few signs being held by legitimate fans, and it was all words of support.

We love you Bellerose.

Save and protect our Bellerose.

Jace, marry me, and I'll shoot the bastards.

Had to admit, that last one made me laugh. Though the best part was the heavyset, bearded man holding the sign and wearing a *Jace Baby* cropped t-shirt. It was funny enough to leave a lingering grin on my lips, even if I would be the one doing the shooting if someone else tried to marry Jace. Or any of my boys.

Mine. Yep, greedy as that might be, now that I knew who owned my heart and completed my soul, I'd be holding onto them with everything I had.

The trip to the airfield was fast, and as the car deposited us right beside the private plane, we found Vee and Giana standing at the base of the steps waiting for us.

I'd never met Giana before, but I knew it was her before she even stepped forward, dressed casually in designer jeans, boots, and a tank with a caramel jacket draped over her shoulders. She was as tall and statuesque as Vee, with dark blonde hair stylishly cut to sit just above her shoulders. Her skin was a golden brown, her eyes dark, and when she smiled, it lit up her entire face. It was the sort of smile that had me smiling in return.

"It's so wonderful to meet you," she purred with just a hint of an accent as she shook my hand. As soon as she released it, she stepped forward and wrapped her arms around me, hugging me like we were long lost friends. "Valentina has talked about you so often I feel as if I know you."

I laughed as I replied. "I feel the same way. It's really nice to meet you."

Vee stepped in next, looking hesitant, and I made the first move to smile her way. "Glad you could make it," I said softly. "Did you get a chance to check the plane over?"

She returned that smile, relaxing slightly. She was wearing black jeans, a white button-down shirt that made her red hair stand out brilliantly, and similar boots to Giana. "Everything is safe and ready to go. I've sent my people off to their flight, and we'll rendezvous in America."

"Let's do it, then."

I was ready to get home. Ready to get Angel back.

On the plane, I chose to sit next to Grayson. He didn't show any surprise by that, even as Jace and Rhett took the seats across the aisle from us. Including all the pre-takeoff checks and a quick drink, we were in the air in about thirty minutes.

Grayson turned in his chair and shot me a slow smirk. "Okay, Prickles. Out with it. What do you need from me?"

Well, wasn't that a loaded question. Something must have tipped him off to the carnal images playing in my mind because the deep brown of his eyes darkened and his stare grew heated. "*That* you'll get whenever you need it," he rumbled, leaning in closer.

"But I also know you're sitting next to me right now for another reason."

He was correct. I should have known that just because he didn't show any reaction to me sitting with him, it didn't mean he hadn't picked up on the strange vibes I was throwing out there.

"I need you to take me shooting again." I said it quickly, prepared with all my arguments for when he refused.

"Great idea," Grayson said, and I blinked at him.

"Sorry, what?"

His laugh was a soft, spine-tingling sound that aroused basically every sense in my damn body.

"Learning to protect yourself fully is an excellent idea. I don't trust anyone else to ensure you're competent with a gun. Not just competent, but comfortable. A lot of gun accidents happen when people are scared of their own weapon."

Guns did scare me. I couldn't imagine ever getting truly comfortable with one in my hand, but hopefully, I'd at least get a little better.

"So, no argument?" I double-checked.

Grayson continued to smile, and it was so disconcerting. "Absolutely no argument from me. We can start the day after we get home."

Okay then.

I relaxed into my chair for a split second before he added, "Just as long as you understand there's not a hope in hell that you'll be on the docks when we rescue Angelo."

Swinging around, I leveled him with my glariest glare, and he just laughed again.

Motherfucker.

"Love, there is very little in this world I can refuse you, but when it comes to your safety... I'm an unmovable boulder."

A huff escaped me, along with all of my arguments. I decided that it wasn't worth fighting him just yet. I'd take the training and keep secretly planning to be there that night.

Grayson let out another laugh, before leaning over and kissing me right on my pouting lips. "Little Hedgehog. You know I love it when you're prickly."

Deciding it wasn't worth the angst of being mad at him any longer, I relaxed under his kiss, returning it with enough force that I think I finally shocked him.

The next two weeks until Angelo returned were going to be interesting, that was for sure, and I planned on using every second of my time very wisely.

GRAYSON

Teaching Billie how to handle a gun was one of my favorite core memories—not only because it was wrapped up with the memory of her handling *my* weapon in the car afterwards, but because the act of teaching her filled me with an inexplicable kind of calm, like every new survival skill she gained settled another of my frayed, anxious nerves.

When we landed in Naples, it took us ages to get back to my house due to dodging reporters wanting the *scoop* on our canceled tour. Again.

The next day we stayed trapped indoors for most of the daylight hours, thanks to the persistent paparazzi camped out on the street outside my gates. So it wasn't until the following day that I finally got Billie out to my secluded property in the woods for shooting practice. Paid security tailed us, but they would wait in their car further up the road, as we'd already discussed.

"Uh, are you taking us out to the forest to kill us and dump the bodies?" Rhett joked from the backseat as I parked my truck near the trail. I exchanged a small grin with Billie at the echo of her question when I'd first brought her here.

Replying to Rhett, I dropped the smile. "I'm not an amateur, Silver. I'd obviously freeze your body, toss it through a woodchipper, then sprinkle the chunks into a shark tank as breakfast for the big fishes."

Rhett was used to my shit and just wrinkled his nose. "Why freeze it first?"

"So the blood doesn't clog up the chipper as quick." I popped my door open and climbed out. This time I'd brought enough guns, ammo, and replacement targets to last us a while.

Jace gave me a sidelong look as he stretched his arms over his head. "You've got a special way of looking at the world, Taylor."

I grunted, then shrugged. "You love it."

I'd reluctantly made a last-minute decision to drag both Jace and Rhett along for this instructional session.

They both sucked with guns, Jace much more so than Rhett, so it could only benefit them to brush up.

Once I had my bag of supplies sorted, I checked that Billie was warm enough in her woolen coat and adorable knitted cap, then kissed her cold nose and led the way into the trees. We'd left in a bit of a hurry last time, so all the targets needed to be reset with the bright paint powder that gave such a satisfying puff of color when hit accurately.

Jace and Rhett messed around with Billie while I took care of that, playing like kids in the frosty grass, but I quickly pulled them into line when I was ready to start.

The satisfaction I felt when Billie showed she remembered everything I'd taught her was all-consuming—especially when I realized she was already displaying better form and superior concentration than both Jace and Rhett. Though Rhett's accuracy was hard to beat. He'd told me years ago that hunting had been a big part of the community he'd been raised in, so he wasn't a beginner. Just sloppy, with bad habits.

I put in some work on both guys, leaving Billie to reacquaint herself with the feeling of shooting. I couldn't stop watching her from the corner of my eye, though, fixating on the way her hands cradled the butt of my Glock, or the way her tongue poked out of her lips with concentration.

"Dude, either tuck that away or go rub one out in the bushes," Rhett muttered, snapping my focus back to him. Startled, I glanced down and realized my hard dick was prodding him in the leg.

"Sorry," I replied with a smirk, reaching down to rearrange. "You know how it is."

Rhett rolled his eyes, then looked in Billie's direction. "Damn right, I do," he murmured, then sighed. "Alright, I've got this. Go rub your dick on her instead; she'll appreciate it more than me."

True. He didn't need to tell me twice; I left him to practice and went to *correct Billie's stance* with my hands firmly on her hips. She groaned, releasing one hand from her gun to tug her earmuffs off.

"Gray, that's very distracting," she scolded. "Now all I can think about is getting you back to the car and... um... stargazing."

I chuckled, holding her tighter against me as I kissed her neck. "Stargazing, huh? Yeah, that's what I was thinking about just now too." My thick erection grinding her ass was evidence of that. "But you need to learn how to shoot with distractions, baby girl. If you end up in a situation where you have to fire on someone, you won't get anything even close to quiet focus. You'll have to—"

She fired, cutting me off as her bullet sent up a puff of pretty, pink dust.

"Like that?" she asked, smug as all hell.

I grinned, then dragged my tongue over my lower lip and decided it was a good day to take my life into my own hands. "You call that distracted? Prickles... love... we can do better than that."

Shifting my hand around her waist, I deftly unbuttoned her jeans and slipped a hand inside. Her panties were silky, and she gave a low moan as I stroked her warmth through the fabric.

"Gray," she whimpered. "This seems unsafe."

All the better. "It is," I agreed. "Hit that target ten times in a row while I *distract* you, and I'll let you finish."

Her breath hitched. "On your hand?"

I smiled against her hair, my fingers already creeping beneath the silky fabric of her panties. "On my hand. Or my face. Or my cock. Your choice, baby girl. But only if you hit that target with accuracy..."

She quivered but quickly squeezed off another shot, and a puff of dust rewarded her direct hit. "That's two," she told me firmly, twisting slightly to look up at me.

I smirked. "Alright, I'll accept that." Then I pushed two fingers into her already hot and wet cunt. Her eyelids fluttered, and she whimpered, but steadied herself against my body as she lined up the next shot. This one *barely* clipped the target, but it gave a tiny puff of color. So I rumbled, "Three," as I found her clit with my thumb.

JAYMIN EVE & TATE JAMES

Billie squirmed and gasped, riding my hand for a moment until I paused my movement. "Gray..." she whined in a needy, sex-hungry voice that nearly made my dick explode.

"Seven more shots, Prickles. You've got this." I dropped a kiss to the bend of her neck, which had become delightfully flushed. I toyed with her pussy, my fingers torturously slow as she tried to set up her next shot.

Number four hit, *thank fuck*, but number five flew wide as I pinched her clit between my fingers.

"Not fair!" Billie protested, her hips rocking against me like she was desperate for my dick. "Gray, you're playing dirty."

I was. But distraction was distraction, and despite how much fun I was having with *this* distraction, the lesson remained the same. She needed to be able to shoot like it was second nature, not only when she was laser-focused and calm.

"Sorry, baby, the challenge was for ten in a row..." I started to withdraw my hand, but the growl she gave as she grabbed my wrist was damn near feral.

"Grayson Taylor, if you leave me high and dry right now, I swear to fuck I'll shoot your balls off."

I grinned. Her threats shouldn't turn me on as much as they did. "Fine. One last chance. You need six in a row, no missing." I wet my lips and slipped my hand back inside her panties. "Let me just..." I plunged two fingers back inside her. My happy place. "Alright, go."

She moaned but tried *really* hard to win my game. Of her next six bullets, though, only two hit the target, and her little roar of frustration when I tugged her pants back into place was echoed in my own soul. She pouted about it but didn't argue. After all, I'd proven my point... she needed more practice.

"So we're clear, little hedgehog, no matter how good you get here, I'm still never letting you stroll into danger." I gave her a hard look as I retreated a few steps, just in case she decided to kick me in the nuts. Her eyes just narrowed with determination, and she shrugged.

"We'll see," she muttered, putting her earmuffs back on and dismissing me.

I watched her a moment longer, then gave my raging hard-on a firm squeeze in a vain attempt to calm the fuck down.

Jace saw me do it, having watched that whole session with Billie, and smirked knowingly. "Maybe if you'd told me this was what shooting practice was like, I'd have tagged along sooner."

"Shut up and hit some targets, Adams," I snapped, my arousal making my patience thinner than air, "before I drag Billie out of here and leave you two to walk home."

He wanted to give a snappy comeback, I could practically see it on the tip of his tongue, but then he narrowed his eyes and pinched his lips shut. Smart man. He knew I wasn't entirely bluffing.

My self-control lasted a whole lot longer than I anticipated, helped largely by my stubborn focus on working with Jace and Rhett, only correcting Billie from a distance. I was smart enough to know if I put my hands back on her body, we'd be done shooting for the day.

Not that I hated that idea.

"Alright, I'm done," Rhett announced a few minutes later. He unloaded his gun, ensuring it was safe before returning it to the oversized duffle bag. "My fucking fingers are cramping and shit. I need to warm them up. Thorn, baby! Got anywhere warm I can put my hands?"

Billie tossed an evil grin my way, then carefully unloaded her own gun. "I sure do," she replied, heading over to drop her weapon and spare ammo into the bag. "Here, try this." She lifted her shirt up to offer Rhett her tits. Fuck. "Boobs are always warm; I don't know why."

Rhett, the fucker, didn't even hesitate in wrapping his hands around her perfect orbs, making her shiver and moan, her nipples hardening instantly through the thin fabric of her bra.

"I don't know either," Rhett agreed, "but I like it." He

toyed with her hard peaks, then reached around to snap her bra clasp open.

"Rhett, for fuck's sake," Jace scolded, but Silver already had a mouthful of Billie's tit, and she was gasping like she was ready to come.

I raked a hand through my loose hair, my own breathing harder than it should have been. "Christ, can we at least take this back to my house?"

"Nope," Billie replied, shooting me a loaded glare. "I'm not waiting. It's not *that* cold out here. Right?" That question was aimed at Rhett, since she was already unbuckling his belt and wrapping her fingers around his dick. Lucky bastard.

"What cold?" he mumbled against her breasts. "I'm not cold."

Then she dropped to her knees right there in the frosty grass and took him in her mouth. *Fuuuck.*

Rhett's laugh was low and smug. "Shouldn't have teased her so hard, Gray. But I'm not mad to reap the benefits." He grasped her ponytail in his fist, using it to push himself harder into her throat, and my balls tightened up with desperate need.

Jace gave me a long look, then shook his head slowly. "This is insane," he muttered but couldn't hide how turned on he was. Our girl had us all firmly wrapped around her little finger, and we were powerless to resist.

Jace seemed *so* torn, though. Had he shared Billie since they'd started fucking again? I didn't even know.

They'd been making huge progress to put their past behind them, though. I desperately didn't want them to slip back into jealousy and hate. So I gave a pained exhale and strode over to where Billie knelt in front of Rhett; her eyes widened as she looked up at me, her mouth stuffed full of my friend's pierced cock.

"Prickles," I barked with authority. "We weren't finished. On your feet, beautiful."

Surprise registered in her eyes, but she didn't immediately do as she was told.

My gaze hardened, and a growl entered my voice. "Now, Billie. Don't make me repeat myself."

"God damn it, Grayson," Rhett groaned when Billie released him from her mouth with a wet pop, pushing to her feet like she'd been told. "Seriously? You couldn't just join in?"

I could have. I absolutely *would* have, but I felt like maybe Jace was going to get weird about it. So I figured I was better off taking one for the whole team this time. It'd be hard. Really hard. But these were the sacrifices we made for our chosen brothers.

ten

BILLIE

Grayson kept his heavy gaze locked on mine as he tossed the truck keys to Jace. He tipped his head to the trail, his command clear even before he said it out loud.

"Head back to the truck and wait for us there," he ordered Jace and Rhett. "Billie and I need to discuss her failure during the distraction test earlier. Don't we, Prickles?"

A shiver of pure anticipation trembled through me, my exposed breasts tightening even more as I nodded. "Yup. We sure do."

Jace and Rhett grumbled their complaints, but they weren't immune to Grayson's authority and did as they were told, no matter how disgruntled they were about the whole thing.

When we were alone, Grayson let his heavy stare rake over my body, pausing at my naked chest. My bra had been discarded, my sweater pushed up, and I'd made no attempt to pull it back down.

"Cold?" he asked when I shivered again.

I shook my head. "Nope." Such a lie, I was freezing. But I was also flushed to the point of sweating with how worked up and turned on I was.

Gray's lips tipped in a tiny smile. "Sure?"

I licked my lips. "Uh-huh. Positive."

His gaze locked on my eyes again. "Good. Strip naked, Prickles. Show me how that perfect body reacts to the wilderness."

Excitement jolted through me, and my hands shook as I quickly tugged my sweater over my head and tossed it aside. Then my jeans and panties came off in a quick motion, kicked off along with my shoes.

"Ta-da," I announced, propping my hands on my hips.

"Cute," he rumbled, gripping my face with his big hand and tipping my head back. His kiss when he delivered it was hot, hungry, and pure torture. He was holding back, and I nipped his lower lip with my frustration.

"Prickles, my little hedgehog," he scolded. "You didn't complete the distraction test. I shouldn't be rewarding you... should I?"

I swallowed hard, my breathing quick. "So punish me instead, Grayson." Heat flared in his eyes, and I leaned into him so that my nipples grazed his shirt. "You want to, don't you? You're all worked up and pissed off that I blew Rhett in front of you. You wanna spank me for making you *share,* don't you, Gray?"

The rumble in his chest was a resounding yes, and a split second later I found myself back on my knees once more. This time, Grayson's huge, thick cock damn near choked me before he even got halfway into my mouth, but I still enthusiastically tried to take him deeper. My hand wrapped around his base, making up for the shortfall of my oral depth, and he gripped my hair firmly in his fist.

He wasn't playing around this time. Not like Rhett had been a moment ago. Nope, Gray *did* want to punish me, and he fucked my mouth hard enough that I gagged and tears streamed from my eyes. Still, I wasn't letting up any more than he was, my fingers gripping his base tight and my moans encouraging him to use my mouth however he wanted.

His grunts and moans as he slammed into my throat over and over were fast and frenzied, but he wasn't letting me off that quick. He jerked my hair, pulling my mouth off his cock entirely before I could make him come. His lust-filled smirk when I pouted up at him said he was in it for the torture still.

"You have been naughty, haven't you?" he murmured, and I nodded eagerly. I liked this game.

"Uh-huh," I agreed, "very."

He gave a huff of a laugh, then stripped off his coat, tossing it onto the grass behind me. "Lie down on your back, spread those legs, and show me how much you want my cock, Prickles."

"Yes, sir," I replied, teasing, but the moan he gave as I obeyed his order was sinfully delicious. I eagerly spread my legs apart, shivering as the cold air reached my wet pussy, but it didn't deter me. I used my fingers to part my lips, my index finger rubbing my clit while Grayson watched with blazing eyes.

"Billie Bellerose," he murmured, getting down onto his knees while stroking his cock. "You're a damn gift from the universe, aren't you."

I assumed that was rhetorical because he didn't give me much of a chance to reply. Gray *usually* took a painstaking amount of time to get me ready for his oversized cock, but not today. Nope, he was in it for the punishment and thrust straight into my tight pussy, making me cry out.

"Shhh, baby girl," he rumbled with a husky laugh, "if you scream too loud, we might end up with company." He pulled back and slammed back into me, deeper, and I hollered louder. Did I want company? Maybe. Grayson just grinned and pressed a hand to my lower belly, firmly pinning me to the ground as he fucked me deeper and harder.

"Gray, holy fuck," I gasped between moans and cries. "So fucking huge, you're breaking me in half. Holy shit... *Gray*. I need to come." My hand snaked down to my clit, but he smacked it away.

"Not a chance," he scolded. "You'll fucking take your punishment like a good girl, Billie. God damn, you feel amazing. So tight. Fuck." He pushed his hand harder on my belly as he thrust, tightening everything even more, and I wondered if he could feel himself fucking me through that hand. Probably yes, with how hard he was rearranging my insides.

His thrusts slowed, and he pulled out entirely when I was just a breath away from coming, and I gave a pained scream of protest that only made him laugh.

"Flip over, beautiful," he told me. "Get on your knees for me."

Again, I did as I was told. He slammed back into me from behind, gripping my ass cheeks and parting them like he wanted to stretch my skin. I moaned, backing onto him as my hair hung down around my face. A warm drip of liquid hit my asshole, his saliva, and then his thick thumb pushed inside as I moaned louder than necessary. His hand gripped my ass with that thumb buried deep, like a handle, as he pounded my pussy.

"You want more, don't you?" he grunted a few moments later. "Greedy girl."

"Yes," I whimpered. "Yes, Gray..."

He slammed into me a couple more times, then slowed. "Jace, get over here and fuck her face."

I gasped, tossing my hair back to find my first love standing there, dick in hand as he watched. I licked my lips, and he needed no more encouragement. He closed the gap between us, getting down on his knees and guiding his cock into my mouth.

"Don't you fucking dare let yourself come, Prickles," Grayson warned me, his thumb pushing deeper. I wanted to laugh—and would have if Jace didn't have my mouth filled right up. It amused me that Gray thought I could *stop* myself from orgasming. I had no control over that shit, but I guess he did. Each and every time I started to get close, he stopped. Or pulled out. Or smacked my ass. Or thrust me forward hard enough I gagged on Jace's cock. Anything to disrupt the moment and chase it away again.

Fucking hell. I didn't like this game anymore.

"You have no idea how badly I wish I'd packed lube on this outing," Grayson confessed when I was nearly out of my damn mind with the need to climax. "I'd be fucking this ass so hard right now."

I jerked at that idea, my pussy tightening around his cock.

He hummed. "You'd like that, I think. My dick buried in your tight little hole, stretching you out. What about this sweet pussy, though? Will you take someone there at the same time? I think yes. You'd be in heaven."

Fuck me, I was in heaven just picturing it. Jace whispered some curses, his hands gripping my face as he pushed his cock deeper into my throat as I sucked him hard. It was getting really difficult to focus with so much going on. But I guess it was good practice, right? I had four boyfriends now. Sooner or later, my body would get more than just two dicks inside it. Hopefully at once.

Two seconds later, as Grayson continued taunting me with the mental image of a foursome—or fivesome —I cracked and detonated. My toes curled and muscles cramped, my eyes rolled back so far I might have blacked out slightly. And then, while I still rode the wave of pure ecstasy, Jace spilled his load in my throat. Grayson lasted a split second longer before letting himself go.

"Billie, Billie, Billie," Grayson scolded as I collapsed in

a jellylike heap. "I told you *not* to come. This was punishment, remember?"

I gave a husky, slightly delirious laugh. "It's cute that you think it works like that."

His answering smile was confident, but it was Jace who translated that smug smirk.

"He knows," he told me dryly. "He set you up for failure there. Now he's got an excuse to *punish* you again later." Jace pushed to his feet with a groan and tucked his dick away before offering me a hand. "But you are turning blue, Rose. So the games can wait."

He tugged me to my feet—albeit wobbly—and helped me dress, not bothering with underwear. Once my jeans, boots, and sweater were all back on my body, I realized I *was* shivering pretty hard.

"Sorry, Prickles," Grayson murmured, wrapping his coat around my shoulders. "I got carried away."

"No complaints here," I assured him with chattering teeth. "Where's Rhett, though?"

Grayson raised a brow, his lips creasing in a sly smile, and I groaned. "I didn't mean like that..." Or maybe I did.

"He was getting the heat going in the truck," Jace said, taking my cold hand in his and tucking them both into his pocket. Grayson draped his arm over my shoulders, and the three of us walked the short trail just like that.

When Rhett saw us—saw *me*—he scowled daggers at both Jace and Gray. "I hate you both," he snapped. "You..." He shifted his glare my way, and it softened. "Okay, I love you. But goddamn, you look freshly fucked and utterly gorgeous right now."

Grayson and Jace exchanged a grin and bumped fists as we approached the truck. It was a subtle gesture, so maybe I imagined it. Regardless, I wriggled out of their hold and went to Rhett, where he leaned against the door with a sexy pout on his face.

"Snuggle with me in the backseat?" I offered, batting my lashes. "I'm cold."

Rhett immediately drew me into his warm embrace, holding me close with his face buried in my hair. "Anything for you, Thorn. Absolutely anything." Then he kissed my cheek and lowered his voice to a whisper. "Will you let me make you come while Gray drives us home? He deserves payback."

I chuckled, nodding. "Fuck yes, he does. You've got yourself a deal, so long as I can sleep in your bed tonight to hide from Gray's wrath."

Rhett's laugh was pure evil, and Jace groaned in dread when we climbed into the back seat of the truck. He knew what was coming, but he'd sit there in the front with Grayson and suffer.

Now who was punishing *whom*?

eleven

BILLIE

It was getting harder and harder for us to leave the house these days. The Bellerose story had started big, but then it'd continued to build like wildfire until the speculation was intense. Big Noise released their statement on the crazed musician-fan theory, but not everyone was buying it. The fans had some huge opinions on who was targeting the band, and the blame ranged from a crazed fan to a jealous musician, and then morphed to guessing it'd been a personal attack on Grayson, Jace, or Rhett. Ex-girlfriends, past acquaintances, high school bullies... the list went on and on. The media was digging hard into their past, and skeletons were falling out of closets faster than any of us liked.

Of course, the one who had everyone the most curious was Angelo.

Giovanni was somehow keeping word of his involvement in the mafia under wraps, but people recognized the lethal predator caged under Angelo's beautiful exterior. It fascinated and terrified them.

So, of course, a lot of OG fans believed he was the reason Bellerose had been having so many issues lately. "I need to make a statement," Jace said a few days after we'd returned from the shooting field. We were all but pacing the living room, about done with being trapped within these four walls. I mean the sex was amazing, but we were also prisoners, and that had to end. "Angel should be back in less than a week," he continued, "and if we can't lose the media circus around us, there's no way we can enact our part in his rescue."

"Is that a good idea, bro?" Rhett asked. "Won't a statement only add fuel to the fucking blaze?"

Jace's jaw was set tightly as he squeezed his eyes closed. "It's a risk we have to take," he finally said. "If we don't say anything and let the speculation continue, then it'll keep growing. A statement might get at least our most loyal fans backing our story, and they'll push the narrative for us, then."

"Yes," Grayson agreed. "I think this is our only option now. It's too dangerous for us to make a statement in public, but we can post across our social media and get the word out that way."

"Run it by Brenda," Rhett added, but Jace interrupted him.

"Fuck Brenda. She's not one of us. I'm done running things through others. This is our band. Ours. No one fucking else's. And *we* will make the best decision for Bellerose."

He caught my eye, and I shot him a gentle smile. Some of the fire died out of him as he strode across and dropped down beside me. "What do you think, Rose? Should I make a statement?"

The stranglehold this guy had on me was dangerous. The simple act of conferring with me before making a huge decision told me that he valued my opinion. "What if I said no?" I checked.

Jace examined my features for a few extra seconds. "Then I wouldn't. You might not have been in the public eye as long as we have, so you definitely see things differently than me. You would see the negatives that I can't and let me know if you truly thought I shouldn't do it."

Grabbing his hand, I held on tightly as I said, "I think

you should make a statement. It's time for Bellerose to step out on their own and do shit their way. It's the best way for the band... and you all. Being controlled almost got us all killed. I say *no fucking more* of that shit. We're done being puppets."

He kissed me fiercely, and I was surprised enough that by the time I was about to return the kiss, he was already up and heading for the soundproof room with all the computers and equipment where they did their recording. The room at Grayson's wasn't huge like the one at the old farmhouse we'd been in, but it had enough space for them to make media statements and such.

"I'll make the statement on my own," Jace said over his shoulder, "so no one questions where Angelo is if only the three of us appear. But I'll run it by you all first."

"No need," Rhett called back. "We trust you to speak for us on this matter."

"We do," Grayson added. "Let's start changing the narrative now."

The mood lightened then, as if the boys had simply been waiting for the right forward movement and now were at peace with the decision. Grayson's phone chimed a second later, and he glanced down briefly, before pushing to his feet. "Vee and Giana are on their way here. I need to let security know."

He left the room, and I spent my time cuddling Rhett while we waited for everyone to return. "Have you had a therapy session lately," I asked him softly, tracing my fingers up and down his bare arm.

"It's mostly been voice chats," he said with a laugh. "Dr. Candace is surprisingly modern with her communication, and I appreciate that. She's helping me shed the guilt I feel toward my mother."

"Guilt?" I questioned.

He nodded, and I felt the movement against my body. "Apparently, the deep-seated hatred I also feel stems from the guilt I experienced when I took off and left her there. In the arms of a monster. I mean, I was all but a damn kid and she was a grown woman, but I also knew she'd been emotionally and mentally beaten and manipulated. She doesn't have the reasoning capabilities of a regular grown-ass woman. If anyone was mentally a child in that situation, it was my mom."

"You tried to save her," I reminded him.

Another nod. "I know. And I know that it's not my fault that I couldn't. Childlike or not, she was given the choice to walk away, and she decided to stay. I've accepted that now, that she chose him over me. I have to let go of my hate toward her because that's what keeps me from moving on fully from that life." He shifted so that we could see each other, and I loved that there was no tension in his features. "I'm letting the anger and pain go so I can have a happy and content future."

"The future you deserve," I said softly, reaching up to press my hand against his cheek. "All the fucking happiness, Zepp."

His lips twitched as he leaned in for a kiss. "What about blow jobs? All of those too, right?"

A snort of laughter was my answer before I replied with, "That was too close in proximity to the conversation about letting your mom go, but yeah, all the blow jobs too."

"Mom was forgotten long ago," he whispered, before his lips crashed into mine, and I groaned against them. One touch. One kiss. I was such a fucking goner over this boy.

Before it could heat up too much, a door banged in the house, and Grayson was back with Vee and Giana. The three of them walked in smelling like snow and danger.

Did danger have a smell? Who the fuck knew, but I felt like it followed these three around, so there had to be something.

"Billie!" Vee exclaimed, hurrying over to throw her arms around me, uncaring that I was still completely wrapped up in Rhett. I liked that he extracted himself from her hold though, as if he didn't like to touch another woman while with me. The possessive asshole inside of me really enjoyed that.

"Hey Vee," I said with a smile as she pulled away and dropped down on the nearby couch. Giana said her hellos as well and sat next to her girlfriend.

Vee and I weren't fixed by any means, but we were working toward healing, and I enjoyed having some female presence in our lives. Especially two badass ones.

"Why are you here?" Grayson asked. Clearly Vee hadn't elaborated in her message to him about coming over.

"Our people have started to arrive," Giana said in her smooth accent. "We will soon have enough numbers to safely take on the Wilsons at the docks. With that in mind, we need to plan the night out."

Grayson didn't sit with the rest of us, choosing to remain a giant statue in the doorway between the living room and kitchen. He did cross his arms over his broad chest, though, just to reiterate his own badass and scary status. "How many people do you have that can be trusted with this?" he pushed. "Angelo isn't like a normal mission. We can't fail here."

Vee's laughter was light. "We never fail, Taylor. And

Angelo is still my husband," Giana grimaced but didn't comment, "so I will be doing everything in my damn power to save him."

Grayson nodded. "That's fair. So what's the plan?"

Vee straightened, Giana did the same, and this *illumination* washed over both. They were excited by this mission. I wished I could feel anything other than terror. All the people I loved most in the world would be in danger, and there was no way I could ever be excited about that.

"My intel says that the cargo ship under Wilson's control will dock at midnight on the twelfth of March. They'll be docking at a small inlet near New Jersey. This dock is regularly used by cartels and mafia since it's completely bought out. That particular dock, though, is too small for a larger cargo ship, so smaller boats will ferry their men and prisoners across. Wilson plans on meeting Giovanni on the docks, under the guise of trading Angelo for weapons, intel, and cash. But we know that he actually plans on killing Angelo, Giovanni, and any and all Ricci members who are there."

"This is step one in taking over a greater bulk of the power, drugs, and control of the region," Giana chimed in. "Once you knock off the top dog, there's a power scramble as everyone works to find the hierarchy again. It will leave the mafia vulnerable for a split second in time, and this is all Wilson thinks he needs to make his big move—which is stupid because Giovanni has a hundred contingency plans in place in case he is ever killed. But some people don't look at the big picture when they've got an axe to grind."

What they were saying made perfect sense, this internal power struggle, but I couldn't shake the feeling that there was a more personal reason that Wilson had targeted the Riccis. If I knew my father at all, and let's be fucking real, I apparently didn't have much of a clue about him, this plan was years in the making. Since the night he'd killed my mother and burned our house down.

What I wouldn't give for five minutes in a room with him for some fucking answers.

Five minutes alone and a borrowed gun, since I still didn't have my own.

"Okay, so if we know the docks and the time," Rhett said shortly, "then we can be ready and waiting for the arrival."

Vee nodded. "Yes, and we think the best option is to cover the docks with a sniper. Long range takes out the guards first, and then the rest of us can move in. We need someone who has no issue with accuracy over distance."

"I can handle that," Grayson said without hesitation.

He was the only one of us who had any kind of experience with that range, so it made sense.

Vee eyed him briefly, before smiling. "Okay good, because there's no one in my crew that I'd trust with such a task. Not for Angelo."

There was an immense feeling of relief at the thought of Grayson being the guardian angel watching over *my Angel.*

"So, we have a sniper placed to take out the main guards," Giana continued. "We will be in the wings waiting, just outside the Riccis' security sweep area so they're not alerted to our presence until we want them to be. Wilson won't show up until the prisoner is on the docks, to prevent any early ambushes. But even so, we will still be up against"—she paused as if doing math in her head—"probably thirty trained assassins."

"If you're waiting in the wings, I'd suggest taking out any men you find on the edges," Grayson added. "Trim those numbers for the final battle. Because they won't let Angelo go easily."

Vee and Giana nodded. "Oh yeah, we totally plan on doing that," they said almost at the same time.

"The aim is to thin their ranks enough for an advantage," Vee continued, "but not enough that the lack of radio chatter alerts them to our presence. We'll also stash some weapons in easy reach for Angelo, provided he's in a condition to fight."

Angel was tough enough to withstand a lot of punishment, so if he couldn't fight, he would be badly hurt. I couldn't think about that, so I would go with their plan. Get a weapon into his hands.

"Will Rhett and Jace be there?" Vee asked, even though Rhett was in the room with us.

"They will." Rhett was the one to answer, meeting her gaze dead on. "We can handle ourselves, and the more people on your side, the better."

Vee didn't look convinced, but she also didn't argue.

And this was my time to shine. "I'll be there too," I said shortly. "This is my Angel, and there's no fucking way I'm letting you all walk into danger without me. I can handle a gun, and I want to help."

The silence was near deafening until Grayson laughed. That asshole of a brute just straight up laughed at me. "Little Prickles," he said with a shake of his head. "There's not a hope in hell. We've already discussed this... do you need a reminder?"

The clenching of my core told me that a part of me very much wanted a reminder, and the punishment that went with it, but this was too serious to get distracted with sex. "We've worked out a compromise before," I tried. "Can we do that again now? Is there a way for me to be there but not right in the midst of danger?"

I didn't have to be down on the docks fighting against mafia assassins. My proficiency with guns wasn't that strong, and my street survival skills were woeful.

No one else answered, leaving it up to Grayson to make this final decision about that night. He let out a deep breath, lips thinning, and I prepared myself for his final no.

"If I'm in position as a sniper, then you can act as my look out," he finally said, shocking the fuck out of me. "I'd prefer you be with me, where I can keep an eye on you. And you will wear a vest and do *everything* I tell you."

Leaping from the couch, I threw myself at him in the same breath, wrapping my arms and legs as tightly around him as I could. He let out another chuckle, but this one was lower, more intimate, as his arms enclosed me tightly.

"Okay," Vee said, ignoring me as I thanked Grayson for his compromise. "It's set then. I'm going to take my people for training sessions at a small dock here, on Lake Michigan, with a similar set up. There will already be Ricci and Wilson goons hanging around the New Jersey area, so it's too risky to head for Jersey yet. But we can train in a similar setup. I'll be in touch if we have further instructions."

I felt her pat me on the back as she left, but I was too busy clinging to Gray like a damn monkey to respond. His hands went under my ass to haul me higher, and then we were striding from the room.

"Time for that punishment, Prickles," he rumbled, and every part of me tightened in anticipation.

Fuck yeah. I got to go to the docks and get punished by Gray. This was turning out to be a great damn day.

twelve

RHETT

When my phone rang, disrupting what was turning out to be a very nice nap, I rolled over and knocked it off the table. These days, sleep was precious to me, and the fact that I could finally nap without Billie told me that my mental health shit was heading in the right direction.

Finally. After too many fucking years of suppressed rage and pain. Therapy was my drug of choice these days, and the fact that I'd been sober for the past week, or longer, had me wondering who the fuck this new Rhett was.

The ringing cut off, and I shook away the last tendrils of sleep brain, pushing myself up to sit. Reaching down to grab the phone once more, I checked the number in case it was Billie looking for me. Not that she didn't know where I was, and we were all in the same house still. But she might have gone out with Gray while I was asleep, and I'd never leave a call from her hanging.

I blinked at the unfamiliar number, before my stomach swirled in dread. I didn't recognize the number, but I knew that area code. It was from my hometown of Townsend, a few hours west of here. The very fucking town where my mother and *her owner* lived.

Why would I be getting a call from Townsend, though? I had no contacts left there, no friends or family that would ever call me. Fuck, my number was almost impossible to even get, so there was literally no fucking explanation for this call today.

Did that bastard somehow know that I was finally, *fucking finally,* starting to move on from my past and had decided to yank me right back in? Yeah, not a chance. I'd kill him with my bare hands before I let that happen again. I'd had that surprise visit from Johnny—a guy I'd grown up with—in Europe, but surely, he wouldn't go passing my number on. He'd said he was out of the cult, long gone, never to return, and I still believed that was the case.

The phone rang again suddenly, and I almost dropped it for a second time as the same number flashed on the screen. For a moment, I pondered the decision I was about to make. Silence this call and block the number so I could keep moving forward and forget that fucking town with its insidious little cult even existed. Or answer, deal with whatever fucking shit was being stirred, and then schedule an emergency therapy session for today.

In the end, my curiosity got the better of me. Maybe it was my mom wanting to finally break free, and if that was the case, I'd do whatever it took to help her. There was no forgiveness in my heart, but I wouldn't turn my back on her like she'd done to me.

"Hello," I said shortly.

There was a slight pause. "Uh, hello. My name is Nurse Nancy from the Provincial Hospital of Townsend. Sorry to call you like this, Mr. Silver, but we have your grandfather here. Jeremiah Townsend."

Good. Hopefully the old bastard was dying. "Yes, okay. What does that have to do with me? How did you even get this number?"

She swallowed hard, her voice a touch shaky. "Your mom gave it to us. Your grandfather is dying and needs a liver transplant. We've exhausted our options for a donor, and your mom mentioned that you're biologically related to Mr. Townsend and could be a match. Would you be willing to get tested, Mr. Silver?"

If this nurse had reached through the phone and punched me in the nuts, I'd have been less shocked and hurt. "My mom thought I'd be inclined to save that sick fuck's life?" I laughed because it was just so ridiculous.

Another pause. "Um, well, we just have to do our best to—" My laughter faded into a furious growl that cut her off, and she cleared her throat quickly. "Look, you're more than welcome to visit with Mr. Townsend and talk with the doctors about both the testing procedure and the actual surgery should you decide to dona—"

I hung up the phone. I'd heard enough to sate my curiosity, and now all I wanted to do was rage and smash this room to pieces. The lamp was in my hand about to be punted at the damn wall, when I took a deep breath and instead hit the voice chat symbol for Dr. Candance. It was convenient to be able to leave her chats, and she could get back to me between clients. I paid her well for this service, and it was worth every fucking cent.

"Doc," I started shortly, the lamp shaking in my hand. "Just got a call from the hospital in my hometown. My grandfather is dying and needs a liver transplant, and apparently, they think I'm the only match." Fucking typical. "I'm kind of flipping out here. I don't know what to do, and my need to smash up this room and smash down a bag of coke is at peak levels."

The fact that I'd chosen instead to chat with her told

me that I was still making progress. I even managed to unclench my fists and release the lamp back to its home on the bedside table.

A beat later my phone rang, and with that sound, rage rose once more until I glanced down to see the doc's number flashing. *Thank fuck.*

"Hey," I said, answering immediately. "You didn't have to call."

Her laugh was low and calming. "This sort of situation warrants a call. A face-to-face session would be even better, but I get the sense you're about to jump into a car and drive to Townsend, so this is the best we have."

That made me pause. "I don't want to go there, doc. I don't want to see any of them, and I don't give a fuck if he's dying. I really don't."

If anything, this was good news.

"I understand," she said, validating my feelings. "You are absolutely entitled to ignore that call, forget the past, and keep moving forward. You have all my support and guidance toward that end goal, but do you wonder if part of you will hold onto this moment if you don't walk into that hospital room, finally face your past, and put it to rest. Completely."

My sigh was long and drawn out as I fought for composure. Dr. Candace had warned me that to truly move forward, I might have to face some of the demons in my past. Literally face them, in some way. And I'd just kept hoping that would never turn out to be the case. But here we were with the perfect opportunity to say what I needed to both of them and then walk away and never look back.

"You're right," I said reluctantly, and she managed not to laugh again at my tone. "Again. I'm just not sure how I'll react when I see them both again. Will I feel like a helpless, terrified child once more, or will the power they've held over me for decades finally be gone?"

Her tone grew even kinder, if that was possible, and I let the calming influence sink into my soul. "No one can answer that for you, Rhett," she started. "But I promise that whatever happens in that room, you will be equipped with the skills you need to face your past, feel the pain, and then grow from the entire experience. Whatever hold they still have, however minor it might be, might be nullified in a single moment. Well, that moment and then all the hours of therapy after."

This time she did laugh, and I joined her because that line was the epitome of *funny cause it's true.*

"So, I should go and deal with him," I confirmed. "This isn't going to send me spiraling?"

"You'll spiral," she told me quickly. "But it won't be the same. It'll be gentler; it'll have more clarity. It'll be facing the demons as a very successful, loved adult, versus a scared, alone, and vulnerable teenager. You need to see the difference, Rhett. You need to see and grow from it."

She was right. I knew it deep in that painful pit of my past that still existed in my chest. The pit she had been helping to fill, but a part of it would always remain like an open wound until I faced them.

Just... rip the Band-Aid off. I needed this. The old fuck dying offered me the exact opening I needed to finally find some closure and put the past in the past.

"I'll call you when I'm done," I said, before closing my eyes and taking a fortifying breath. "Thank you for calling."

"Any time, Rhett. Let me know how it goes, and send a chat whenever you need a little helping hand."

"Will do, doc. Talk soon."

When she hung up, I took a few more deep breaths before I got my ass out of bed and headed into the bathroom. Twenty minutes later I was dressed and ready to face the past so that I might have a fucking future.

Speaking of, as I stepped into the living area, my future was there, curled up on the couch, napping just as I had been before my life was brutally smashed into once more. Someone had taken the time to cover Billie with a throw, and I just watched her breathe for a few seconds, wishing with everything inside me that I could crawl in beside her and lose myself in her.

Billie was a very big part of the reason I was determined to claw my way out from under the shadows of my past, and for her, I'd face these fucking demons. Face and slay.

Unable to leave without a kiss, I pressed one to her cheek, gently, so as not to wake her. But of course, my girl was a light sleeper at times. "Rhett," she mumbled, opening one eye and squinting at me, before she blinked a few times. "When did I fall asleep?"

Lowering myself closer, I brushed some of her messy hair off her face. "I'm not sure, love. I was napping as well, so it seems we both needed a little sleep."

Probably thanks to the four hours of sex we'd had in the early hours of this morning. Night sex and day naps were the stuff of my fantasies.

"Oh good, you slept," she mumbled again, before yawning.

"I did," I replied, brushing her cheek once more before I straightened. "I've got to duck out quickly for the rest of the day, but I'll see you later tonight, okay?" I'd left a note for Gray to let him know where I was going... just in case.

The sleepiness faded from her face in a near instant, and she focused sharply on me. "Wait, what? Where are you going?" She studied me closely, pushing herself up to sit. "Your expression is odd. Is everything okay?"

I really didn't want to drag her into my shitty past. "All good. Just got some shit to deal with, and I don't want to add to your worries. It's not important, just... maybe necessary for me to keep healing."

My words did not deter her at all. "Perfect, I'll get ready and come with. Give me five minutes."

"Billie, love, there's no need——" She was gone before I could finish, rushing from the living room into the closest bedroom. She had clothes and toiletries in all of our rooms. True to her word, she was back in just over five minutes, dressed in jeans, boots, and a sweater, with her larger coat draped over her arm.

"Ready!" she trilled. "Where are we going?"

"Townsend," I said, my fucking heart swelling with pure love for this damn miracle who'd stumbled into my life. The fact that she didn't even know where we were going or why, but she knew enough to be there for me, told me that Dr. Candace was right. I wasn't going to face my family as the same scared kid. This time, I'd be able to deal better.

"Isn't that where your family is from?" Billie asked, her expression falling.

I nodded. "Yep. I'll explain in the car."

It took a few more minutes to leave; after telling the

guys so they didn't panic and sneaking out past the press and security, we were finally on the road. "Grayson looked like he wasn't going to let us leave without him," Billie said with a chuckle as she adjusted the vents, snuggling into her seat. "Lucky he's a little distracted with the Angelo mission."

That and he knew I wasn't dumb enough not to take security with us, albeit at a distance. I knew it was safer to have the back up, but I also didn't need an entourage for this shit. No one would touch us in Townsend; it was owned by Jeremiah, after all, and *he* needed my liver to survive.

"Yeah, this is going to be hard enough, and I don't want one of them to go postal and tear up the hospital room." My bandmates were my brothers, and they would take out my grandfather for me. I knew that without any doubt. But this was a mental battle, and the only one who could win that for me... was me.

"Maybe I'll be the one going postal," Billie said with a shrug. "It's going to be hard not to punch your grandfather in the face, if I'm being honest."

Capturing her hand, I held it tightly. "You are a miracle, Thorn. Please don't ever change. But there isn't a need to punch him in the face anymore. The old bastard is finally dying. We're heading for the hospital."

She spun to face me, eyes wide as she stared,

unblinking. I looked away from the road for longer than was probably safe, enjoying that wide-eyed look of shock. "You're just going there to see him die? What did Dr. Candace say about that?"

I also loved that she knew and was so supportive of my therapy crutch. A crutch that I was assured would fade once I found my path through the darkness.

"Not exactly. I got a call from a nurse..." I explained everything that I knew so far and what the doc had said about facing the past to move forward. When I was done, Billie was huffing and puffing in her cute little angry way.

"How dare she call you and ask for you to give a piece of yourself to that fucking monster," she raged. "He's old and evil. It's time he was gone from this world."

I completely agreed, which I reiterated by squeezing her hand tightly in support.

Billie raged for a few more minutes before she calmed and let out a huff.

"It's all good, baby," I promised her. "This is just another step forward in moving on from the past. It's time to show them that I don't need them, I don't want them, and that there is no *little boy* left who can be emotionally manipulated into saving his grandfather."

"Okay, good." She nodded a few times. "But *Christ,* you're a bigger person than me. The fact that you're even considering showing him mercy when he gave you none?

You're a fucking saint, Rhett Silver. I aspire to be as mature as you one day. Now, let's talk about anything else."

We spent the rest of the few hours journey chatting about music, saving Angelo, and where Bellerose was headed once we dealt with everything else in our lives. "I really hope we go indie," I said, having thought about it for a few months now. "Our true fans would follow us, and I think authentic music, not studio compromises, is exactly what drew people to Bellerose in the first place."

"I totally agree. Even if most of those songs were about Jace's hatred for me, the emotions were so strong that they dragged you in."

"They were about his love for you, Billie," I reminded her. "He just thought it was hate."

She sniffled a few times before clearing her throat. "We have it figured out now, at least."

They did, and their healing was almost as beautiful to me as my own. All of us were growing to be better fucking people and couples than I'd ever expected, and I was totally here for it.

thirteen

BILLIE

The trip to Rhett's hometown was a bust. First, we got delayed countless times by road construction, then we arrived at the hospital after the doctor we'd been sent to see had gone home. He'd apparently just finished a thirty-hour shift, so neither of us had the heart to make a fuss.

The nurse on desk duty apologized profusely, but we had also arrived after visiting hours and had to come back in the morning. After a polite discussion with Grayson on the phone, Rhett and I checked into a lakeside B&B about forty minutes away from Townsend.

Okay, who was I kidding? The phone call had quickly devolved into a shouting match between Gray and Rhett over our safety and resulted in Gray barking at us that he was sending a bodyguard to meet us, and Rhett snarling that he could take care of me just fine without a bodyguard.

After the call ended, though, Rhett sheepishly admitted he was relieved that Gray was sending backup. A few people had stopped him for autographs at the hospital, and it was making him nervous about our security. He'd thought that in this town he'd be immune to fame, but Bellerose was too big for that, even in the town controlled by his evil family.

The next morning when we returned to the hospital, Mr. Townsend's doctor whisked Rhett off for the testing, which was a surprisingly easy blood draw. It wasn't until *after* they'd taken his sample, though, that the doctor told us Rhett's mom and grandfather—or father, if we were being accurate—had declined access to visitors.

They'd lured him all the way here, kicking him in the face with the life he'd worked so hard to leave behind, then didn't even have the decency to look him in the eye.

It made my blood boil, and as I'd predicted, I lost my shit.

"It's not worth it, Thorn baby," Rhett soothed, grabbing me before I could slap the unapologetic doctor right in his smug-as-shit face. Based on little things he'd said, I guessed he was fully drinking the Kool-Aid of the

Townsend Community, aka cult, but blocking our entry to the room really took the cake.

"Like *hell* it's not!" I raged. "You get your ass back there, and you tell that sick, predatory *fuckstain* that he doesn't deserve to live. Bad people shouldn't get second chances."

Rhett swiftly guided me out of the hospital, not slowing or looking back once. As we drove away, I ranted and raved all kinds of expletives about the doctors, his grandfather, even his mom... but then I cut short when I saw the silent tears tracking down his face. Then I demanded he pull the car over and, when he did, climbed into his lap to comfort him.

We probably would have stayed there on the side of the road all day—cuddling, crying, and making love in the cramped driver's seat—if Grayson hadn't called to ask what the fuck we were doing. He'd been tracking us on GPS and worried the car had broken down. Our newly acquired security car was behind us, so he could have just called them, but clearly, he wanted information direct from the source.

"Let's just... forget we ever took this trip, okay?" Rhett asked quietly as we pulled back into Grayson's driveway later that night. It had been a *long* drive to Townsend. "It was fucking dumb of me to think she'd actually see me.

JAYMIN EVE & TATE JAMES

That's not how excommunication works, right? Even if they want my liver."

I hated that they'd done that to him. Hated that he'd had his hope dashed when he'd been so brave to take that massive step. "Is that why she's never reached out before?" I was curious and wanted to understand more about the Townsend Community. "They like... pretend you're dead?"

Rhett nodded, kissing my hair as we entered the house. "I don't know if you remember, but when we were in Dublin, there was a guy waiting at the hotel to talk to me."

I blushed. Yes, I remembered, because that'd meant I was alone in the elevator with Jace, which had resulted in us fucking on camera for the hotel security. Whoops. "He was part of the cult?"

"Yeah. He apparently got out a few years after me. He's been living over there ever since because Jeremiah destroyed his name here. He couldn't get a job, couldn't get anywhere to live. That's one of the many things the vindictive shit of a leader does to control people. If you leave, sooner or later you'll come crawling back because he'll *make* you desperate. But Johnny was smart and moved overseas, started fresh. He just wanted to... I dunno. He saw Bellerose was in town and took the opportunity to just say hello. Tell me he got out. Say he was sorry." Rhett paused, swallowing hard. "That's the first time I've so much as set eyes on anyone from the community since the day I left."

Fuck. I'd had no idea. "That's what gave you the push to talk with Dr. Candace?"

He nodded, his hand squeezing my waist. "And I'm so glad I did. The peace I achieved when I was able to tell *you* about my past... it's unlike any high I've gotten from drugs. So I don't need to face my mom. You've already given me the closure I needed, Thorn."

Oh geez, my heart.

He pinned me against the wall, his kiss deep and slow, full to overflowing with affection and appreciation, and I didn't realize I could fall harder than I already had. And yet, there I went... tumbling into the abyss of warmth and happiness that was Rhett Silver's love.

Grayson, of course, scolded us for the unexpected overnight stay without security. He gave up on his bad mood pretty quickly, though, as we dove back into preparation for Operation Save Angelo.

Three nights later, I found myself head-to-toe in black and looking like some kind of badass mercenary. My hair was braided tightly away from my face, and Grayson had personally seen to strapping me into a bulletproof vest. Then he'd made me take off my pants and fucked me hard and fast while I was bent over the end of his bed wearing the vest.

It'd been hot and dirty and played to some seriously naughty fantasies since he'd been decked out in weapons when he railed me.

"Stay still, Prickles," he murmured sometime later as I squirmed beside him on the rooftop where we waited. We were set up on the roof of a high-rise office building roughly a *mile* away from the docks, and I was already grumbling about how I should have known there was a reason he'd agreed to let me come along so easily.

"Why?" I replied, huffing with irritation. "We are literally a mile away from the action; no one can see if I squirm. Or hear us, for that matter. I *knew* you agreed too easily to let me come along. Why am I even wearing a vest, Gray? No one can shoot me here unless they also have a sniper rifle."

He turned to look at me with a quirked brow. "They *do* have a sniper, but he's just focused on the wrong location. Here." He passed me the long-range binoculars. "Third floor from the top, sixth window from the left."

I brought the binoculars to my eyes to look at the building he was pointing out. Sure enough, the window he directed me to had a small section cut out and the long nose of a rifle protruded. Holy shit, how'd he even spot that?

"How do you know he hasn't seen us?" I asked, swallowing a flash of panic.

"Because he hasn't fired," Gray replied with a half smirk. "So stay still, and stay hidden, my impatient little hedgehog. Besides drawing attention if he starts scanning for threats, you're distracting me."

I rolled my eyes. "Maybe I wouldn't be squirming if I didn't have your cum soaking my panties right now." His gaze heated, then his eyes narrowed with a warning glare. Okay, maybe that information wasn't helping the whole distraction thing. "Still don't think I need to be wearing a fucking Kevlar vest, though."

"Yes, you do," he murmured, shifting his attention to the rifle scope and scanning the area for the hundredth time.

I sighed. "Because someone might shoot at us all the way up here?"

"Because you look fucking hot in it," he corrected. "And it helps *all* of us to know you're protected somewhat. Now, *hush*, Prickles. Much as I'd love to, I can't go shutting you up with my dick in your throat right now."

That actually did shut me up. As much as I loved getting my mouth fucked by Gray's huge cock... we were here to save Angelo. Nothing was more important than that, and I needed to stop splitting Grayson's focus. So for the next *hour* I sat there as still as a statue and tried to practice some of the meditation techniques that Dr. Candace was teaching me.

Finally, though, Grayson grunted and reached for his radio. "We have action," he said into the microphone.

I scrambled over to the ledge where he was set up with his sniper and backup rifles. He silently handed me the binoculars again, and my heart sat right in my throat as I found the *action* he was talking about. Three blacked-out cars had just pulled up to the meeting point. The doors opened, and sharply suited Ricci men climbed out.

"Giovanni," I whispered, recognizing Angelo's sleazy father surrounded by goons.

"Wilson won't be far behind," Gray commented, his eye glued to the scope. We'd all made an unspoken agreement to continue calling my back-from-the-dead father *Wilson*. As far as I was concerned, Bruce Bellerose had died in a fire nearly nine years ago. That man... the one who'd pointed a gun at me and kidnapped Angelo? That was not my father. He was a stranger. A monster.

Sooner or later, it was a topic I needed to tackle with Dr. Candace—not just that he'd faked his death and *never contacted me again*... but that he was obviously the guilty party in the murder of my mother. And my unborn baby, whether that had been intentional or not. Some things were just too big to work through all at once, though, and this was something I'd tabled until Angelo was home safe.

Then... well, then I could fall to pieces over the whole thing. Right now, he needed me to be strong—all the guys did—so we could *focus* and save our fallen Angel.

"Boats incoming," Giana's voice sounded in my ear. Gray and I both wore earpieces connected to the radio, and I was appreciative not to be left in the dark. "Looks like it's go time. We've taken out a few of their men around the edges but left enough so it's not radio silent on the docks. We still good up there, Big Bird?"

I snorted at her chosen codename for Grayson and caught his glower in the corner of my eye.

"All good here," he replied. "I'll take down their birdie once all the pieces are on the board."

"Mixed metaphor," I whispered, and he ignored me. Fair call, his meaning was clear enough.

"Cars approaching from the south," Rhett advised from his position as lookout on another elevated position. "Two sedans and one SUV."

"Wilson," I murmured, anxious nerves coursing through me like a live wire. "This is it. Isn't it?"

I'd be devastated if this was a false lead. All the buildup and then no climax. Those were the kind of bullshit plotlines sadistic writers used to draw out a story and fuck with their audience, not real life.

"Looks like it," Gray confirmed, his eye still locked on the scope.

I brought the binoculars back to my eyes, searching for the boats Giana had mentioned. Two zodiacs with outboard motors approached slowly through the inky water, each carrying a half dozen black-clad guys. Or I assumed they were all guys because these crime lords were all misogynistic as fuck.

My breathing hitched when they tied off against the dock and a bound, hooded man got manhandled off the zodiac. "There he is," I said in a strangled whisper. "Angel. He's..." I wanted to say *he's alive,* but as the guys started down the dock toward Giovanni and Wilson, who'd just gotten out his car, I realized that Angelo wasn't walking himself. Two broad-shouldered guards held him up by his biceps, his wrists cuffed together behind him, but his boots dragged as they escorted him along the dock.

"He's hurt," I squeaked out, my emotions choking me. I blinked rapidly to clear my cloudy vision, trying to keep Angelo in sight. What good was all of this if he was already dead?

"He won't be dead, Prickles," Grayson reassured me in a gruff voice. "Wilson wouldn't waste his opportunity like that. He didn't go through all that effort to transport Angelo back here only to have him killed in transit."

Okay. Yes, that made sense. He was right. They'd probably just had a struggle with Angelo and knocked him out. That sounded plausible, right?

"Alright, all our guests have arrived," Vee said in our comms. "Ready to set off some fireworks?"

Grayson drew a deep, steady breath, settling his shoulders and grip on the gun. I knew from the hundred times we'd gone over the plan that the first strike was taking out any ranged weapon guards, like our sniper across the way. Then he'd target anyone close to Angelo. To our utter frustration, we'd concluded we couldn't kill Giovanni yet, but Wilson was fair game. If anyone could kill him, they would. But our primary objective was saving Angelo, so those guards would be the focus.

One shot and the tinkle of breaking glass in the distance, and our rival sniper was taken care of.

"Birdie down," Gray confirmed after waiting a beat to see if there was return fire.

"Everyone else in position?" Vee asked. A chorus of quiet, grim responses from everyone confirmed their readiness, and Gray lined up the first guard in his sights. Something wasn't right, though. A pool of dread filled my belly as I studied the scene through my binoculars. I couldn't put my finger on it, but... something was wrong. Why were all the guards from the boat masked so thoroughly? Why would they care who saw them?

Wilson paid their salaries, and Giovanni was about to be killed... So why bother disguising themselves? The two guards holding Angelo even had gloves on... *as did Angelo.*

"Let's do this," Vee gave the command.

"Wait!" I exclaimed, bumping Grayson in my panic. His shot went wide, hitting a drum of gasoline further down the dock. It was enough to alert the scene to our attack, and within the space of a second everyone was shooting at one another while also diving for cover.

"Billie!" Grayson roared. "What the fuck?"

"It's not him!" I shouted back, absolutely convinced of my evidence-less theory. "It's not Angelo!"

Gray looked at me like I'd lost my fucking mind, then turned his eyes back to the rifle scope. It took him a moment to find "Angelo" again, now that everyone was locked in a full on firefight, but then he breathed a curse.

The man who'd been dragged from the boat, hands bound and a hood over his head, lay in a dead heap on the dock, but there, hiding behind the gas barrel that Gray'd shot? My Angel. He'd ripped his ski mask off, and his handsome face was set in a mask of grim determination as he gave hand signals to another of the "guards" from the boat.

"Son of a bitch," Gray whispered, then picked up his radio. "Pick your targets carefully. Angelo has his own plan in place. *Only* shoot Wilsons and Riccis; leave the boat guards untouched."

He then shifted his rifle, searching for a new target. I suspected he was looking for Wilson. My father. Was this how he died for real? Would I watch the man I loved shoot the man who'd raised me and I'd thought loved *me*?

"Over by the container," I told Gray, locating the two-faced bastard. "Hiding behind the SUV."

Gray waited patiently, then took his shot when he got the chance. It hit Wilson right in the chest, knocking him off his feet and flat onto his back. I felt nothing. Fucking nothing. No grief or fear or even regret. I was numb.

"Figures," Grayson grunted as Wilson slowly pushed himself back to his feet like something out of a zombie flick. "Should have gone for a headshot."

It took me a moment to understand his meaning. Wilson, like me and all our team, wore a bulletproof vest. And now it was too late for another shot because he'd already disappeared into the back of the car and a driver was gunning it out of the area.

Gray still popped another shot at the vehicle, though, aiming for its engine, maybe? Either way, it did nothing and I had to watch silently as my father—the man who'd just been about to execute Angelo—disappeared into the night.

"Anyone got eyes on that car?" Gray asked into the radio.

There was a pause. Then Jace responded, sounding puffed. "Just lost them. Sorry."

Grayson glanced at me for a reaction, but I was still cold as ice and shrugged. "We'll get him another day. All that matters now is Angelo."

He gave a thoughtful nod, then started packing up his rifles. "Let's get down there. By the time we arrive, it'll all be over with and you can check your Angel over for injuries." He winked. "I bet he'd be more than happy to let you kiss all his scrapes better."

Fuck yes. *Fuck yes.* Finally, it was like I could see light at the end of the tunnel. Our family was almost complete once more, and god help anyone who tried to break us apart again.

fourteen

BILLIE

Grayson was right about it all being over by the time we arrived at the docks. Blood and bodies littered the area, and several fires burned from where gasoline had caught alight and exploded—we'd heard them go off on our way—but otherwise, it was all relatively calm.

"Angel!" I cried out when I spotted him, gun still in hand as he nudged a dead body with his toe. He glanced up, a huge grin on his face, then quickly fired two bullets into the dead man's head before putting his gun away.

"Bella, you're here! Why are you here? Where the fuck is Grayson, and why did he not keep you somewhere safe?" He closed the gap between us and wrapped me up in a massive hug, lifting me clean off the ground.

I hugged him back just as tight, tears rolling down my face. "He's not the boss of me," I informed him in choked sobs. "As if anyone could stop me being here for you, Angel."

"Silly, gorgeous girl," he scolded, pulling back far enough that he could kiss me without ever putting me down. Then those kisses quickly heated up, and I hitched my legs up around his waist.

"Okay, okay, enough," Vee interrupted, striding over, looking like the femme fatale she was. "We need to clear the area. Angelo, you seem in one piece. Go with Billie and Jace to get checked over by our medic at the safety point, please."

Angelo stared at her with wide eyes, then gave a slow nod. "Yes, ma'am." He still didn't put me down, though. "Was that Giana I saw slitting a man's throat earlier?"

Vee smirked, the love and pride for her partner shining through. "Sure was. My baby is ruthless."

"So much for keeping her out of this life, huh?" Angelo remarked sarcastically. "You got this all handled?" He gestured to the mess we'd all made. There were *a lot* of bodies to take care of.

Vee's grin was pure arrogance. "Please. I think I know

how to scrub a crime scene, A. What do you take me for, an amateur?"

Roaring with laughter, Angelo carried me away without ever trying to set me down on my feet. Old bruises discolored the side of his face, but otherwise he seemed totally healthy. How had he managed to flip the guards to his side?

I was so fucking overwhelmed with emotions I buried my face in his neck and just let him carry me, literally stepping over bodies to get us to where Jace waited with a running vehicle. Only once we got there did Angelo set me on my feet, and Jace grabbed him in a tight hug of his own.

They exchanged a sweet moment of bromance, whispering gruff, manly endearments to one another, and my heart nearly fucking burst out of my chest to see their love rekindled.

The angry way Jace had lived his life for the past near decade was clearer than ever for me—along with his attitude when we'd returned to his life. We'd broken his heart, for sure, and that was a pain that never went away. But it was more than that... for all of us. We'd been living as half people, missing parts of ourselves and not even realizing how much impact that had on us until we were back together.

Together and able to truly be whole again.

"Let's get out of here," Jace said, releasing Angelo and nodding to me to get in the car.

"Where's Rhett?" I asked, scanning the area to ensure all my boys were safe and well. I spotted him chatting to Grayson beside a burning drum and gave a small sigh of relief. "Okay. Good. Everyone's accounted for, then."

"Not quite," Jace replied as we climbed into the car and set off. "Vee lost a few from her team, which isn't ideal."

Angelo grunted. "A few isn't so bad. You see how many Wilson lost?"

Jace grinned, giving Angelo a quick fist bump. "What happened to your dad in all that, Angel?"

"Regretfully, I made the decision to let him go. Not before making a hell of a point that I was *letting* him go and could have killed him if I chose. But it's never so easy... there's all the—"

"Contingency plans," I finished for him, leaning forward from the back seat. "Vee went over it all with us. The entire hierarchy system and the people your father has already set in place in the event of his death. You made the right choice... even if it feels anticlimactic."

Angelo shifted in his seat to face me with a curious look on his face. Then he grabbed the back of my neck and crushed his mouth to mine in a searing kiss. I moaned, parting my lips and letting him dominate my mouth with his hungry tongue.

"Come on, guys, save it until we get home," Jace complained, his hands gripping the steering wheel with a white-knuckled grip.

Angelo made a frustrated sound. "Fuck that, we're hours away. Where's this secure point Vee mentioned?"

Jace gave him a long look, then laughed softly. "Not far. Keep it in your pants until then, big boy."

My breathing sped up with excitement, and I squirmed in my seat, making Jace shoot me a knowing look in the mirror. "You too, Bellerose. Angelo needs to be cleared for injuries. Don't even fucking pretend you're not limping, dickhead. I saw it."

He was? Shit, now I felt like an asshole for not noticing. Especially since he'd been carrying me. That killed my overflowing arousal a little, and I forced myself to sit back in the seat while Jace drove us to Vee's safe house. It was an unfinished mansion in a new development area near the docks. She'd set this up as a base of operations for this mission. It was currently being used as a mini-clinic, utilizing the enormous open space of the unfurnished living/dining/lounge area.

"Keep an eye on him," Jace murmured as Angelo sat down on one of the makeshift beds that had been set up near the kitchen. "He'll try to bullshit them, but it's his knee that is hurting him."

"From the bomb at Big Noise?" I asked, double-checking I understood. Angelo had spent a couple of weeks walking with a cane but had recovered enough to walk without it before we'd even left for Europe.

Jace nodded. "I'd guess so, unless it's a new injury from the cargo ship. I need to go shower. I've got someone else's blood on me, and I'd rather not."

I blanched, gagging. "Good idea."

Angelo was surprisingly well-behaved for the medic. He wasn't too roughed up, and the bruises he did have were more than a week old, almost healed already. His knee was puffy and swollen, but ultimately, the medic just strapped it with tape and advised him to take it easy.

"Where's Jace?" he asked when they were done. He stood and walked toward me, this time not trying to hide his limp, and I scowled.

"Went to shower upstairs," I told him, nodding my head to the stairs. "Vee was smart enough to have the water turned on along with power. She's good at this shit, you know?"

He smiled. "I know. Show me the way? I could definitely use a shower right now. Two weeks on a cargo ship took its toll, even if we did have cold showers."

Jace was already out when we reached the upper-level master suite. He had a towel wrapped around his waist and was inspecting a nasty bruise on his shoulder in the mirror when we found him.

"You should get that checked out," Angelo told him, already stripping out of his clothes without waiting for Jace to exit the bathroom. As badly as I craved seeing Angel naked, I needed to stay in my lane and respect the gravity of all that'd happened tonight. So I averted my eyes and retreated into the bedroom. Vee and Giana had been sleeping there, so a big mattress sat on the floor, neatly made up with a quilt and pillows as though it were a proper bed.

I yawned as I kicked off my boots, then reached for the myriad of Velcro tabs on my Kevlar vest. It was *heavy,* and my body ached from sitting with Gray on that roof so long. I wanted it off.

"Here, I'll help," Jace offered, coming up behind me and brushing my fingers aside. He tugged the straps free but stepped away before I could lean back into him. "I'm going to go raid Vee's supplies for fresh clothes."

He disappeared out of the room, and I peeled my vest over my head with a groan, then tossed it aside.

"You gonna take the rest off too?" Angelo asked, making me spin around with a squeak of surprise. He stood in the bathroom doorway, a towel barely concealing his nakedness as he patted bruised skin dry.

I wet my lips, trying not to stare. "That was quick."

"I had other things on my mind," he admitted, "and you didn't look inclined to join me in the shower, so..." His gaze ran down my body, and my belly flipped with excitement. "Fuck, I'm glad to see you in one piece, Bella."

A couple of strides across the room saw him close the gap between us, and my arms banded around his neck as our lips met. He held my waist with one hand, then dropped his towel to hold my face with his other.

The damp fabric touched my toes, and the realization that Angelo was totally naked flushed heat through my body. Fuck waiting for another date, I wanted him *now*. Here. Wordless, I lifted my own shirt, breaking my kiss with him just long enough to pull it over my head.

"Bella," he groaned, his hands cupping my breasts through the simple black bra I wore. "I want you so fucking bad, but this—"

"Don't you dare turn me down, Angel," I growled, kissing him hard and biting his lip. "You're going to toss me down on this mattress and fuck me. Right now. Or I swear to god, I will—" My threat cut off with a yelp as he did exactly as I'd instructed, lifting me off the ground and dropping me onto my back on the bed.

He followed, sinking to his knees to tug my pants off with a hungry expression on his face. I was horny and impatient enough to let him, but then I frowned when I saw how he winced from leaning on his left knee.

"You're supposed to be resting that knee," I scolded, sitting up to remove my own bra. Now we were both naked and on equal footing. Unable to control my own hands, I reached out and grasped his impressive erection with a sure grip, making him moan. "Is this a piercing?" I rubbed my thumb along the underside of his shaft, finding two pairs of metal balls studding his silken skin.

"Uh-huh," he groaned, his eyes closed as he rocked into my hand. "It was meant to be a full ladder, but I never got around to doing the rest of the rungs."

"Fascinating," I murmured, exploring the jewelry. They weren't studs, but barbells threaded under the skin of his dick. Different from Rhett's, which went through the tip with a much thicker bar, these were almost delicate.

Angelo gasped as I stroked him again, then gave a hiss of pain when he shifted his weight on his knees.

"Shit, that's right. Sit down, idiot. I don't need you doing any more damage." I released my grip on his dick to drag him down onto the mattress. I'd apologize to Vee and Giana later for fucking Angelo in their bed, but manners were low on my priority list right now.

He got situated, his back resting on the pillows as I took his erection back in hand once more. "This doesn't feel fair, Bella," he protested with a groan as I worked my hand up and down, still fascinated with how the metal of his piercings moved with my motions. "I wanted to worship *you*. I wanted our first time together to be *special*."

I wriggled down the mattress and lay on my belly between his legs to lick the tip of his hot, hard cock. "This is special, Angel," I told him with a smirk, then circled my tongue around his crown while holding his gaze. "You're alive. We're alone." Sort of. "I can't think of anything I'd rather be doing right now than this." Then I closed my lips around him, sucking him in as I lowered my head.

He hissed a sharp breath, his fingers flexing against my hair like he was torn between stopping me and making me take more. He ultimately decided on neither, just bucked his hips and whispered curses in Italian while I blew him enthusiastically. Eventually, though, he yanked me back up until I was seated across his hips, and his mouth crushed to mine.

I moaned into his kisses, my lips puffy and sensitive from the work I'd just done, but he just kissed me harder. My body rocked against him, my aching pussy crushed against his cock, still slick from my saliva. He was so close to just slipping right into me that I was about to lose my mind with anticipation.

"Bella..." he breathed against my lips. "I'm sorry, beautiful girl."

"What for?" I asked, my voice hitching with worry. Was he turning me down?

He shook his head slowly, his tongue running over my lips like I was made of honey. "I'm so sorry, Bella," he repeated. "But I can't take this slow. Or gentle. I need to be inside you so fucking bad it hurts."

He reached down between us, lining himself up, and then thrust up as I sank down. The immediate stretch and fullness of taking his cock made me squeak, my nails digging into his neck as I fought to relax my inner walls and let him in fully. The added sensation of his dick piercings only confused my senses further, in the greatest of ways, and I worried I was going to come already.

"Angel," I yelped as he gripped my waist, holding me tight as he slid out halfway and slammed back in. Hard. Fuck yes... I was here for this. "Oh my god. Angel... I missed you so much."

His answer was another soul-sucking kiss as he started to pump his cock into me from below, finding a hard and fast rhythm that made my tits bounce and my skin flush.

A sharp knock on the door a moment later made us both still, and I rested my forehead against Angelo's as he grinned at me.

"That you, Jace?" he called out. Jace must have closed the door when he left, no doubt *knowing* this was about to happen. Very thoughtful of him.

"Yeah, it's me," Jace called back. "I've got clean clothes out here for you when you're done. But like... take your time. Rhett and Gray are downstairs sorting out casualties, but Vee and Giana will be a while yet."

Angelo studied my eyes a moment, his cock still moving in and out of me with a lazy, unhurried pace. It was still driving me wild, though, and my breathing was sharp pants. "Can we invite him in?" His question was quiet, intended only for me. But without even the slightest hesitation, I nodded.

"Join us then," I called out. There was a pause, like I'd confused him. Then his groan was barely audible. I licked my lips, grinning as Angelo shifted our position enough to wrap his lips around my nipple. Holy hell, who knew a big muscular guy like him was so flexible with his dick still buried in my pussy?

"Please, Jace," I gasped out. "Heal with us."

There was a slight pause again, and I thought maybe he would refuse. Sharing me with Rhett on an alcohol-fueled hate fuck, or even fucking my mouth while Gray screwed me in the forest... that was different. That was hot, no question, but it was *sex*. This... sharing me with Angelo... it was facing our past. Coming full circle to the stupid teens who'd broken each other's hearts. It was a huge step, but one I was more than ready to take. As was Angelo.

But was Jace?

Right when I started to feel crushed and rejected, the door opened. Hope soared in my chest as Jace closed the door once more behind himself, then took in our position with wide eyes. His nostrils flared and his jaw clenched, then Angelo gave my nipple a gentle bite that made me moan.

That sound seemed to snap Jace out of his shocked trance, and he reached for the hem of his t-shirt to pull it over his head.

"Are you sure?" he asked in a darkly sexy voice, approaching the mattress.

Angelo slammed his dick up into my pussy, making me gasp. "I am," he said. "And I *know* Bella is." It was a purred statement, and I whimpered my agreement. He'd felt how my body reacted when Jace entered the room. "You want to see for yourself, brother? Get your dick out and sit. She'll show you... Won't you, beautiful girl?"

I nodded eagerly. "Please, Jace. Don't make me beg. We need this... all of us need this."

Swallowing visibly, Jace shucked his sweats and joined us on the mattress. Even before Jace was settled, Angelo lifted me off his dick and deposited me on Jace's lap. My mouth met his desperate kiss, and I reached down to grab his already leaking dick beneath me. He needed no further encouragement, pushing up as I sank down on him, my walls hugging his intense thickness as I took him all the way to the hilt.

The familiarity of the scene filled me with bittersweet nostalgia. Our threesomes had always been like this... where the boys shared me back and forth. We'd been kids then. We didn't have the time or experience to take things further than that.

We were older now. More adventurous. And I knew damn well what I wanted from them tonight.

"Rose," Jace moaned against my lips as I rode his dick, my knees planted wide so I could really get him deep. "Holy fuck, you feel incredible. Your pussy is pure heaven, babe."

"I want to feel you both," I confessed between kisses, glancing over at Angelo, who stroked his cock while he watched. "I want you *both*." Surely my meaning was clear enough. The flash of excitement on Jace's face said he understood, and Angelo just looked like he wanted to eat me alive.

"Are you sure, Bella?" Angel asked, cautious even as he strangled his trouser snake in his desperate grip. "Have you—"

I shook my head. "No. Not yet. But Rhett and Gray have been... um... playing around with it."

Anal. I was talking about anal. I'd yet to take a dick there, let alone at the same time as one in the pussy, and yet here I was... practically choking on my need to try it out.

"It might hurt..." he murmured, though the interest in his eyes was undeniable.

My pussy tightened just at the mental image, and Jace gasped. His hands cupped my breasts, playing with them as I answered Angelo.

"I don't care," I told him truthfully. "I like a little pain, just ask Gray." Angelo's face flashed with jealousy, and I grinned back. "Angelo... are you gonna fuck my ass or not?"

Jace gripped my chin, bringing my lips back to his and thrusting up into my cunt like he was about to lose his cool just from talking about anal. Or more. Double penetration was what I was asking for here. That idea was definitely turning him on just as much as it was me.

Angelo murmured something too quiet to hear, then leaned off the mattress to flip open one of the girl's suitcases. I broke my kiss with Jace to peer over and see what Angelo was doing.

"...must have some in here," he was muttering under his breath as he rifled through women's clothing.

"Uh, Angel?" Jace asked with an edge of laughter. I was confused enough that I'd stopped riding him entirely, but he seemed content to let me just grind for a minute. "What are you searching for?"

Angel hunted a moment longer, then clicked his tongue in satisfaction. "Bingo." He held up a bottle of lube. "Those two use *a lot* of toys; I knew they'd have lube."

I coughed a laugh. "I would have been okay with spit."

He rolled his eyes. "Sorry, Bella, but if we're doing this here and now, you're damn well going to enjoy it. I'm not taking any chances with you getting hurt, because once we cross this line..." He smirked, crawling across the mattress to where I still straddled Jace, pussy full of his cock. "Oh baby, once we cross this line, you better believe it's going to become a regular thing."

Christ. I nearly came.

"Lean forward into Jace for me, Bella." Angelo pressed a hand to my lower back to give himself better access, then he deposited a heavy squirt of lube right down my crack. I shivered, then gave a shuddering moan as he started to massage the lube where it needed to be. He wasted no time pushing that first finger in, and I convulsed against Jace's chest as Angelo fucked me with his finger.

"Does that feel good, Rose?" Jace asked in my ear, his voice husky. "You like that?"

I nodded, gasping for air as he pumped his dick in and out of my cunt with a calm, slow rhythm, just enough to keep me feeling fucking fantastic while Angelo lubed me right up. "So good," I confessed, moaning, then Angelo pushed a second finger in with the first. He took his time to stretch me while I panted and trembled against Jace. Then he gave me another heavy squirt of lube.

"Angelo," I whimpered as he returned his fingers to my ass. "You're teasing now. Please, Angel, I need your dick. Please... I'm losing my freaking mind here."

He gave a deep chuckle, then sucked in a sharp breath of pain as he tried to shift his position.

"Switch," Jace ordered him in a no-arguments tone. "You can't be on your knee."

Fuck, that was right. Where was my head at? I nodded emphatically, sitting up and manhandling Angelo until he was back in his original position against the pillows. He pouted, but that sad face melted into a smile when I climbed back onto his dick and tensed my walls around him to hold him inside a moment.

"Ah, goddamn Bella, you're going to make me blow my load." He chuckled, gripping my hip to hold me still while Jace took up residence at my back. "Here." He offered the bottle of lube to Jace, squirting it into his friend's open palm like a real helper.

"You good?" Jace asked, kissing my spine as I imagined he was slicking that handful of lube all over his dick. Fuck me, was I really doing this? Yes. Yes, I was.

"Amazing," I confirmed, leaning forward further to give him access.

Jace hummed a thoughtful sound, then tugged me up off Angelo's dick to put my ass higher in the air. "Just until you get used to it," he told me with an edge of amusement. "Walk before we run." Then something a whole lot bigger than a finger pushed against my lube-slicked asshole.

"Relax, Bella," Angelo purred, stroking my hair in a soothing way when I squeaked. "Don't tense up, beautiful. Let him in. Let Jace work that fat cock into your tight little hole."

I moaned long and low, trying really hard to do as I was told. Jace *did* have a thick cock, but Angelo's was pierced so... same, same. At least it wasn't Grayson's monster breaking my anal virginity because that'd really destroy me.

Jace stroked my ass cheek, whispering to me that I was *doing so good*, and I relaxed incrementally. Then I realized it was feeling *really* good.

"That isn't so bad," I commented with a grin. "I like it. It feels good..."

Angelo arched a brow, and Jace coughed a laugh. "Uh, Rose baby. That's just the tip. Hold onto Angel for me while I just..." He pushed deeper, and I cried out. Now I understood why he wanted to do it for the first time *without* Angel in my pussy. Holy fuck I was so full, so stretched, it was unlike anything I could have imagined. "A little more, Rose," Jace grunted. "That's it, beautiful, you're doing great. Push back on my cock, baby, oh *uh,* yeah. Just like that. Fuck, you take my dick in your ass *so fucking good.*"

My face burned with all the praise, and my whole body trembled, but I was floating on cloud freaking nine. Cloud dirty-anal-sex nine. Fuck yes, achievement unlocked, and I was *into it.*

"Are you okay, Bella?" Angelo asked in a low rumble, his hands playing with my tits as he kissed my neck. "Still having fun?"

"So much fun," I panted, nodding emphatically. "Jace..."

"I've got you, baby girl," he replied, echoing the kind of endearment Grayson often gave me. "I'm gonna move now. You tell me if it's too much." Then he slid out a little way before pushing carefully, slowly back in. I moaned long and low and rocked against him. Jace chuckled. "I take it you like that, huh?"

Another long moan from me and he moved faster with the next thrust.

"Christ, Rose, you were made for this. Look how responsive she is, Angel. Touch her clit; I bet she comes."

Angel did exactly as he was told, and I didn't disappoint. Jace spluttered a curse, gasping the flesh of my ass tight as he rode out my intense orgasm, which locked up my whole body with convulsions.

My head spun with dizzying speed as I came back to earth, and I reached eagerly for Angelo's dick. "Angel," I gasped, my breathing harsh and heavy. "Please..."

He didn't need to be asked again. With a gentle grip he shifted me back down to his lap, and Jace moved his position to accommodate without ever having to pull out of my ass. Then Angel was pushing up into my pussy, and panic flashed through me. It was too much. Too tight.

"Angel, shit, you won't fit!" I protested, sandwiched between the two of them and unable to close my legs. "There's no space!"

He chuckled, then cupped the back of my head to bring my mouth to his. He kissed me long and hard, then pushed a little further into my slick pussy. I gasped again, and he swallowed the sound with his kisses.

"It'll fit, Rose baby," Jace reassured me, his own

breathing rough. "You'll adjust, and it'll feel amazing." With that confidence, I melted into Angelo's kiss and let him push his pierced dick in further.

"Shit, what the hell?" Jace muttered a few moments later when Angelo got his full length buried in my cunt. I was full to bursting, and one hundred percent, I wouldn't be able to walk in the morning, but Jace was right. It felt *amazing* to have them both inside me at once. "Is that thing pierced?"

Hysterical laughter bubbled out of me. "You didn't notice?"

"I wasn't exactly looking," Jace grumbled. "Fucking hell, you and Rhett must share a masochistic streak."

I had to agree. Then another thought occurred to me. "You can feel him?"

Jace's response was just a grunt. Then Angelo smirked, catching my lips in a kiss as he started to move under me. Jace muttered a curse, then resumed his own movement. Within a moment, they found their rhythm, fucking my holes like they were composing a song. Goddamn musicians and their sense of timing. I bet if Grayson were here he'd be smacking out a beat on my ass for them, too.

"Oh my god, I'm going to come again," I protested with a gasp, feeling the intense sensation building deep within me. Deeper than I'd ever felt it before, which made sense given all the firsts I was ticking off my list. Apparently anal gave me a different kind of orgasm, and *that* was fun.

"Do it," Jace ordered, "Because I've been holding myself back since the moment you presented this perfect peach for fucking."

I whimpered and trembled as the two of them picked up the pace, fucking me hard as our skin slapped together. The intertwined sound of our rough breathing filled the room, and I was powerless to resist the soul-shaking climax that stole through my body. My toes curled, my shoulders tensed, and I gave a soundless scream against Angelo's neck while they thrust harder and deeper, fucking me right through the orgasm and out the other side.

Only this time, the sensations didn't fade away like they usually did. They lingered, my body lit up with sensitivity as my orgasm drew out longer, fluttering on the edge like there was more to come. Was that even possible? Fuck, who was I kidding, after all the back-to-back orgasms I'd been having lately, I could probably cross into another dimension if I tried hard enough.

"Oh fuck," I groaned, licking my lips desperately, "you're going to make me come again already. Holy *shit...*" That was all I gasped out before I came so hard I momentarily blacked out.

"...need to come," someone was saying as my hearing slowly returned, "...can I..."

That was all I made out, but I could guess the rest. "Yes," I cried out, my voice hoarse. "Yes. Finish inside me. Please. Both of you. Fill me up until I'm dripping, and then do it again. And again. And—"

Deep masculine grunts rolled through me as their bodies jerked and their hips slammed into me at the same time. Hot jets of cum lashed my inner walls, both front and back, and pure joy and satisfaction unfurled in my chest. I'd never felt so worshiped or precious in my whole life. I'd never felt so loved and adored, or so fucking filthy. It was glorious. Angelo was right, we'd definitely be doing this again... I couldn't wait to get Gray and Rhett to join in.

Next time, though. Because as we all collapsed in a sweaty, cum-slicked pile of limbs, I seriously questioned how sore I would be when I woke up. Worth it, though. So fucking worth it. Maybe I just needed more practice, and I was confident I had four very willing training buddies up for the task.

fifteen

JACE

I've been an obsessed motherfucker for most of my life. Obsessed with music, obsessed with fame, obsessed with proving myself.

And above all of that, obsessed with Billie Bellerose.

She'd been a sassy little shit of a kid, and from the first fucking moment she'd wandered into my life and bossed me around, I'd been a goner. Like all genius guys, I'd pretended that she was an annoyance, when really... she was the fucking reason I got out of bed most days and stumbled my way through this life.

The darkness I'd felt when she'd left me had been indescribable. It was so complete, and I'd acted so destructively in that darkness, that I'd lost parts of myself I probably would never get back.

I'd almost lost the best part of myself: her.

If I hadn't been so goddamn stubborn, I'd have forced her to explain everything to me years ago and maybe we wouldn't be in this sort of situation where now I had to rebuild everything between us. It was my penance for my weakness. I'd been too weak and scared to face Billie again, and in doing so, I'd punished both of us.

But I was no longer that scared piece-of-shit boy. I was a man now, and I would show Billie what it was liked to be loved by this version of Jace Adams.

Even if I did keep referring to myself in the third person and by my full fucking name.

Yeah, some rock star traits were ingrained.

"How are you feeling today, baby?" I asked late the next morning after we'd rescued Angelo and the three of us had connected in a way that forged new fantasies in my head. We'd returned to Naples and Grayson's in the morning, and Billie had decided to stay in with Angelo. I'd slept on the couch and given them their time together.

She shot me the sweetest smile, wearing one of my shirts and, I would guess, nothing else. Her hair was messy, her face sleepy—we weren't giving our girl much rest these days—and she was the most beautiful sight I'd ever seen.

There was no replacing a first love, no matter how fucking hard you tried.

"You know, I'm feeling *all kinds of things* this morning," she said with a laugh, before her expression calmed, and she smiled gently at me once more, "but mostly what I'm feeling is loved. Thank you for..." She cleared her throat and shook her head. "I don't even know. Everything. For showing me the potential of the man I always knew you could be."

Shot straight in the goddamn chest.

"I'm not even close to done making up for my behavior in the past," I reminded her. "This is only the beginning, and I promise, I will never let you down again. Not if it's within my power."

She stumbled over and dropped down next to me, and I couldn't stop from reaching out and lifting her so she was on my lap. Almost immediately she tensed, but then she relaxed. Her first instinct was still to worry that I might hurt or reject her, and until she knew that would never happen again, I had my work cut out for me.

My hand splayed across her belly as thoughts of our child entered my mind once more. Despite everything over the past few weeks, my thoughts kept drifting to it. I decided it was maybe time for us to have a more serious conversation about the past.

"I know I apologized for my reaction to you telling me about the baby," I said softly.

Billie tensed again, and I stroked my hand across her stomach, lifting the shirt so I could touch her bare skin. "I can never truly make that up to you, I know that, but I want to explain what was happening in my life back then, the reasons that caused me to not be there when you needed me the most."

Billie twisted just enough that she was resting on her side against my shoulder, able to stare at my face. "You said that you refused to allow anyone to talk about me around that time."

I nodded. "Yeah, I couldn't handle hearing about you. Seeing you. It just hurt so damn much, and it took everything inside of me to not go after you, Billie. I wanted to respect your wishes, even if I was furious about them, and I reasoned that the only way for me to do that was to walk away and never look back."

"That was my fault too," she whispered, her words husky. "Fuck, I was so stupid. Now, I can't believe the choices I made and the reasoning I gave myself for doing so. It's amazing how incredibly underdeveloped my brain must have been at the time."

Tightening my arm around her, I pressed a kiss to her forehead. "You've always been smart, Rose. The smartest fucking person I knew. But you're also emotional, and while I love that about you, those circumstances were ripe for an overemotional state. You were a pregnant, hormonal sixteen-year-old, and no one could have expected you to make a clear, rational decision."

"And they would have been right," she said sadly.

"I was a dickhead then too," I reminded her. "Hyped up on my talent as a musician, thinking I had the fucking world in my hand."

"You did," Billie said readily. "You still do, and I never had a doubt you'd make it as a musician. Your talent is unsurpassed, Jace. Even now, all these years later."

Fuck, I'd missed my biggest cheerleader. "You are the reason I made it. Your help, your encouragement, and your songwriting abilities are the foundation on which I built the rest. Don't ever forget it, Rose. I owe you more than I can ever repay, but I do plan on spending the next seventy to eighty years giving it a shot."

She sniffled, and there were tears in her eyes as she lifted herself a little higher to kiss me. My cock throbbed at the first taste, but that bastard would have to wait. I had some serious shit to discuss with my girl, and there would be no fucking until I got this out.

"I can't believe this is happening," she whispered when she pulled away. "It feels like a dream, and I'm scared to wake up."

I knew the feeling all too well.

"No dream," I reminded her, "this is our new reality."

Another of those brilliant smiles forced its way across her face, some of the tears drying up as I brushed a few stragglers away. "That's the best information to wake up to. But what did you want to tell me about that day? You said you had something else to explain."

Right, right. We had gotten a little distracted there. My usual state when I was around Billie.

"Right around the time of the fire, my family was going through a bit of an... upheaval."

There was no other way to really explain it.

Billie pushed herself higher, hand on my chest as she examined my face. "Your family always seemed super boring and stable. You had high school sweethearts for parents, your dad the retired veteran, loved by the community, and your mom an English teacher who baked cookies on the weekends. I legit would not expect the slightest upheaval to darken your door."

I chuckled at the picture she painted. "You're not wrong. My parents are still stupidly in love, happy as newlyweds, but they actually almost got divorced that year."

Billie just blinked at me like I was speaking another language before she shook her head. "Nope, I can't see it. Must be a mistake."

That sobered me up. "Yeah, one of them did make a

mistake, and the aftermath of that was a trying time for us as a family. Did I mention I have a sister?"

Her blinks slowed as she stared wide-eyed at me. "I think I'd remember if you had a sister, Jace," she said softly. "I spent more time in your house than my own, growing up."

She had, and our games of hide and seek definitely took a different turn in our teenage years.

"Yeah, turns out that dad had a child he didn't know about." It had been years since the discovery, and it was still a little mind-blowing. "Teresa was discovered through an ancestry test, and it all blew up about the time of your fire. It was the hugest distraction, and it made it even easier for me to brush mom off when she tried to talk about you. I kept saying we needed to focus on our family."

Billie was still wide-eyed. "Are you fucking with me? Greg Adams had an affair? I've never known a man to love his wife so damn hard. I honestly can't believe it. I refuse."

Fuck, she was so damn cute. "So, Teresa is a couple of years older than me. It was during college, and they hadn't been super serious as a couple at the time. It was messy, that's for sure, and Teresa's mom never had even told dad. Let me tell you, I thought he was about to have a heart attack when he found out."

"Your mom was still upset, though?" she asked, no doubt wondering about the divorce comment earlier.

I shook my head. "Not really. A little upset at first, but when dad refused to contact Teresa, she got pissed. Said he wasn't the man she thought he was if he could turn his back on his daughter, and she moved out for three days."

Billie pressed her hand to her chest as small gasp escaped. Fuck, it would have been a different situation back then if I'd had her to talk to. "Your dad would have lost his mind."

My laugh was dark. "Bastard stayed drunk the entire time, until eventually he got his shit together, acted like a damn adult, and got his wife back. He also made contact with Teresa, and she's been part of our lives ever since."

She relaxed against me once more. "I'd love to meet her."

Fuck, I'd really hoped she'd say that. "Awesome, because they're going to be in town next week, and I know my parents are dying to give you a hug and welcome you back in as their favorite daughter-in-law."

It slipped out before I could stop it, and there was no fucking surprise when Billie went as stiff as a damn board. But fuck, it was the truth. She was the only woman I'd ever marry, and from here on out, the only one in my life. End of fucking story.

"It's only ever truly been you," I reminded her softly. "They've never met even one other woman. I've never mentioned one to them. Not a single name. Just yours Billie. Or 'our Rose,' as they always call you."

"Fuck, Jace," she sobbed, pressing her face into my chest. "You are going to kill me with kindness."

She had no clue. I was only getting started.

"Will you come out to dinner with us?" I asked her, more formally than was probably needed for a simple dinner. "See the parents and meet Teresa. She's desperate to meet the woman who stole my heart when I was a dumbass kid." I tightened my arms around her and laughed briefly. "I'm still a dumbass kid, according to Teresa. Nothing like a sister to humble you."

Billie sobbed a few more times, before she calmed, her face still pressed against my chest. "I'd love to go for dinner with you all," she finally whispered. "I'm actually really looking forward to it."

"Me too, baby. Me fucking too."

This moment was the full circle of my old and new life, just like last night had been, and I almost couldn't believe I'd spent so many years without Rose and Angel in my life.

No wonder my music had been shit after I'd run out of anger and pain to fuel my songs. I'd lost my true muse. My true love. The music in my soul.

Now that I had it back, I wouldn't give it up for anything.

Rose thought me mentioning *daughter-in-law* was a big deal, but she had no idea.

It was *'til death do us part* for me. Now and always.

BILLIE

The next few days flew by in a happy little bubble of bliss. I had my boys all under one roof—and in my bed—and I was so *fucking* happy it made my teeth hurt with all the sweetness. Logically, I knew it couldn't last. Not with everything hanging over us like a guillotine, just waiting to drop and sever our heads at the neck. Sooner or later, that blade would fall and send our heads rolling, our decapitated bodies falling to the floor, blood soaking into the dirt as the Bellerose fans looked on and wept.

"I'm officially getting cabin fever," Rhett commented with a yawn, flicking off the TV. "I can't believe I just watched a whole season of a historical regency drama. I don't even *like* history."

I smiled, leaning my head on his shoulder. "You watched it because I let you eat my pussy out every time someone curtsied to the king." It'd been a very good day. Exhausting, no doubt, but one for the core memory bank.

Rhett laughed. "Good point. Season two?"

"We should get out of the house," Angelo suggested. He'd also gotten in on that action around episode five when he found Rhett and I all sweaty and naked in the media room. "Bella, you want to get some fresh air? This house is starting to stink of semen."

Despite the fact that I was largely to blame, when he put it like that, I gagged a little. "Thanks for making that seriously unsexy, Angel. So yes. Gimme a few minutes to shower and change." Rhett started to follow, and I laughed as I pushed him back into the sofa. "Alone, Zepp, I meant alone. My poor pussy is about to malfunction from all that attention she just got."

I was bouncing back a whole lot quicker than I used to, though, which verified my whole *practice makes perfect* idea and meant I no longer spent days walking like a cowgirl. Now I just rode reverse cowgirl and begged for more. We called that *personal growth*.

An hour later, Angelo, Rhett, and I were heading out of the house in one of Grayson's highly secure SUVs with blacked-out, bulletproof windows. A second car filled with security was behind us, but they weren't going to follow us to *wherever we were going* since this was apparently an incognito mission.

"So, where are we going?" I asked, just realizing I had no clue what Angelo's idea of *fresh air* actually was. Rhett grinned, so clearly he knew, but they both just told me to *wait and see*. Which... okay sure, it was cute. I didn't love surprises, but I did love both of them, so I was excited.

Twenty minutes later, I got my answer when we pulled into Siena's most extravagant mini-golf park. Grinning, I climbed out of the car with the guys and looked up at the big, goofy characters looming over the entryway. "Mini-golf, huh?"

Angelo shrugged. "Why not? You used to love coming here."

I snickered. "When I was eight, sure. I can't even remember the last time I came here!"

His brows raised. "Really? I do." He reached into the back of the car and pulled out a costume hat with a sandy-blond mullet attached and tossed it to Rhett. For himself, he put on a fedora and fake beard. It was a truly comical disguise, but it did the trick, considering how famous Bellerose was.

"What happened the last time you were here?" Rhett asked, making sure his hat-mullet combo covered all his distinctive hair, then pulling a pair of sunglasses on. He handed me some sunglasses as well, and a cap, and reminding me that I was kind of famous now too. Not in a positive way, of course, but as the harlot who was fucking all of Bellerose, taking them from the masses who loved them. But it still meant I needed to keep myself somewhat disguised or I'd give the whole charade away.

Angelo cast a wistful look my way. "Billie kissed Jace on the cheek and asked if he'd marry her when they grew up. I was so jealous I never wanted to come back."

Oh shit, I vaguely remembered that day. I'd been nine and the boys eleven. Because Angelo had been listening Jace had laughed and told me I was being a silly *girl*. Then later, he'd held my hand and said that if he ever got married, *of course* it would be to me.

I smiled at the memory, then hugged Angelo's waist as we headed for the entry booth.

The first part of the plan went smoothly. Angelo used cash to pay for our entry, and we grabbed some clubs and balls and got started on the first hole—all of which sounded very sexual after the last few days, and for sure, the jokes were flowing from both guys every single time they missed.

"Aw, missed the mark," Angelo said with a laugh when Rhett's ball all but rimmed the hole and then bounced out. "So close, Silver. But, I guess you're used to that."

"Shut it, asshole," Rhett said, flipping him off. "Your last shot didn't *even come close*. Again, though, no surprise there."

The biggest surprise was that I was still pretty good. We'd played a ton as kids, and being the competitive chick between two guys, I'd always worked hard to beat them. And today, it looked like I was going to do the same.

"Your stance is a little off," Angelo said when I was lining up the seventh hole. "You need to twist your hips like this."

He pressed in behind me, hands landing on my hips as he moved them into the position he suggested. "And keep them relaxed as you swing."

The hard length pressed to my ass told me that there was nothing wrong with my hips or stance, and fuck, it was nice to have men in my life who took every opportunity they could to demonstrate their need for me.

I never had to worry I was the only one all in.

"Can you show me that again?" I asked with a soft chuckle. "I think I missed some of the pointers."

His chest shifted behind me as he groaned low. "Fuck, Bella. You're going to be the death of me. We're in disguise; I can't throw you down on this green and fuck you how you deserve. So, behave."

"Rich coming from you, mafia," Rhett said with a snort of laughter. "You're all over there with the hips swaying as you 'correct' her stance. That's from the oldest playbook in history."

Angelo shrugged, not seeming offended. He just smirked and stepped back to let me finish my shot. Of course, I was so turned on and distracted that I completely missed the mark. Judging by Angelo's smirk, that had been his aim all along, and I silently promised him payback later.

By the time we reached the twelfth and last hole on this course, I felt somewhat calmer and more relaxed. Our lives had been *a lot* the last few days... fuck, weeks and months, actually. It was nice to let loose and just act like normal people.

Even if there was no way Bellerose would ever be able to be "normal" again, we could hopefully find our own normal in the future.

"Have you heard from your father?" I asked Angelo when we were heading toward the exit, dropping our equipment off in the return slots.

"Not a word," he said shortly, adjusting his hat. He pushed it up on his forehead, briefly, before letting it settle into place once more. "He'll be in planning mode, and I know from Vee that there're lots of rumors skirting along the dark web about his next moves."

Fuck, that made me so nervous. Part of me just wanted the plan to drop so we could deal with it, while another knew that was super dangerous, and I couldn't handle having any of my guys in danger any longer.

"Is Vee ready?"

Angelo hesitated briefly, and that did not fill me with confidence. "She's getting there," he said, sounding surer. "I think we have a decent plan brewing."

We started toward the car then, the boys framing either side of me, as they tended to do in their protective way. I barely managed to stop myself from reaching out and taking both their hands.

It annoyed me that society made this perfect love we all shared seem like something dark and depraved. As if there was only one correct formula for love and relationships. But shit, we were all adults, more than consenting, and I had never been happier.

As if my fucking happiness was too much for the universe to allow me in one go, the second I had that thought, a girl who was standing a few yards away let out a shout. "Bellerose!"

"Fuck," Rhett muttered, and Angelo picked up the pace, trying to get us back to the car before anyone managed to reach us. Unfortunately, though, there were fans ahead on the path, and there appeared to be nothing that was going to stop them from stepping right in front of the boys.

Angelo barely managed not to bowl them over, and I would guess it was only the thought of bad publicity that had him grinding to a halt. "Excuse me," he said soft but firm. "We really need to get to our car. I'd appreciate it if you'd move out of the way."

There were two of them, both young, blonde, and dressed in skimpy dresses, despite the fact that the temperatures here were still unpredictable. "Can we get a photo and autograph first," the closest girl to Angelo said, reaching out as if to touch him. Like he wasn't a person and didn't deserve the right to privacy and personal space.

He stepped back before her hand could land, pulling me with him, and that was the moment she noticed me there, sandwiched between the two of them.

Her excited and open expression fell, eyes narrowing as she leveled them on me.

"What about you, Rhett Silver," the other chick asked, not having seen what her friend had yet. "You're the sexiest guy ever. I will literally blow you in this car park if you want me to."

Rhett let out a low laugh. His fake, stage-presence laugh. "Ah, darling, as tempting as that offer is, I really need to get home. But we appreciate your support of Bellerose. Keep rocking out."

He tried to step past her, but she dodged to get in his way, and that was when his fake personality vanished under his regular one. "I will ask you nicely one more time to please get out of our way. Then I'll call security."

"Forget about it, Trisha," the first girl snapped, still glaring at me. "They have the Bellerose whore with them. You must have one hell of a fucking cunt on you, bitch, if you think you can keep four rock stars pleased."

No one could sling an insult like another woman. It was fucking sad, really.

"It *is* one hell of a cunt, thanks for noticing," I said as pleasantly as I could. "Though it is rather sore right now after Rhett tongue fucked it..." I turned to him. "What was it, twenty times today? God, it's hard to keep track."

He chuckled, before he stepped in front of me, not completely blocking me, but keeping me in a position of safety. Angelo did the same, and I saw the way his hand rested near the spot he always carried his gun. Bellerose's regular security might still be in their car across the way, but with Angelo, I still felt safe.

"You're just the slut of the hour," the other chick said with a shake of her head. "I wouldn't get too comfortable in their beds. Rock stars tell everyone they love them, and it's all just for the puss—"

Rhett brushed her aside, shutting her off mid-sentence, and she burst into tears almost immediately. "How fucking dare you touch me," she shouted.

His entire expression went hard, and when he turned toward her, she shrunk back, her friend running to protectively stand at her friend's side. "Security cameras captured everything," Rhett said, his voice scarier than I'd ever heard. "If you try to spin this any other way to the media, I will destroy your life. I have the money, time, and the power to do just that. Consider this before you make your next move."

She let out an angry screech before throwing her phone right at his head. My cry was lost in the noise, but thankfully Rhett managed to catch the device and drop it to the ground before we started to move again, leaving them crying off to the side of the path.

As the adrenaline died off, I realized I was more shaken than I'd expected from that little interaction. "Is it always like this with your fans?" Angelo asked gruffly. "They're both persistent and fucking psycho."

Rhett let out a long breath, keeping his hand firmly wrapped around mine as we made it into the car park. "It's been worse lately, with all the drama and the Dirty Truths blog, but yeah, a lot of the time they think of us as their property. Like, a piece of fucking meat they can manipulate how they will. It sucks that we can't make music without the other shit getting in the way."

He sounded tired, and I didn't like that sound from my sweet knight.

I wanted to comfort him, but we did need to get to the car before those chicks recovered and did something even stupider. Of course, as I had that thought, a flash went off almost right in front of our faces as a pap jumped out from between two parked cars, shouting, "Rhett, do you have a statement about the recent article stating that Billie Bellerose is causing the band to break up?"

Another flash in our faces, and Rhett let out a low roar before he swung back suddenly and punched the man right in the face. The camera shattered to the ground as the guy fell back, shouting out in what I had to guess was shock and pain.

"Don't fucking come near us again," Rhett spat, standing over the top of him. "And never mention Billie. She holds us together, not the other way around."

I was thrown over Rhett's shoulder in the next second as he took off jogging, Angelo following behind, and it didn't escape my notice that he had his gun in his hand now. Any other celebrity drawing a gun to deal with press and rude fans would seem like they're totally lost the plot, but given how many times our lives had been at risk lately? Yeah, it was understandable. Who knew when our enemies would disguise themselves as fans *or* press?

Fucking hell. The night had started out so well, and yet the ending was more fucked up than I could have imagines. This life of fame and fortune wasn't all it was cracked up to be, and I wondered if this was my reality from now on.

This was the reason Jace wanted to make a statement to calm some of this crazy down, but here tonight, seeing all of this, I wondered if it was just too late.

The tidal wave had started, and we could do nothing but stand on the shore and get swept up in the crash.

seventeen

BILLIE

The fallout from our mini-golf trip was insane. Not only had Grayson lost his shit at our security that had failed to intervene when the paparazzo showed up—they'd been on their phones in the car, not even looking our way—but also because the photographer filed charges against Rhett.

Brenda and the Bellerose legal team went back and forth with the photographer's lawyer until it was finally resolved when the guy agreed to drop assault charges if Rhett replaced his camera. And made a public apology. Slick fuck just wanted his five minutes of fame, and he got it when Brenda dragged Rhett out on camera to say *sorry.*

Not a single person who knew Rhett would have believed his apology, though. Though the words were scripted, his meaning was crystal clear. He wasn't sorry, and he *would* do it again.

I got so caught up in that whole saga I nearly forgot about going to dinner with Jace's family until the day they got into town. He reminded me after breakfast, then I spent the day stressing out over what to wear.

"You look beautiful, Prickles," Grayson reassured me as I checked the mirror for the hundredth time that evening. He was reclining on my bed, having quietly watched me get ready for my dinner. "But there's one little thing I'd change, if I can?"

I spun around, panicked. "What? Is it the lipstick? It's too much, right? Too bright? I should have gone with nude."

Grayson smiled, crooking his fingers to beckon me closer. "The lipstick is perfect, baby girl. You're perfect. But I wanted to help Jace out... I know he's a bit stressed about seeing his parents."

When I stopped at the edge of the bed, Grayson sat up. His hands pushed the skirt of my knee-length green dress up, and I moaned in protest. "Gray, I don't have time to—"

"Tempting as that is, Prickles, I'm not going to make you late. I'm just taking these." He tugged my black panties down and indicated for me to step out before smoothing my skirt back over my ass. "Much better. No panty lines, and Jace will have easy access if he needs any *distraction* during dinner." He shot me a wink, and my belly fluttered in response. How had I never realized what a sex addict I was? These days it was like I was *never* not in the mood.

"Jace is not going to try and fuck me halfway through dinner with his family," I grumbled, but I also didn't put my panties back on. I liked the secret knowledge of being totally naked beneath my demure dress, and I knew Jace would enjoy that discovery if he *did* need a little distraction.

My guy in question knocked on my door a moment later, asking if I was ready to leave, then paused with his jaw dropped as he took in my outfit.

"Rose... holy crap, you look incredible," he commented, licking his lips. "Maybe we should tell them we'll be late." He reached for his pants, jokingly, and I laughed.

"Stop it. I just wanted to make a good impression... The last time your mom and dad saw me was, uh, probably at my parents' funeral." I blanched. "I mean, my mom's. I guess my dad never got buried, huh?"

"They loved you then, they'll love you now," Jace reassured me, dropping the joke. Okay, maybe it wasn't totally a joke because he needed to rearrange his growing erection as we headed out to the garage. Grayson told us to take the Mustang, and there was no security since we were heading for a swanky restaurant that had their own staff. Jace grabbed the Mustang key from the peg board on our way.

He kept stealing glances at me while he drove, and I had to hide my smiles so we didn't end up late. It was unbelievably hard to keep our hands off each other at the moment.

"Just so we're clear," he told me as we pulled into the valet parking of the restaurant, "if you get up during dinner to use the ladies' room... I'm going to follow. And we *will* fuck."

My heart fluttered and my pussy heated. "Noted," I replied with a grin.

Laughing, he handed the car keys to the attendant, then offered me his arm. "You think I'm joking, but I'm not. I'll be sitting there trying to talk to my fucking family with a raging boner. So, thanks for that."

I blushed when an older woman nearby gasped. Jace hadn't even tried to keep his voice down as he'd said that. He ignored her, though, heading straight to the hostess station to give his name.

His family had arrived before us, and his dad stood to greet him as the waitress showed us to a table near the back of the restaurant. I recognized Greg and Lydia Adams, Jace's parents, but the pretty blonde woman seated beside Lydia was a stranger to me.

"Hi, you must be Billie," she said with a smile, standing up to offer me her hand. "I'm Teresa, but call me Tess."

I accepted her hand and cheek kiss. "Tess. Nice to meet you!" Then I turned to Lydia, who had tears in her eyes. "Hi, um, Mrs. Adams."

She burst out crying, grabbing me in a huge hug. "You stop that, Billie Bellerose, it's Lydia and you darn well know it." I relaxed into her embrace, hugging her back with tears in my own eyes. I didn't realize how worried I'd been about their reception until now. They had once been like family to me, and I hadn't seen them, outside of the funeral, in years.

"Liddy, let the girl go," Greg gently scolded his wife. "We're in a fancy restaurant."

Lydia sniffled but nodded, releasing me. "Sorry, Billie. Gosh, this is all very overwhelming. Sit, sweetheart, sit down." She flapped her hand to one of the seats, and I did as I was told while she greeted her son with a big kiss on his cheek.

"Mom," he said softly as he sat in his own chair beside me. "Did you guys find the place okay?"

His dad gave him a long look. "I know we aren't

celebrities, son, but Naples isn't that far from Siena. We've been here before."

"Once," Lydia added with a smile. "On our twentieth wedding anniversary. Really, though, we'd have been just fine to meet you two at a diner."

"I know," Jace sighed. "But places like this are more... *respectful* of, um, recognizable people. Billie had an uncomfortable interaction with a Bellerose fan earlier in the week, so I wanted to try and avoid that happening again."

Tess nodded. "I saw that on the Dirty Truths. Rhett beat up a photographer?"

Jace grimaced. "Don't tell me you follow that bullshit gossip site, Tess; you're too smart for that shit."

She just shrugged. "Gotta stay up to date with my rock star little brother somehow. Besides, you know they have like six million followers now?"

"They're parasites," Jace growled, "preying on our private lives and spreading bullshit rumors."

I placed my hand on his knee under the table, giving it a squeeze to tell him to change the subject. "Tess, Jace told me that you work closely with a women's shelter. How'd you get into that?"

Her smile was bittersweet as she started telling me about her work and how her mom had suffered through a string of abusive relationships while Tess was growing up. Eventually, she and her mom had ended up in a shelter. "The people who ran that shelter saved our lives. Without the care and support they provided, who knows where we would have ended up. My mom was my biggest supporter when I decided to venture into trauma recovery, and specializing in domestic abuse survivors. Every day when I go to work, I see my mom in the women I try to help. I hope she would still be proud of the woman I became." Tess cleared her throat, her eyes glassy.

"Her mom's passing was the reason Tess started to search for me on the ancestry site," Greg said with a soft, and clearly proud smile. "Clara only told her about me just before she died."

"She didn't want to leave with secrets," Tess said huskily. "I don't have any family left on my mom's side. It was just us."

I wanted to hug her. I seriously wanted to get up and walk around this damn table and hug her. Instead, I settled for reaching out and grasping her hand. "Your mom would be *so* proud of you," I whispered, unable to speak louder with how choked up I felt. "And I'm so happy you found Greg and Lydia. And Jace. They're the best kind of people."

Her smile was beautiful. "The absolute best. I'm one

lucky girl to have found light in my darkness. I think that was mom's doing."

I gave her hand one last squeeze, and then, thankfully, the conversation shifted to something a little lighter.

"Tell us how you and Jace reconnected after all these years apart," Lydia said.

Okay, maybe not lighter, but different...

"Um..." I glanced at Jace, who was sipping his whiskey with a smirk on his lips. "Uh... it was an accident, actually. I bumped into Rhett outside a club and didn't know who he was."

Tess laughed. "I bet his ego took that well."

Jace found my hand under the table, his fingers linking with mine. "We had a bit of a rough reunion," he admitted honestly, if a little understated, "and it took some time to work through some pretty heavy misunderstandings. But we're stronger for it, now. I'm just glad Billie could be patient with me."

I met his tender gaze, my heart in my throat as I nodded my agreement. I couldn't have spoken even if I'd tried, so I just leaned in to brush a light kiss across his lips instead.

He returned my kiss, then reluctantly released me since we were sitting at the dinner table with his parents watching us. Awkward.

"Well, it looks like things worked out," Lydia commented with a gentle smile on her lips. "I couldn't be happier for you both. Even with all his success and fame, Jace was never quite as happy as he was with his Rose, isn't that right, Greg?"

Jace's dad gave a curt nod of agreement, sniffing like he was getting a bit choked up himself. "That's right, Liddy." He raised his glass to us in a toast. "Here's to you two, Jace and Billie. Don't waste this second chance."

"Not a chance," Jace whispered, his eyes on mine even as he clinked glasses with his dad. I blushed and tapped my glass with everyone's, then took a sip right as Lydia asked her next question.

"So, when can we expect wedding bells and a baby?"

I choked on my Champagne. It went right up into my nasal passage, making me cough and splutter in a seriously unattractive way.

"You okay, babe?" Jace asked with a grin, handing me his napkin.

Holy hell, Champagne in the sinuses *burned*. "Fine," I croaked. "Yep, good. All good. I'm just... uh... excuse me a moment." I was still coughing, my eyes watering and running my mascara, so I slid out of my seat and hurried to the restroom to clean myself up.

I'd barely finished wiping up the dark smudges under my eyes when the door swung open again. The ladies' room had multiple stalls, so I didn't even look over until Jace grabbed my waist.

"Jace!" I exclaimed as he spun me around and boosted my butt onto the long counter in front of the mirrors. "What are—" My question cut off as he kissed me, and I melted into his embrace. My knees fell open, and he surged closer, his hands sliding up my thighs.

"I warned you, Rose," he murmured against my lips. "I'm so fucking hard right now. All I've been able to think about is how to get you alone."

I gasped as his hard length ground against me, his suit pants straining with the bulge. "Jace, we can't! Anyone could come in and see us!"

"Then we should be quick about it," he replied with a devious smirk, his hands pushing my skirt right up over my hips. "Billie... Rose... where are your panties?"

It was my turn to grin, and he dragged his lower lip through his teeth as he moaned a curse. Then in a flurry of motion, he loosed his belt loosed and thrust his thick cock into my aching cunt. All good sense flew out the window as I wrapped my legs around him, leaning my shoulders back against the mirror to pull us closer together.

"Jace..." My voice was pure lust. "Holy fuck, you feel so good."

"Hold on, baby girl. I wanna make you fall apart

before we get caught." His voice was low and rough, his hips rocking as he started to fuck me right there on the vanity. Just the idea of getting caught had me so worked up and tense I already knew it wouldn't be hard to make me come.

His mouth claimed mine as he thrust hard and fast, my high heels hooked together behind him to hold on tight. At some point, I thought I heard the door open, but when I peeled my lids open, there was no one there, so I said nothing and continued to kiss my guy. Continued to rock against his intense rhythm as he chased both our releases.

"Fuck, Rose," he moaned a few moments later. "Tell me you're close; I need to feel your sweet pussy locking up on my cock."

I nodded, kissing his throat. "Close," I agreed, "really close. Don't stop, Jace. Don't fucking stop for anything; I'm right there..." He continued pounding me into the mirror, and a split second later I spiraled into a hot, hard orgasm. My walls spasmed, clenching around his dick just like he liked, and then he slammed deep as he joined me in sweet release. His cum pumped into me, and he gasped out a curse.

"That was dangerous," I whispered, licking my buzzing lips with a gasp. "We could have been caught.

Then kicked out. Then your family would know what we were doing."

He smirked, smoothing a hand through my messed-up hair. "It won't be hard to guess as it is, Rose." Then he leaned in and kissed me sweetly, his cock still twitching inside me. "I love you so much it hurts. Even if it takes our whole lifetimes, I'll prove that I'm worth the second chance."

My pulse raced even harder, and tears pricked at my eyes. "You've already proven it, Jace. But tell your mom to cool it on the marriage and babies talk, okay? She must not know I'm also in love with your whole freaking band."

He chuckled, reluctantly separating from my body, and helped me off the counter. I grimaced as I wiggled my dress back into place, feeling the slick mess of his cum on my inner thighs already. Fucking Gray could have left me a pair of panties to put on *after*.

"I need to clean up," I admitted, cheeks heated. "I can't go back out there like this."

Jace frowned in confusion, then grinned when he understood. "Oh. Baby. You are *absolutely* going back out there like that. Christ, now I'm getting hard again just thinking about you walking around with my cum coating your pussy. You'll be sitting there eating dinner, and it'll be dripping out... *Fuck*. Round two?" He grasped himself through his pants, which he'd only *just* done up, and I laughed as I pushed him away.

"Stop it! We can go for round two in Gray's car on the way home." I laughed, pushing him again, but he caught my hand, reeling me in for another breathtaking kiss.

"Fine," he grumbled. "Come on. They already probably know we were fucking; no use hiding it by sneaking out separately." He guided me out of the restroom and back to the table before I could even tidy my hair, and the knowing look Tess gave us said it all.

Damn it, Jace!

The rest of dinner was amazingly enjoyable, once I got past my embarrassment. Jace kept giving me soft looks of adoration, his hand on my knee under the table, and I found myself gazing at him like a lovestruck idiot on more than one occasion.

Eventually, though, the dinner ended, and we all got up to leave. Jace and his dad handed their valet slips in to get their cars, and I chatted with Tess about her new puppy, which she needed to get home to feed. He was a twelve-week-old Spoodle she'd named Jonas after a character in a book she was reading. After seeing pictures, Lydia and I cooed over how cute the little floof was, and Jace's dad spoke quietly to him on something or other.

The first car to arrive was Lydia and Greg's, so we bid

them farewell with hugs and promises to stay in touch. Lydia gave us a wink and told us that we'd make beautiful babies, then climbed into the car as my panic surged *again*.

"Alright, well, I better get going," Tess told us with a wide grin. "Ignore Lydia. She's just desperate for grandbabies at the moment; must be a phase of life."

Clearly Jace hadn't told his parents about Penelope, but I couldn't blame him for that. It wasn't the sort of thing to casually drop in conversation.

"Can we give you a ride?" I offered, since she'd said she would walk the few blocks back to her hotel. Lydia and Greg were driving back to Siena, but Teresa was staying for a few days. "It's late, and Naples is full of crime these days."

She shook her head, declining. "Nope, I enjoy the night air. But I hope I can see you guys again while you're in town?"

"Absolutely," I agreed emphatically. "I'd love that."

Tess hugged us goodbye just as the valet pulled up with Grayson's Mustang. The attendant hopped out and handed over the keys, then gave a horrified gasp.

"You're Jace Adams," she exclaimed, still clutching the car keys in her hand as she glared up at Jace. "You're Jace *fucking* Adams. From Bellerose."

Jace winced, glancing around. "Yeah. Did you want a

selfie or...?" He hunched his shoulders and clutched my hand tight, uncomfortable with the girl's attention but also trying to be polite and not brush off a fan.

"A *selfie*?" she spat like he'd just proposed shitting on her bed. Maybe not a fan, then. "You ruined my whole fucking life! You think I want a *selfie*? I want you to pay for what you did!" Her eyes shifted from Jace to me, then to Tess, and her expression twisted with a cruel coldness. "Teresa, right? Jace's half-sister from Baltimore?"

Tess frowned, a flash of fear in her eyes. "H-how do you know that?" She turned to another member of the valet staff. "I think maybe we need security." But the restaurant was crazy busy, and the guy barely even glanced over as he spoke on the phone with a guest.

"No. No we don't," the enraged valet snapped. "No, this is perfect. Fucking perfect. Better than anything I had planned." She gave an unhinged laugh, reaching into her pocket. "You ruined my life, Jace. Now I'll ruin yours."

From her pocket she pulled out a switchblade, pressing the release to flick out the blade. I shrieked, and Jace acted lightning fast. He grabbed me, twisting our positions so his broad form shielded me, but it was pointless.

I wasn't the target.

Tess screamed, the kind of scream I would never forget, and I shoved at Jace as I fought to get at the crazy bitch. Jace realized what'd happened a split second after me, but the girl was already gone. She took off running into the night, leaving Tess on the sidewalk with a pool of blood rapidly spreading across the middle of her silver dress.

The hoarse cry that tore out of Jace when he crouched beside his sister, his hands desperately pressing her injuries to apply pressure, was the sort of sound that haunted the world. It ripped through my soul and squeezed my heart, and I had to *force* myself to move. To snatch the phone from the other valet's hand and dial an ambulance, all the while praying to gods I didn't believe in.

She couldn't die. Jace didn't deserve this. Tess needed to be okay.

The lifeless way her hand flopped onto the concrete spoke a different story, though.

Sirens sounded in the distance, and I sank to my knees beside Jace, at a loss for what to do as gut-wrenching sobs shook his whole body. Maybe... maybe it would be okay. I had to have hope. Without hope... where were we in this life?

eighteen

ANGELO

When Billie called me, sobbing and choking out her words, I'd thought the worst. For a horrible, harrowing moment, I'd thought something had happened to her. Or to Jace. When she finally got the relevant information out, that it was Jace's sister Teresa who'd gotten hurt, I could finally breathe again.

My heart ached for Jace, and for Billie to witness such a shocking act of violence, but I was relieved. Rhett had gone out for an evening appointment with his therapist —apparently, he was more inclined to talk about his feelings in the dark or some shit—so Gray and I waited for him to return before heading to the hospital.

We approached the nurse's station and asked where we could find Jace's sister, but she denied us access. The Adams were only allowing family to visit, she said. I searched the waiting room that she'd directed us to but couldn't see Billie anywhere, so they must have let her through.

It wasn't much of a wait before Jace came storming back through the double doors with a haunted look on his pale face. Blood stained his shirt and hands, and his eyes were red-rimmed. He didn't see us at first, then Rhett strode over and hugged him.

Jace flinched, then recognized his friend. His expression crumpled as he hugged our eccentric guitarist right back. I joined them, wrapping my arms around both men, and Gray clapped Jace on the shoulder in a stoic display of love and support.

"How's Tess?" Rhett asked in a rough voice. Of all of us, only Rhett knew Jace's sister well. I'd never met her, and Gray had given her a wide berth since she'd made a drunken pass at him back when the band was new. Rhett considered her a friend, though.

Jace sucked in a shuddering breath, released the hug, and ran a blood-stained hand over his hair. "Um, I don't know," he confessed. "Not good. They just took her in for surgery, so we won't know until... until they're done."

"What happened, and where's Billie?" I asked, trying

really hard not to lose my shit. They'd taken Tess to an expensive private hospital, the kind with heavy security and a strong police presence in the waiting room. It reassured me that we, as Bellerose, would be left alone for once.

Jace swallowed hard, his eyes on the ceiling as he searched for words. "She's with mom, safe. And... uh, it was... fuck, I don't even know; it all happened so fucking fast."

"I'll get you some coffee," Gray rumbled, rubbing Jace's shoulder in another gesture of comfort. "Sit down. Take your time."

Jace nodded, still anguished. He made his way over to the seating area with us and sat down to lean his forearms on his knees. "It was some chick. The valet attendant. She recognized me, then... I still don't get it. She started snarling about how I ruined her life and then pulled out a knife." His eyes pinched and his jaw ticked with tension as he rolled the events over in his head for probably the thousandth time. "I thought she would attack Billie. Everyone has been attacking Billie, haven't they? So I grabbed *her*. Protected *her*. And this bitch... she went for Tess instead."

"Shit," Rhett breathed, scrubbing a hand over his face. "Jace, man, I'm so fucking sorry. She'll be okay, though. Tess is a tough chick; she'll fight."

Jace inhale, his whole body shuddering like he was right on the edge of tears. I didn't blame him.

"What do we know about the attacker?" I asked quietly. I refused to call her a girl because that implied some kind of humanity that this psycho clearly lacked. "Was she arrested?"

Jace shook his head, murderous anger flashing across his face. "No, the deranged bitch took off running and just left Tess lying there in a pool of her own blood. I have no clue what happened afterward, but the nurse mentioned there were cops on the scene. I don't... I wasn't paying attention. I don't know."

Gray returned with a little paper cup and passed it to Jace. "The coffee sucks, but sometimes it helps to have something to do. Even if that something is drinking shit coffee."

Jace took a small sip, then winced. "You speak the truth."

"Will Billie be out soon?" Rhett asked, looking around with a frown of worry.

Jace nodded in the direction he'd come from. "Yep. Mom was having a breakdown, so Billie's sitting with her."

Almost on cue, the automatic double doors opened again, and our precious girl came out with her arm around a weeping Lydia Adams. I held back my urge to go to her and grab her in my arms, sensing that she was focused on getting Lydia settled in a seat in the waiting area. Jace's dad, Greg, followed them out with puffy, red eyes himself.

When Greg saw us all there, his expression softened. Then he saw me, and his eyes narrowed with anger.

"Angelo," he said in a rough voice.

I stepped away from Jace and the guys, taking a few steps toward Greg. "Mr. Adams." I put my hand out for him to shake, but he just eyed it like I'd offered a spitting viper.

He inhaled sharply, glaring daggers. "I heard you slid into Florence's place in the band. Just like a Ricci, exploiting a tragedy for their own gain."

Ouch. Then again, Greg had never been my biggest fan. Back in high school, he'd thought I was a bad influence who'd eventually get Jace hurt. Turned out he was right. I'd let Billie break my best friend's heart and accepted all the blame, pretending like we no longer loved him. All of it was painfully untrue, but it meant Jace got to live his dream of being a rock star. I would never regret that.

Tightening my jaw, I dropped my hand back to my side. "Sir, whoever hurt your daughter *will* pay. That is something I can promise you."

He stared at me for a long moment, then gave a small

nod. "Good. If there is one and only one thing your family is good for, it's this. Find her, kill her, make it hurt. You do that, and I will look past the shit you put my boy through all those years ago, since, clearly, he's forgiven you and Billie both."

I nodded. "I can do that."

Greg looked over to where Billie sat with Lydia, rubbing her back and speaking in a soothing way. His expression softened dramatically as he stared at the two women. "Hear me when I say this, Angelo. If you hurt that girl again, or my Jace, I'll gut you myself. Not everyone deserves a second chance."

I said nothing back to that because not a shred of my being doubted him. Greg might not be mafia, but he was a veteran and a hard-ass at that. He'd string me up by my balls and not flinch. Greg Adams loved hard, and Jace took after him in that respect.

Greg left me with that thought, crossing over to Billie and Lydia to wrap his arm around his shaken wife and let Billie step away.

My beautiful girl scrubbed her eyes, smudging her makeup further, then crossed to Jace and Rhett. She started to sit down, but Jace hauled her right into his lap and hugged her like his security blanket, his face buried in her breasts. She closed her eyes, resting her chin on his head and stroked his back. It warmed my heart to see their bond growing stronger with every day that passed. Billie and Jace were the kind of couple fated in the stars.

I was just glad the stars were plentiful and fate had brought all of us together with her.

"What's the plan?" Gray asked quietly.

I glanced at him. "Let's find this crazy bitch. Jace said she recognized him from Bellerose, so she could still be a threat to all of you. We can't risk her running around out there."

"All of *us*," Grayson corrected with a firm set to his lips. "You're Bellerose, too. She's a threat to *all of us*, Billie included. So let's take care of it."

Rhett was looking our way with suspicion and curiosity, so I jerked my head to call him over. Gray and I gave him a quick update on our plans and instructed him to stay and support Jace. He agreed without complaint, telling us to be safe, then returned to his seat beside Jace and Billie.

Grayson and I headed for the exit, but before we stepped out, I overheard two uniformed officers asking the desk nurse where he could find the family of Teresa Cramer. Jerking to a stop, I tapped Grayson's arm, then hurried back to the desk to intercept.

"You're here about Tess's attacker?" I asked without preamble.

One officer eyed me with suspicion, taking in my

numerous tattoos, visible even with a dress shirt and suit pants on. He clearly didn't like what he saw, because his lips tightened. "Who are you and what do you know?"

I glanced at his partner, who was squinting at me in confusion like he recognized me but couldn't quite place why.

"Apologies," I purred, switching on the Ricci charm. "That was rude of me." I extended a hand. "Angelo Ricci. And you're Officer Simpson?" I read it off his badge.

"Oh shit," the partner murmured. "The new Bellerose bass player."

"And son of Giovanni Ricci, notorious underworld player," Simpson sneered. "We've heard all about you."

"Great," I replied with a cold smile. "Then you know I'm not inclined to play games. Jace Adams is distraught; he just watched his sister get stabbed by an insane Bellerose fan, so he's in no state to be questioned. So, I'll ask once, just once, nicely. Then I'll call your boss." I paused to let that sink in. "What do you know about who attacked Tess?"

The officer swallowed visibly, then chose to be smart. "She's been apprehended and taken to Naples General."

Confusion rippled through me. "The hospital? Why?"

The officer glanced at his partner, who gave him a quick nod. "She was hit by a car while running from the scene. It was pretty brutal."

Well fuck, that was unexpected.

"I take it she's still alive?" Grayson asked in a deep rumble.

The cops nodded. "For now," the second one added. "She's in surgery, but it doesn't look good. Seems like karma caught up quick, huh?"

"We still need to talk to Mr. Adams, though," Simpson said with an uneasy frown. "And his girlfriend, Miss Bellerose? They witnessed the attack and—"

"And are currently distraught," I cut him off. "You have the guilty party in custody—I assume you have officers at Naples General? So questioning *witnesses* can wait, don't you think?"

The cops exchanged another look, and then Simpson sighed. "Sure, I guess you're right."

Pulling a business card from my wallet, I flashed a tight smile. "Call me if Tess's attacker makes it through surgery. I want to be updated if she doesn't die."

"So you can kill her yourself?" the second cop asked with an uneasy laugh.

I just stared at him, totally deadpan. "Yes."

Their smiles evaporated, and Simpson flinched. Then they both murmured a polite farewell, and Gray sighed. "Perks of being a Ricci, huh? All the Bellerose fame gets us is loose women that pale in comparison to Billie."

I snorted, then bumped him with my shoulder. "Now

that the crazed fan is dealt with, we can grab Jace and Billie some clothes. " She had distinctive splotches of dark blood staining her tight green dress, and that had to be playing on her mind. She used to faint at the sight of blood, but I guessed things had changed.

Gray grimaced, then nodded. "Yeah. She might want some underwear too." Then he threw his hands up defensively at my accusing glare. "I didn't know it would end up like this. Fuck. I just wanted to help Jace out."

Fair call, and I'd bet Jace had been all too pleased to find our girl was flying bare under that sinful, demure dress. Jealousy sparked in my chest, but it wasn't dangerous. It was just healthy.

nineteen

BILLIE

Tess was in surgery for fourteen hours. There were complications, bleeding they almost couldn't get under control, and the few updates that were relayed to us had us all expecting the worst. Jace and his family were a mess, and I felt absolutely devastated and helpless in the face of their pain and grief. Pain I felt as well, but clearly on a much smaller scale since I barely knew Tess.

But from what I did know, she would be a great loss to this family and the world.

Fuck, why was it all so unfair? Why could none of us catch a damn break?

"Mr. Adams."

Jace had been dozing against my shoulder, but he was alert immediately when the surgeon emerged and softly called for his father.

"How is she?" Greg rasped, on his feet, arm wrapped around Lydia as if they were already ready to hold each other up if needed.

The doctor, who looked absolutely exhausted, wore a serious expression that gave away nothing. "She made it through surgery."

Jesus fuck. The suspense before he said that really hadn't been necessary.

Greg's face crumpled before he pulled himself together. "That's wonderful news," he managed to choke out.

The doctor nodded before reaching out and placing a hand on the other man's shoulder. "It's very good news, but she's not out of the woods yet. Teresa lost a lot of blood on the table, and we had to make multiple unexpected repairs..." He continued on with a lot of medical jargon that went over my head and sounded scary as hell, but in the end, she was still alive. "She's in the intensive care unit now," he finished, "and she'll have round-the-clock monitoring for the next twenty-four hours. Those are our most critical."

"Can we see her?" Lydia asked.

The doctor nodded. "I recommend immediate family only. And one at a time. She's unconscious and will be for another few hours. We have to let her body heal in more ways than one after such an attack."

Jace was holding me tightly, and I felt the sigh of relief that his sister was, for the moment at least, still alive and fighting.

"Tessy is strong," Greg said with a nod. "She's dealt with more than most people should have to. She's going to make it. I know it."

The doctor nodded. "A patient's will to live is almost as important as the excellent medical care she's receiving."

He left us then, advising the nurse to allow the Adams family back one at a time. Greg went first, and I returned to my seat between Rhett and Jace. Gray and Angelo had left briefly to bring us a change of clothes, and when they'd returned, they'd sat as our new security, never taking their eyes off us, arms crossed over their chests, their badass stare firmly in place, as they kept watch.

Our new security, two men I loved, both born into bloodied families.

I'd never felt safer.

Not to mention there was a literal army out the front

of this private hospital ensuring that no media or press made it inside while Bellerose was here.

"You should all go home and shower, change, and get some rest," Lydia said with an exhausted smile. "Tess will be unconscious for a few hours."

"I want to stay," Jace said firmly. "I'm going to make that statement to the media today as well, and I want to do it from the hospital. This has gone too fucking far."

"I'll stay with you," I said immediately, but he shook his head, leaning down to press a kiss to my forehead.

"As much as I'd love that, you're exhausted. You should get some rest and then come back to me."

I'd always come back to him, there was zero doubt about that. "We'll take Billie home and bring her back later," Gray said, already on his feet. He reached out a hand to me, and I took it without hesitation, even though I really didn't want to leave Jace.

"Is it safe for them here?" I asked Grayson as I stood. "She's still out there, right?"

His expression never wavered. "Perfectly safe. She was hit by a car as she fled the scene, and the police aren't sure she's going to make it."

I had no idea when he'd spoken to the police, but the end result was the same. I didn't have to worry about that bitch any longer. I didn't give a shit what her reasons were; Tess was an innocent, and she'd hurt her just because she could. That wasn't a person I wanted in this world.

"Okay, good," I said firmly, before realizing that Lydia was close enough to hear this conversation. Jace's mom no doubt thought I was straight up depraved.

Except she nodded decisively and rasped, "Love when karma does its job."

I couldn't help but smile and give her one last hug. "See you soon," I told her, and she squeezed me tightly.

"Stay safe, honey."

"Always."

Not entirely true in our current situation, but I was doing my fucking best to make it true.

Jace got one last hug from all of us, and then we left the hospital. Rhett, Gray, and Angelo surrounded me in a circle of protection, even though we were only heading into the secure parking lot in the basement. Gray's bulletproof car was back in action, and I got the sense we'd be taking it everywhere from now on.

It was a quiet ride home, the stress and exhaustion getting to all of us. By the time we arrived home, I was near delirious. "Come on, Thorn," Rhett said, opening my door and helping me out. "Let's get you to bed."

For once, there wasn't an ounce of sexy in that tone. He meant it literally, and I was ready to rest up so I could get back to Jace and his family as soon as possible.

"I'm going to do a little investigating into the chick who stabbed Teresa," Grayson said when we were inside. "I don't trust the cops to do a thorough job now that she's essentially been caught."

"I'll put some calls into my contacts," Angelo added.

It was a relief to know both of them were following this all the way to the end. Even if she did die, we needed to know the why of her attack to make sure it didn't happen again. Maybe with another member of her family. Or another deranged fan who believed the same shit.

Grayson wrapped an arm around me, his strength holding me up. "Get some sleep, Prickles," he ordered. "I'll wake you in a few hours so we can head back to the hospital."

I cleared my throat to speak. "Wake me if you hear anything from Jace, too."

"I promise." Grayson was a man who kept his promises, so I knew I could relax. Angelo kissed me solidly on the lips as well and then patted my ass, sending me into the bedroom with Rhett.

Rhett undressed me with care and love and stood under the shower holding me while I sobbed against his chest. It had been hours of staying strong for Jace, Greg, and Lydia, and now it was all catching up to me. "It's okay, baby," he whispered, running a hand up and down my spine as the water crashed down on us. "Let out your pain and sadness. I'm right here to keep you safe."

He was perfect, and that, of course, made me cry harder until, eventually, the tightness that had been plaguing my chest for hours eased. I did feel better after releasing that pain, and when we emerged and dried off, we both fell naked into bed. I was asleep before my head hit the pillow, and I slept the sort of dead sleep where you wake up wondering what century it was.

The only reason I woke at all was the loud ringing of a phone, and in my delirious state, I panicked thinking it was Jace, and I reached out to answer before my eyes were open. "Is everything okay?" I slurred and half shouted into the phone.

There was a brief pause, and then a female voice asked hesitantly. "Oh, sorry. I must have dialed the wrong number. My apologies."

The line went dead, and I managed to shake the rest of my brain awake as I looked down at the phone in my hand. It wasn't mine, but Rhett's. Shit, that was awkward.

"Who was it, baby?" Rhett asked with a yawn, lifting his arms above his head in a long stretch.

"Sorry," I said quickly, "I thought it was my phone. I didn't mean to answer yours."

He relaxed and rolled over to face me, soft smile gracing his gorgeous face. "I have no secrets from you. Answer my phone, read my texts, check my emails. I don't give a fuck."

"You're too good to be true, Zep," I said, leaning over to kiss him because I couldn't help myself. "And I have no idea who that was. Female voice, she thought she had the wrong number."

I held the phone out, and he checked the number. "It's the hospital where my grandfather is."

There was no inflection in his tone, and I had no idea what he was thinking. "Are you going to call them back?" I checked.

He stared at the screen for a beat, before shaking his head. "If it's important, they'll call again."

As he finished that sentence, the phone rang, and I had to laugh. "Apparently, they think it's important."

Rhett let out a low rumble before sucking in a deep breath, and he answered on the third ring, putting it on loudspeaker. "Yeah," he said bluntly.

"Rhett Silver?" the same female voice from before asked.

"Yeah."

Another awkward pause, and I wanted to laugh so badly but somehow managed to contain myself.

"Uh, this is Nurse Radcliff from the Townsend hospital. We have your test results back. Would you be able to pop in and discuss them with us?"

"Not a chance in hell," Rhett said bluntly. "I'm three hours away. I'm sure test results can be given over the phone in these circumstances."

Another pause, and I wondered if the nurse was counting to ten. "Of course, Mr. Silver," she finally said, still as professional as ever. "I will just check with the doctor. Could you hold for a moment?"

"Yeah."

This time I did laugh, muffling it in my pillow as Rhett shot me a slow smirk.

The nurse was gone for about two minutes before she returned. "Okay, thanks for holding, Mr. Silver. The doctor wanted me to let you know that you're a match for your grandfather. We'd appreciate if you could visit again and discuss the transplant as soon as possible. He said he'll make himself available to you whenever you have time."

Rhett hung up the phone without another word, and I was no longer amused.

Fucking hell. I'd really hoped he wouldn't be a match, because now he had a huge decision to make. He remained silent, staring at the phone, and I let him have his thoughts. All I did was take his hand so he knew I was here supporting him, no matter what decision he made.

"The irony of this is fucking insane," he finally said with a sad laugh. "I've wanted that old bastard to die so many times that I've lost count. I planned on killing him with my bare hands, and now he's about to die if I don't step in to save him."

A selfish part of me, the same part that ranted and raved about it the other day, really hoped he wouldn't save that bastard. The less selfish part, though, knew that this wasn't my decision and that I shouldn't influence Rhett. I had to support him.

Wiggling closer, I wrapped my arms around him, and he rested his head against me. "I need to see them both, and then I'll make my decision. At this stage, I honestly can't imagine one reason that would make me risk my own life and health to save that fucker, but without seeing them, it's hard to know."

"I'm here for you, no matter what you decide," I told him, even as I closed my eyes and sent out every hope that he wouldn't do this. "When do you want to see them?"

"As soon as fucking possible," Rhett snarled. "We need to get this over with so I can move on with my life, one way or another."

I just hugged him harder. "You've already moved on," I told him. "This is just one piece of the past that needs to be buried."

Along with that old bastard in the hospital bed. Dead and buried was the only fitting ending for him.

I'd changed a lot over the past few months, hardened in some ways and opened up in many others. I wasn't the same person who'd stumbled into that alley the night I met Rhett. Not even close. This version of myself was fierce in a way that old Billie hadn't been.

I now had a life I was desperate to keep and men I'd die to protect.

There was a knock at the door a second later, and Rhett called out for them to come in. We were both naked, the sheets pooled around our waists, but it would only be Gray or Angel, and they were not going to mind.

It turned out to be both of them.

"Jace is making his statement," Gray said shortly. "It's blowing up across social media."

He was wearing just a pair of sleep shorts, all of his gorgeous skin, muscles, and ink on display. Angelo wore a shirt and shorts, which for my suit-loving mafia man was practically naked.

They crowded into the bed as well, and Gray lifted the tablet he'd been carrying, hitting play on the screen. Jace's face came immediately into view, and I saw that he was set up like he'd called for a media presence. He stood at a podium, mics visible in front of him.

"Thank you all for hearing me out today," he started, and my heart ached at how tired and sad he looked. I mean, Jace Adams was never anything but extraordinary, in both looks and talent, but in this moment, he looked beaten.

"I've wanted to make a statement for a while now, to speak directly to our fans and to those who have loved and supported us for the past near decade. You are the ones we care about, and this message is for you."

He took a deep breath, and then lifted his gaze so those piercing blue eyes were staring right into the screen. Right into our souls. I really wished I was there to hold his hand right now, but it was better that this statement came from the man himself. Alone. No distractions.

"For the last few months, Bellerose has been under attack. Not from the fans who love and support our music, but from the media, from other bands, and from a group of zealots who want to destroy everything we have worked for. Florence, our incredible bassist, was murdered in such an attack. It was staged as a random home invasion, but I'm so sure she was targeted for who she was. Who we are. She was ripped from us, and last night, I almost lost another important person to me. My sister."

Another pause, and I saw the way his throat moved as if he was composing himself before continuing. "She was stabbed by a woman for no reason other than she is related to me. To Bellerose. We've never shied away from what fame brings to us, always sharing our lives and giving parts of ourselves to you all. But this is where it has to end. We are not property for you to take, touch, hurt, and murder. So, I'm here today to ask the true Bellerose fans, those who are here for the fucking music and nothing else, to back us in this new change. Don't give the media more power, don't allow the masses to take another Bellerose member from us, and stand by our sides as we fight for a different future. I promise, there's new music coming from us, and it's sound is right back to our origins. A promise I will keep, no matter what."

When he broke off this time, the media he was vilifying started to shout out messages.

Jace ignored them all. "And you might be wondering why I have the media here, since I'm certain they are more than half the issue. Well, the truth is, they've been camped out here since the story broke about my sister, trying to worm their way inside the hospital, bribing, lying, and all the rest to get the first scoop. I figured that I might as well give this message directly to them as well.

Bellerose is done with your shit, and we will fight back now."

He turned and walked off, ignoring the hundreds of shouts and questions that followed him. Security stepped in and stopped anyone from following Jace as he returned to the hospital, and I wondered if shit was about to get better.

All I could hope was that it didn't get worse.

BILLIE

J ace's message did what no other media statement had been able to. It created an army of Bellerose fans hellbent on keeping their precious band safe. The initial response was an outpouring of love and support for Jace and all of Bellerose, and I kept reading the comments with the biggest fucking smile on my face.

How dare they hurt our Jace, one commenter said, *I will personally be deleting any media outlet who talks shit and creates drama. They can't be allowed to take away our music or our boys. #BellerosiesForLife.*

#BellerosiesForLife was trending as a movement to

stop the violence against musicians and famous people in general.

I have loved Bellerose since I was twelve years old, and now... now I am an adult who will personally go to fucking jail to protect their precious souls. Look at Jace's face. LOOK AT IT. How dare they break our man. If I have to commit a crime to protect them, I swear to fuck I will.

The comments went on and on, with only a few random ones sneering at how *famous people hated fame.* For the most part, there was so much love I couldn't even be mad about how many women called my guys their "husbands."

"How are you feeling about everything?" I asked Jace the day after his statement, when we were leaving the hospital after visiting Tess. I still hadn't seen her, but Jace had, and she'd even woken briefly to speak with him. His relief was palpable, and his step was more lighthearted as we left. Gray was with us since I wasn't allowed to go anywhere on my own these days ,not even to wait out in the lobby while Jace visited Tess.

"I feel good," he said nodding. "This is the right path forward. I can feel it. Tess is going to be fine. We will sever ties with Big Noise, and there is a fucking bright future waiting."

For once, I felt like that might be true. As soon as we

dispersed those last few dark cloud hovering over our lives.

"We have a meeting today with Brenda," Grayson said when he got behind the wheel of his car. After thoroughly checking it over first, of course, even with the monitors underneath to alert of any tampering. "She wants to figure out our next steps toward dissolving the contract."

Jace nodded. "Okay, sounds like a plan. Where are we meeting?"

"At my house," Grayson said shortly, before he reached over and checked my seatbelt and then pulled out of the parking lot.

When we arrived back home, Rhett and Angelo were already in the living room but no Brenda. "She canceled," Rhett said when we walked in. "Her baby started throwing up, and the husband is useless."

"She rescheduled for tomorrow or the next day, depending on the kid," Angelo added.

The four of them looked blankly at each other, clearly unsure of what they should do next. "I could really use a jam session," Jace said suddenly, rubbing a hand across his face. He hadn't caught up on sleep yet, still at the hospital more hours than he wasn't. He and his parents were taking round-the-clock shifts so that Tess was never alone. "I've got some fucking angst to pour into song lyrics, if anyone is keen."

"Fuck yes," Rhett said, leaping to his feet and rocking his hips like he was about to dance. "My soul bleeds when we're not making music." There was my dramatic musician.

"I'm in," Grayson said, reaching over to grab one of the many pairs of sticks he had stashed around the place.

"Me too," Angelo nodded. "It's been a rough fucking week, and I think we could all use the reprieve."

Four sets of eyes turned my way, and I had to fucking smile. It wasn't often I had all of them in the same room together, and when their attention as a whole was focused on me, it was hard to keep thoughts straight. "Baby?" Rhett said in a questioning tone. "You want to sit in with us?"

I was about to nod and reply when my phone buzzed in my hand, and I saw Vee's number. "Hold that thought," I said, lifting a finger at them. "Hello?"

It was on speaker so the guys could hear too.

"Billie! Girl's day at the spa. You in?"

My initial reaction was to freeze. We so rarely left the house these days that I felt like I was developing a slight fear of the outside. Especially the outside without my boys.

When my hesitation went on a little too long, Vee

continued in her same breezy tone. "We will pick you up and deliver you back, this spa is under my control, and I have a veritable army around me at all times. You don't need to worry about safety. I promise."

Lifting my gaze, I met Grayson's, needing to know his thoughts before I agreed. Probably because, in part, I just wanted to stay with my boys and have a music session. But was it actually healthy to have no other friends or outside hobbies?

"Vee will keep you safe," Grayson assured me, and the others relaxed then too.

Angelo backed him up. "Yep, this is a safe option for a girl's day."

It wasn't that I needed their permission, but I also didn't want to take any stupid risks that could hurt all of us. We were a team now, and teams checked in with each other.

"Okay, great! I'm in. When will you be here to get me?"

Vee let out a little shriek. "We're out front now! Get your gorgeous ass in the car."

I should have guessed she'd already be out front. Vee was nothing if not uber confident.

"I'll walk Billie out," Angelo said to the others. "Meet you guys in the studio in ten."

Jace, who was the closest, wrapped his arms around

me and lifted me off the ground, pressing a solid kiss to my lips. By the time he pulled away, I'd forgotten all about Vee and the girl's day. My head was still spinning as Rhett, followed by Grayson, took possession of my mouth, each of them branding their lips against my skin.

Angelo laughed as I stumbled after him toward the front door, before he took pity on me and loped an arm around my shoulder, keeping me steady. "I don't know where the hell you came from Bella, but we are four lucky dudes."

I was the lucky one.

Vee was with Giana, and I loved that we were going to have a day together, continuing to build on our friendships. "Hey husband," she said to Angelo, and I didn't even flinch.

Their relationship was kind of cute, actually, like best friends and family, but without any sexual attraction for me to worry about.

"Look after Billie with your life," he warned her. "She's precious."

I waved him off. "Come on, I can take care of myself too. We still need to get me a gun."

Vee squealed again, and the contrast between her girlie side and the mafia queen who killed people was shocking and fucking amazing. I liked the duality of her personality. "I can do that! We'll gun shop after we get our facials and massages. Get in, bitch, we're going day spa-ing."

Giana dissolved into laughter too. "She's been waiting so long to use that line. I can't even tell you."

Vee shrugged before turning back to start her car up and get us moving. Angelo deposited me into the back seat, buckling me in, his knuckles grazing across my nipples in what was definitely a deliberate move. "Stay safe, Bella. See you back here later."

He kissed me even more thoroughly than the other guys had, no doubt leaving his mark a little harder. Not that it mattered; all of them owned me, and as long as we were working out our dynamics, I'd never complain.

"Bye," I called breathlessly when he finally pulled away. Vee didn't wait for him to say anything else, taking off with the door still half open. I managed to get it slammed shut as we turned the first corner, laughing at my crazy friend.

It had taken some time, but the trust was finally returning between us, and I was able to relax fully in their presence. "So, any reason for the spa day?" I asked as Vee sped up, ignoring virtually every road rule ever invented.

She wasn't a fan of rules, and this was just one small demonstration of that.

"One, you need to get out of that testosterone-filled

house before they break your pussy," Vee said as she took a corner super-fast.

I spluttered out some laughter, Giana joining me as she turned in her seat to look back at me. "Vee loves you and she feels guilty for what happened in Europe. She's going to keep trying to make it up to you for as long as you'll let her."

Some of Vee's high excitement faded then, as she let out a deep breath. "I really am sorry about what happened there, Billie. I took risks that I shouldn't have with your lives, and I regret doing so."

The genuine remorse in her tone had the last of my reservations falling away. "It's okay. Seriously, it is. You did what you had to in the situation, and who the fuck would have expected Wilson to just show up like he did and kidnap Angel?"

Wilson. The father I still wasn't thinking about or dealing with because I seriously couldn't handle one more thing this week. Month. Year. Lifetime.

Yep, all of the above.

"And Angel is safe," I added, "so we can move forward. Just next time... make sure you discuss the plan with us first."

Vee took her eyes off the road, scaring the fuck out of me since she was still flying along. No lie, I was white knuckling the back of Giana's chair. "I promise, Billie. I will never make plans that involve you or Bellerose without discussing them with you first. And that leads me to part two of why we invited you here today."

Thankfully, she returned her eyes to the road, probably saving our lives.

"Part two," I reminded her as she negotiated an intersection. And by negotiated, I meant she drove straight through it to the sound of horns and shouts. I returned my hands to the back of the chair, since, clearly, there was no time to relax with Vee behind the wheel.

"We want to deal with Tom." Vee grinned.

It had been a while since I'd heard that name, but I knew immediately what sleazy piece of crap she was talking about. Tom the fucker. The one who'd lured us all to the Big Noise meeting where we almost got blown sky high by an Altissimo/Wilson bomb.

"What's the plan?" I asked, my fear of dying in a massive, seventeen-car pileup fading as I focused on Vee. Tom was a sore point for all of the band, with his current control of Florence's share of royalties.

"We need to kill him," Giana said with a small laugh. "We should do it today after we get Billie her gun."

She said it so casually, and I was instantly reminded of the vast difference in my upbringing from these two badass ladies.

"Oh, he's definitely going to die," Vee said with her

own laugh, "but I think we can use him to our advantage before we make that happen. That bastard got in with my family, with the Wilsons, and with a few others, all so he could rip off Florence, Bellerose, and who knows how many others. I would like to see him used to our benefit before we bury him alive."

I had no idea if she meant that literally or not, but I was interested to find out more and also to get to the bottom of his sleazy dealings. The secret marriage to Flo, the inheritance that she probably didn't know about. It was all a lot of shady fuckery.

But first, we were getting facials and massages. Girl's day out with two mafia chicks, and I'd never felt more at home.

twenty-one

RHETT

J am session with my boys was exactly what I needed after getting that call from the hospital, but as much as playing music calmed my tense, confused soul... my mind needed work. Needed *help*. So I sent a tentative SOS message to Dr. Candace when we were finished in the studio.

Her assistant replied immediately and let me know that Dr. Candace had an opening at her room in an hour, so I jumped in the car to go see my shrink in person. Video appointments had been a lifeline while we were in Europe, but it was easier to open up in person.

"Head straight in, Mr. Silver," the receptionist told me with a professional smile when I arrived.

I gave her a nod of acknowledgement, not even bothering to take off my sunglasses until I was safely inside Dr. Candace's office.

The doc herself was pouring a coffee from the pot set up on her sideboard. "Want one?" she asked, glancing over her shoulder at me.

"No," I replied, plonking my ass down in one of her armchairs. "Thank you," I added, remembering my manners.

She wasn't bothered, just finished making hers before coming to join me in the matching chair.

"So... what's happened to spark an SOS from you?" She wasn't making fun or annoyed, just calmly interested. She genuinely seemed to *care* about fixing me. No, that wasn't accurate. She cared about helping me fix myself. I liked that about her.

I drew a deep inhale, bracing my elbows on my knees. "The hospital called. I'm a match for Jeremiah. He wants my liver, or a piece of it anyway, to save his life."

She gave no reaction, just nodded thoughtfully. "That must be something you considered as a possibility when you got tested."

I blew out a harsh breath. "Yeah, I guess? But that was before he refused to let me see my mom. I really thought..." My voice croaked as bitter disappointment welled up in my chest.

"You thought that they would repay your kindness with kindness themselves," she said, understanding me perfectly. "I think that is the natural human expectation, especially for someone like you, Rhett, who does always seek out the best in people. It's understandable that you'd hope they'd at least extend some basic courtesy while you considered it."

I nodded, at a loss for words. I *did* think that my showing up to be tested would be enough. Enough to just *see* her... my mom. "It feels like he's using her as leverage to get what he wants," I admitted in a rough voice. "Like he's blackmailing me to force me into saving his life. What if..." I trailed off, not wanting to voice the horrible thoughts in my mind.

Dr. Candace waited patiently, then gave me a little push when I didn't continue. "What if what, Rhett? What are you thinking?"

I wet my lips. "What if she's not even alive? He could have easily killed her, and I'd never know. I haven't spoken to her or even laid eyes on her since... Since the night I left his cult. She could be dead, and I wouldn't know."

The doctor's brows raised, and she gave a thoughtful breath. "You're right."

I stiffened. "I am?"

She nodded. "Yes. You *don't* know... The last time you

saw her was over ten years ago. Anything could have happened in that time, and from what you've told me, Jeremiah sounds capable of hiding a murder."

I frowned. "Um... doc, I don't know if that's... uh... That isn't really helping my stress levels."

Her answering smile was kind. "I know. But it's the truth. And you're being presented with an opportunity now, after more than a decade, to find out for sure if she's still alive and well. Can you cope with turning your back on that chance?"

My lips parted in shock. "You think I should do the transplant?"

She was quick to shake her head. "No, that's not what I'm saying at all. I just want you to weigh *all* sides. And maybe it's not an all or nothing situation. You're smart, Rhett. I bet you can come up with a decision that you can live with long term. Just... sit on it. You don't *have* to make a choice today."

I swallowed hard. "And what if he dies while I'm thinking about it?"

Dr. Candace shrugged. "I'm not professionally permitted to say what I want to say on that matter, Rhett. But I urge you not to make any rash decisions here. Talk it over with Billie or with Jace and Grayson. They could attack it from a whole different angle. Maybe there's an outcome that would make it worth the sacrifice. Maybe there's not. But I do know that you'd regret not considering all the options."

She was probably right. I should talk it through with the whole band... Angelo included. They would have a different perspective.

"So. Tell me about this photographer you attacked in the street last week," she suggested with a twinkle of amusement.

I groaned and flopped back in the armchair dramatically. "What an asshole. Did you see that he tried to file *assault* charges? He was the one who jumped out in front of us and stuck a camera in Billie's face."

Dr. Candace gave a knowing smile. "I suspected as much. You're very protective of her."

"With good fucking reason," I grumbled, toying with my lip piercing as I frowned. "She never asked for all the shit we put up with for being famous, and the fans were tearing her to shreds for the relationship dynamic we've all entered into. I just hope she hasn't seen the worst of it, the keyboard warriors.

Silence echoed through the room while I stared at the ceiling, thinking that over.

"I'm scared," I finally admitted, still looking at the AC vent above my chair. "I'm scared that the press and the intense scrutiny will all be too much for her one of these days. I'm terrified that she'll get tired of having to leave the house with security or in disguise, and one day we won't be enough to balance it all out. Does that sound stupid?"

"The right answer here is no," the doc said with a hint of amusement. "But since I personally *know* Billie and know how deep the love runs between you all... yeah, Rhett, it does sound stupid. That girl won't get chased off by some persistent paparazzi any more than you'll leave her for a groupie when you next go on tour."

I made an exaggerated gagging sound, and the doc chuckled warmly.

"I think you see my point." She smiled, crossing her legs. "That's not to say you won't have challenges and hardships ahead. But you two are more than capable of staying strong no matter what comes your way."

I coughed as emotions welled up in my chest. "Shit, doc, you're going to make me cry."

"Nothing wrong with crying, Rhett," she told me. "It's a normal human reaction to strong emotion. I'd like to hear more about how things are going with the band, though. How is the dynamic now that Angelo has joined?"

This was a topic I was much more comfortable discussing. "Honestly, to my surprise, the dynamic is great."

I must have paused a little long there, so she added. "Why is that such a surprise?"

Letting out a long breath, I shifted to get more comfortable. "On the surface, Angelo is about as far from a rock star bandmate as one can get. He's all polished lines and scary intentions. Too smooth and cold for the fire of making magic through song. It appeared there was zero music in his soul, and yet... it's there. Fuck me dead, it's actually there. That guy kills it on his bass, and now that I'm not worried about him trying to poach lead from me, I can appreciate the beautiful sounds he can create."

"How is he fitting in with the everyone?" she asked. It was a loaded question, on multiple fronts.

"Jace has his OG best friend back, and it's brought almost as much happiness to him as Billie being back." Fuck, I hadn't ever seen Jace like this, and despite the bastard being all sappy and filled with joy, my heart was damn happy to see him so happy. "Grayson appears to enjoy another"—I cleared my throat—"*alpha male* in the group for him to share bonding time." Two murderous bastards discussing their pastime of burying bodies. "And Billie has loved Angelo since they were children too. If it makes my girl happy, then..." I shrugged.

Dr. Candace shot me the kind of smile that made me feel warm inside. Not in a creepy crush on your therapist way, but in a *you're showing some real growth and I'm proud of you* way. Like a mom. Since I definitely had some fucking mom issues, it wasn't a huge surprise that I was projecting that need onto the older, caring, female figure in my life.

Didn't need a PHD to diagnose myself with that one.

"Before our time is up, is there anything else you want to talk to me about?"

A million thoughts tried to smash into my head at the same time, leaving me all but blank as I stared at her. "I don't think so. I just needed some clarity about my grandfather and this situation. I have spent a lot of years not thinking about them. They were as good as dead to me, and yet... I never fucking slept, I still had nightmares when I did manage to sleep, and I was self-medicating with drugs and alcohol. If anything, I feel like I held them tighter in the years I was away from them than I did while living there."

The doc nodded twice, expression calm. "That's understandable because you never allowed yourself to truly let go of the trauma. You tried to grow from it, but you just grew around it, leaving it as the center of your being. But that is changing, Rhett. The last month speaking with you has been truly wonderful for me as a therapist. You are a textbook case of acknowledging there is an issue and then putting everything you have into dealing with it. I'm proud of you."

Fuck. Fucking hell. The tight sensation across my chest wasn't new, but this time I didn't get pissed at myself for it. Bottling up my damn emotions and hiding from my pain is what got me into this position in the first place.

"I'm ready to face him," I said finally, when I got myself sorted. "Ready to look them both in the eye and release them from my life one last time. Jeremiah might think he can control everyone, from the damn police to the doctors to the fucking IRS..."

A sudden thought occurred to me as I was listing out how deep Jeremiah's corruption went, and with that thought, I wondered if maybe there was a way to twist this entire situation to my advantage.

"You were saying?" Dr. Candace prompted.

"All his to control, but not me any longer," I finished in a rush. "I'm no longer his to control."

But he might be mine. The fact that he was literally dying and I was the only one who could save him gave me the sort of advantage over that old bastard that I'd never had before.

An advantage that I might be able to use to right a lot of fucked up situations in our lives.

First things first... I needed to find Angelo and Grayson and discuss this idea with them.

Second thing, I was heading for Townsend.

twenty-two

BILLIE

The planned meeting with Brenda didn't happen for a few days. Her baby was sick for longer than expected, and finally, Jace decided just to go to her house for a quick chat since mom life was kicking their manager's ass these days.

"You want to come with, Rose?" he asked as he shrugged on a jacket.

I was on the couch next to Rhett and Grayson, listening to them while they smashed out a new beat for the song they were working on, but jumped up quickly. "Yes! I'd love to."

Jace including me in his life would never get old. They'd all decided that it wasn't worth everyone heading to Brenda's while she was dealing with sick kids and generally being overwhelmed, but the fact that Jace wanted me there made me stupidly happy.

"Don't forget a jacket and security," Grayson said gruffly. "For what those bastards are worth. But at least they might act like a human shield if bullets start flying."

Angelo let out a laugh from the kitchen, where he was fixing himself some coffee. "I love when they're useful like that," he called back.

Some of my men were a little unhinged, and I was okay with it.

"We'll be back in an hour or so," Jace said when I returned with my boots on and jacket in hand. He took the tan wool trench coat from me and helped me slip it on before we were out the door. A car waited in the driveway, one of the security team behind the wheel. It seemed today, Jace wanted to arrive rock star style.

A second car was waiting on the street, and I could see at least five men inside, all of them wearing sunglasses and black jackets. "Angel called in some better-trained security," Jace explained as he held out the back door for me. "We should be fine."

Ever since Tess, we'd all been paranoid. Jace's speech to the world had helped to calm some of the situation, but it never left our minds that Wilson and Giovanni were still out there. Out there and ready to fuck us up when the right time presented itself. Vee and Giana hadn't been worried when I'd spoken with them the other day. We'd spent most of our time coming up with a plan to use Tom to take out some of the loose players in this game, so I knew they were still working toward their end goal.

All of our end goals. Freedom from the bastards controlling our lives.

The patience to wait for our opportunity to put these plans into play, though, was harder to find than I'd expected.

"Have you spoken to Tess this morning?" I asked Jace as the cars pulled away. It was weird having a driver again and having to be careful about what topic of conversation I brought up. Tess was safe though, and I liked getting regular updates on her condition.

"Mom called just before Brenda did," he said quickly, looping his arm around me so we were snuggled together in the leather seats. "She's out of the ICU now and in a regular room. She's improving so fast the doctors are continually shocked, but in a good way. She's doing amazing." He leaned down and pressed a kiss to my head. "She's also ready for more visitors now, and she asked for you to stop by."

I'd been in the waiting room while Jace visited her many times but hadn't seen her myself yet. It would be nice to see her not covered in blood and dying. "That would be great. I'm so happy that she's recovering so quickly. It feels like the sort of miracle and good luck we don't usually have."

"We were due a fucking break," Jace grumbled. "Outside of you stumbling back into my life and dragging that stubborn suit-clad bastard with you, these past months have been a series of asshole events one after another."

Where was the lie?

We arrived at Brenda's surprisingly quickly, with the midmorning traffic a fraction of what Naples normally had. It was odd how quickly this town was starting to feel like home to me, in a way that Siena only ever had when Jace and Angelo were there.

Maybe that had been the secret all along. As the old adage says: *Home is where the heart is.* And my home and heart existed with four arrogant, gorgeous, incredibly talented, and amazing men.

Four. My mom used to call me an overachiever, but I bet she had zero clue how that would manifest in my adult years. I shut that thought down quickly because thinking of my mom had me thinking of Wilson. And I was only surviving the unknown of him and his current *alive* status by keeping it far from my thoughts.

Until we had more information to go on, I'd only

drive myself crazy pondering all the millions of questions I had.

At Brenda's security gate we buzzed to be let in, and the second car stayed out front to ensure that no one entered the premises while we were there. Our driver waited in the car at Jace's request. "We'll be back shortly," he said, helping me out and closing the car door firmly behind me.

Brenda answered the door as Jace was knocking, looking exhausted in a stained pair of gray sweats. "Fucking hell, finally some adult people not vomiting on me," she exclaimed, waving us in. "Sorry that my house is a disaster zone, but baby James is down for a nap at least, so we can chat uninterrupted."

"Where's Humphrey?" Jace asked, looking around as we entered the front foyer. Brenda's house was nice, not rock star millionaire nice, but her success was obvious in this two-story Hamptons-style home.

"He's here," Brenda said, wrinkling her nose. "I asked him to help clean up, so I think he went out back to sweep the lawn. You know, the really useful jobs that are needing to be done around this place."

Jace shook his head. "No idea why you married him. You deserve so much better."

Brenda stilled, blinking a few times as if she was unsure of what she'd just heard. She finally tilted her head and regarded Jace like she hadn't seen him before. "I'm sorry. Who the fuck are you, and where is my moody lead singer?"

My laughter burst free before Jace could answer, and he shook his head at me. "Come on, I wasn't that bad." He was trying to defend himself, but it was a tough crowd.

Brenda joined me in laughing, her entire body shaking as she leaned over and dropped her hands to her knees in an attempt to catch her breath.

Eventually Jace joined us. "Yeah, okay. Whatever," he grumbled. "I was a cranky bastard, and I can own it. But... shit is different now. I'm fucking different, and you're a good person, Brenda. Don't let Humphrey drain that from you."

Jace wasn't different so much as he was *my Jace* again. The one I'd fallen in love with, only slightly older, more handsome, if that was possible, and extremely successful. This was the best version of Jace, and I had never been so happy to witness it in all its glory.

Brenda sobered up then, and she looked closer at Jace. Really looked at him. "Fuck, I'm so happy to see you like this," she finally said, letting out a little sigh. "I've waited a long time for that angry kid to fade into the incredible man you are. It's finally happening."

The emotionally charged air shimmered between

them, and Jace nodded before waving her off. "Okay, okay. Enough of that. Let's get to business."

He headed out of the foyer, knowing his way since he'd been here before, and Brenda's gaze met mine. *Thank you,* she mouthed, and I didn't pretend not to know what she was talking about.

We were both grateful for the change in Jace.

The *messy house* that Brenda had apologized for was actually fairly tidy. There were only a few pieces of clothing and some toys in the living area where we all sat. Brenda's house must usually look like a show home.

"How's everything been?" Brenda started. "Since you made the speech at the hospital?"

Jace leaned forward, his hard thigh pressing hard against mine, and I had to force myself to focus on the conversation at hand. "Honestly, I think it made a difference. The negative comments online have died down, the fans in the streets are being more respectful, and Tess received a thousand cards and gifts to her room, all from those expressing their sorrow about what happened."

"Do we know why it happened?" Brenda asked.

"We do, actually," Jace said, before repeating what Grayson had told us all a few days ago. "The chick who stabbed Tess was the sister of the fan who tried to break into Florence's funeral and got shot by security."

Grayson had been digging into the reason for days.

"Did she die from her injuries?" Brenda asked. "I've barely had time to even breathe the last few days, let alone watch the news."

"She did," Jace confirmed. "She blamed us for her sister's death and became obsessed with *Dirty Truths*, believing all the shit about us and our *depraved lifestyles*. Her friends told Grayson's investigator that her rage built until she was consumed. She had dozens of plans in place to enact her revenge, but running into us at that restaurant was pure coincidence. She'd worked there for years."

Brenda shook her head. "So many deaths that could have been avoided. I'm just happy that Tess is going to be okay."

For that, we were all grateful.

"It does lead us back to the issue of the media, though," she continued. "To the issue of how toxic *Dirty Truths*, in particular, has become. It has too much inside information, which in turn has given people too much access to you all. Now one girl is dead, Tess could have been as well, and on top of that, you've all been attacked late—"

A gasp from the doorway stopped her midsentence.

Brenda swiveled in her chair, hand pressed to her heart as if she expected her baby to be there vomiting everywhere. Only there was no baby. It was a middle-aged man, only a little taller than Brenda herself, with a receding hairline and an unassuming face. He was slim and wore a pair of jeans and a polo shirt. In his hands was a leaf blower, so Brenda wasn't far off on her assessment of him sweeping the grass.

"Honey?" she said, half out of her chair. "Is everything okay?"

He did look a little stunned as he took a stumbling step into the room, the leaf blower smacking against the door frame as he did. "What did you say about *Dirty Truths*?"

Brenda quirked an eyebrow at him, expression confused. "What do you know about *Dirty Truths*? Are you secretly a gossip site fan?"

Humphrey paled considerably. "No! I mean, yeah, not at all, but did you say someone died?"

Brenda was upright now, and she crossed her arms over her chest as she regarded her husband. "What the fuck is wrong with you, Humphrey? You're acting even more scattered than usual, and that's saying something. What do you know?"

Her husband shook his head and seemed to pull himself together. "Sorry, sorry. I just heard you say that *Dirty Truths* has been causing the sort of trouble that got people killed. But maybe I heard wrong. That's crazy, right? It's just a gossip site, and there are thousands of them."

I don't think it escaped any of our notices that he hadn't directly answered Brenda's question. "No. You heard right," Brenda said shortly, still staring her husband down. "Fans have been obsessing over all the dirty laundry, so to speak, and from that obsession at least two people are dead. And Jace's sister is in the hospital after being stabbed. All the *inside information* that blog site has been sharing seems to have worked the hardcore-obsessed fans into a frenzy unlike ever before. We're working on how to get that damn site shut down permanently."

The leaf blower dropped to the floor, landing with a clang, but neither Brenda nor her husband even glanced at it. Their gazes were locked.

"It was me," he whispered, tendrils of what sounded like regret and panic in those three words.

Everything went very still and silent. Jace was so tense at my side that I wondered if he was about to lose his shit.

"What the fuck did you just say?" Brenda rage-whispered.

Humphrey swallowed hard, his throat moving as held both hands up in front of him, like that would ward off the raging bull. "I'm sorry. I've just been so bored stuck at home that I decided to start a little gossip blog. You're always chatting loudly on the phone, and I hear tidbits before they're released to the public. And then, um, you left your email logged on when you used my laptop... I figured it wouldn't hurt to make a little side money, and maybe even help with some publicity. Isn't all publicity good publicity? Isn't that what you're always saying?"

Jace was on his feet in the next second, and I followed, throwing myself at Jace in an attempt to stop him from killing the much smaller and far more pathetic man, who was literally shaking as he shifted his gaze from his furious wife to the furious rock star in the room.

"How fucking dare you," Jace snarled. "You almost got my sister killed. Now I'm going to kill you!"

He started to move, half dragging me across the room, and only stopped when I winced. He hadn't hurt me at all, but I figured that was my best option to slow the rage. "Baby, you okay?" Jace grit out, as he paused and eyed me closely.

In that time, Brenda was across the room and in front of her husband. "Humphrey, you are the dumbest fucking moron I've ever known in my life. I'd let Jace murder you, if it didn't mean I had to clean up the mess afterward to keep my biggest star out of jail."

Jace let out a rumble, but he didn't try to move again,

since I was still wrapped around him and feigning an injury.

"I'm so sorry," Brenda's husband wailed. "I honestly never meant any harm. It was just a stupid gossip site."

This fucking idiot clearly had no idea how powerful the media could be to people who worshipped the famous. It was where they got all their information and formed all their opinions. Brenda pinched the bridge of her nose and closed her eyes, taking a few deep breaths. "Here's what we are going to do," she finally said.

I kept one hand on Jace's chest, just in case this wasn't the news he wanted to hear.

"We will use *Dirty Truths* to our advantage," she started. "I've got everything in the works to dissolve Bellerose's contract with Big Noise, which we were supposed to discuss today, but I don't see a point since it's actually moving through quite well. Giovanni is not fighting us, for a change, and I should have everything finalized by the end of the week."

"What does that have to do with *Dirty Truths*?" Jace bit out.

"When we dissolve this contract," Brenda continued, "you will be looking to rebuild as an independent band, correct?"

"Yes." Jace confirmed what all the band had decided

the other day. "No one to control us. No one to dictate anything about our music any longer."

Brenda nodded. "Great. Well, *Dirty Truths* is one of the leading fucking sites for Bellerose gossip at the moment. A lot of your fans are on there, and that means we can take control of the narrative and feed them the stories that we want them to know, including the when, how, and why of your new indie status."

Jace was silent as his chest heaved once and then again, before he finally relaxed. "Yeah, okay. I can see the benefit there. But seriously, get your fucking husband under control, or you'll soon be a widow."

Brenda flashed him a smile over her shoulder before she returned her glare to Humphrey. "Oh, don't worry. He's about to learn what happens when you piss off your exhausted wife. He'll suffer."

The poor man was so pale now I was worried that he might have had a stroke. Or maybe he was hoping for a stroke, since I got the sense that Brenda's wrath might be worse than Jace's.

A quick death versus a long, slow, drawn-out punishment.

Yeah, Humphrey Daniels was going to suffer more than enough.

twenty-three

BILLIE

Returning home after that eye-opening visit with Brenda was a relief. The mood instantly lightened when we told the rest of the band that the information leak for *Dirty Truths* was none other than their manager's bored house-husband. Rhett laughed so hard he cried, then apologized profusely to Jace for laughing when Tess had nearly died from the whole thing.

Grayson was somewhat more sedate about the information.

"Just because we've gotten to the bottom of *that* blog site doesn't mean that crazy fans aren't still going to exist," he warned us with a deep frown. "Brenda's dead-shit husband didn't make them obsess so hard they were literally willing to kill over us. He just fanned the flames, but the fire was already alight."

"Gray's right." Angelo nodded. "This isn't reason to let our guard down. Nor is that man solely responsible for all the shit going on right now. Even if it would feel good to blame him." He arched a brow at Jace, who sneered back and extended his middle finger.

"Well, in other news," Jace changed the subject, draping his arm over my shoulders where I sat beside him, "Brenda thinks she's come to an agreement with Giovanni to release us from our Big Noise contract."

The shocked silence was so quiet you'd be able to hear a mouse fart.

"Bullshit," Angelo growled. "And why is this the first I'm hearing of it?"

Jace screwed up his nose. "Why *wouldn't* it be the first you're hearing of it? Do you and Brenda have something going on that we aren't aware of?"

Oh shit. Angelo's deal with Brenda meant she should have run *any and all* deals through him before taking it to Jace. But Jace didn't know that, and he sure as fuck wouldn't be happy if he *did* know that...

"Angelo and Brenda had a thing," I blurted out, trying really fucking hard to save my Angel's ass. And Brenda's.

She was a good manager, even if her husband was an asshole. "They, um, slept together."

Angelo quirked a brow at me, his lips twitching like he was holding back a laugh. He understood, though, and nodded slowly. "Billie's right. It was more than a year ago... Our paths crossed in a bar, and one thing led to another."

Jace wasn't buying our shit. "Okay so why would that have any bearing on her telling you Bellerose business before the rest of us? Unless it's ongoing?"

Ah fuck, well that hadn't been well thought out.

"It's most definitely not," Angelo replied firmly. "Billie is *it* for me."

Rhett let out a loud, exaggerated yawn like he could sense there was something more going on and wanted to provide a distraction. It worked, too, with both Jace and Angelo turning to look at him with puzzlement.

"Um, so, I had a thought..." Rhett started, toying with his lip ring. "Or I had a thought the other day, during my session with Doc, and then I was going to ask you guys what you thought, but then I second-guessed my thought, so went on a whole research mission to figure out if my thought would actually work out or not, and then I realized that it did seem to work, you know? But then I got all confused because it seemed like a really easy answer and nothing in life is ever easy, right? So I figured I must have overlooked something impo—"

"Bro," Jace interrupted, shaking his head. "Take a breath. That was a lot of words without ever actually saying anything."

Rhett swallowed visibly. "Sorry. Um. You left Giovanni alive at the docks for a reason, right?"

"Correct," Angelo agreed. "Because it's not as easy as just killing my father. He has people in place to take over should anything happen to him. We need to deal with the whole hierarchy, not just the man at the top."

"Right," Rhett agreed. "So... we need to do that."

"Get to the point, Silver," Grayson snapped, stroking a hand over his short beard in a gesture of impatience.

Rhett extended his middle finger Grayson's way, then refocused on Angelo. "You need to take out *all* your fathers' henchmen, right? All his enforcers or... whatever the fuck they're called in the mafia. Lieutenants? Managers? Whatever, you know what I mean. You need them *all* taken care of before we can get rid of Giovanni. Right?"

"Right..." Angelo replied, his brows still dipped with confusion as he was not following Rhett's frazzled thought process. "But they're not easy men to get at, and if we shoot one, then the rest go into hiding."

Rhett rolled his eyes. "Okay, mafia prince. I wasn't

JAYMIN EVE & TATE JAMES

suggesting we go out on a purge and shoot them all before the sun comes up. I dunno if it'd be enough, but what if they were just locked up? They couldn't take over the Ricci empire if they're behind bars... could they?"

Hope flared in my chest, even though I had no idea how the fuck we'd achieve that. Surely, it'd be better than trying to *murder* them all, right? I didn't want to ask that much of my boys. They already had so much blood on their hands.

"It could work," Angelo mused, "if they were all locked up at the same time. And even then, it'd leave us a very specific window within which to rid ourselves of my father and stake a claim on his company through inheritance rights before his hierarchy gets released..."

"How?" I asked, unable to sit quietly any longer. "How would you get them all arrested?"

Rhett gave me a tentative smile. "Well, I figure these mafia guys, they're always on alert for criminal activity, right? Like if they're watching for someone taking shots, they're looking at the underworld and gang activity. So I thought, what if we hit them above ground. Tax evasion."

Again, silence reigned. Then Angelo started laughing.

"Tax evasion?" he repeated, chuckling. "I mean... it's brilliant. White-collar crimes would be the last thing they'd ever think to get arrested for, but *how?* My father has the right pockets greased to make sure the tax office looks the other way."

"On a local level, sure. But I know someone with connections to a much, much higher position in the IRS. Someone who could, with the right pointers, stage some sort of sting operation, which would see them all grabbed and all locked up, all within, like, a day of one another." Rhett shrugged nonchalantly. "Then it'd just be Giovanni we need to kill."

My jaw dropped, and I had a sick feeling I knew how he could get those connections to do what he wanted. I shook my head. "Rhett... no."

He avoided my eyes as he looked at Angelo instead. "My grandfather, Jeremiah Townsend, has some of the high-level directors in the IRS firmly under his thumb. They're part of the Townsend Community, along with other very high-level law enforcement. Right now, Jeremiah is critically ill and needs a liver transplant. I'm a match."

This was my worst fear come to life: that Rhett would be put in a position to save that bastard, all for someone else.

Only this someone else was, at least, Bellerose, the band he loved and that had saved him many times.

Not that it made it any better.

"We don't need you to do this," Jace said firmly.

"We'll figure out another way. It seems that the mafia might be leaving us alone anyway. Once we're out from under Big Noise, it should all be fine."

Angelo cleared his throat, and Jace let out a long sigh. "Or not."

"Definitely not," Angelo said gruffly. "My father is letting me play band right now because he has other pressing shit on his plate, but when he clears up the Wilson issue... and he'll definitely clear it up, then he will come back to this. To us. Not to mention Vee's family will be plotting her death as well, as soon as they get the Wilson drama dealt with. Giovanni is calling all families to unite against the larger threat, but once it's dealt with, we will be back on their agenda."

Rhett nodded, seemingly so calm. "Exactly, and we have this fantastic opportunity now to take them out in a different way. While they're distracted."

"It could work," Angelo confirmed. "I know people who have the sort of information we need. Fuck, I can access a lot of it, but I'll probably be implicated right along with the rest of the families."

Everyone remained silent as Rhett continued, "That's the brilliance of this, I can ensure you remain safe, especially if you're part of putting most of the Riccis, Altissimos, and whatever other main mafia families behind bars. With what we could dig up on them, they'll all be going away for a long time."

And all it would take was for him to sacrifice a part of his body... and a larger part of his soul.

This wasn't my decision to make, but I still sent out a prayer that another solution would fall into our laps, and soon.

Before Rhett was forced to make a decision that no person should ever have to make.

To save the life of a great evil.

One that had almost destroyed him more times than I cared to think about.

Fuck.

twenty-four

GRAYSON

I lay in bed early the next morning after learning a fuck ton of revelations, including that Humphrey, the fucking house-husband extraordinaire, had somehow found the balls to create *Dirty Truths*. That fucker had caused us so much trouble and almost got Jace's sister killed.

I was tempted to pay him a visit and really remind him that he was *nothing*, and I destroyed *nothing* without a second thought. I'd leave it for now because Brenda had no issue busting those balls back to his normal puny size, and I'd let her have a shot at getting him into line.

If she didn't, then I'd step in.

Another revelation was Rhett's plan to take down the

mafia world using the very family he'd run from so very long ago. The Townsend Community had been on my radar for a very long time. They didn't run in the same circles as my family, so I'd rarely crossed paths with them, but I still knew that in the areas they did *run in,* they were considered to be powerful and dangerous.

It wouldn't surprise me if their ties in the IRS and other government departments went a hell of a lot higher than the Riccis'. Jeremiah was known for having connections all the way to the fucking president, depending on who was in office at the time.

Hence he'd never been convicted of anything.

Rhett's plan had some substance to it, especially if Angelo could dig up extra information to get that investigation rolling. That was his job for the day, and the rest of us were to stay put.

Staying put had never been a strong suit of mine, but at least there was one shining light in the house that kept all of us occupied and distracted.

Billie Bellerose.

Speaking of...

She was up and moving, heading for the shower, and I wondered if anyone else had joined her this morning. My cock was reminding me it had been a few days since we were deep inside her, and that just wasn't okay.

Pulling myself from the bed, I brushed my teeth and

took a piss, before padding naked from the room into the dark hallway. Billie was showering in the main bathroom, which was usually a fairly good indication that she was alone.

Fairly good. But it wasn't an exact science.

Whatever. All of us would have to get used to seeing the others naked, if we were going to start having this sort of *inclusive* relationship with Billie. A relationship that would have normally driven me crazy, but for some reason it worked. She made it work.

As I eased the door open, I got the first blast of a song as Billie launched into a rendition of a popular 80s track about dancing with somebody. She started low, but by the time she hit the chorus, a chuckle escaped me.

It was nice to know she wasn't perfect at everything, because even though our girl could write songs like no one's business, when it came to singing, she was woeful. In an adorable way.

A snort of laughter echoed behind me, and I looked over my shoulder through the open bathroom door that I hadn't closed yet to find Jace and Angelo standing there, both dressed in shorts. Angelo had a shirt on as well, of course. "She's really something," Jace said with a shake of his head. "I actually think she's gotten worse with age."

Angelo crossed his arms over his chest, looking less

amused. "She's fucking perfect. Not everyone has to know how to carry a tune."

That set Jace off again, and he shook his head. "I never said she wasn't perfect, bro. She fucking is. But let's be real, the girl lives with four rock stars, and she's the worst singer I've ever heard."

Angelo's lips twitched, before he shrugged. "Yeah, the fuck. I can't argue. My Bella is a goddess, but not in any sort of tonal sense."

A rumble escaped me. "*Ours,*" I reminded him bluntly, before I stepped further into the bathroom and shut the door in their faces. The low sounds of their laughter still drifted through to me.

My presence finally got Billie's attention, and her song cut off as she poked her head out of the shower stall. "Gray," she gasped, gaze sliding down my body to where my dick was already rising to greet her.

"Little Hedgehog," I rasped in return. The sight of her soaking wet, water dripping down her face and across her perfect tits, had me completely forgetting that our girl had been butchering a song not two seconds earlier.

Billie pushed the door all the way open and stepped back in a clear indication that she wanted me to join her. "How long have you been in here?" she asked, tilting her head back as I crowded in with her. "I didn't hear you enter."

The smallest of smiles appeared on my face. "I can understand why."

She smacked me on my chest. "Shut up. I'm a songwriter, not a singer, but that doesn't mean I don't enjoy a good dance ballad every now and then."

I held both hands up; my palms were almost the size of her damn head, reminding me of the vast difference in our size. A fact I appreciated most of the time. "Baby, everyone should sing for joy, and fuck knows, you are a brilliant songwriter. No one expects you to be able to do everything. All I know is that with you on our team, indie-Bellerose is going to take the damn world by storm."

Her laugh was gentle as she stepped into me, snuggling closer, and I wrapped my arms around her, just holding her under the rain of water. "All of you can do everything," she whispered, her words barely audible against my skin. "Jace especially. Fucker has the voice of an angel and can play multiple instruments, and he writes songs as well. Not really fair."

Yeah, Jace was usually referred to as a musical genius. "Don't compare yourself to him," I said. "He's the exception."

Billie chuckled. "A truth that he'll be the first to remind you of."

"Enough about Jace," I grumbled. "I want to hear you sing again. Only this time, in a different tune."

She stilled as her breathing went a little raspier, eyes wide. "I can't carry a tune," she whispered, licking her lips.

"Not an issue."

I kissed her before she could reply, and she opened up for me like she'd been desperate for this touch. My arms wrapped around her tighter, pulling her higher so I didn't have to bend nearly in half. Billie wrapped her legs around me, groaning against my lips. I was so fucking hard, tingles racing across the head of my cock as it strained to get closer to Billie.

"Baby," I groaned, "I don't know if I can wait. Are you ready?"

My size didn't allow for me to just fuck at will. But Billie destroyed my control, and I was afraid to hurt her.

"So fucking ready," she moaned, rocking against me. "Please, Gray."

I released one hand holding her and palmed her ass, sliding my fingers down the crack, thankful for my extra reach so I could touch her pussy. She was wet, thick moisture coating my fingers as soon as I touched her.

Straightening, I returned my hold to her ass cheeks, using both hands to lift her slight frame so I could slide inside her. As ready as she felt and as badly as I wanted to fuck her hard, I took my time with the first stroke, sliding in small increments as her body adjusted. Ready and *ready* were two different things with me.

The only pain I wanted to cause Billie was pleasure-pain, not outright breaking her.

"Gray," she panted. "Slow is for snails, not fucking. Come on."

A chuckle escaped me. "My impatient little hedgehog. Are you calling me a snail?"

I thrust up harder, and she gasped and dropped her head back, words beyond her. I hadn't pushed her against the wall, choosing to hold her so I could move her body as I wanted. With that in mind, I lifted her hips so I could fully thrust into her again, the walls of her pussy catching my cock before she relaxed into the movement, and then I was almost fully inside.

I continued this slow—not snail-slow but normal-fucking-slow—movement of lifting her off my cock and then thrusting deep inside, until I could feel her cunt pulsing around me. She made little noises that might have been begging, but it was hard to tell as she gasped and cried with each thrust.

Her nails dug into my shoulders, and I welcomed the small bite of pain.

"Sing for me, Billie," I whispered, and in the next beat, I picked up the pace, pushing her against the wall finally so I could thrust into her without pause. I fucked her until she sang my name, and we both came in a wet, groaning mess.

Fucking hell, this chick destroyed me. She owned me. I hoped that I'd get to hear her off-key singing in the shower for the next seventy years.

That way I could die a happy man.

twenty-five

BILLIE

The shower was starting to be *our place.* Grayson's and mine. There was something about him crowding his huge body into the smaller stall and taking me to the height of pleasure as the water streamed over us that really fucking did it for me. Even if I was hobbling out of my bedroom an hour later, dressed and walking like I'd been really fucked.

Which I had, and I had zero regrets.

"Hey baby," Jace said when I entered the living room. He had just left the kitchen, and he dropped the two cups of coffee on the small glass table so he could give me a morning kiss. "Angel just headed out to start gathering information," he said after that delicious greeting. "He wanted me to tell you that you are his tonight, since Grayson stole his morning with you."

I laughed and shook my head. "Why do I feel like we need an actual schedule at this point?"

Jace shrugged, before wrapping his arms around me and hauling me up into a more thorough kiss. "As long as I get every fucking night, a schedule is fine by me."

There was no time for more laughter as his kiss deepened, and I groaned, sad that I needed a little recovery time after Grayson's huge dick had almost destroyed me in the shower. Next time, no matter how ready I felt, maybe some prep wouldn't hurt. Not like foreplay with any of my boys was a hardship.

When Jace dropped me down, I had to force the disappointed pout off my face. I really wasn't in a position for more loving, but later, I'd demand he finish what he started, that was for sure.

"So, what are we doing today?" I asked as we took our seats, and Jace handed me a coffee. If I didn't love him already, his thoughtfulness in always having a coffee ready for me would definitely do the trick. "And is Angel safe going out on his own to gather intel against his family?"

"He took Gray with him," Jace said. "So it's just you,

me, and Rhett here today. We're apparently allowed to do whatever we want, as long as none of us leaves this house."

I shook my head. "Let me guess, that was Gray's rule as he walked out of the door."

Jace smirked. "Yep. But what Gray doesn't know won't hurt him."

"Gray knows everything," Rhett groaned as he wandered out of the kitchen, his own cup of coffee in hand as he dropped down beside me and leaned over to press a kiss to my lips before he took his first delicious sip.

We were quiet for a few seconds as we indulged in our second favorite morning ritual. Our favorite was, of course, what'd happened in the shower this morning.

I needed a schedule.

The peace of the morning vanished when Jace placed his cup on the table and turned to face me. "Do you think it's time we discussed Wilson? I mean, I know you well enough to know when you're compartmentalizing to deal with life, but that doesn't mean we can ignore it forever. Ricci is our first priority, but Wilson has to come soon after that."

Rhett was quiet on the other side of me, and the fact that he didn't immediately jump in to shut Jace up told me that he was in agreement. It was time to discuss Wilson. *Fuck.* After spending nearly a month pretending my father hadn't just popped up from the grave and stolen one of my boyfriends, my time for denial had run out.

"Have you chatted with the doc about it?" Rhett added gently. "Because if you haven't, Jace is right, you have to start talking to someone about it. Or eventually the trauma will eat you alive."

He knew that better than most. Better than I would ever wish on someone as kind and beautiful as Rhett. Though I did often wonder if it was his upbringing that had given him such an empathetic and loving soul. Or would he have been this way no matter how he was raised?

That old nature versus nurture argument, and for me, there was never a clear answer.

"What the fuck am I supposed to say?" I finally said flatly. "I have questions of course, including wanting to know why he killed my mom and then faked his own death."

"Probably the most pressing question," Jace agreed with a shake of his head.

I shrugged. "Probably, but in all seriousness, what's the point of going over and over the questions when I will never get answers. At least, I won't until I stand face-to-face with *Wilson*. And in all honesty, I don't want to do that. I wanted Grayson to kill him at the docks and end it all once and for all. It would have been, you know, easier."

As though they'd planned it together, both boys reached out and took one of my hands. Jace was still turned toward me, and Rhett mimicked that pose, until I was surrounded by rock star hotness. They certainly knew how to distract a girl from her evil father.

"We will deal with him once we deal with the Riccis," Jace said, his words lit with promise. "Gray has already said that there will be no true freedom from the underworld life, unless we wrap up every single loose end. And your dad is one of the biggest still floating out there."

I nodded raggedly, clutching their hands tighter. "I know we have to deal with him, but I also know that finding out the truth changes nothing. My mom is still dead. Our baby is still... gone." My voice cut off as I fought for composure. "And my father still betrayed his family and left me alone for the better part of a decade. No truth changes any of that, and I don't think I care to face him again. I kind of hope he gets shot walking to his car and his brains end up splattered on the sidewalk."

After another moment of silence, a dark laugh

escaped Rhett. "Why does it turn me on when you get all bloodthirsty?"

Jace's laughter followed a beat later. "Because we're all fucked up with enough trauma to write decades of hits."

Wasn't that the truth.

Before we could continue this conversation, my phone, which had been thrown on the coffee table last night and promptly forgotten, started to ring. Leaning over, I saw that it was Vee's number, and I answered on the next ring, putting her on speaker.

"Hey!" I said quickly. "Everything okay?" My immediate panic that she was calling about Angelo faded as she laughed warmly.

"Girl, everything is fucking golden. Want to hang out with us again today?"

I glanced at Jace and Rhett, who wore neutral expressions. None of them had ever really tried to tell me what to do–except Grayson, who wasn't here, the poor bastard–but we still checked in. To me, that's what you did when you were dating someone.

"Sure, what did you have in mind?" I finally asked. "As long as it's safe, since Gray gave strict instructions for me not to leave the house."

His punishment would be so damn delicious this would not be the last time I broke his rules.

"Perfectly safe. You'll be at one of my houses downtown. G is pulling into your drive as we speak to pick you up."

I had to laugh at that. "You only call when you're already here. Okay, I'll be out in five."

Vee hung up, and I turned to the boys. "This is cool, right? I don't want to be the stupid chick who ignored some excellent advice to run right into a dangerous situation. We're not on high alert or anything at the moment, right?"

Jace gently lifted me up and into his lap, pulling me against his firm body. "Baby, you have to stop stressing. Vee is one of the safest friends for you to have these days. No one is fucking with her, and she knows how to stay off the radar. Go and have some fun with your friends."

He was leaning in for a kiss when Rhett stole me away. "Love you, Thorn," he whispered against my lips, before he kissed me.

Jace dragged me from his grasp after that, and I got my kiss from him as well, and then both boys walked me out the front, after ensuring I had a coat and my bag. "You've got cash and credit cards in your purse," Jace told me as he opened the front door of Giana's Porsche. "Call us if you need anything."

I squinted at him, brows furrowed in confusion. Had he just said *credit cards*?

Before I could ask him what the hell he was talking about, he shut the door firmly in my face and smirked at me the entire time Giana backed out of the drive. "Girl," she said, sounding a lot like her girlfriend. "You are so fucking done over that boy. All of them. I know why the media is calling them the Boys of Bellerose now. And it has nothing to do with the all-male lineup."

Sucking in a deep breath, I shook my head. "I'm fucked. It's too late to back out of this, and I wouldn't want to even if I had the chance. They're it for me."

Giana smiled broadly and, thankfully, despite her supercar, drove at a much more reasonable pace than Vee as she navigated the streets. "I get it," she said. "I really do."

We chatted comfortably for the rest of the drive, and I didn't ask what Vee was up to, knowing that Giana wouldn't give it away. Their loyalty to each other was unbreakable, and the fact that Vee wasn't here to pick me up told me there was more to today than just a random hangout.

We ended up in a newly built suburb that I'd never been to before, but all the houses reminded me of the safe house in New Jersey—which was my second clue that today wasn't about any normal, chick stuff.

This was mafia stuff, and I wondered if the boys would have been as willing to let me go if they'd known.

When Giana pulled in, she turned the car off and turned toward me. "Okay, Vee is a little busy right now. I'm going to take you round back so we don't disturb anyone. Stay quiet, okay?"

Flutters started in my gut, but I just nodded. As much as I wanted to ask questions, I had the sense that I'd find out soon enough.

The house was quiet and had the look of a place that wasn't quite ready to be moved into yet. The paint finishes weren't done, and plastic still coated some of the windows. The side yard we walked through was mostly dirt, and when we entered the back door, it was to find a completely empty room.

No furniture or personal touches. This was definitely a house used for business and not for living.

Giana didn't creep or anything, but she was quiet as she padded through that room and into a hall. Off to the side was a set of stairs, and she led me up them with a wink.

If I didn't trust these ladies, I'd be getting really nervous about now.

At the top of the stairs there was an open landing, and here, Giana moved much slower, gesturing for me to slow as well. I forced my breathing to remain steady before I took very light steps after her, both of us edging near the balcony that looked down into a near empty living area below.

Vee, dressed all in black, a smirk on her face and a long, lethal-looking knife in her right hand. She swung it round casually as she said, "... no other choice, asshole. You chose the wrong family to ally yourself with, and now that I control the streets, you've put yourself right in my target."

Giana crept even closer to the railing, and I did the same until I could see who she was talking to. I clapped my hand over my mouth to stifle a gasp. Because I knew exactly who that was strapped into the chair. Tom Tucker the fucker.

Looked like Vee's plan was in motion. "See, I was going to just kill you," she continued. "It'd be so damn easy, since the Riccis gave up your name and safe house without a second thought, but then I figured... we could help each other."

Tom stopped struggling against the cable ties holding his arms to the chair and met her gaze full on. "Help each other?" he repeated, and it was fucking clear she had his full attention.

Vee took a step closer and sliced across his arm with her blade. Tom flinched as if expecting pain, but all she'd done was free that hand. "Yes, Tom. You're a slimy piece of shit who sells out to the highest bidder, and today that bidder is me."

Tom no longer looked stressed. If anything, he was caught in her web, just like so many other poor suckers.

Vee leaned in even closer. "I have a plan, Mr. Tucker. One that involves you getting the entire Altissimo family to a certain place at a certain time. See, they want to get rid of the Riccis, and you're going to offer them the chance to do just that. Here's the plan..." She leaned in closer, and I could no longer hear her. By the time she was done whispering, Tom wore the creepiest, smarmiest smile on his face.

"If I agree to this, what's in it for me?" he asked, smirk growing.

This creepy-as-fuck opportunist was going to end up dead, and he didn't even realize it.

"You get a place at my table," Vee told him. "The table that will rewrite the underbelly of this city. I'm doing things differently, and I'm bringing on those who know how to follow orders and do what needs to be done. With that comes protection, power, and riches."

She was speaking his fucking language there. Pretty sure I saw a tiny, shriveled-dick hard-on in his pants.

"I'm in," Tom said with enthusiasm.

Vee leaned in even closer. "If you betray me, Tom, then I will find you and I will carve your balls off and make you eat them. Before I take your dick and fuck you in the ass with it. Do you hear me? I take betrayal very personally, and my idea of revenge will haunt your fucking dreams."

She never flinched, not even once, still twirling that fucking huge knife around in her hand like it was a lollypop. Tom went paler than usual, before spluttering out his promises to never betray her.

Vee let him go for a beat before she sliced through the final cable tie, allowing the weasel to get to his feet. "I'll be in touch tomorrow," she said as he rubbed at his wrists. "Don't miss my call."

"I-I won't," he said hoarsely before he seemed to recover some of his cockiness. "I'm the man for this job."

Vee's return smile wasn't nice. "Oh, I know you are. Now fuck off out of my sight."

Tom scurried from the living room, and when the front door slammed, Vee glanced up to where we were perched on the balcony area above. "Step one initiated," she said with a laugh. "Now it's time for cocktails."

Giana relaxed, even though I hadn't realized she'd been tense at all before that moment. "Fucking hell," she sighed. "I need ten shots. That guy makes me super fucking happy that I love pussy."

Vee snorted out laughter as she dropped her blade on the chair Tom had just vacated, one of the only pieces of furniture in the room. "Come on, bitches. Let's get out of here, and I'll explain the rest to you over lunch."

Something told me this was going to be an interesting lunch. Time to deal with Tom the fucker. Once and for all.

twenty-six

JACE

Brenda's phone call woke me up way faster than any coffee could manage, and I damn near leapt out of bed before remembering Billie was curled up fast asleep beside me. Slowing my movements, I turned to check whether I'd woken her.

Angelo cracked one eye in curiosity but held our girl closer against his chest possessively, his silent gaze telling me to shut the fuck up.

"Gimme a second," I whispered into my phone as I slid carefully out of bed and grabbed a pair of pants off the floor. I didn't wait to put them on, just quietly exited the room stark naked, pants in hand, and hurried down the hallway toward the kitchen. "Okay, say that again. The *label* wants to meet? Or—"

"No," Brenda corrected as I hopped on one leg to pull my pants on. Rhett was in the kitchen brewing coffee and pretended to be offended that my dick was out. As if he wasn't used to it by now. "No, I said *Ricci Corp* wants to meet *at* Big Noise to discuss your contract. You know I've been pushing to get them to release you from this last album, and it finally sounds like we've reached an agreement. This is good news, Jace. Can you guys all be there by ten?"

I glanced at the time on my phone. Nine o'clock. Big Noise was a half hour drive... "Yeah, if I wake everyone up now, we can."

"Well, hurry up!" she barked down the line at me. "I'll be waiting in the foyer at ten to."

Fucking hell, now I had even less time.

"Why are we waking everyone up?" Rhett drawled as Brenda hung up on me without a goodbye.

I slid my phone into the pocket of my sweatpants, then grabbed the fresh mug of coffee out of his hand before he could react. Grinning, I took a gulp. "Mmm, you're getting good at this. Thanks. Go wake Gray up; we need to leave in fifteen." Better to keep five minutes up my sleeve.

"Dick," he grumbled, glaring daggers at me. "Gonna tell me why I'm risking my neck by waking the big man?"

Excitement bubbled in my chest as I took another gulp of Rhett's coffee. "Big Noise wants to meet about dissolving our contract. Although, it definitely crossed my mind they might try blowing up the building again, I also really want to believe that this is actually the meeting we want. So, you know, go put a suit on or some shit; this is a big day for Bellerose!"

I left Rhett gaping at me in shock and took his mug with me back along the hall to wake Angelo and Billie up. We needed to haul ass if we didn't want to be late, especially with how long Angelo spent in the shower, doing fuck knows what. Polishing his dick piercings or something.

As it turned out, I didn't need to wake either of them up.

"Harder," Billie moaned when I opened the door to find her hanging halfway off the bed while Angelo pounded his dick into her sweet cunt. "Yeah, like that, fuck..." Her words morphed into a groan as Angelo went harder, grinning at me as he fucked our girl.

"I came to wake you two up," I said, closing the bedroom door behind myself and meeting Billie's eyes from her upside-down position. Her hair pooled on the carpet, and her tight nipples jutted up at the ceiling as her tits rocked with Angelo's motion. "But I can see you're already *up*." I narrowed my eyes at Angelo, but he didn't miss a beat as his flesh slapped against Billie's.

Billie gave a throaty laugh. "How about you, Adams? Are you—" She gasped and whimpered once, "Do that again, Angel."

My friend smirked, circling his hips as he thrust in, and she rewarded him with a long groan of ecstasy, her fingers twisting in the covers.

"Jace," Billie gasped out a moment later. "Are you *up?*"

My gaze snapped back to her eyes, away from the mesmerizing sight of Angelo filling her greedy cunt with his cock. Was I up? God, yes. I'd pitched a tent the moment I'd heard her moans. I licked my lips, trying to remember why I came to wake them in the first place. It was important. Wasn't it?

Billie held my gaze, then licked her lips and opened her mouth... inviting me to fuck it.

"Big Noise," I blurted out, remembering. "Fuck, damn it. We need to meet Brenda at Big Noise to discuss our contract release."

Angelo stopped. "Seriously?"

"That's great!" Billie exclaimed.

I smiled at both of them. "Yeah, it is. But we're in a rush, so... damn. Maybe we could be quick? No, shit, nope we'll be late. I'm going to take a shower. A cold one. Freezing. But we need to leave in ten minutes, so..." I waved to them as if to say, *quit it and get dressed.*

"Got it," Angelo nodded. "Stop messing around and make our girl come."

He immediately grabbed Billie's thighs, hitching them up until her knees met her chest, and then started fucking her again. Hard and fast. Christ... the sounds she made...

Reluctantly, I left them to finish and headed for my shower. My ice-cold shower that did nothing to soften my throbbing dick. A situation that wasn't helped when Billie wobbled into the bathroom a few minutes later dazed, satisfied, and dripping cum down her leg.

Fucking hell, now I'd just have to tuck my dick into my waistband until she could sort me out.

Angelo was all lazy smiles and casual kisses with Billie as we piled into Grayson's SUV, and I couldn't stop my knee from bouncing anxiously. I had a bad feeling about this meeting, and I couldn't put a finger on *why.* Aside from the obvious fact that we nearly died in one of the Big Noise buildings recently. Maybe because everyone kept telling me it was a good thing? Good things didn't happen to us... did they?

Fuck, that wasn't even true. We were world-famous rock stars, and Billie was back in my life. Good shit happened all the damn time; maybe we needed all the bad to balance it out. The harder we loved... maybe the harder we had to hurt.

Worth it.

"You should have taken an extra ten minutes, bro," Angelo murmured as we stalked into the foyer of Big Noise Records—not the recording studio that had been blown up by the Altissimo-Wilson scheme. This was their office building. "Maybe you'd have a little more chill if you dealt with this." He whacked me in the boner, and I flinched. Hard. Fucking asshole.

Angelo laughed when I shot him my middle finger. I'd get my payback as soon as this meeting was done.

Brenda met us near the elevator, looking considerably more nervous than usual. "We all ready?" Her gaze flicked to Billie ever so briefly, but she didn't comment on our girlfriend tagging along. Technically, she wasn't involved in the record-label bullshit, but neither was Angelo. Didn't mean it'd crossed our minds to exclude either one of them from this meeting.

"Jace only gave us the briefest details," Grayson commented as we all boarded the elevator car. "That Big Noise is willing to discuss terms for releasing our contract. Is that right?"

"It certainly seems that way," Brenda confirmed with a tight smile, pressing the button for the twenty-sixth floor. "I've been going back and forth with them a lot lately, through the legal teams, and we seem to have finally come to an agreement. Maybe. Or that's how it sounded when their lawyer called me this morning."

Angelo squinted at her, frowning. "Why do you seem so anxious, then?"

Brenda gave a shuddering exhale, her eyes glued to the display as the numbers climbed. "Because unlike you, Angelo, I'm not used to dealing with the Ricci Corp sharks on a daily basis. They scare the crap out of me, and I can't think why *they* are asking to meet instead of just the label lawyers."

Angelo jerked like he'd just been slapped. "What did you say?"

"You heard me. Ricci Corp are sharks." Brenda quirked a brow. "This isn't new information, Angelo."

"You never told us that part!" Angel barked at me, and I raised my hands defensively.

"I was distracted, Angel! Remember? And so what? We already knew that Ricci owned Big Noise; it makes sense for them to be the ones dissolving our contracts. Chill, dude." I rolled my eyes, and the elevator dinged our arrival. "We're here now. Just don't shoot anyone, and we'll be fine."

Grayson rumbled, "Easier said than done, these days."

He wasn't wrong there. But still... this meeting was a *good thing*. Right?

"Come on," Brenda urged as the doors opened. "Conference room."

We'd been to enough meetings and negotiations at the Big Noise office that we were well familiar with where to go, even without the polite receptionist who tried to escort us. It was all new for Billie though, and she stared wide-eyed at all the gold and platinum records displayed on the walls.

I smiled, looping an arm around her waist as she paused in front of Bellerose's first one.

"I wish you could have been there the day we got this," I whispered in her ear, touching a finger to the metal plaque displaying our name. *Bellerose*. Then, with a heavy pang of sadness I traced over the name *Florence Foster*. We still needed justice for her. Tom couldn't get away with his shit for much longer.

Billie turned to press a soft kiss on my lips. "I'm here now," she replied. "And I'm never leaving. I'll see the next one, and that will be the sweetest because it'll be *all yours*."

Fuck. How good would that feel, to be out from the oppressive control of a record label? It was terrifying taking away our safety net, but I couldn't wait to see what new creativity it opened within us all.

"Oh shit," I heard Rhett exclaim, and a lightning bolt of dread shot through me. I hurried to catch up and entered the conference room just in time to grab Angelo's hand before he could reach for a gun and shoot his father.

"Let me go," Angelo growled, but I shook my head.

"Not yet," I replied from behind gritted teeth. He knew what I meant. It was too soon to kill Giovanni; we needed to play out the rest of the plan first. Plans. Plural.

"Oh good, the whole band is here," Giovanni purred, kicking his feet up on the conference table and folding his hands over his belly. "You even brought your whore along. Was she on offer? Maybe I'll change my price if you're throwing in some fertile, child-bearing pussy."

This time it was Angelo who stopped *me* from killing Giovanni. With my bare fucking hands.

"Ah-ah-ah, none of that," Giovanni scolded as Angelo restrained me. "We're here for a civilized business negotiation, are we not?" He looked to Brenda, who shook herself free of the shock she'd entered into.

"Yes, we are," she confirmed, placing her briefcase on the table and taking a seat. "I understand that our legal teams have gone back and forth quite a few times to iron out the agreement that will see my clients released from their remaining contractual obligations. The most recent—"

"I don't care what the lawyers told you," Giovanni cut

her off. "You want out from *my* record label? It'll cost you."

"Name your price, father," Angelo snapped, his fists clenched at his sides. It didn't escape my notice that he and Grayson had formed a human shield in front of Billie and that she was more than happy to *let* them. "Whatever it is, we will pay it."

Giovanni smiled like the shark Brenda had just mentioned. "I hoped you might be agreeable, son. Here." He slid some papers across the table, then tossed over a pen. "No need to read it, if you're so confident. Just sign on the dotted line."

Angelo snatched up the page and pen with one swift movement, but I yanked it out of his hand. "You're not under contract, dickhead," I muttered softly. "You can't sign for Bellerose."

I had been inclined to agree with him, though, that no matter what price Giovanni was setting on our freedom, we would pay it. But as I brought the pen to page, I paused. Then I sucked in a breath and skimmed the page of tiny text and legal jargon. Maybe I wasn't a lawyer, but even I knew when we were being screwed.

Swallowing the acidic taste in my mouth, I ripped the papers in two. "Fuck you, Giovanni," I sneered, slamming the pen back down. "You can go straight to hell where you belong."

Stuffing the ripped paper into my pocket, I stalked out of the conference room, trusting that my family would follow. They did, and no one spoke a single word until we were clear of the whole cursed building.

"Do I want to know?" Angelo asked, his shoulders slumped.

I shook my head. No one needed to see what Giovanni had tried to push through so brazenly. Certainly not Angel. Or Billie, for that matter.

"Fuck it," Rhett commented with a sigh. "Back to plan A, then: Kill Giovanni, and let Angelo inherit the company."

twenty-seven

BILLIE

Jace was tight-lipped about what Giovanni had tried to push through in that contract, but he did say that it was an insult. Giovanni had *known* the band wouldn't agree to it, so he was just being a smug shit by pretending to offer a way out for them. As long as Giovanni Ricci owned the label, he'd find ways to keep Bellerose under his thumb, purely for pride. I'd seen the dark, disgusted look he gave Angelo when his son had stood with us, and it scared me.

"Can we stop for bagels?" Rhett asked out of nowhere when the silence stretched thin. "I'm craving one of those poppyseed ones with chicken and cranberry that they sell over at Hole-y Crunch."

My stomach rumbled, and I remembered that I'd run out of time for food before we left the house, too busy getting fucked senseless by Angelo... not that I was complaining. But damn, bagels sounded great.

"What's the security threat level like this morning?" Jace asked, his hand gripping my knee like he was worried I might disappear.

Grayson gave a one-shouldered shrug from the driver's seat. "Low, to be honest. Or as low as possible, given all the shit going on. We should be fine for bagels, though. If we're quick. Maybe not everyone goes in so we aren't as recognizable." He flicked his turn-signal, moving us off the path home and toward the bagel shop.

"Good idea," Jace agreed, his fingers flexing on my knee. "Get me one of the salmon ones with dark rye."

"Got it," Rhett nodded in agreement. A few minutes later, Grayson pulled into the parking lot outside the cute building with a big, cartoon bagel creature sitting on the roof. Rhett and Angelo got out, and I joined them, shutting the door against Jace's protest.

"What?" I shrugged at Angelo's quirked brow. "Jace and Gray are the most *recognizable* of Bellerose, aren't they?" Then I frowned at Rhett with his tattoos, piercings, and bright blue mohawk. "Uh... maybe you should wait too, Zep, baby."

He rolled his eyes and tugged a black knit cap over his

distinctive hair. "See? Now I'm just an alternative rock fan." He winked and slung his arm over my shoulders as we headed into the store.

Angelo remained alert, and I knew perfectly well that he was more than adequately armed to act as a bodyguard, so I tried to force some tension out of my posture as we browsed the menu board. They served coffee, thank goodness, so I quickly added that to my order on the touch screen.

"For me, too," Angelo murmured from behind me. "Someone distracted me this morning, and Jace wouldn't let me grab one."

"I heard," Rhett said with a sigh. "Do you think the jealousy will go away? I'm not the only one who feels it, right?" His question was directed at Angelo and seemed genuine, despite the easy smile on his lips.

Angelo hummed thoughtfully. "It's not just you. When I heard Billie in the shower with Gray the other day, I nearly burst in there and knocked him out."

My jaw dropped, and I made a squeak of... something. Shock? Panic? Worry? Something. This was all new territory for me, though, and I really, *badly*, wanted it all to work out.

"I hope it doesn't go away," Angelo continued, brushing a kiss over the bend of my neck. "Jealousy means we give a shit. It's how we *handle* our jealousy that matters to the group dynamic. Right, Bella?"

I nodded, at a loss for words.

Rhett grunted in agreement. "That's a good way of looking at it. Okay, so do we need to add anything else to this?" He turned his attention to the screen, scrolling through our order to double-check it all. There was *so* much food on there, but I guess four grown dudes who spent a lot of time working out needed lots of fuel.

We placed the order, then Rhett pulled me into his embrace while we waited. He leaned his ass against a half wall, and I snuggled against his chest while he chatted with Angelo about the song they'd all been working on this week. The music seemed to be flowing freely now that we were all in Grayson's house once more, and it only made them more determined not to release under Big Noise.

A group of teenage girls entered the shop, chatting and laughing loudly as they ordered, and my guys fell silent in some kind of attempt to blend into the background. I laughed quietly against Rhett's chest, thinking how silly that was. Even if they *weren't* Bellerose, they were still straight up sexy. Girls would see them regardless of their fame, so it was amusing to think they could go unnoticed simply by not discussing music.

Sure enough, a few minutes later Rhett stiffened, his arms tightening around me.

"Um, excuse me," a young girl said, and I raised my face to look at who was speaking. She was red-faced with embarrassment and chewing her lip like she was about to flee... or cry... or something.

"What?" Rhett snapped, and I gave him a sharp pinch on his side. He frowned at me, and I tipped my chin back defiantly.

"Manners," I hissed, then turned to the girl. "He *means*, hello."

Her eyes went huge, and her gaze darted between me and Rhett several times, then to Angelo and back to Rhett again. "Um, I'm so sorry. I just... are you Rhett Silver? From Bellerose?"

"No," Rhett replied, totally deadpan.

The girl's expression fell, as did her shoulders. "Oh, sorry. God, this is embarrassing now; my friends said you weren't, but then I thought... sorry. Ignore me." She turned to leave, her face flaming even brighter, but I shrugged out of Rhett's embrace to grab her arm gently.

"He's being an asshole," I told her quietly, offering a sympathetic smile. "We've had a rough time lately. Yes, it's him."

The girl sucked in a sharp breath, her eyes widening

even more as she stared, starstruck at Rhett. She didn't seem like the kind of crazy to go stabbing any of us, nor did she seem like paparazzi, since she was all of thirteen at most. And in a prep-school uniform. And I felt bad for how rude Rhett had just been.

"Bella..." Angelo warned with a frustrated groan.

"Shut it," I told him quietly, then nodded to the girl's phone. "Did you want a picture with Rhett? I can take it for you."

She practically dropped her phone with how fast she unlocked the camera and handed it over to me, babbling thanks and yeses. Rhett shot me a dark look but extended an arm for the girl to step closer for the photo. Poor thing nearly fainted when he draped his arm over her shoulders for the picture, and I took a few to make sure I captured a good one of her.

"What's your name, hon?" he asked politely now that I'd shamed him for being a dick.

The girl was practically hyperventilating as she replied. "Um, it's, umily. I mean. Oh my god. Emily. I'm Emily. My friends call me Em."

Rhett turned up his charm as he shook her hand. "It's nice to meet you, Em. Sorry for being a dick before. Did you also want a photo with Angelo? He's the newest member of Bellerose and quite the heartthrob, don't ya think?" He indicated to Angel with a grin, waggling his brows.

There was no time for Angelo to flip him off as Emily gasped. "Yes! Oh my god, I wasn't sure... He seemed like a bodyguard. Can I? I'm such a huge fan. Is it true that you and Jace grew up together?"

Angelo smoothly answered her questions and posed for photos before I handed her phone back. Then she looked at me with a shy smile.

"You're Billie, right? Like... Billie *Bellerose*? Could I take a photo with you, too? My friends are going to *die* when they see these." She waved her hand to the outdoor seating area where her friends must have gone to eat.

I winced, not wanting to say no but also not wanting to feed the online Billie-haters. These pictures *would* end up online before the end of the day, after all.

"How about one of all of us?" Rhett quickly offered as he grabbed the shop worker who was refilling the condiments nearby. After asking them to take the picture, he pulled me into his side, and we all smiled for the shot right as our order number got called.

Emily gushed her thanks over and over, mostly to Rhett, as I grabbed the bags of food from the pickup counter, then the three of us hurried back out to the car before Emily's friends heard the news.

"What happened?" Jace asked with a worried frown when we climbed back into the SUV. How he knew something had happened, I had no idea. Maybe he was just guessing based on our track record.

"Nothing," I replied with a frown. "Chill, Adams. No one tried to kill us at Hole-y Crunch."

He narrowed his eyes suspiciously. "Nothing?"

"Rhett got spotted by a fan," Angelo spilled casually, "and then was a dick, so Billie smoothed it over and let the girl take a pic. No big deal, bro."

The panic in Jace's expression was undeniable as he inhaled. "No big deal? What if she'd tried something? What if she'd been like—"

I cut him off with a firm tone. "She wasn't." My hand cupped his cheek, bringing his wild eyes around to meet mine. "Your fans love you, and while your fear after what happened to Tess is totally understandable, you can't keep hiding from them. And you especially can't treat them all like they're your enemy. This girl didn't mean any harm, okay?"

He scowled back at me, his eyes glassy with unshed tears. "What if she did? I can't lose you again, Rose."

"We can't live our lives afraid of what-ifs," I replied with a small shrug. Because we really couldn't. If we were too scared to leave the house, that was no way to live.

"Billie's right," Grayson agreed as he drove us home. "We never have guarantees. A meteor might hit the earth tomorrow and wipe us all out, ending our story right then and there. We can't live in fear of the unknown, so the important thing is to make the most of every moment we have."

"Deep, bro," Rhett murmured, his mouth full as he nodded.

Jace still frowned, though, so I pressed my mouth to his, licking along his lower lip and coaxing him into kissing me back. He groaned, then slid his hand into my hair to take control.

"So... did you want me to save your bagel for later, then?" Rhett asked amusement in his voice.

Jace's response was to unclip my seatbelt and haul me into his lap so I straddled his hard bulge. He was really taking that "make the most of every moment" advice literally, and he wasn't getting any complaints from me. Thank fuck I was in a stretchy knit dress, because it took nearly no effort at all to hitch it right up over my hips so I could grind against him better.

"Are you two planning on fucking or just dry humping?" Rhett drawled from his position in the passenger's seat. "I'm okay with both, just deciding whether I should put my bagel down or not."

Jace's fingers trailed over the thin, wet fabric of my

panties, his lips leaving mine ever so briefly. "Shut up, Silver." Then he tugged my panties aside and plunged two fingers into my pussy, making me moan like a porn star.

I tipped my head to the side, letting Jace kiss my throat as I locked eyes with Angelo. His gaze was pure fire, and I knew I'd get no complaints if we *did* fuck properly. Grayson was more than capable of keeping us on the road without getting distracted. Probably. Screw it, I was already so turned on I'd lost all sense of restraint.

Grinning, I unbuckled Jace's belt and freed him from his suit pants. He wore no underwear and was so hot and hard in my hand I wondered if he'd been sporting that erection all morning.

"Seriously?" Grayson growled when Jace made a shuddering moan as I pumped my hand.

"Shut up, Taylor," Rhett snapped, putting his food away and turning in his seat to watch. "Keep going, babe. Can you ride him like that?"

"Yes..." Jace urged, holding the fabric of my panties aside to allow me to line him up. Yep, that'd work. I shifted my weight onto my knees, sinking down onto his thick length as I whimpered and moaned at how fucking good it felt.

The car jerked ever so slightly, and Grayson cursed.

"Angelo, you better cover her mouth, or I'll crash this car before we make it home."

I laughed, and Angelo smirked, but he shifted over to the middle seat and did what he was told. Yeah, my guys might get jealous, but they were *definitely* handling that emotion well. So far.

twenty-eight

BILLIE

Unsurprisingly, little Emily's photos with us at Hole-y Crunch hit the internet before the sun went down. By morning, they were on every gossip site, and even a few that pretended to be *news* sites. But what was surprising was the tone of the articles, which largely quoted from Emily's TikTok and Instagram posts.

In them, she hadn't played to the common narrative of Billie Bellerose the homewrecking whore. Instead, she'd gushed over how *nice* I had been and how all the haters needed a reality check because Rhett Silver looked happier than he'd ever been.

I hadn't expected my staunchest supporter to be a

thirteen-year-old fangirl. But it was nice to show Jace and prove that *not everyone* wanted to hurt us.

"Good morning, Bellerose!" Vee sang out, letting herself in the front door well into the afternoon. "I have good news for you all!"

Giana followed, then made a gagging sound and pinched her nose. "Oh man, you need to open some windows. It reeks of semen in here. Fuck, I'm glad I don't have to deal with that in my sex life."

The boys exchanged grins that told me they were more than happy with our current sex life, semen-fucking-splattered walls and all. Not that there was literal semen, but clearly this place was turning into a bit of a sex-den, despite Grayson's twice a week housekeeper —the only staff he trusted to service this place with everything happening.

"It's afternoon, you weirdo," Angelo said as he dropped his phone from where he'd been sending multiple messages to the few trusted contacts he still had in the mafia world. Angel had been quiet since our meeting with his father, quiet in a contemplative way, and I had a feeling he was all in on Rhett's idea to get Giovanni and everyone else involved locked away for a very long time. He exhibited a new level of motivation I hadn't witnessed before today.

"We finally have a plan underway and working

exactly as hoped," Vee continued, dropping on the couch and grabbing chips from a bowl on the coffee table. She delicately ate one before continuing. "What are you all up to tonight? Fancy a party?"

I sat a little straighter when I realized that she was here to enact part two of the plan she'd started with Tom. Over lunch that day, she'd explained a little of what she wanted to do, but I didn't know the finer details. Vee thought it was safer to keep those under wraps until the very last second.

"Heading out in public when we're dealing with so much publicity sounds like a recipe for disaster," Jace said drily, his expression neutral. "What sort of party are we talking about, here?"

Vee's smile grew, and Giana just shook her head as she sat next to her girlfriend. "Now you've done it," she said, "went and gotten her all excited about her—"

"Murder party," Vee said gleefully, interrupting Giana, who shook her head again. "We're hosting a real-fucking-life murder party. It's going to be wonderful."

Everyone went silent, until low laughter emerged from Angelo. "You have our interests, Vee. Why don't you give us a little more detail."

She wiggled in excitement and ate another chip before continuing, "Tom the fucker is working for me, rounding up members of some important mafia families and getting them all in one spot: an extravagant yacht that will be the scene for our murder party. Oh fuck, it's going to be so much fun."

Vee was a loveable psychopath, and I'd never been so grateful that she was on our side.

"My father?" Angelo snapped, leaning forward, laughter completely gone.

Vee sobered a touch. "No, sorry, love. Giovanni is the big dog, and he's super paranoid at the moment— not to mention, the entire premise of this party is meeting to discuss how to knock Giovanni off the top spot so that an Altissimo can take his place. Tom has been my fathers facilitator on that from the start, and now he's going to facilitate their last fucking moments."

"You can't trust Tom," Rhett said softly. "He betrayed Florence, and I still believe he was the reason she was murdered. That whole claim on her inheritance? Shady shit."

Vee's expression softened, and she shuffled forward on her seat so she could reach out and take Rhett's hand and give it a brief squeeze. "I don't trust Tom. Not even a tiny bit. But I do know the exact sort of person I'm dealing with, and he's what I need to get what I want. Once that's over, we can dispose of Tom however you see fit."

"He deserves nothing less," Grayson rumbled, sounding scary.

"What do you want us to do?" Angelo asked, his expression neutral once more now that he knew this wasn't a Giovanni takedown. That was still to come, probably in a less *murder party* kind of way.

"You don't have to do anything but be there. I just think we should all be together for this ending," Vee said, her smile returning. "All the pieces of our plans are finally coming together and I know this will give you all some closure about Florence's death. We've been through bombs, shootings, betrayal, loss, and so fucking much more. And we're still standing, together. This is how the full circle should go."

No one argued, and she slapped her leg in excitement, standing as she did. "Fuck yes! That's settled then." Leaning over, she scribbled something on one of the many pieces of blank sheet music that littered every table in this house. "We'll meet you at this address at 6:00 P.M. sharp. Don't be late. You won't want to miss out on the show."

Murder and a show, we were lucky. Or was murder *the* show? Vee had me all kinds of confused about how this was playing out.

Either way, we would be there, that was for sure.

I stood when Vee did, accepting her hug and then

317

Giana's before they left in the same rush as they'd arrived.

"What do you know about this, Rose?" Jace said as he eyed me closer. "You were the only one not surprised."

I shrugged, managing not to laugh, even though I was amused. "Vee has fed me bits and pieces of information, but she appears to be saving the full plan for us to witness with her tonight. I honestly don't care as long as her family and Tom get dealt with. They all tried to kill us, and they actually killed Florence. That shit needs some karmic justice."

"It will be done," Grayson rumbled again. "I'm going to sort some weapons for tonight. None of us will go in unarmed." He turned to meet my gaze full on. "You should consider staying here, Prickles. We don't know what danger might arise from this. Vee treats you like you grew up in our world, and you didn't. I don't want you getting hurt."

Walking toward him, I wrapped my arms tightly around him, and he only hesitated a beat before he hugged me back just as hard. "I choose to be with you," I whispered against his chest, "through danger and beyond. For me, there's no safer place than being with my boys of Bellerose." Sweet enough for a cavity, but it was the fucking truth. "Don't cut me out of these darker parts of your life. I can deal with a lot, but I can't deal with that."

He released a huge gust of air as he continued to squeeze me half to death. "Fuck, okay, little Hedgehog. You can be there as long as you promise to stay close to me or Angelo. At all times."

I let out a happy sound. "I promise! I'll be careful and on my best behavior." Pulling back, I had to fully crane my neck to see his face. "I get a gun though, right?"

Grayson laughed before bending himself nearly in half to kiss me. "Yes, baby. You get a gun."

Fuck yeah! All my practice at his shooting field was turning me into a decent shot and a *more than decent* fuck, since that was always the second part of our training sessions.

The next few hours were spent with Grayson outfitting us all with vests, guns, and a few other weapons. I got mace and a taser, both of which were small enough to fit into my pocket. Backup weapons were apparently as important as your main piece.

Speaking of, he handed me a smaller Glock than I was used to, one much lighter than the weapons I'd been training in the field with. "So you can strap it to your thigh," he told me, handing over the leather case with a belt attached to it. "Wear thick pants underneath because it can chaff until you get used to it."

By the time we had to leave, everyone was dressed in black, decked out in weapons, and I wondered if I was in love with a rock band or a criminally inclined group of hot friends, preparing to steal all the money from the underground networks of Vegas casinos.

They had a dangerous vibe tonight, and I was into it. My kinks went much darker than I'd ever expected, and if we all survived—no, fuck that, *when* we all survived—I would be asking for them to keep their black clothes and Kevlar on for a few more hours.

And the guns. Especially the guns.

Maybe just naked and guns... Fuck, I needed to focus or I'd get us all killed.

We piled into Grayson's armored SUV, and I ended up in between Rhett and Jace. Everyone was silent while the last of the setting sun sprinkled over us, and it felt like maybe winter was finally easing up.

I took that as a good omen for tonight. Evil never thrived as strongly in warmth and light. They were its natural enemy. Or some shit like that.

Rhett reached out and took my hand, and I held on tightly, the silence comfortable enough that no one felt the need to chat. If the boys were anything like me, we were all caught up in thoughts of what the next few hours would look like.

A murder party didn't sound like the sort of party any

of us wanted to attend, and the fact that we weren't dressed fancily told me that no one expected to be there for long. We'd just be Vee's backup, or witnesses, since she apparently really wanted to share this with us. It wasn't like we were about to go mingle with the Altissimos.

It took about fifteen minutes for Grayson to pull up to a swanky marina located on the largest river system in this area. The *Grand Viper River*.

There was a valet near the main gated entrance, but Grayson didn't stop there, moving further along until we were out of sight from that gate. Finally, he broke the silence. "This is where Vee said to wait."

We sat quietly, none of us daring to do anything more than breath and look out the window for danger. Vee and Giana popped out of the bushes a second later. I was surprised to see they were dressed in black too—hoodies and tight pants, definitely not party attire, though an excellent color palette to hide blood.

Grayson opened his door slowly, and Vee crooked her finger on her right hand while pressing her left index finger to her lips to indicate we should remain quiet.

Everyone exited the car and followed the pair around the side of the large boat yard, which was dark and shadowy outside of lanterns set up around a huge yacht docked a few hundred yards away. When we reached a set of bushes on the most eastern point of the docks, a shadowed figure stepped out.

Gray and Angelo reacted immediately, drawing their guns before we all recognized that slimy intruder: Tom.

"What the fuck are they doing here?" he snarled, and Vee responded with a hard crack across his face.

"Shut the fuck up and speak only when spoken to," she said coldly. "You're here to ensure that this plan is fulfilled; it doesn't matter why anyone else is here."

Tom shut the fuck up as suggested, but his furious gaze drilled into all of us, and the boys returned that glare with much scarier ones. It only took that dumb asshole five seconds to realize he was outgunned, so he stopped glaring and went back to peeking through the bushes, a skill he had clearly practiced many times in his life.

"I think our decoys worked," he said to Vee, who dropped in next to him, a set of binoculars in hand. "Having the valet and steward to greet them and hand out initial drinks means they've all gotten on board."

"How many?" Vee asked shortly.

"Everyone invited is there," he replied quickly. "Except for Wilson."

Vee didn't appear worried. "I never expected him to show when there's so much heat around. He's always been smarter than the others. As long as my family is there, we can proceed."

It surprised me that my father had been issued an invitation, and I figured Vee hadn't mentioned it to keep me from overthinking it since she hadn't expected him to show up.

"Your parents were the last to get on," Tom confirmed, "and..." He looked again closely, nodding like a fuckwit. "Yep, your guy on the inside has set sail already. He should bail out in a few seconds."

A smile that was one part joy and two parts evil lit Vee's face. "Perfect. Now it's time for part two."

The yacht was out on the lake now, drifting along slowly. Music playing on its deck grew fainter as they sailed away.

Vee kept a close eye on everything through her binoculars, until she eventually turned to Giana. "It's time, love."

Giana shrugged a small backpack off her shoulders and slowly unzipped the top.

"They're moving out onto the main balconies," Tom said, leaning forward like that might help him see better through his binoculars. "I think they're starting to realize that there's no staff onboard, just a soundtrack playing across the speakers."

Vee laughed darkly. "Finally, their arrogance in

thinking they're the tops of the food chain is coming in useful. Bastards never even saw it coming."

I was distracted by Giana as she pressed a button on the small device she'd pulled from the backpack. It reminded me of a video game controller, and I wondered what she was doing as a whirring sound reached my ears.

Giana handed the device to Vee, who took a final glance through her binoculars before she pressed another button on the controller.

"Boom," she said softly.

Grayson wrapped his arms around me and yanked me back away from the hedges. He turned his back toward the docks so that he stood between me and—

The world exploded.

The sudden burst of noise shocked my senses, and I screamed as my mind tumbled back to the last explosion we were in. To that gut-wrenching fear that I'd lost my boys once and for all, making me momentarily forget where and when I was.

A second explosion followed the first, but Grayson held me the whole time, shielding me from any fallout.

When the noise and light subsided, I turned back with my ears ringing to find nothing but debris and flames left of the yacht. And half the damn docks.

There was no way Vee's family or any other person onboard had survived. *Murder party* made a hell of a lot of sense now, and I admired her cold calculation in taking them all out at once like that. Nothing personal, no need to face them one last time. Just a bomb dropped by a drone, and the justice in that, when they'd tried to kill us with a bomb, wasn't lost on me.

The murder party was over, and now we only had Tom to deal with.

ANGELO

The echo of the explosions faded quickly, leaving burning debris scattered over the dark water, and that slimy shit *Tom* whooped with laughter.

"Yes! That's what I'm talking about! Fuck yeah!" He danced around like an idiot, grinning from ear to ear like he'd just won the lottery. *Oh. I see.* That's how Vee had secured his assistance in this... he thought he was in a *partnership* with my ruthless wife. I almost felt bad for the little skunk when she cracked a sharp right hook across his face to shut him up.

"Very dramatic, Vee," I commented with a shake of my head. "We should get out of here before authorities turn up. What's your plan for that?" I nudged Tom with my boot where he lay whining on the ground.

Our mafia queen just grinned. "I thought maybe you guys would want a chat with him. Little Tommy let slip a few details about your former bandmate that might warrant further questioning... After that, I have no use for him. Chuck his body to the pigs or something."

"What?" Tom screeched in outrage. "You said—"

His protest cut short with a solid hit from Grayson that knocked him clean out. Thank fuck for that; we didn't need his noise drawing attention.

"Take him to the warehouse," I told Gray with a nod. He knew what I meant; we had tortured plenty of assholes in my secure facility after the farmhouse attack. It was a fitting place to extract some information from the snake Vee had just handed over. Tom wasn't strong enough to withhold the truth under pain, even if he wanted to.

Giana and Vee exchanged a quiet word, then grabbed their bags. "We'll come with you," Giana told us with a nod. "Lead the way, Angelo."

I quirked a brow but didn't question them on it. They didn't *need* to tag along if we were just squeezing Tom like the pus-filled sore he was, but I got the feeling the dynamic duo just wanted to witness some bloodshed.

A dozen or so first responders zoomed past us as we

drove away from the docks, but they were way too late. No one could have survived that strike, just as Vee had intended. While I was content to play the long game as I picked Ricci Corp to pieces, Vee gave zero fucks about taking the heat for wiping out her family. She knew it would create a power vacuum, but that was a void she and Giana had already taken steps to fill. The key to it would be me replacing Giovanni in the Ricci family and supporting my wife's power grab.

Tom woke up en route to the warehouse and started screaming, so Jace gagged him with a sock. Did he need to use a sock? No. But there was a smirk on his face as he crammed the sweaty garment into Tom's mouth.

Grayson hauled the smaller man into the warehouse when we arrived, waiting while I keyed in the access code to my little soundproof torture chamber, then shoved him into the waiting metal chair. It was bolted to the floor, unable to be tipped over, because I wasn't a fucking amateur.

"Uh... do I even want to ask?" Billie whispered to Rhett under her breath, but with the absence of other sounds, it was easy to hear her. It made me pause and exchange a long look with Grayson.

He exhaled heavily, running a hand over his hair with a grimace. "Prickles... do you think maybe you could head home with Rhett and Jace? Let us handle this."

"Fuck no!" she snapped back. "You can't just push me away right when it gets—"

"That's not what I'm doing!" Grayson roared, his usual control slipping for a moment. "But for fuck's sake, Billie, there are some things you *don't need to see.* This is going to be one of them. You already have enough nightmares as it is; can you *please* just let me protect you from this one, totally unnecessary-to-be-seen evil? Please?"

Her expression saddened, her eyes going huge, and I silently thanked Grayson for taking the heat of this argument for me. I was in total agreement with him. It was one thing to *know* we would be torturing Tom before killing him, it was another for her to witness each cut and scream.

"How about a compromise?" Giana suggested with a placating smile. "I actually agree that Billie doesn't need to *see* this, nor does darling Rhett—baby, we both know you don't have the stomach for this—but the answers Tom has are important for them to hear. So what if they just wait outside and we leave the door open? They can *hear* the information but not be left with the visuals to haunt their dreams. Hmm?"

"What the fuck? I'm fine," Rhett grumbled, but Jace gave him a sharp elbow to tell him to shut the fuck up. The compromise would be easier for Billie to swallow if she weren't being singled out. He got the message and nodded. "Yeah, actually now that you say it, I've literally only just started sleeping through the night. I probably don't need to start having nightmares about Angelo ripping my fingernails out. Come on, Thorn; I'll play with your pussy while we wait."

He grabbed her arm and tugged her out of the room without giving her a chance to refuse. It was better this way. All of us could see how conflicted she was between wanting to *prove* she was strong versus the truth of Grayson's statement. Her dreams were haunted enough without piling more violence into her head.

We all knew she was strong; she didn't have to prove anything to us.

"I was going to go wait with them," Giana commented with a frown. "But now I feel like I'll be blocking Rhett's game, so maybe not."

I smiled because she was right, then arched a brow at Jace. Was he leaving?

He shook his head. "I'm staying," he said firmly.

I didn't question his choice, nodding as I pulled open my tool drawer at the side of the room. Inside, I had a whole range of torture instruments, all sparkling clean and arranged perfectly, thanks to my cleaners. To start, I grabbed out a handful of thick Zip Ties.

Once Tom was secured, I tugged the sock from his

mouth, and he immediately started shrieking again, so loud it made me wince and Vee cover her ears.

Grayson punched him again, just to shut him up, but accidentally knocked the weak bastard out instead.

"Bit hard," I muttered, rolling my eyes. "Someone go grab us a bucket of water to wake him up again."

Jace sighed. "I'll go. Point me in the right direction."

Grayson told him where to find the tap and a bucket, then turned to me with a shrug. "I didn't mean to hit him that hard. Sometimes I don't know my own strength."

I snorted. "Save the preening for when Bella is in the room, bro; I'm not interested in your big, manly muscles."

Jace came back a minute later with the cold water and seemed to take great delight in dousing the unconscious Tom Tucker with it. The weasel woke up spluttering and coughing, then turned an accusing glare on Vee.

"You lied to me!" he snarled. "You said we were going to—"

"Oh, blah blah," Vee drawled, flapping her hand dismissively. "I lied, you murdered your ex-girlfriend, none of us are good people, Tom. Sharpen up."

"Not true, babe," Giana countered, shaking her head. "Billie is a good person."

Tom's lip curled. "That *slut* ruined everything for me. She's the reason Flo had to die. If she hadn't fucked it all up, I never would have had to take such drastic steps."

Well. That confirmed that.

"So you admit it? You sent those guys to the farmhouse to kill Flo?" Jace folded his arms over his chest, scowling down at our prisoner. "Why go after the rest of us? Why have Billie stabbed in the belly?"

Tom's sneered. "In the fake belly, you mean? I wanted to offer my allies a gift by killing the Ricci heir, and it turned out the baby never fucking existed."

"Your allies," I murmured. "You mean the Altissimos."

"I think we've already well established that's who I was working with, yes." Tom clearly wanted to kill us all, but bound to the chair as he was, he'd already accepted defeat.

Jace made a frustrated sound. "Why kill Flo? You already had a ton of debt against her name; she was worse than broke. What the fuck did you gain from killing her?"

Tom's lips locked up tight, and I smiled. Thank *fuck*, I thought he was just going to sit there and spill his guts without letting me rough him up.

Gleeful, I grabbed a pair of pliers from my drawer. "Teeth or toes?"

"Teeth," Grayson rumbled without hesitation. "I'll hold him still."

"Wait! No! No, no no, I'll talk! You don't need to do that!" the spineless fuck exclaimed, shaking his head frantically. "Inheritance! Flo had money, lots of it; she just didn't know about it. Technically, we were married, so I got it all when she died!"

"What money?" Grayson demanded, grabbing his jaw like he was preparing Tom for an unpleasant trip to the dentist.

"Sh-she didn't know," he babbled again. "Her grandmother died the day you all went to the farmhouse. I was at her place and took the call. She was left millions in the family estate."

Jesus. Poor girl. I'd barely known her, but shit... that was slimy.

"Hold him," I told Grayson, then forcefully ripped out two of Tom's teeth anyway. Because he fucking deserved it.

For several moments, the asshole just screamed and wailed, sobbing about *his* pain like he hadn't tried to murder my unborn baby—fake or not. To shut him up, I circled the chair and took three fingernails with my pliers, causing him to pass out.

"Good call," Jace commented with a grimace, rubbing

his ear. "Do we care about the rest of the information? How he conned Flo into marrying him? Any of that? Because I kind of think it doesn't matter now. Not now that she's dead."

"Agreed." Grayson nodded.

I shrugged. "Fine by me." Then I pulled out my gun to finish the spineless prick.

"Wait!" Billie's sweet voice exclaimed, freezing me in place. "You can't kill him."

I frowned, turning to glare at her. "Bella, baby, I love you. But this is why I didn't want you here. I know that you have a good heart, but—"

"I didn't mean *keep him alive*, you condescending ass. I meant you can't kill him *yet*. He needs to sign over all of Flo's royalties and shit to you guys before he dies, otherwise they'll pass to whatever greedy bottom-feeder is Tom's next of kin." She propped her hands on her hips, giving me a fierce scowl.

That... made me pause.

"She's got a good point," Giana agreed, shooting me a hard look.

"Sorry, Bella," I mumbled. "I jumped to conclusions. That *is* a good point. How quickly can we get legal paperwork drawn up and then notarized?"

Jace already had his phone in hand. "I'm getting Brenda now; I bet she already has something drawn up that will only need a few edits."

"I can help on the notary," Vee offered with a grin.

Grayson gave a rumbling laugh. "Of course you can. I'll hang here with Angelo to keep our little friend company while you get that contract, Jace."

Everyone jumped into motion, and Grayson and I spent the next few hours reminiscing about old times together. Old times of just a few months ago, torturing assholes until we had squeezed every last thing we wanted to hear, true or not, from their sorry sacks of skin.

After Jace returned, Tom barely remained conscious long enough to sign his name, let alone try to escape. Vee had called in her favor with a notary who "witnessed" the signature and rubber stamped the papers on the spot. Sometimes it paid to be a gorgeous, ruthless mafia queen.

I waited until we heard the car drive away, then brought my gun back to Tom's forehead.

"No, not you," Vee barked, gently moving my gun away and nudging me to step back. "Let Billie do it."

"Why?" I argued, even as I let her take the gun from my hand.

Vee just rolled her eyes, like the reasoning was too complex for my silly man brain to comprehend, then pressed the butt of my pistol into Billie's grip instead. "All yours, girl."

I wasn't a fucking idiot, I could see my wife practically frothing at the idea of luring Billie into her new female powered mafia. She was barking up the wrong tree, though.

All of us just stared, watching our love with bated breath to see what she'd do next. She focused only on Tom, though. I recognized the steel in her spine and determination in her face as she stepped forward, raising the gun to aim.

Would this really be her first kill? I wasn't so sure I wanted that for her... but I also wouldn't stop her.

thirty

BILLIE

Tom was barely conscious; in fact, he was barely alive, if the shallow breathing and slumped form were any indication. Maybe he knew that this was his last moment and he just didn't care to fight any longer.

Maybe it would be easier for me if he were fighting. At least if his ratlike face was snarling and spitting as it had been a few hours ago, I wouldn't be standing here with shaking hands and lack of disposition to do what I fucking needed to do.

"Bella, baby, you don't have to do this," Angelo said, but he didn't move closer or attempt to take the gun from me.

My voice was high and stiff. "I do. I have to fucking do this. He killed Flo, and he deserves to die. Not to mention that all of you have killed for me, to protect me and for other reasons. I don't want to be the fucking princess you all baby through life." I looked away from Tom for a brief second and found Vee nearby, her face impassive as if she didn't want to encourage or discourage me further. "I want to be badass like Vee."

"Vee is badass, but she's also a psychopath," Jace said drily.

Vee's impassive expression morphed into a pleased smile. "I thought you'd never notice."

Oh, we'd all noticed. Not for the first time, I was grateful that she was on our side.

Sucking in another deep breath, I turned away from my loved ones and stared down at Tom. Only this time, he'd managed to lift his head, and it was so much worse.

My hand, slippery with sweat, shook as I tried to keep the gun level. No one ever told you how damn heavy these things are or that standing with a gun held out before you isn't exactly comfortable. I needed to hit the fucking gym or something.

But first, I had to kill Tom. *I had to do it.* I couldn't be the weakest link any longer.

Double gripping the gun now, I aimed for his head, ready for a clean kill. He just stared at me, eyes dark and empty, expression slack, though that fucker had somehow found the strength to stare into my soul as I killed him. Like he knew this was going to haunt me forever.

Goddammit! Fucking shoot him, Billie. Pull the damn trigger. This is just like target practice.

My finger twitched on the gun, but no matter how hard I tried to squeeze that trigger as Grayson had taught me, I couldn't do it. I had to face the truth: I couldn't kill someone like this, no matter the reason or how much he deserved it.

An angry sob escaped me at my own fucking weakness, and when the trembling in my arms became too much, I let the damn gun fall to the floor, along with my pride.

I hadn't put the safety back on. *Oh fuck.*

Grayson had warned me that this model could misfire if it was dropped and hit the ground at the right angle.

What the fuck were the odds of that though?

In what felt like slow motion, I watched the gun flip once and then again before it landed butt first, and the bang that emerged near deafened me as I screamed and threw myself backward. A strong arm wrapped around me and swung my body away from Tom and the gun.

What the fucking fuck! Had it actually gone off? Had I killed him without meaning to?

As the rapid and panicked thoughts flooded my head, I started hysterically sobbing and trying to draw air into my lungs. What if I'd shot someone else? What if I'd killed someone I loved because I was too fucking weak to do what needed to be done?

Before I could descend fully into hysteria, laughter rang out in the room, and I was fairly certain it came from Vee. I was also fairly certain that Grayson was the one who'd grabbed me, since it felt like I was surrounded by a giant. Protected and safe.

"Prickles," he rumbled, sounding fully pissed off. "Are you okay?"

Vee's laughter increased, and a second later Giana joined her. "What happened?" I asked. "Why are they laughing?"

Grayson released me from his protective hold, apparently satisfied that if I was talking, I was fine. "What happened is you and I have a lot to talk about regarding gun safety. I think you need a few more lessons, baby girl."

Damn, I couldn't be thinking about his lessons when I had to figure out what I'd done. Drying the tears on my cheeks, I forced myself to look Tom's way, only to find him groaning and crying out, and there was a fucking bullet hole in his leg. Blood slowly seeped from his pants, and I swallowed hard, wondering if I was about to vomit.

"Great work, babe," Vee said, shaking her head as she pranced a little closer. "You decided to throw in some extra torture first. Want a position of power in my cartel? We're pussy heavy here, and I love it."

Her words echoed in my head as my heart squeezed tight in my chest, and everything went a little hazy as I struggled to breath. *I'd shot him.* I fucking shot someone. In. The. Leg.

If Tom hadn't been half dead anyway, he'd be screaming, and it was all because of me.

A new round of sobs burst from me in the next second, and I was immediately surrounded by men. Lethal, deadly, talented men who could make music and kill assholes in the same day.

Meanwhile, here I was unable to carry a fucking tune while accidentally shooting someone in the leg. *What the fuck?*

"Billie, sweetheart," Rhett crooned, wrapping his arms around me. "Don't cry. You didn't do anything wrong."

"I c-couldn't sh-shoot him p-p-properly. I'm the w-w-weakesttt." More sobs escaped me, and the rest of my words were drowned out in a jumbled mess of *feeling sorry for myself.* Yeah, I was doing that, and I couldn't stop it.

Rhett held me tighter as Jace, who pushed closer to

my right side, said, "Baby, you have it all wrong."

For some reason, his gently spoken sentence slowed some of my hysterical sobs as I turned my head to find him wearing a serious expression. "What d-do I have wrong?"

He brushed his thumb across my cheek, chasing tears. "You are our heart and our soul, and neither of those are weak. In fact, they're the strongest parts of us. Not shooting him even though you thought it was expected of you is strong. Your moral compass is strong. Without you, the rest of us would just be fucking savages. You make us better. You are our strength."

It was Grayson's and Angelo's turn then, the two who were the most bloodthirsty of this group, and I felt shame all over again when I stared at them. Rhett held me around the waist, Jace still cupped my face, and those two reached out to place a firm hold on other parts of my body, as if all four wanted to have a place to hold. "We love you, Bella," Angelo said seriously. "All four of us. If you were weak or not worthy, that would not be the case. And I promise that you will never have to kill scum like Tom, because you have me to take care of that for you."

"And me," Grayson added gruffly. "I don't even like you being in the same room as that piece of shit. He shouldn't get to breathe the same air as you, Prickles."

There was a muffled shot then, and we all turned to

see Vee standing with her gun in hand and a smile on her face. "What?" she said with a shrug. "I was just making sure he doesn't breathe the same air as our Bella."

Giana looked like she was desperately trying not to laugh as well.

It was official, my friends were insane. And... Tom was finally dead.

As he slumped forward, I waited for panic and disgust to rise up again. Vee had been able to do what I couldn't, and that would have broken me a moment ago, but now, as I stood in a circle of love, respect, and warmth, there was no room for anything but happiness.

The fact that these four men, exceptional in every way, loved me... meant everything to me. I'd been strong on my own before, when I'd had to scrape through life and fight for survival, but this was a different sort of strength. One built on love. Fuck, as sappy as it was to say, we were stronger together.

No need to stand alone and kill someone to prove anything, because I already had everything I needed.

Thank fuck.

It didn't seem that the boys were planning on moving away from me any time soon, and despite my revelations about *my* strength being different than what I'd expected, I wasn't quite ready for them to step away either.

Tonight had been a lot, from Vee scaring the shit out

of all of us by dropping a literal bomb on her family to Tom's torture and death, and now we were here.

"I'm just going to clean this mess up," Vee chirped happily, nodding for Giana to follow as they approached Tom, "and then we need to get out there and see what's happened with the bombing. Such a tragedy. We'll chat tomorrow, okay?"

By the end of her speech, she had Tom unchained and was dragging him across the floor.

"Be careful," Angelo warned her. "Taking out your family in such a manner is a recipe for street violence; keep your guard up."

Vee's smile was scary and dark as she continued to haul the dead body out of here. "Oh, I'm counting on it, husband. Have fun, friends."

Then they were gone, a trail of blood the only indication that they'd even been in the room.

Our lives were fucking weird.

"You okay, Thorn?" Rhett asked, his focus all on me as he stared down, eyebrows bunched and concern on his face.

The pressure in my chest had eased along with the disappointment in myself. "Yeah, actually, I think I am. I'm certainly glad to have Tom and his hold on Flo and Bellerose dealt with. As long as he's dead, it doesn't matter that I couldn't do it."

Rhett leaned down closer. "I'm so proud of you," he whispered, and when he kissed me, my eyes burned once more. But for a different reason.

As his tongue caressed mine, desperate need became the dominant emotion flooding my system as I groaned. Nothing like a little murder party and a torture scene to get the libido raging.

I'd seen it happen in movies and always thought it was insanely farfetched, and yet here we were, and I was both horny and needy, with zero fucks given that there'd been a dead body in the same room as us not five seconds ago.

"Did you forget we were all here too?" Jace's voice was strangled, but he hadn't moved away.

Rhett couldn't answer because his tongue was busy with mine, and still no one moved away.

"I don't think they care," Angelo said with a laugh. "As long as we can join in, I don't care either."

The moan that escaped me this time was longer and more drawn out based on the mental image he'd just painted.

All of them joining in?

Four men and one.... me.

Fuck. Was I ready for this?

Yes. Holy shit. The answer was always yes.

thirty-one

BILLIE

I t was all too easy to melt into their kisses, touches, caresses, and I almost forgot where we were. But when I gasped, then the tang of urine and blood reached my nose, and it was like a bucket of ice water over the sexy mood.

"Um, maybe we should relocate for this," I suggested, gagging on the smell that now flooded my nose. The body might be gone, but it was far from clean in Angelo's torture chamber. "Just... you know. What if Tom had a bloodborne disease or something? We should all shower. Preferably together."

"Sold," Rhett agreed, yanking me free of the others and sweeping me up in his arms. "Come on, losers, our girl wants an orgy." He gave a whoop of excitement, carrying me out to the SUV while I laughed uncontrollably in his embrace.

The others followed, and I heard Angelo mutter something to Gray about it being a good idea, since he didn't stock lube in his torture-tool drawer.

"Really? Why not?" Jace asked, overhearing. "I'd have thought that was, um, something used in torture. Isn't it? Or am I being a sick fuck right now?"

Angelo and Grayson both chuckled, then Angelo whispered his answer to Jace too quietly for me to hear. Whatever it was, Jace blanched and hissed a breath through his teeth.

"Ouch," he replied. "Forget I asked."

We piled into the car, Rhett pulling me into his lap as Grayson grudgingly took the driver's seat with Angelo beside him. Jace had been quickest to the car and had taken the other backseat spot, and he grabbed me out of Rhett's lap swiftly.

"Home?" Gray asked with an arched brow, and I barely got my confirmation out before Jace claimed my lips in a searing-hot kiss.

I moaned against him, letting his tongue plunder my mouth as I sank deeper into his embrace. All the intense emotions of the night had left me coursing with adrenaline, and my hands shook as I threaded fingers into Jace's hair. I needed *more*, but we definitely needed to shower. I could still smell blood but wasn't totally sure if it was my imagination or not.

"Don't be selfish, Jace," Angelo scolded from the front seat. "If you're getting Bella warmed up, sit her in the middle so we can all see."

Jace continued kissing me, ignoring Angelo for a moment, but I *liked* the idea of letting them all see, so I laughed and pulled away from Jace's lips. "Sharing is caring, Adams," I whispered, then slid out of his lap and into the middle seat, where I met Angelo's hungry gaze straight on. "But I don't know what you think you can see when I'm dressed like this. Not really easy-access, car-fuck sort of clothes."

Rhett clicked his tongue. "Nonsense, Thorn. We can work with this." To prove his point, he slipped a hand beneath the ink-black knit of my top and peeled it up over my breasts. I wore a sensible black bra underneath, but it was far from dowdy and pushed my tits up perfectly.

Jace grabbed my jaw, turning my face back to his so he could keep kissing me, but Rhett was focused on getting my bra undone. I arched my spine off the seat, and he popped my clasp, but then Jace had to let me go so Rhett could strip my top off entirely. It was weirdly fluid, the way they worked together, with Rhett claiming my mouth and Jace unbuckling my thigh holster next.

"Play with her nipples, Jace," Grayson ordered, and I looked up to find him watching us in the rearview mirror. "Suck them."

"Watch the road, Gray," I replied, trying to make my voice stern and only achieving breathy and lustful. Close enough.

Jace did as he was told, though, cupping my breast and closing his lips around my nipple while Rhett sucked the skin of my throat. Hot sparks of desire zapped through me, and I tipped my head back with a moan. Fuck, that felt good.

I threaded my fingers back into Jace's soft hair to hold him there, then squirmed as he tugged my nipple with his teeth.

"You like that, huh?" Angelo asked from his position in the front. He'd turned almost entirely around, his seatbelt forgotten as he watched us with hungry eyes.

I moaned my agreement, my back arching as Jace's fingers rolled my other nipple. Why did we need to drive home, again? Surely, we could make the backseat work if we pulled over somewhere. Hmm, then again, if I really did want all four of them... maybe not.

"How much?" Angelo pushed. "Rhett, check how wet she is already. Show us."

Rhett had already popped the fly of my black jeans, but I still muttered curses about my shitty clothing choice as I lifted off the seat to let him wrestle the stiff fabric down. Gray had better keep his eyes on the road because if we got pulled over, there was no chance of me re-dressing in any hurry.

Jace had to sit back and let us have a moment to get my boots undone and the jeans over my feet, because otherwise, he'd have copped an elbow to the face in the process. Sexy, it was not. But we quickly recovered it the moment my jeans were safely discarded on the floor, along with every other stitch of clothing that I'd worn out this evening. The boys hooked my legs over theirs, spreading me wide open for Angelo to see.

"Rhett," I gasped as he slid his fingers down the length of my pussy. I moaned, rocking my hips forward with encouragement as he circled my clit with his thumb, then thrust two fingers deep inside me.

Jace's teeth grazed my neck, his hand grasping my breast, but I kept my eyes open long enough to see Rhett withdraw his fingers from my cunt and offer them, glistening wet, through the gap in the seats to Angelo. When Angelo grabbed Rhett's wrist and sucked those two fingers into his mouth, I nearly died.

"Gray, please tell me we're nearly home," I whined, desperate for cock. Four of them, to be precise.

His gaze flipped to the mirror, then he watched for way longer than *safe* because Rhett had pulled his fingers from Angelo's mouth and thrust them straight back into my pussy, making me cry out with delight.

Gray bit his lip hard as he dragged his gaze away from the mirror. "I reckon we have enough time to see you come at least once, Prickles," he replied. "You really can't be *too* warmed up for what we have in store."

I squeaked an embarrassing sound of excitement, but then Rhett started pumping his hand, fucking me rough with his fingers while Jace joined him to play with my clit. My whole body sang with arousal as they worked me up, swapping kisses between them like I was dining at a buffet of sexy men. It seriously wasn't a hard request when Grayson growled at us to *hurry up and finish before we crash,* and my gasping moans echoed through the car while he parked us securely behind the gates of his home.

My climax quaked through me, my inner walls clenching tight around Rhett's fingers like I wanted to keep him there forever. But Grayson had other ideas, barely waiting for the garage door to shut before he yanked open the back door and snatched me out.

My world tipped sharply upside down as he tossed me, naked and still trembling, over his shoulder, then strode into the house.

"Grayson! What the shit? I can walk!" I protested, despite the fact that I probably couldn't just yet.

His only response was to smack my ass. Hard. Which made me moan loudly, so he did it again.

Fuck... we were off to a great start.

With monumental effort I lifted my head, shaking my hair away to find the other three guys following quickly behind, Rhett already shirtless and starting to strip his pants. It was nice to know I wasn't the only one desperate for an orgy. Was that what this was called? Or was it a gang bang if they weren't fucking each other?

Either way, I was excited. So were they, judging by the hard dicks being set free of restrictive pants.

Grayson literally *tossed* me into the middle of his bed, and I bounced high enough that I worried about my landing. But then he was right there on top of me, kissing the very breath from my lungs as my legs pulled him closer. Then my skin caught on one of his knives, and I hissed in pain.

"Dammit," he rumbled, sitting up to inspect my scratch. It was barely even bleeding, but his brow was dipped in a deep scowl, nonetheless.

"It's fine," I quickly reassured him. "Doesn't even hurt. Promise. But if you're worried, let me help..." I sat up, pushing him off the bed to standing while I sat on the edge, unbuckling his weapons from his thick thighs.

Then his belt. Then I wrapped my fist around his monster cock and tried to take him in my mouth.

"Jesus Christ," Angelo muttered on a laugh, clearly getting an eyeful of Grayson's trouser snake for the first time. "I'm gonna run a shower because I have Tom's blood under my nails."

Ew. And yet, there was Rhett with his dick out, so I smoothly shifted onto my knees, keeping Grayson in my hand as I took Rhett in my mouth. He fisted my hair, pushing deeper into my throat than I was able to take Gray, and I gagged a little before he let up.

"Shit," Grayson groaned, his hips rocking as I worked him with my hand. "I should wash up too. Hold this thought, Prickles."

"And that pose!" Angelo yelled from the bathroom where water was already running. "I want in on that!"

Grayson slipped away, but Jace was right there to take his place, and I hummed happily as I swapped back and forth between Rhett and Jace, sucking them deep, exploring Rhett's piercing with my tongue, letting Jace choke me a little. Eventually they both came, taking turns to shoot their load down my throat, and I swallowed eagerly, like I was starving for their cum.

When they shifted away, Grayson and Angelo were right there to take their places, and I went to work once more. Surely, if they expected me to orgasm multiple

times in one night, they could do the same. Right? Well...
we were about to find out.

I took my time, keeping one hand wrapped tight
around each of them as I swapped my mouth back and
forth between them, and when Grayson tried to pull
away, I gently applied some teeth to remind him who
was really in charge.

The edge of pain—or maybe danger—made him
snap, and he filled my mouth with his load only a
moment later, grunting like he'd shocked himself. I
couldn't help my grin of victory as I swallowed and
released him, but his narrowed gaze said he'd get
payback soon. I could hardly wait.

"You want me to come, Bella?" Angelo murmured
with a wicked grin, his hand stroking my face as I took
him back into my mouth once more. My tongue flicked
over each of his piercings, and mentally, I made a note to
book him in to finish the ladder. If these few felt as good
as they did, I could only imagine the fun we'd have on a
full stack.

Angelo seemed to want my answer, so I nodded,
humming an *mm-hmm* around his thickness. He smirked
down at me, then grabbed my hair in a borderline painful
grip and took control of the pace. Suddenly, I wasn't
sucking his dick anymore; he was fucking my throat
instead. It was all I could do to flatten my tongue and

protect my teeth from his piercings as he thrust in and out of my mouth with dizzying speed.

Then someone's hand snaked between my legs from behind, two fingers filling my soaking wet cunt while another found my clit and rubbed it like a fucking magic lamp.

I screamed around Angelo's cock, and he came without warning, making me choke and splutter on his hot load as I crashed into my own orgasm, thanks to whoever was finger-fucking me.

When Angelo released my head, I gasped for air, coughing while grinning like a loon. He bent down and kissed me hard, his tongue sweeping through my mouth and not flinching once at the fact that I'd just swallowed four different dude's cum.

"Fuck, you're sexy, Bella," he groaned, pressing extra kisses to my lips as he withdrew. "What did we do to deserve a queen like you?"

"Absolutely fucking nothing," Jace commented from behind me, making me realize it had been his fingers inside my pussy a moment ago. Of course it had been. Jace and Angelo shared a bond deeper than human.

I swallowed hard, licking my swollen lips, but before I could say anything, a strong pair of hands lifted me up off the carpet and deposited me onto the bed, where Jace had just scooted back to recline against the pillows. His fist stroked his dick, pumping it hard once more as he watched me with heated, feral eyes.

"Bend forward, babe," Rhett told me while dropping a kiss on my shoulder. "Kiss Jace. Let him taste us all on your tongue."

To his credit, Jace didn't hesitate as he leaned in to meet my kiss; his tongue slid over the seam of my lips and plunged deeper as I parted them. Cold, wet lube dropped onto my flesh as I kissed Jace, and I gasped at the initial contact. Then I groaned with ecstasy as Rhett massaged it in, pushing the slippery substance inside me —both holes—with forceful, impatient fingers. He dragged his lips over my butt cheeks, kissing my flesh as he made a thorough job of lubing me up, and I rocked eagerly onto his hand, desperate for more.

"Patience, Thorn." He laughed as I tried to coax him deeper. "Don't worry, baby, we'll fill these up for you."

As if that was the magic password, Jace wrapped his hands around my waist, pulling me forward and turning me around all at once until I was straddling him reverse cowgirl. With my back to Jace, I had an unobstructed view of my other three lovers.

Rhett grinned at me from his position on his knees, cock hard and straight in front of him already. Gray and Angelo stood back, taking a hot second to recover, but that was more than okay with me. Baby steps. Jace gripped my hips, moving me to where he wanted, and his hardness slid against my lube-soaked crack, making me pant with anticipation. Was he going to...?

"Want a hand, baby?" Rhett asked in a husky voice, moving closer to smack a kiss on my mouth. "Lean back; brace your hands on Jace's chest."

I did as I was told, shifting my weight onto my feet, like a horny frog, while Rhett dipped his head to suck one of my nipples. Moaning, I arched into him, and he chuckled.

"Sorry, you distracted me. Alright, don't mind me, Jace." He shot a wink at my first love over my shoulder, then just boldly reached down and grabbed his best friend's cock in his hand. I gasped when that action computed in my brain, sitting up to get a better look. Sure enough, Rhett's tattooed fingers curled around Jace's dick as he guided the thick head to where he wanted it.

I sucked in another sharp breath, but then Rhett's mouth was against mine and Jace was applying pressure to my hips to hold me tight, to push me down as he surged up and his tip stretched my asshole open. I screamed into Rhett's kisses, but that didn't stop me from spreading my legs wider and desperately trying to stay *relaxed* enough to let Jace push deeper into my ass.

"That's it," Rhett purred against my kisses, "good girl,

Thorn. You're taking him so fucking well. Christ, I can't wait to take a turn in that tight little ass." I whimpered, so turned on it hurt as Jace finally exhaled heavily as he reached his limit. "Yeah, you want that, don't you? You want us all to take turns in *every* hole, Thorn?"

Shit. Here I was thinking *I* nailed the dirty talk thing, and Rhett just swooped in and upped the game. Words totally failed me as he played with my clit, his fingers rubbing, tapping, pinching.

"You gonna move or just chill there all night, bro?" Angelo asked Jace with a smirk, coming to kneel on the side of the bed as he stroked his quickly hardening, metal-studded dick.

Jace grunted his response and, presumably, flipped Angelo off, then started to fuck me from underneath. Rhett whispered more praise, then kissed his way down my body until his mouth reached my pussy. I cried out as his tongue thrust into me, timed perfectly with Jace's thrust in my ass, and Rhett just laughed. Then he pushed his fingers into my pussy while he french kissed my clit and made me see stars. No... not stars, he made me see fucking *planets,* and then, while I was still coming, he sat up and slammed his cock inside my cunt with a feral roar.

I spiraled right into another, more intense climax, and even Jace spluttered curses beneath me as my muscles all tensed.

"Holy shit, that's hot," Angelo moaned, shuffling closer and stroking himself like he was possessed. I knew exactly what he wanted, so I parted my lips and beckoned him with my eyes until he shoved that pierced length down my throat once more.

Yep. That was a whole new experience. I whimpered and moaned as Angelo filled my mouth, Rhett pumped my pussy, and Jace slammed into my ass all at once. Then Grayson was at my other side, his firm grip guiding my hand from Jace's chest to wrap around his hardness again. I pumped him with my hand as well as possible, but my balance was all messed up.

With a groan of frustration, I pulled away from Angelo just enough to rebalance myself between Jace and Rhett, somehow managing to take them both at a new angle that nearly made me climax. But it also meant I now had both my hands free, allowing me to alternate between hand job and head job on Gray and Angelo again.

Jace's breathing came hot and hard at my back, his fingers biting into my hips as he thrust harder and harder, then exploded with a rush of wet heat inside my ass.

"Thank fuck," Angelo moaned, giving Jace a nudge. "Rearrange."

As if by a rehearsed arrangement, Rhett sat back,

Grayson lifted me, and Angelo push Jace clean off the bed to take his place against the pillows. Jace hit the floor with a heavy thump and a moan of protest, but I was already climbing onto Angelo's lap, facing him as he threaded his pierced dick into my sensitive, overstimulated pussy.

Moaning as those metal rungs teased my flesh, I adjusted my position onto my knees so I could rock on him slowly a few times. Then Rhett slapped my ass and made me yelp.

"Fuck," Angelo coughed. "Dammit, Silver."

Rhett chuckled, then palmed my stinging butt cheek and pushed his way into my ass. I whispered curses at the new sensation of his pierced tip in my back hole, but it wasn't a bad thing. Not even a little bit. Then Angelo started moving in my pussy, and I got treated to the double sensation of their piercings stimulating all different spots at the same time. Holy hell, how was a girl to handle that much pleasure all at once? Fuck if I knew, but until I had a better idea, I just gave myself over to yet another intense, stomach-clenching, toe-curling orgasm that left me practically speaking in tongues as my vision faded in and out.

Rhett and Angelo fucked me faster, riding my high as they chased their own, and then Grayson was there, gagging me with his huge girth while I moaned and convulsed as the meat in one hell of a sexy sandwich. Rhett's control snapped a moment later, and his cum joined Jace's, painting my insides as he thrust deep and cursed.

"You good, Ricci?" Grayson rumbled, stroking my hair back from my face as I sucked his tip and sucked quick gasps of air through my nose.

"Yessir," Angelo muttered back, his fingertips digging into my hips as he gave my pussy a few more slamming thrusts.

Grayson made a satisfied hum, cupping his hand under my chin. "What about you, Prickles? You want more?"

He popped free of my mouth as I nodded quickly, not even a fraction of hesitation in my mind, regardless of how hypersensitive every damn inch of my body now was. "Yessss," I moaned, licking my lips. "Please..."

"Good girl," he praised. Then he and Angelo were both shifting positions again, almost like they'd all had a discussion about this ahead of time. Had they? The idea of them sitting around, discussing how to fuck me all together... it was a major turn on. I groaned my arousal as Grayson pulled me onto his chest like a Billie blanket, then hitched one of my knees up to give himself easy entry into my cunt. Even with how warmed up and well stretched my pussy was, his size made it a tight fit. Real tight. So when Angelo pushed my knee higher and pressed his tip to my ass, I sucked in a gasp of panic.

"Shhh, little hedgehog," Grayson murmured, "you're fine. You've got this. Like you were made to be fucked by all of us... over and over, in every possible way..."

My panic morphed into pleasure as Angelo pushed inside with little resistance, thanks to how slick things were getting down there. It was safe to say, though, the combination of Grayson and Angelo together was pushing the limits of what I could safely take. Right? Surely.

Wait, where had Jace and Rhett gone? The shower was running again. Were they in there together? Oh fuck. Why did that mental image make me want to identify as a loofah?

"Bella," Angelo moaned, gripping my hips as he thrust deep. "I fucking love you so much." Thrust. Then he smacked my ass, and I squeaked, my teeth sinking into Grayson's lip, since I'd just started kissing him.

Angelo chuckled. "That's it, baby, stay with us. Fuck, you feel good strangling my cock with your tight ass." On that note, I tightened up my muscles—as much as possible—and he gave a low moan in response. Nice.

Grayson kissed me hard, his tongue tangling with mine and stealing my air as he rocked his hips beneath me, fucking in shallow thrusts while Angelo went harder on top. In fact, the harder and faster Angelo went, chasing his release and driving me wild, the slower and shallower Grayson went. Like he was trying to hold off his own climax. Shit. Did that mean...?

"Bella, baby, I'm gonna come," Angelo exclaimed. "But I wanna feel you fall apart again. One more time."

Rhett and Jace sauntered out of the bathroom, smelling like soap and glistening with water, and my mouth watered. Their gazes locked on me with predatory instinct, and Rhett sat casually on the bed, his towel barely covering his groin.

"Baby, you're all strung out on touches, huh?" he pouted, but his eyes sparkled with mischief. "You're like a livewire, right now, like you haven't totally come down off your last climax, so all it'd take to spark one again..." He trailed a finger down my side, then tweaked my nipple. Hard. I screamed as my orgasm crested *again*. "That's it, Thorny babe. That's our girl. So perfect. So responsive."

Angelo slammed into me, unloading his release with grunts and moans, then kissed a line of sweet caresses down my spine as he whispered his love.

"Oh man... That's one for the spank bank," Rhett admitted with a lustful sound, watching Angelo pull out of me. Or maybe watching the ooze of too much cum dripping out of me.

"Beautiful Rose, are you still alive?" Jace teased, stroking my hair. "I can take you to clean up, if you want...?"

I moaned, then shifted to sit up more and gasped when Gray sank deeper into my cunt. Wash up? No. Not yet. "But we aren't finished," I replied, giving Grayson a shy smile. "Are we, Gray?"

His lips curled in an evil grin. "Good girl," he purred. Then he banded his arms around my waist and flipped us. My world spun on its axis for a moment, and then I was on my knees facing the headboard with Gray at my back. "Hands on the headboard, Prickles. Hold on."

Fear and anticipation curled through me, reviving my boneless body once more as I did as I was told. Gray pressed a hand to my lower back, urging me to arch and push my ass higher, and then he went to work tearing me in two with his anaconda.

"*Fuuuuck!*" I screamed out as the intense sensation of being stretched got to be almost too much. "Shit, holy hell, Gray... you don't fit!"

"Shh, baby, you can take it," he rumbled, stroking his hand over my butt cheek soothingly, even as his breath came in sharp pants. "I know you can, Prickles; you were fucking made for my dick. Just breathe."

"Or don't," Rhett suggested, tossing his towel aside and getting to his knees beside me. "Distraction might help, Thorn. Wanna suck my cock to take your mind off things?"

I nearly laughed, then Gray pushed another fraction in, and I panted. "Yes. Fuck. Rhett, choke me."

Thank fuck he'd just showered because he didn't hesitate to grab my hair and thrust into my throat. He was right, though; as I focused on not *actually* suffocating while also sucking his cock, I wasn't focused on Grayson pushing the biggest cock on earth into my ass. Before I knew it, he was *in*, and goddamn, it felt good. He grunted, gripping my hips, then set a pace to pump in and out, while Rhett lazily fucked my face and crooned sweet nothings about what a perfect little fuck doll I was. It was dirty, *filthy*, and I'd never been more comfortable in my own skin. Never felt so loved, cherished, adored, protected, and *owned*.

Between the four of them, they dragged one final climax out of me, then Grayson emptied himself inside my ass alongside the other three.

I collapsed then, unable to find even a second more of strength. Vaguely, I was aware of the guys gently carrying me into the bathroom and thoroughly cleaning me up in the bathtub, petting my hair and all gushing the sweetest words about their love for me. But I was on another planet. Planet Orgy, meeting with their leader, President Orgasm. It was a happy place to be.

thirty-two

RHETT

In the days after that night with Billie and our big family bang, as we lovingly referred to it, the dynamics did change between all of us. Not in the way I'd expected though. The jealousy and petty bickering were never going to end between the four of us, since there was only one Billie and none of us were particularly good with long-term sharing, but there was a new comfort in our group dynamics.

It was as if we'd all decided at that point that we were really doing this, it was *for fucking sure* happening, and now we just had to figure out how to ensure that we could continue to live like this for another seventy or so years.

With Billie as our center, I had no doubt that we could make this work. We'd been through hell together and come out the other side. We could do this, no worries.

"Are you heading to the hospital today?" Jace asked when I strolled into the kitchen that morning. "Today is the day, right?"

I nodded, reaching for coffee because I needed it fucking badly. Last night had been my worst sleep in a long time, and I'd been grateful to have Billie with me. She'd let me lose myself in her body all night, and I'd left her exhausted in our bed this morning so I could try and sort my mental space before we left for Townsend.

"You don't have to do this, bro; you know that, right?" Jace was leaned back against the bench, hair mussed up like he'd just rolled out of bed too. I might have kept them all up last night with my Billie distraction. She wasn't exactly quiet.

Fuck, I loved that girl.

"I don't know how I'm going to react when I see them," I said, taking a huge gulp of coffee. The soothing caffeine started to work a few seconds later, and I managed to relax a touch. "It's been so fucking long and so much of my trauma is wrapped up in that fucking town and my grandfather. The doc told me to expect triggering moments but that I should be able to pull myself out of them much faster than I would have been able to before."

Jace's expression remained serious, and he didn't say anything for a few seconds. "You've changed a lot. For the better. You've always been the best of us, Rhett, but with the most broken soul. Now you're still the best of us and all those pieces are repairing."

I'd bet my left nut some variation of that line would appear in one of our songs soon. Bastard talked poetically when he was in the middle of composing.

Grayson entered the room, sweaty with a towel over his shoulders. Of course, he'd already worked out; why the fuck wouldn't he have. Asshole overachiever.

"We should go with you," he said for the tenth time since we'd last discussed this. "Keep those fucking Townsend sycophants from interfering with you and Billie."

It had been decided that just Billie and I would go, with a few of our usual security, of course.

"I don't want you on any of their radars," I said quickly, shaking my head. "I'm sure they're aware of Bellerose, but they just think of you as loser musicians. I don't want to change their perception of that."

Not to mention that this felt like a journey I had to take on my own. I'd been hiding from my demons in

Bellerose for too long, and it was time to stand on my own. The final part of my healing journey.

"Call us if you need us," Grayson grumbled, before he poured his own coffee. "That's a fucking order."

"Yes, sir," I chirped back and was rewarded with a glower.

"I'd watch yourself," Angelo said, strolling into the room, the only one of us fully dressed because he was clearly a psychopath who probably slept in a three-piece suit. "Grayson is a little cranky that you kept us up all night with Bella's screams. He was slamming that boxing bag pretty hard this morning."

Slept in a suit *and* managed to work out before 6:00 A.M too. Another sign of being a psychopath. We were fucking rock stars; we weren't supposed to crawl out of bed until midday.

"No better distraction than our Billie," I said with a shrug. "You all better get used to hearing her scream from my room."

"Going to hear you scream in a minute," Grayson threatened before he took another sip of coffee, as if to calm himself.

The disgruntled look on his face had me laughing, and for the first time today, some of my uneasiness faded as I relished this moment of brothers bonding—a part of the new, deeper bond between us all that had me as fucking sappy as Jace and his emo love songs.

When I finished my coffee, I left to get ready and to wake our sleeping beauty. "Thorn, we have to leave in about fifteen minutes," I whispered, pressing my lips to hers. She opened her eyes and smiled so sweetly at me.

"Okay, Zepp, I'll jump in the shower."

We showered separately because there was no fucking way we'd make it out of this house before lunchtime otherwise, and then it was time to leave.

"Call me when it's done," Grayson said sternly. After kissing Billie firmly, he deposited her in the passenger seat of his bulletproof car. "Security will be in the car behind you guys."

"You got it, bro," I said, deciding not to be a smartass for once.

"Here are all the documents you need," Angelo said, leaning over Billie to hand me a thick folder. "I think this is more than enough to get the IRS investigation started." When he pulled away, he kissed Billie long and hard, then leaned back out of the car.

Jace was around the back loading up our suitcases, since we weren't sure how long we'd be away. I could tell it was bothering Billie to leave the others for a week or so, and I let out a long breath. "Maybe you guys should come visit midweek, depending on the schedule. I'll let you know after we've convinced the old bastard to help us."

Everyone's faces brightened then. "That's a great idea," Jace said, reappearing at Billie's window to lean in for his own kiss. "I think we'd all feel better if we could stay for a night or two later in the week."

It went against every instinct I had to put my loved ones in the same vicinity as that bastard. It was bad enough Billie was here, but she'd flat out refused to let me go without her. And my weak ass wanted her there too.

"Okay, I'll let you know," I said, starting the car and shifting it into drive. "We'll call when we get there."

"Love you," Billie called through the window. The boys all leaned in for one more kiss, and then it was time to go.

The drive there was fairly quiet as we held hands and listened to music and Billie let me have my thoughts in peace. The security car stayed behind us, and we encountered very little traffic on the drive.

Part of me wished some disaster had closed the road so I didn't have to go through with this, but I knew that I'd have found a way around it, no matter what. I had to do this for my family... and myself. This closure had been a long fucking time coming.

When we reached the hospital, the security stayed in

the waiting area with Billie while I went off to speak with the doctor, the same Townsend asshole as last time. "We just need you to sign off on the consent form," he said when we were in his office, as he shoved a clipboard in my face.

Technically, there should be a whole lot more involved in the process. Psych evaluations, counselling sessions, in depth discussions about the lengthy hospital stay and recovery that would follow. But apparently the Townsend Community hospital was cutting corners to save time. Well... tough shit.

"I need to speak with my grandfather first," I said bluntly, ignoring the clipboard, even as he shook it.

The doctor's jaw ticked and his suddenly brittle smile did a piss-poor job of covering his anger. A seamless transition for one brainwashed loser. Every single person in this cursed town was under Jeremiah's control, so the slip from professionalism was no shock. "There's no need for that. What would talking to him do?"

My smile was not a nice once. "That's none of your fucking business. Now, organize the meeting, or I'll take my compatible liver with me out the fucking door and let your *leader* wither and die."

Not that I wouldn't put it past these assholes to try and ambush me and take the liver anyway, but hopefully it wouldn't come to that. I wasn't asking for a lot, after all.

Well, not from this fuckwit of a doctor.

The doctor muttered something before tossing the consent form on his desk. "Come with me," he grumbled, walking out the door without looking back.

I followed because I needed this dealt with. Pulling out my phone, I checked in with Billie on the way, and she texted back that she was still safe and sound, surrounded by men in suits.

Good. Hopefully no one would approach her while they still needed something from me. My grandfather would ensure our safety for as long as it took to get his liver. After that, of course, we'd all be fair game.

As the doctor led me down the hall, I mentally prepared myself for this meeting. It wasn't my grandfather, but my mother who had me the most worried. She was the one who'd hurt me, and it was her face that had kept me awake many nights, the anger and pain eating me alive.

When we reached the end of the corridor, the doctor opened a set of double doors, and we entered a hospital room at least four times the size of any hospital room I'd seen before. It was almost set up like a fancy hotel, with a king-sized bed, couches and tables in the corner, and a small kitchenette.

Was I surprised to see Jeremiah Townsend dying in the lap of luxury? Not even a little.

He was propped up in the bed, wires and drips attached to him, the monitors around him beeping as they did whatever they were doing to keep that old asshole alive.

His beady eyes locked on me, and there was no surprise on his face. Clearly the doctor's job had been to try and dissuade me from seeing him, but Jeremiah knew me better than that.

"Make it quick; he's quite frail," the doctor snapped as he stepped aside.

I turned back and looked at him. "Get the fuck out of this room or the deal is off."

He bristled across every feature, but glanced toward the bed, then nodded stiffly. "Do not touch him," he warned before he left the room, closing the door behind him.

And now I was alone with the evilest human I'd ever known, and considering the last few months, that was saying a fucking lot.

"Son," Jeremiah said softly, and my own morbid curiosity forced me to look at him again. Not just look, but step closer, until I had no choice but to see him clearly.

"Don't call me that," I said without inflection, determined not to let him know the turmoil inside me.

I examined him for a few seconds, surprised at how frail and small he actually looked. In my memory he was larger than life, the epitome of fear itself, and yet here he lay... dying, with just wisps of white hair on his head. His skin was a sickly yellow that I could only assume indicated acute liver failure. His face was reasonably unlined for an eighty-year-old—having a decent plastic surgeon in your cult helped with that—but he still looked old.

Old and sick. Weak.

I felt nothing as I stared down at him.

"Where's my mom?" I asked, unsure how I felt that she wasn't here.

"In the community, doing her duty," he said shortly before he waved me closer. "Why did you want to see me, son?"

I'd made a mistake in letting him know that "son" bothered me. Fucker would use it every time, and I decided to ignore it as best I could going forward. It was that or reach out and wrap my hand around his throat and choke him to death.

There'd be time for that later, along with figuring out if he'd just told the truth about my mom or if she had long since died and been buried by his hand.

"You need something from me," I said in the same monotone. "Something very important that will save your life. I'm willing to donate it to you, but nothing comes without a price. You taught me that."

Jeremiah smiled, yellowing teeth a similar color to his yellowish skin. "You are a chip off the old block, aren't you, son. I expected you'd come back into the fold eventually."

Delusion was his middle fucking name.

"What do you require of me?" He was playing that affable fatherly figure now, the one he'd perfected to draw in the weak and unsuspecting with promises of a better life, prosperity, and eternal peace.

There was no sense in beating around the bush, and I didn't want to linger a second longer than necessary. "I need you to orchestrate, through your contacts in the IRS, the takedown of a few key families in Ricci Corp."

I let that hang in the air for a few minutes as Jeremiah tried and failed to hide his surprise. "You're involved with the mafia?"

"My involvement is none of your concern," I continued. "All I need is for you to make some calls. You and I both know you have the contacts to initiate this investigation, and I need you to fast track it—which is really in your best interest, since I won't consent to any liver transplant until everything is signed and sealed and the perpetrators are all arrested."

His surprise was hidden once more, and he regarded me carefully before he nodded. "If I do this for you, I have one further stipulation."

Of course he fucking did because me cutting out a piece of my body for him wasn't enough.

"You come back to Townsend. You come back and take your rightful place with us as my heir."

I laughed. It burst from me and grew out of quickly control, until I was near gasping for air. Just the thought of that request had me nearing hysteria.

"It's a simple request, really," Jeremiah said, a snap of anger underlying his words now. My lack of respect or fear was finally getting to him. "You don't even have to live with us, at least not at first, but you must promise to visit. To learn how to lead."

A promise wasn't worth shit, so I'd indulge this asshole to get what I wanted.

"Fine. If that's what it takes, I will visit the community on occasion, outside of my normal commitments. Baby steps, Jeremiah. Baby steps."

He nodded. "I never like when my sheep leave the flock. There's always something missing."

We were sheep to his wolf, which was the part he never told anyone.

"So, we're agreed?"

Not like he had a damn choice, but I wanted him to feel as if he had power here still. At least until I got what I wanted.

"Agreed," Jeremiah said, before he coughed a few times and sank back into the bed. "Hand me the phone, and I'll call my contacts."

Two hours later I'd gone over everything with Jeremiah's people in the IRS and emailed them copies of everything in the folder of information from Angelo. With their assurance they'd have a plan of action in the next few days, I made my way out to Billie, who was reading a book on her phone. When I called her name, she jumped up and smiled brightly. "Zepp," she said. "I've been worried."

Before I could say anything, the doctor emerged from somewhere. Probably the depths of hell.

"Time to sign that consent form and schedule the surgery," he said, thrusting it at me one more time.

I shifted Billie so she was behind me, and I was grateful that our security stood on either side of us.

"Jeremiah knows what I need from him," I told the doctor. "We'll be back when his side of the bargain is complete. I'm staying nearby."

Nearby but not in Townsend.

"Wait, no," he spluttered. "He doesn't have much time."

I shrugged before looping my arm around Billie's shoulders and pulling her into my side. "Guess he'd better hurry then."

We left the hospital without another word to anyone, and when we sat in the car, I let out a long sigh. "Fuck," I groaned.

Billie reached over and took my hand. "Did everything go okay? Do you need to talk about it?"

I shook my head. "No, it went exactly as planned. He agreed to facilitate the takedown of the Riccis and their associates and called in his IRS contacts. They were literally falling over themselves to get the information Angelo had collected. Unsurprisingly, there's already an ongoing investigation, but they've never found their smoking gun."

"Did you make sure Angelo's immunity was part of the deal?"

I nodded, smiling down at the cutest little concerned expression on her face. "Yep, our mafia prince is safe, as long as they get the rest of them."

Billie settled back into her chair, and I made sure she was buckled in before starting the car.

"So, now we wait," she said.

I shot her a wicked grin as we pulled out of the

parking lot. "Don't worry, Thorn baby, I know exactly how to pass the time."

Her breaths grew shallow as she looked at me and then out the front window. "How long until we reach the hotel?" she asked in a rush.

Fuck. I planted my foot as soon as we hit the street, the powerful engine loud around us. If I had to deal with my fucking family and this transplant in the next few days, then these days before with Billie were about to be the best gift.

Maybe I should donate a liver more often.

thirty-three

BILLIE

One day with Rhett at the little B&B an hour outside of Townsend morphed into two, and then into three. The doctors called multiple times a day, pleading with Rhett to come in for the procedure because every day *might* be Jeremiah's last. But he stubbornly refused each and every plea.

On the fourth day, we got the call we were waiting for.

"It's done," Jeremiah croaked over the phone, sounding like he was literally on death's door.

Rhett arched a brow at me, the phone on speaker in his palm. I shrugged, then shook my head, not trusting the word of a desperate, dying man.

"Good to hear," Rhett replied with a sigh. "I'll wait for confirmation from *my* people before returning to the hospital. I'm sure you understand."

A rattling wheeze came down the line, which I guessed might be a laugh. "I do." Then the call ended, and Rhett scrubbed a hand over his face.

"Are you really going through with this?" I asked softly, still somewhat in disbelief that he was willing to save that man's life. We could have come up with another plan, couldn't we?

He just shrugged. "I guess we'll find out. Check in with Angelo? I'm gonna take a shower."

I nodded, then brushed a kiss over his lips. As he walked to the bathroom, his shoulders sagged like he was carrying the weight of the whole world. I wished I could take some of that from him, but only he could see this through. All I could offer was a shoulder to lean on.

Sinking down onto the end of the bed, I unlocked my phone and pulled up Angelo's number.

"Jeremiah says it's done," I told him when he answered. "Have you heard anything?"

Angelo grunted in surprise, and the clank of metal in the background told me he was in the gym. Of course he was; the boys all spent a *huge* amount of time in there to keep their cheese-grater abs firm. I was just glad none of them tried dragging my lazy, unfit ass in there. Unless it was for sex. That happened plenty.

"I haven't yet," he replied, puffing slightly. "But that doesn't surprise me, if they all got picked up at the same time. Let me make some calls, and I'll let you know."

"Okay, good idea," I agreed, shifting on the bed. My butt hit the TV remote, and the screen lit up as a loud sex moan echoed through the room. Panic flashed through me, and I fumbled for the remote, switching it to the news channel instead, but Angelo had *definitely* heard it.

"Bella..." he purred, and I could *hear* his grin. "What was that?"

I groaned, rubbing my eyes. "Um... Rhett and I might have been watching porn last night. Anyway, call me back if you find anything." I quickly ended the call, then focused on what had just come up on the TV. Then I hit redial.

"Bella, baby, it's rude to hang up like that. I wanna hear more about this porn you've been watching. Is it kinky shit?" Angelo was chuckling, and I rolled my eyes.

"Focus, Ricci. Turn on the news. Looks like Jeremiah did followed through." I tapped the volume button up, listening as the reporters gave brief details of what was a years-long case being built against some key players in the Siena mafia.

Angelo scoffed, clearly watching the same thing now.

"Years long, my ass. They'd be nowhere without our help. Still... it does look like he held up his end of the deal. What will Rhett do now?"

I chewed the edge of my thumbnail, anxiety curling through my stomach. "Sign away half his liver, I guess. Save an evil man's life." I gritted my teeth, hating that Rhett was in this position. We never should have agreed to his plan.

"Well... tell him we're thinking of him," Angelo murmured, his voice rough. "And we appreciate him." Cute. "NI wanna know what sort of porn you've been watching with him. Give me a hint, Bella. Just boring, intro porn? Or is he tossing you in the deep end with gang bangs to give you ideas for our next family bonding session?"

Oh man. Now I was getting all worked up. "I'm not talking about this with you, Angel," I groaned, then laughed. "Go back to your workout; I'll call from the hospital."

He gave a horny moan, then started chuckling. "Fine. I love you, Bella. Today, tomorrow, and always."

Oh geez, he was going to make me cry with an out-of-the-blue sentimental statement like that. "Love you too, Angel," I replied in a whisper, then ended the call and started packing up my little suitcase of stuff.

When Rhett returned from the bathroom, I showed

him the news story, which was still playing out on the TV, and he nodded without any emotion. "I guess... I guess that's it, then. We should go."

I grabbed his hand, pulling him in close, and pressed my forehead to his. "You don't have to do this, Zepp. He doesn't deserve mercy."

Rhett inhaled deeply, then gave me a weak smile. "I know. Come on, let's get this over with."

I had to bite my tongue to stop pushing the issue with him when his mind was already made up. So I just held his hand silently as we drove back to Townsend and checked in at the hospital reception. All of a sudden, we were swept up in a flurry of motion as they pushed and pulled Rhett, getting him ready for *urgent* surgery. Apparently, Jeremiah was right at the end, so if we waited another day, he would probably not make it.

It was a shame. I'd quietly hoped the old fuck would die before the IRS pulled off their sting.

As it was, I got pushed aside into a waiting room while Rhett was admitted as a patient and stripped down to a hospital gown. I hovered in the doorway, watching at a distance while a nurse inserted an IV line into the back of his tattooed hand, and someone in a suit waved a clipboard of paperwork under his face.

He took the pen from the suited douchebag's hand, then looked over at me across the space to where I'd been told to wait. We locked eyes, and I tried to convey to him how much I fucking loved him. How he could walk away right now and I'd have his back. We all would. But then he just gave me a sad smile and scribbled his signature on the forms.

The social worker—presumably that's who it was—whisked the clipboard away and exited the room, leaving the hospital staff to start pushing Rhett's bed out into the corridor. As soon as he came close, I grabbed his hand, linking our fingers together as I walked alongside while they pushed his bed toward the operating room.

"Ma'am, you need to go back to the waiting room," one of the nurses informed me with a pinched expression. It took all my strength *not* to punch her in the mouth. Normally I had the utmost respect for nurses, but this *entire* town gave me the creeps. Every single person within it was complicit in Jeremiah Townsends disgusting abuses, so my patience had worn right out.

"Fuck off," Rhett snarled. "She can come as far as the operating room doors. Or would you like me to cause a scene and delay things further? Because I am in *no* hurry. Can you say the same for Jeremiah?"

The nurse narrowed her eyes like she wanted to argue —if only for the sake of arguing—but one of her colleagues pulled her aside and the orderlies started pushing the bed once more. No one else spoke the whole way to the operating room, where Jeremiah was already waiting in the corridor outside, frail and weak in his bed, waiting to be wheeled inside with Rhett.

This was the first time I'd seen Rhett's grandfather, and he looked like the slimy fuck I expected. With veneers, whisps of hair transplants, and an obvious face lift, he would have worn the crafted face of an extremely successful older man, if his liver hadn't decided to do us all a favor and peace out on him.

"Okay, good, there's no time for delays; we need to get started immediately," the smarmy fuck of a doctor from the other day announced, spearing me with a hate-filled look. "Why is she here? This isn't a visitor's area."

"Shut up," Rhett barked, glaring daggers as his fingers tightened on mine. "I have another request before we do this."

"No!" the doctor snapped back. "No more stalling. You got what you wanted—whatever that was—and now you need to follow through. Mr. Townsend doesn't have any time for more games, and you've signed your consent form, so, I'm sorry, but we're doing this. Now."

That wasn't true. Rhett could remove consent any time he wanted. But I got the feeling they'd force the issue then rely on the *consent form* to justify the surgery and discredit me as a witness of Rhett's refusal.

Jeremiah seemed so weak he barely even managed to

roll his head to the side to look at Rhett. His *son*. Fucking hell, evil came in all shapes. Right now, it stared at my love with yellow eyes like the demon in him was finally showing through. "What do you want?" he whispered.

Rhett remained cool and calm, the only tell of his anxiety in how tight he held my hand. "I need to see my mom. I can't just trust your word that she's alive. Bring her here, and then we can continue."

Jeremiah didn't respond for a few moments, and the doctor opened his mouth as if to throw his authority around again. He shut up when Jeremiah raised a weak hand.

"Fine. Get Mary here," he told the staff, not directing the request at anyone in particular. Why bother when they all worked for him?

One of the nurses whispered a quick, "Yes, Father of Good," before scurrying away, and I nearly gagged on my disgust.

"Sir, we don't have *time*," the doctor pushed, "and he signed the consent so—"

"Did I?" Rhett interrupted. "How confident are you?"

The color drained entirely from the doctor's face, and Jeremiah hacked a laugh.

"You did," the doctor insisted. "I saw you sign it myself. Our hospital lawyer has already filed it in our system." He snatched a tablet from one of the nurses and tapped furiously on the screen before beaming with relief. "Ah, see? Here. Signed and dated."

He twirled the tablet around to show us, and I frowned. I'd seen enough of Rhett's signatures on posters, merch, fan's skin, to know that wasn't it. My confusion cleared up as Rhett leaned forward and swiped the screen to zoom in.

Sure enough, on the signature line instead of his usual *Rhett Silver* scrawl that *any* self-respecting Bellerose fan would recognize, the document read: GoFuckYourself.

"Whoops," Rhett murmured with smug sarcasm. "Someone really should have verified that before accepting it."

The doctor's face turned a deep red that suggested he was seriously thinking about just knocking Rhett out and cutting the liver out of him, consent be damned.

"Whatever you're thinking," I said quietly, squeezing Rhett's fingers, "don't. We have security parked out front, and they're fully prepared to do *anything* to protect Rhett. And the media would have a field day with this story... with how famous *Bellerose* is, and all."

With that line drawn in the sand, Jeremiah ordered the staff to leave until Mary could arrive. At least he was smart enough—or defeated enough—to see when Rhett wouldn't be moved.

Time ticked past, minute by minute, soon turning into an hour. Jeremiah didn't try to speak, seeming to doze while we waited, so I just sat on the edge of Rhett's bed and waited silently with him. When two hours had passed and a nurse came by to check Jeremiah's vitals, Rhett sighed in frustration.

"Why is it taking so long?" he snapped. "If she was in the commune, she should be here by now."

Jeremiah cracked his lids open, his wrinkled lip curling up in a slight sneer. "She's working, son. And your mother takes a lot of pride in a job completed thoroughly."

Rhett's jaw clenched so hard it clicked. "Working *where?*"

Jeremiah gave him a sick smile. "At the temple, where she's worked every day and night since you left the community."

Whatever happened at "the temple," it was bad. Real bad. Enough that Rhett lurched off the hospital bed and vomited into a nearby trashcan. I stared, shocked speechless, and Jeremiah just chuckled to himself. The sadist.

Before I could suggest to Rhett that we just leave now, a frail, emaciated woman started along the hall with one of the stern-faced nurses escorting her. With the way Rhett jerked like he'd been shot, I guessed that was her. Mary.

"Mom," Rhett croaked, extending a hand to her as she drew close. But the woman with sunken eyes and limp hair walked straight past him like he didn't exist, going to Jeremiah to fall to her knees beside the bed.

Her whispers were panicked and pleading, but I couldn't make out the words. I was too fucking shocked at how she'd totally ignored her son like he was a ghost.

"I don't know what you expected, son," Jeremiah croaked between heavy breaths. "You know the rules. You died that day, and your poor mother has had to pay your debts ever since. But see? I gave you what you wanted. She's alive."

As if summoned by magic, the social worker was back along with the doctor.

"Sign the form," the doctor snarled, shoving the clipboard at Rhett's chest.

My love just brushed right past the doctor, stalking across to where his mother still knelt on the floor, her hands clasped together on the side of the bed and her head hung low.

"Mom," he tried again, crouching down beside her. "Mom, it's me. It's Nathan." His voice broke with emotion, and my heart ached for him. *Nathan.* I hadn't known the name he'd gone by in this community, and I had to say, *Rhett* fit him so much better. He'd been reborn the day he left Townsend, and my Rhett was too good to even set foot back in this place.

Mary gave no indication that she could hear him, just continued whispering her *prayer* over and over. When Rhett gently touched her frail shoulder, she flinched so hard he shook his head and stood up.

"How long does he have left?" Rhett asked the doctor, nodding to his dying sperm donor. His abuser. His worst demon. "Without the transplant. Weeks? Days? Less?"

The doctor visibly swallowed, then frowned. "Less," he growled. "Hours."

Rhett nodded, thoughtful. "Well. Let's see how long it takes, shall we? Take your consent form and shove it up your ass. You're not getting my liver, old man."

Gasps of shock rippled through the nearby staff, then Jeremiah started laughing. His laughter then morphed into coughing, which went on and on and then... stopped.

The monitor beeped long and low, and medical staff leapt into action to try and revive the *Father of Good*, but Rhett just turned his back on them all. He knew, like I did, that it was too late. Karma had come calling, and that demon had just breathed its last gasp.

thirty-four

BILLIE

Jeremiah Townsend was dead, and the whole Townsend Community was in shock—even more so when they realized he'd left no will. According to his personal-estate lawyer, it was something he'd been urged to do several times in the past weeks, but he'd refused. He'd been so supremely confident that Rhett would save him, so arrogant in his immortality, that he'd seen no *need* to complete a last will and testament.

This left the hospital staff at a loss for what to do. The doctor initially tried to have Rhett arrested—with absolutely zero plausible grounds—but a scuffle ensued when Bellerose security stepped in. When one of the hospital staff timidly reminded them that Rhett was, unfortunately, Jeremiah's next of kin, they'd reluctantly backed off. Which was how we found ourselves back in the VIP Suite of the hospital, only this time it was Rhett's mom in the bed.

"She still hasn't said anything?" I asked softly, coming back into the room from my coffee break. Mary had gone catatonic when Jeremiah died, so the hospital had admitted her for assessment. Rhett had stayed by her side the whole time, pleading with her to hear him, to *see* him, but she just stared blankly at the wall.

He shook his head in reply, sniffing hard. "Nothing. She barely even blinks."

I was at a loss for what to say, so I just sank down into the chair beside him and took his hand in mine. "Have the doctors been back to check on her?"

He shook his head. "Not yet. They're in chaos mode trying to work out who the fuck they all answer to now, like it even matters. This whole town is not *normal*, though, so it's stupid of us to think their hospitals operate anything like what we'd expect. Don't forget, every single person living and working here in Townsend has lived under his influence their whole fucking life. They don't know anything but how to follow his will."

Silence fell over us, and I rested my head on Rhett's

shoulder as he sat there watching his mom like he was just waiting her out.

"She won't talk to me," Rhett eventually said in a hoarse voice, "not until she gets told she's *allowed* to. Per the Townsend Doctrine, her son died when I left the community. If she acknowledges my existence, she is going against the word of Jeremiah. And that... carries punishment. Until his successor—whoever the fuck that is—tells her otherwise, I may as well be a ghost."

I hated that. I hated the whole creepy, pod-people vibe of the whole town. But that lined up with the cult situation. It still made me furious for Rhett and his poor mother for whatever horrors she'd endured in the name of religion.

"The guys are on their way here," I told him, trying to shift his focus even for a moment. "They're worried that the people here will do something. I don't know. The guys are just worried. So they'll be here in a couple of hours."

He pressed a kiss to my hair, with a soul-weary sigh. "Good. That's good. They'll know what to do next."

I swallowed hard at the empty hopelessness in his voice. This was far from the reunion he'd probably imagined with his mom. After all these years...

"Sounds like Giovanni is freaking out, too," I said, picking up a different thread in our fucked up tapestry of life. "His office at Ricci Corp looks like every document got shredded in a hurry, and he's disappeared. Angelo thinks he got tipped off early because he hasn't been seen since *before* the arrests started."

"Probably gone to try and strongarm the IRS into letting his guys go with a warning," Rhett murmured distractedly.

I chewed the edge of my lip, searching my brain for another line of conversation to help pull him from the pit of despair that only got worse with every second that Mary stared into space. Before I could go commenting on the weather—it was raining and dull, very appropriate— the door to the room opened and a broad-shouldered man with a bushy beard stepped through.

The shift in the room was undeniable as the emaciated woman on the hospital bed shrank smaller, her hands clasping in her lap and her eyes lowering. Rhett sucked in a sharp breath, then gritted his teeth and stood to face the imposing man.

"Garth," Rhett growled with undeniable hatred in his voice. "You're not welcome here. Get the fuck out of my sight before I drive my fist through your sorry skull."

The man barked a laugh, but it was cold and cruel. "Look at you, Nathan, all grown up. Found a set of balls out there in the world, eh? Well, save it. Your *fame* means nothing within Townsend. I've come to collect my property." He looked over at Rhett's mother with disgust. "Mary, *come*."

He treated her like a dog, and she responded in kind, scurrying out of the bed and crawling to him on all fours. It made me nauseous to watch.

Before she could reach the newest asshole in the room, Rhett reacted with lightning speed, getting between them. "There's no fucking way I'm letting you touch my mother," he snarled. "You might think you own this town, but unless Jeremiah left his estate to *you*, there's no paperwork to back that up. And I'll use every dollar to my name to have you destroyed."

Garth's *I'm-the-top-fuck-here* pose didn't falter, but I was fairly sure there was a flash of unease on his face. So brief. But Rhett had hit him hard enough to leave a mark with that statement. It also had Mary hesitating in her animal-like crawl to the next *messiah*.

"You don't scare me, boy."

It was a weak statement by a man who had nothing fucking else to throw Rhett's way.

"Liar," Rhett murmured. "You always did have a tell, you old bastard."

Garth went for him then, hands held out in front like he was going to attempt to strangle Rhett. Good fucking luck with that. Rhett might not be the largest of the

Bellerose boys, but he was hardly small, and he worked out just as fucking hard.

Still, just in case, I was already searching for a weapon to use if needed. Being a hospital room, I was sure there'd be something in one of the drawers, but I didn't have time to search cabinets during a fight.

The hospital door slammed open then, just as Rhett was straightening up to meet the asshole face to face. I swung around to find the doctor there, two suited men behind him, and all of them looked grim.

It was enough to stop Garth and Rhett in their tracks as they both swung on the newcomers. "What are you doing here?" Garth snapped at the doctor. "I told you to leave this usurper to me."

These people had so many screws loose their entire town was falling apart.

"Uh, these are the lawyers," Dr. Dickhead said with a rasp. "They've been working out the logistics of Townsend Community now that Townsend has ascended."

Well, fuck, that had old Garth raging again as he started for the doctor this time. The first suited man spoke before he could reach them. "I am Donald Osbourne of Osbourne, Schultz, and Myer Legal. We have all the paperwork as filed through us by Jeremiah only a few weeks ago."

If looks could kill, the lawyers would be preparing their obituaries because Garth apparently was not keen on this information getting out into the world when there were two outsiders in this room. Especially one who'd been excommunicated from the cult.

Rhett, meanwhile, was trying to coax his mother up off the floor and didn't seem to give a single fuck what the lawyers said. My heart ached for him, but I knew I needed to leave him to fight this alone. At least for the moment. Mary hardly needed a stranger in her face when she was barely functioning.

"Normally, this would take more time," the second suited lawyer stated, "but considering the sensitive nature of this inheritance and the current distress within the Townsend Community, we have hastened the process."

Get. The. Fuck. On. With. It. Then.

Lawyers, totally in love with the sound of their own voices. And charging by the minute, no doubt.

"As per the paperwork filed at seventeen hundred hours, on this date," he rattled off a bunch of numbers, which apparently translated to two weeks ago, "Jeremiah listed one Nathan Townsend as his next of kin. This was paperwork filed as part of his application to have the testing done for a liver transplant. Nathan Townsend inherits Townsend Community and every asset it contains."

This got Rhett's attention, his head snapping up, and while he didn't smile, he was satisfied about something. "Allow her to speak with me. Allow her to acknowledge her damn son."

Garth opened his mouth, then slammed it closed again before he released a few harsh breaths. "Mary, you can acknowledge Nathan Townsend. He is no longer banished from the community. He is the new Father."

Garth stormed from the room in the next second, and that was when everything went to shit.

Mary finally looked up and met Rhett's gaze, and when she did, her eyes widened so much that in her gaunt features, it almost looked like her eyeballs were going to pop out of their sockets. She started to scream.

A hysterical, gut-wrenching sort of scream that just went on and on, no matter how much Rhett talked to her. He wrapped his arms around her and tried to rock her back and forth, but she was beyond his help.

A few seconds later she started to seize, the wide-eyed stare fading as she spasmed, and Rhett bellowed for a doctor.

Dr. Dickhead rushed over, clearly hoping to garner favor with the new "leader," and he managed to get Mary stabilized as he assessed her. Nurses rushed in as well. All of them helped to get Rhett's mom up onto the bed, and she was immediately hooked up to drips and a bunch of machines.

"What's wrong with her?" Rhett demanded.

I was no doctor, but she looked like she'd suffered years of horrific abuse. That had to have taken its toll, and with the shock of today, it was clearly all too much.

Dr. Dickhead confirmed my thoughts a few seconds later. "It's the shock; she needs rest and medication," he said quickly, no disdain in his tone when he addressed Rhett now. The man was an excellent actor. "I think it's in her best interest that we treat her immediately for her health issues, and then afterward, we will commit her to our psychiatric ward for further testing. Much of this, I would guess based on her history, is psychological. We will need to work through her many"—he hesitated briefly—"issues and assess where to go once her physical health, at least, is back on track."

Rhett looked a lot like he was about to wrench his mom out of that bed and run from this place. For the first time, I moved closer, needing to show my support now that his mom was off the floor and being assessed. Rhett wrapped his arms around me as soon as I got close, and I felt the tremble in his limbs. "Do you want to leave her here?" I asked in a whisper.

He hesitated, before his chest rumbled in annoyance.

"Under other circumstances, I'd have her out of here so fast this hospital would spin, but now that I'm the sole beneficiary of Jeremiah's estate, she'll get nothing but the best treatment here. Jeremiah only ever had the best and most qualified people working for him."

Dr. Dickhead almost preened at that, before he seemed to realize that there was still so much fucking loathing in Rhett's voice that he'd be a fool to do anything except keep his head down and shut the hell up.

"I support whatever decision you make, Zepp," I whispered to him. "No matter what. Trust your instincts."

He leaned down and kissed my forehead. "I love you, Thorn. I couldn't do this without you."

I hugged myself hard against him, my throat so tight I wondered if I could keep it together any longer. I'd been trying so hard not to react to Rhett's pain and the absolutely heartbreaking scene with his mom, but the tears were near refusing to remain on the inside any longer.

"I love you too," I choked out. "Should I grab us some coffee while you chat with the doctor? We might be here a while."

He kissed me again, a little longer this time then we parted to watch as the doctor and nurses fussed around Mary as they continued to take all her vitals. "That would be amazing," he murmured. "Don't go far, though, and take security with you."

"I will," I told him, and with one last kiss, I hurried out of the room, desperate for a second to fall apart somewhere I wouldn't make Rhett feel any worse than he already did.

In the corridor, though, there were people everywhere, and they were rushing around like the end of days had arrived. I guess when a cult's leader dies, it kind of is the apocalypse for them. The noise was loud, and as the *newcomer* who'd brought Rhett back, I was the center of freaking attention. It seemed word had already spread about the new *Father of Good*.

I had no idea how Rhett was going to handle this, since for the moment, he was focused solely on his mother and getting her the help she needed. My chest tightened again, and I desperately searched for an empty room or small hidden space to break down.

Just when the burn of my emotions got too much to handle, I spotted a door that had "STAIRS" printed on it in large letters. Surely, a stairwell would be empty.

Ducking inside and hoping like fuck no one followed, I let out a choked sob as soon as the door closed behind me. The stairwell was empty, and I gave myself the moment I'd needed for hours now and broke down, all the way down, as I fell to my knees and sobbed so hard my chest hurt and my eyes burned.

Rhett had been through so much in his life, more than most people would ever experience, and to have it all resurface in such a heartbreaking way like this, right when he was getting therapy and healing himself, just felt too horrible. Too much.

What would be left of my Zepp when this was all done?

No matter what it was, I would be there for him, and I would fight every fucking secon—

"Appropriate to find my son's whore on her knees."

My head jerked up at that dark voice, shock rocking me since I'd been so sure I was in here alone. Even worse, it was a voice I fucking knew. Giovanni Ricci stood on the landing, less than two feet from me.

Jumping up immediately, the pain I'd been releasing was replaced by fear so fast that my head spun. "What are you doing here?" I whispered, taking a minute step back, even though there was only a wall behind me and no chance of escape.

Giovanni smiled, and even in the dim light of this stairwell, I could see that he looked tired and more disheveled than normal. "I'm here to take away my son's life, since he decided to take away mine."

Jesus fuck. He sounded completely unhinged, and

considering I'd already thought he was unhinged before, that was terrifying. "I know it was Angelo," he continued conversationally, and with it, he stepped closer to me, until I was backed against the wall. "No one else could have procured the documents they're using to put me away." His voice trembled as rage lifted it higher. "There was no one I trusted more than my own flesh and blood, born of my fucking bloodline."

There was no reasoning with someone like this, and I had stupidly put myself into a place with no witnesses, security, or the chance of being discovered. Even if Rhett eventually came looking for me, it'd take him so long to figure out where I'd gone.

I had to save myself.

"You want to kill Angelo?" I queried, since he'd said he was going to take away his son's life.

Giovanni's off-kilter smile grew. "Ah, women are so stupid it's almost amusing. No, you dumb bitch. You are his life. You've been his fucking life since he met you as a child, and I wish I'd followed through on my desire to drown you in the backyard pool. I came close a few times, but back then you were more of an annoyance than a threat, and I figured it was easier to keep you around as leverage to get Angelo to do whatever I wanted. Worked for a long time."

Now I wanted to drown this asshole. One evil fuck had died here today; it was time to make it two.

Before he could say anything else, I leapt into action, heading down the stairs, since he stood between me and the door to this floor. If I could just get down to the next level, I'd get out into the main hospital and scream for help.

Giovanni was quick, though, and he must've anticipated my escape route. He lurched forward and wrapped his hands around my biceps, jerking me back so that I landed hard against the steps, my ribs screaming in protest as they took the brunt of the impact.

Adrenaline was on my side as I got back up just as fast, this time lashing out at the older man. Fuck, he had to be nearing sixty. Surely, I would have a shot at making this harder for him. No way would I go down without a fight, not when I had so much to live for.

Not when I had everything to live for.

Used to submissive women, he was shocked by my willingness to fight, and he stumbled back a step, which gave me another chance to scramble to safety. This time I went up, back to the door I'd entered through, and I got my hand on the handle, a scream on the tip of my tongue, when he fisted a full hand of my hair and jerked me almost off my feet.

He expected me to struggle against it, so based on

some weird fucking instinct, I went with his momentum, getting my feet on the door to push off it and really smash into Giovanni.

It was a huge risk because I was going down the stairs with him, and all I could hope was that he broke my fall somewhat, giving me a chance.

We went backward in slow motion, and that scream I'd been holding onto finally tore free from my throat, Giovanni's shouts joining in. It took us so long to fall, and the whole time, I was praying. Praying and thinking of my boys, their faces crossing my mind one by one, surrounding me with so much love that if this had been a fantasy world, I'd have floated down the stairs filled with the power of our bond.

Unfortunately, this was no fantasy world, and in that regard, our slow fall finally came to an end when Giovanni hit the stairs under me, and then we rolled and tumbled until everything went dark.

thirty-five

GRAYSON

As soon as Billie called, letting us know that Rhett's grandfather was dead but that Rhett couldn't leave until his mom was looked after, we jumped in the car to drive out there. To Townsend Community, the creepiest town in the country and not somewhere I'd ever have willingly ventured. Everyone knew it was a cult-owned, cult-run town, where law enforcement casually looked the other way.

Jeremiah Townsend had somehow amassed a staggering number of powerful connections in his lifetime, meaning he ran the community like his own little empire.

Picturing Rhett growing up in that toxic, abusive

environment made my chest ache. The fact that he'd come out as kind-hearted as he was blew my mind.

"Where's our girl?" I asked Rhett, after giving the little shit a hug. A manly hug. He'd just exited his mom's hospital room to greet us in the hall and frowned at my question.

"She..." He squinted, shaking his head. "She went to get us coffee, but shit, I don't even know how long ago that was. I told her to take security, though. I don't fucking trust this town."

"Agreed," Angelo muttered, rolling his shoulders like he could feel the slime of the brainwashing on his skin. "We'll go find her in the cafeteria. You wait here."

Rhett jerked a nod, already turning back to the VIP suite where his mother was being assessed by a team of doctors. Angelo, Jace, and I made our way along the corridor, ignoring the stares. All that mattered was getting our family home safe.

The cafeteria was on the floor below the VIP wing, and when we stepped out of the elevator, we found a whole commotion going on near the fire stairs. Uniformed Townsend police were gathered in the hallway, and a sick feeling curled through my gut.

"What's going on?" I asked one of the closest cops. He glanced at me dismissively, then did a double-take, his eyes widening.

"You're Grayson Taylor," he said, shocked.

I narrowed my eyes. "I know. What's going on here?"

The cop flinched like he'd just remembered he was on duty. "Can't say, sorry. Crime scene."

Not in the mood for shit, I pushed the cop aside and shoved my way through the crowd, knowing my bandmates were right behind me. My instincts were dead on, too; I pulled up short when I found my heart sitting on the floor with tears and blood streaming down her face while a bored-looking cop stood over her with a notepad in hand.

"What the *fuck* is going on?" I roared, and the hum of the crowd died off instantly.

Billie looked up, gasping when she saw me, then a moment later, she leapt into my arms. Sobs wracked through her as her legs gripped my waist, and my arms held her tight.

"This young woman was just found in the stairwell with a dead man," the cop informed me with a sniff. "She needs to be questioned. Please put her down."

"Fuck off," I snarled.

Jace stepped forward with a more diplomatic expression than I was currently feeling. He spoke smoothly, laying on the signature Adams charm as he threw around phrases like *legal representation* and *press release* due to the public nature of our band. Then he asked the important question.

"Who was the dead man?"

"Unidentified," the cop snapped back, clearly incensed by the challenge to his authority. "But if you let me question the suspect—"

"I can identify him," Angelo called out from further along the hallway. I hadn't even noticed the sheet-covered body on the gurney parked a few yards away. Angelo had taken it on himself to lift the sheet and take a look, though, and his expression was grim. "And she's not a fucking *suspect,* she's a victim. Pull up your security footage; whatever happened will be a clear case of self-defense. We'll take her with us now to get some *real* medical attention, since she is clearly hurt."

The cop spluttered, his face darkening with anger and outrage. "How can you possibly make that leap?"

Angelo rolled his eyes, dropping the sheet as he returned to us. "Because your dead man is Giovanni Ricci, head of the Siena mafia. Trust me when I say he's no victim."

Oh shit. *That* I hadn't been expecting.

"Jace," I rumbled, still holding Billie against me like a scared animal. "Head upstairs, and let Rhett know what's going on. Angelo and I will take Billie out of here and get her checked on by people we can trust to actually do their job."

We didn't hang around waiting for consent. In fact, Angelo ended up decking an orderly who tried to prevent us leaving. But then we were driving away from the hospital and didn't stop until we were outside the Townsend Community borders. Only then did Angelo pull over onto the shoulder and turn to scowl at me. Or at Billie, still curled up in my lap and sobbing into my chest.

"Bella, honey, you're safe," he said, running a gentle hand down her spine. "It's us, baby, we have you. But we need to know if you're okay."

Billie sniffed back her tears, pulling away from my chest enough to look at Angelo. "I'm fine," she croaked. "I just... Angel, I killed him! Your father, I just, he was, it all happened s-s-so f-fast. I'm sorry, I didn't mean—"

"Shhhh, Bella, hush," Angelo smoothly cut her off, a tender smile touching his lips. "Baby, I don't know what you're apologizing for. We all knew he needed to die, but *you're bleeding.*"

"I am?" She touched a hand to her forehead, then peered at her fingers in confusion. "Oh. I am. I'm okay, though. Probably just a cut. We fell down the stairs, but Giovanni took the worst of it." She swallowed audibly, wincing. "His neck snapped like a glow stick."

Good visual. I was a little sad I didn't get to see it, after all that man had put us through.

Putting my full focus on Billie, I kept her wrapped up tight enough for comfort but, hopefully, not so tight it put pressure on any injuries. Knowing that she'd fallen down the stairs with that asshole had my blood both boiling and iced over in fear.

It was pure luck she was still with us and not in the same condition as Giovanni.

"Tell us everything that happened," Angelo said in a soothing tone. "Rhett said you went out to get coffee."

She sobbed a few times, lifting herself up off me so we could see her face clearly. "I had to leave the room because it was so devastating to watch him beg his mom to look at him. Beg her to stay alive. It broke me, and I really didn't want to add to Rhett's turmoil by bawling like a damn baby when he has so much other shit to deal with. I just went out for a five-minute cry. Swear to fuck. I have no idea how that old bastard knew I was in the stairwell."

Angelo's features tightened, and I wondered if he, too, was trying not to think about how fucking bad this could have gone for our girl. Our lives could have ended today.

"He knew it was you who gave the IRS the information they needed for their investigation," Billie whispered, turning closer to Angelo. "He said he wanted to take your life."

Angelo's laughter was derisive. "Old bastard never did miss a trick. How did you manage to fight him off?"

She shuddered as if the sudden memory of what had happened was almost too much. "I tried to get down the stairs first, and he managed to grab me and yank me back." She pressed a hand to her right ribs and winced. I made a mental note of these additional injuries that needed to be assessed. "I shoved him and got some space and went back up to try and go through that door, but he grabbed my hair. I think he expected me to fight against him, but for some fucking reason I decided to just go with the momentum and kick off from the wall to really send us flying. Giovanni was the unlucky bastard on the bottom of the pile, and I got a little knock to the head on my way down. That and my ribs is it. I'm fine."

Yeah, I'd be the fucking judge of that.

Reaching for my phone, I dialed a number I hadn't used in a long time. It was answered on the first ring. "Maker."

Single word. She wasn't much for small talk.

"I'm calling in my favor."

Yeah, okay, small talk wasn't for either of us. There was a brief pause, and then... "Where?"

I rattled off the address of the bed and breakfast that

Rhett and Billie had stayed in while they were wading through the Townsend crap.

"I'll be there soon."

The line went dead.

"Who was that?" Billie asked, smiling and shaking her head. "You seriously both said about six words, but it was somehow an entire conversation."

"An old acquaintance I trust to assess your injuries," I told her, forcing a smile so she wouldn't see the pure rage lurking beneath the surface of my skin. If Giovanni wasn't already dead, I'd be cutting him into little pieces before this day was done.

"Head for that location?" Angelo asked, starting the car again.

I nodded, and when Billie made a move to get off my lap, I tightened my hold on her. "No," I growled.

She tilted her head back to see me better, and I fought not to drag her closer to me and kiss those puffy lips. To fuck her senseless so I could pour all of my pain and love and worry into this one, perfect fucking human. But she didn't need that from us right now. She needed comfort and support and medical attention.

All of which I'd provide, until she was ready for the monster inside me. The one who wouldn't be sated until we tasted her, until we heard her screaming our name. Until the entire fucking world knew she was mine.

Well, mine and the rest of Bellerose's.

Some forty minutes later we reached the accommodation, and it was lucky that they hadn't canceled their room there yet. "I wasn't sure if I might have to come back and stay here while Rhett was in the hospital," she said as we entered the room. Angelo checked for danger as I carried her in, still refusing to let her out of my arms.

When it was safe, I placed her on the bed gently. "Strip," I ordered.

She stared up at me, her eyes darkening as she sucked her bottom lip into her mouth.

Angelo let out a low chuckle beside me. "He wants to check you for injuries, Bella. No time for porn just yet."

Her cheeks flushed pink as she let out a disappointed sigh. "I told you I'm fine. Just a little bump to the head."

My control was hanging on by a thread, and she clearly saw that as she stared up at me. Without another word, she started stripping her clothes off. First the ragged, bloody shirt, and then Angelo helped her with the jeans, since I was still using all of my control to keep myself contained.

When she was just in a bra and panties, I allowed myself to move closer, taking my time to assess every inch of her body until I was satisfied that, at most, she had a cracked rib and a mild concussion. She did have some bleeding on the back of her head where some hair had been torn out, but otherwise, she was okay.

Some of my panic died off as I collapsed in a chair beside her bed. "Fuck, Prickles. You fucking scared me. Don't ever do that again."

Her smile was mischievous. "Maybe everyone who wants us dead is dealt with now. Right? Maybe we can just take vacations and watch porn like normal people."

Angelo snorted in laughter, relaxing too, even though he was always armed. As was I.

"We're getting closer, Bella," he said, the laughter fading. "Closer to an actual future. I can almost taste it."

There was still the issue of Wilson being out there, but Angelo was right, we were much closer.

A few hours later there was a knock on the door, and I woke the dozing Billie. "The doctor is here," I whispered as she blinked and rubbed her eyes.

"Did you sleep?" she asked me.

I hadn't taken my eyes off her, just like a fucking creeper.

"Got a little," I lied.

Angelo stood when I did, palming his gun, and both of us moved toward the door. "Do you trust this person?" he whispered to me.

I gritted my teeth. "As much as you can trust anyone in our world. More so, it's that she owes me a big favor, and she'll want this debt paid. That's why she got here so quickly." Leah Haliver would have taken a damn helicopter to get here and settle old debts. I wanted it gone too, if I was being honest. It was lucky that I still had this outstanding favor, in all honesty, since my usual contact for all things medical, Morgana, was out of the country.

Checking the peephole first, I saw a familiar olive-skinned face, dark hair pulled back into a severe bun, and a neutral expression. I took a second longer to ensure there were no other threats present before I opened the door. My gun remained in hand, but she didn't even blink, just strode inside, pushing her sunglasses up on her head.

"Bed?" she said in lieu of a greeting.

Leah Haliver was a child prodigy, having finished high school at the age of fourteen, before going on to start medical school at sixteen. By the time she was thirty, she'd paid off all her medical debt and other family debt by patching up my family whenever they got hurt—not only paid it all off but was now rich and coveted by all underworld groups.

Turned out she enjoyed the cartel life and now stayed full time with whatever group could pay the most. She'd moved to this side of the world a couple of years ago, and

I'd saved her life in a shootout, to which I'd been given a favor to cash in one time.

There was no greater reason than Billie.

"She fell down a flight of stairs and hit her head," I said as we walked. "She has injuries to her ribs, the back of her head, and possibly some muscle tearing in her calf." She'd winced when I assessed there earlier.

"Does she want you guys to leave while I check her over?" Leah asked.

We were close enough for Billie to hear. "Not a chance," she said.

Leah nodded, taking it all in her stride. Over the next twenty minutes, she thoroughly examined Billie, before declaring that everything was minor or superficial. When she was done washing her hands and packing up, I walked her to her car, leaving Angelo to watch over Billie.

"I'm surprised you would cash in such a major favor for such a minor injury," Leah said in her blunt way. "Is there another reason?"

She dropped her medical bag in the backseat, and I waited until she was facing me to answer. "My life lies on that bed in there," I said simply. "Any injury to her is major."

Leah's hard features softened just a fraction as she nodded, those piercing blue eyes of hers delving deep inside me, as her too-smart-for-comfort brain saw a bunch of shit I'd rather she didn't know. But I trusted that it would, for the most part, stay with her.

"I also want any final ties to my old life done," I continued. "I don't want the family coming after me or interfering in my life any longer. You can assure them the debt is wiped, and I am out of the system for good."

This time she did smile. "The Kahulu Cartel is heading back to Hawaii," she said simply. "They've decided it's too hot here now with the IRS investigations and new players taking over the Siena mafia scene without due process. It seems that their plan to diversify into the Midwest is going to be put on hold for a long time. They're not going to bother you, Maker. You're the least of their concerns."

She opened her door and got in. I didn't thank her, because she'd be offended. This was not a favor. We'd also probably never see each other again, and I was more than okay with that.

Her information turned out to be way more valuable than any debt she'd owed me, and I realized that one more piece of our puzzle was dealt with.

Which just left one to go.

Wilson.

thirty-six

BILLIE

Giovanni was dead. His hierarchy had been dismantled, and the Siena mafia was scrambling. There was no time to take a breath and assess the situation; Angelo and Vee needed to act quickly to secure their leadership before any lower-ranking members acted on their delusions of grandeur.

Much to all our reluctance, Angelo had to leave us and return to Siena before the news broke of his father's happy accident. Grayson insisted that I sleep the rest of the night, but by morning, we were faced with a decision. Rhett couldn't leave Townsend. Not yet, anyway. Not until he'd worked out a plan for the whole cursed community to rehabilitate and de-program their cult brains, all the while ensuring someone as evil as Jeremiah didn't take over.

Jace had stayed at his side, paranoid someone like Garth would try to murder him in the night, but they both insisted I was *not* to come back.

"We should just take a vacation," Grayson mused aloud as he checked the cut on my head. "Rhett doesn't want you in Townsend because it's too dangerous. Angelo, though he hasn't said it, doesn't want you in Siena because it's too dangerous. Maybe we just take a vacation and let them sort it out?"

I chuckled, tipping my head back to kiss him. "Grayson Taylor choosing to vacation over getting his hands bloody? That doesn't sound right. Are you feeling okay?"

He huffed, kissing me back deeply until I moaned and melted against him.

"If it means never seeing you with blood dripping down your face again, Prickles, I would happily walk away from any and every fight." He cupped my face in his huge hands, his dark eyes locked on mine. "You are the most precious thing in my life, Billie. I'm quickly coming to realize there is nothing I wouldn't do to keep you safe."

Oh, my heart. "As much as I love the growly protective thing, you know I'd never leave the guys to handle shit on their own."

He released me, gusting a long sigh. "I know. Worth a try, though. So... who are we pissing off? Rhett or Angelo?"

I screwed up my nose, hating that it was even a choice. "Angelo," I finally decided. "I know he's got a lot to handle with the Ricci Corp takeover, but with Giovanni dead and his lieutenants all locked up... it's kind of safer now than ever before, right?"

Grayson stared at me a long moment, like he wanted to argue that we were *never* safe—not while Angelo was a Ricci, my father was Wilson, and Bellerose was *Bellerose*. But he respected my intelligence enough to just grimace and shrug. "Sure. That's plausible. Call Rhett and let him know we're heading back to Siena, then. See what Jace wants to do."

He packed up our things while I made that call, then we were back on the road. Heading home. I hadn't been back to Siena since the whole fake-baby-mama situation we'd pulled to keep me safe from Giovanni's men. The closer we got, the more nervous I grew, like there was a heavy, dark cloud hanging over the whole fucking city in the form of my not-so-dead father.

"Why are all our fathers these sick, power-hungry psychopaths?" I mused aloud as fat droplets of rain started to fall outside. The weather was moody, like me.

"Do you think that's why the universe brought us all together? Shared fucked up family trauma?"

Grayson arched a brow, giving me an amused smile. "Jace's dad seems normal."

True. "Good point." I sighed. "That's so typical Jace, staying all squeaky clean while the rest of us are the children of murderers."

"Technically, it was my *mom's* family running a cartel, not my dad's," Grayson commented thoughtfully. "But I see your point. Nah, the universe brought us all together because we're just fractured parts of one heart."

"I like that." I hummed a tune that'd just popped into my head, then quietly tried out some combinations of his words, incorporating the "fractured parts of one heart" line he'd just handed me. Grayson stayed quiet, listening, then a slow grin curved his lips.

Huffing a sound of irritation, I glared. "I'm well aware I can't sing; there's no need to smirk about it. At least you know I'm not just angling for a place in the band."

"It's cute," he told me with way too much patronization for a man who liked to sink his dick inside me. Guess who wasn't getting said dick sucked on this road trip now.

Angelo hadn't replied to our message asking where he was, but Vee had sent us back an address that turned out to be one of the flagship *Giovanni's* restaurants in Old

Siena, on the south side of the river. It wouldn't be open to the public for hours yet, but Giana met us at the door with a wicked smile on her perfectly painted lips.

"Remind me again how Vee wanted to keep you *out* of the mafia?" Grayson muttered with a dry voice as Giana let us into the restaurant, then locked the door behind us.

Giana snickered. "Silly woman was taking a page out of your book, Gray, acting all growly and protective, as if I can't hold my own. Come on through; the meeting is almost done."

"What meeting?" I asked, genuinely curious as she led the way through the vacant dining room and into the kitchen.

She turned around to flash me a wide grin. "Changing of the guard, baby girl. I used to date an Australian girl in high school who'd say, 'We're not here to fuck spiders.' In other words, there's no time to pussyfoot around. With Giovanni dead, we need to move fast."

I shared a glance with Grayson, who was frowning with concern. Giana didn't wait for us to question what she meant, just slid open the false wall at the back of the kitchen. The room beyond appeared, and I quickly noted the long conference-style table with a dozen gray-haired and balding old men seated and my Angel standing at the head of it.

He glanced up when the door opened, locking eyes

with me as the tiniest flicker of surprise crossed his face before he slapped his hand down on the table top. "Now's your chance, ladies."

For a moment I thought he was speaking to Giana and Vee, but then twelve women stepped out of the shadows, each standing behind a man seated around the table. Each with a gun to that man's head. Then they collectively fired their weapons, painting the room red and deafening me momentarily.

I screamed, burying my face in Grayson's chest as he instinctively guarded me with his body. Suddenly, Giana's comment made sense. They were *literally* changing Giovanni's guard for a whole new set of leaders, all handpicked by Vee and Giana, I was going to bet. They'd hinted at it often enough, but now I saw their plan coming to fruition. They didn't just want to disrupt the gender rules of *their own* places within the Siena mafia, they wanted to rewrite the whole fucking rulebook.

Angelo spoke, addressing his new enforcers, I guessed. But my ears were still ringing, and Grayson held me in an iron grip. Then a moment later, I was being guided back through the kitchen to the dining area, where it was quiet and blood-free.

"What the fuck..." I caught Angelo snarling as my hearing started to return. "...waited for me back at..."

How were their ears not suffering? Was the ability to stand sound just like building up a callous? "...fucking Vee."

Grayson released me, and then Angelo had his hands on my face, tipping my head back as his lips crashed against mine. My hearing might be spotty, but there was *nothing* wrong with my appetite for these men, so I groaned and kissed him back, our tongues intertwining as he effectively made me forget the mass murder I'd just witnessed.

Until he released me, then I winced as I remembered.

"Why are you here, Bella? You didn't need to see that." His tone was caring and full of love, not scolding me like a child. I appreciated that.

"Apparently, your wife thought she did," Gray muttered, sounding pissy.

Angelo rolled his eyes but didn't seem shocked. Maybe it was a discussion he and Vee had already had. After all, she was tits deep in building a female-led mafia; it made sense—in her unique friendship way—that she was trying to toss me in the deep end. Or recruit me.

"Are Rhett and Jace here?" Angelo asked, directing his question to Grayson. "I've got something for you all back at my house. Can we meet there in a couple of hours? I need to make sure this mess gets cleaned up first."

Grayson huffed a laugh. "They stayed back in cultville

to try and get *that mess* sorted. I don't think Rhett will be leaving for a while, but Jace should be on his way here soon." He cleared his throat. "So, yep, you have fun with *your mess*; I'll take care of Prickles until you're back. Keys?"

Angelo handed over his gate clicker and front door key, then told Grayson the alarm codes while keeping me snuggled against his designer shirt. He'd rolled the sleeves up, and his strong, tattoo-covered forearm sat warm against the back of my neck as he held me. It was a good look for him, all *mafia chic,* but I preferred the rock star Angel. Or the naked one.

"Do you need help with anything else?" Grayson asked, his question loaded with meaning.

Angelo only hesitated a moment before shaking his head. "Nah, we have it handled. The women have been fantasizing about this day for so long it's like I've barely had to lift a finger to tug all the strings together. By the time dusk falls, there won't be a single person in Siena willing to question the change of leadership."

"Good," Grayson rumbled. "That's what we need."

Angelo shifted his grip on me, leaning down to kiss me again. And again. Then he got a little carried away, and I found myself boosted onto a table as his hand snaked under my shirt. The only thing that stopped us was Grayson's pointed throat-clearing.

"Fuck," Angelo groaned, reluctantly peeling away from me. "Bella, you make it easy to forget the whole world outside of your orbit."

"Yeah, yeah, save it until you get home," Grayson rumbled, giving Angel a teasing smirk as my mafia prince needed to adjust his dick inside his suit pants. "I'll keep our girl entertained in the meantime."

Angelo made a frustrated sound, then dipped back in to kiss me again. "I'll hurry. Tell Jace to hurry the fuck up, too. He needs to be there."

My brows rose. "For... Okay, yeah, I'm game. Should we pick up lube on the way, or...?" I trailed off, squinting between them. "Not what you meant. You weren't... Yep. I'll just... see myself out."

Angelo barked a laugh, grabbing my wrist to prevent me from fleeing back to the car in embarrassment. "Bella, baby, if that's where our evening ends up, I won't say no. Just give me a few hours to reinforce my new position, and I'll be right there."

Grayson clapped him on the shoulder in a manly gesture of support. They exchanged a few words that gave me warm fuzzies inside as I watched their bromance solidify before my eyes. Then Angelo released my wrist and unlocked the front door for us to leave.

"Be careful, Ricci," Grayson told him as we exited. "Come home safe."

I nodded firmly. "What he said. I wanna fuck all of you tonight, and we can't do that if you're bleeding out, alright?"

Angelo scoffed another laugh, then dipped his head to kiss me sweetly. "I love you, too." To Grayson he offered a fist bump, then retreated inside and locked the door once more.

Gray and I slid back into the car, and I nervously chewed the edge of my lip until he dropped his big hand to my knee, giving me a squeeze of reassurance. "Don't worry about him, Prickles. That man was born for this day. He's got it handled."

I didn't disagree with that statement, but part of me was terrified he was *too* good at it. That maybe he'd change his mind about getting out of the mafia. And then where would that leave us?

No. I had to have faith in Angelo and in how strong our bond was. Even if he did choose to retain his new position of power, he'd always make space in his life for me. For *us*. We were a family, tighter than any blood bonds. Of that, I was sure.

thirty-seven

BILLIE

Angelo's *gift* that he'd been so excited about was for Bellerose and came in the form of shredded paper. A whole bag of shredded paper that he gleefully dumped out on his coffee table when he arrived home. Jace, who must have driven like a crazy person to get here so quickly, arrived at the same time as the mafia man. He poured himself a drink and stared down at the paperwork, just as confused as the rest of us.

"Bellerose is free."

Angelo's simple statement told us everything we needed to know. The shredded paper was what remained of the entire Bellerose-Big Noise contract and our elation was high. So high that we all ended up fucking right there on the table on top of the shredded documents. Then again in Angelo's big old bed in the opulent master suite.

At some stage in the night, Jace and I had a quiet discussion over a midnight snack. We came up with a plan for how to reel in our last remaining enemy and immediately woke Gray and Angelo up to discuss.

As the sun rose, I was buzzing with nervous anticipation. Part of me really hoped this would work. We couldn't ever feel safe with my father—Wilson—out there painting targets on us. Or on Angelo and Vee, at any rate. Surely, if he wanted me dead, he could have done it long before now.

Then again... he'd had his hand in that bomb at Big Noise. He clearly didn't care enough to protect me should I end up as collateral damage. So, with that knowledge in mind, I needed to harden my heart against the memory of my sweet, caring father. Bruce Bellerose was dead; he'd died nearly a decade ago in a house fire.

"He will expect a trap," Angelo warned me as I stared at the phone in my hand. "No matter what you say, no one reaches the level Wilson has and still trusts people. Even family."

It wasn't completely true. Giovanni had trusted

Angelo—to some extent—and that trust had gotten his entire operation either dead or behind bars. But I understood what he was saying. My father and I hadn't seen each other in almost a decade, and he knew where my loyalties lay these days. But I would do this on the small hope that somewhere deep inside was still the man who used to take me to school when mom was too busy and who'd taught himself to braid my hair so I could wear it the same as other girls in my third grade class. The man who had said he loved me every single night as he tucked me into bed and sang me a lullaby.

It might have been a front, but I doubted anyone was that good of an actor.

Fuck, it was our only hope.

"I understand, but I have to try," I finally told Angelo. "I think I know what to say to convince him, but I'm banking hard on parts of my old dad still being inside him. However deep, I need to dig it out."

Angelo's dark eyes bored into mine, holding me captive, and I could see his internal struggle. He didn't want to have me anywhere near such a dangerous man, but I might be the only one with any hope of drawing Wilson out.

He was the last dark cloud hanging over our lives now, and I needed him dealt with.

"There's no better time than during a change of

leadership," Grayson rumbled from his perch near the kitchen. "As much as I hate to admit it, because it requires Billie to step further into the darkness with us, this might be our only chance."

We all knew it, even if none of us liked it very much.

"Do you want us to leave or stay?" Jace asked, his expression soft as he watched me closely. He did that a lot these days, watched me with a mixture of love and respect, and it really reiterated how much he had kept his word to me about changing. It had taken us a fucking long time, but we were finally growing up. Together.

"I think I might try it alone," I said quietly. "If I have to say some nasty shit to convince him, I don't want you guys to hear those words from me. Even when they're fake."

The three of them stood or straightened and made their way to me. They each kissed me and, without another word, left the room, and I stared down at the phone in my hand.

I'd gotten this number from Vee; it was Wilson's last known contact information, which she'd found in her parent's house. She was all in on our plan, and if anything, more excited than anyone to have a clear path to take out Wilson.

Knowing that if I hesitated any longer, I wouldn't go

through with it, I dialed the number. My hand trembled as I pressed the phone to my ear, and when he answered on the third ring, the quiver in my voice only added more legitimacy to my story.

"Yes."

I sucked in a deep breath before I asked, "Dad?"

There was a pause, longer than I'd expected, and I wondered if maybe this number was no longer his. Then... "Billie..." He sounded hesitant, as if he wasn't sure this was real.

It hurt more than I expected to hear that name from him again. There had been so much going on in Europe that I hadn't really paid attention to him, but now, with nothing to distract us, it was like a blade to my chest. All of my months of compartmentalizing his existence, ignoring my feelings, and shoving him down into a box inside were destroyed in that moment.

A sob escaped me. A real sob.

His voice was sharper. "Are you okay? What's happened?"

"Dad," I choked out. "What happened to you? What happened to our family?"

He ignored the questions, though his voice sounded softer. "Are you okay, Billie Jean? Do you need me to come and get you?"

I nodded, even though this was not a video call and he couldn't see me. Stupid frazzled brain. "I'm scared, daddy," I whispered, reverting to the childhood name in hopes of reestablishing old bonds and memories. Of reasserting those protective instincts of a father to his child. "He's out of control, just like last time, and I have nowhere else to go."

I knew he was going to be suspicious, but he was also a man who believed himself smarter and more capable than anyone else. He trusted his instincts, and he had always hated Angelo. It wouldn't take much to convince him that I needed help.

"Tell me what happened." Wilson's words were short. He sounded legitimately angry, and I hated how easily he could fall into the role of *dad*. A dad who'd fucking abandoned me and killed my baby. One who'd never looked back, no matter how rough things had gotten for me.

"I'm pregnant again," I choked out. "Angelo doesn't seem to want this child, and I'm scared that I won't survive this time. No one here believes me when I say that he's unhinged, and I think it'll be too late soon. You're the only one he's afraid of. The only one with the money and power to get me out of here."

I gasped then, like I'd heard someone. "Dad, I've got to go. Shit."

As soon as I hung up, I had to suck in a few deep lungfuls of air. This was the point where it could go either way. If he believed me and if there was enough love still there somewhere, he would figure out a way to get back in contact with me, and the guys and I could initiate stage two of the plan.

If he didn't believe me, I'd have to cross paths with him a little beaten and bruised and hope that would do the trick.

I called the boys back into the room. "First contact made," I said quickly. "He's bound to be a little suspicious that I have his number, so we'll see if he calls me back again."

None of them smiled; they just sat beside me, all of us waiting to see if we'd calculated this correctly. An hour later I'd almost given up hope when my phone buzzed. A weird little bubble popped up onscreen, and Grayson leaned over, cracking his first smile.

"Encrypted message," he said.

That got Angelo to smile as well, but I had no idea what this meant.

"Only you can open it," Gray told me. "It'll require some form of identification."

Turned out it was my thumbprint, and I didn't even want to know how my creepy father managed to have that fucking print on file after all these years.

When I got it open, a short message appeared.

Billie. Use the money I left for you and get a vehicle. When you're away from the house and danger, call me, and I will come to save you.

There was another phone number at the end, and I had to assume this was what I was supposed to use to contact him next time.

"Now we plan," Angelo said standing. "Wilson won't go alone, no matter what you said to get him to meet you. But we can't give that away when he's scouting. I have an idea of how we can conceal our people, if we use a certain location."

"Could he be watching us now?" I asked.

"Definitely," Grayson growled. "We will need Vee and the others to covertly set this up for us."

I nodded. "Do you think it's a good idea for us to be out and about doing normal rock star shit, and I can look kind of quiet and broken, so that Wilson's spies can report that back to him? Keep Wilson from thinking I'm plotting how to trap him."

"Excellent idea," Jace said, jumping to his feet. "With that in mind, I've got dinner reservations booked at the *Gilded Rose* for us tonight, and then we can hit the clubs after—normal band activity. Meanwhile, the rest of Siena will be prepped."

"How will we let Vee know all of this in a safe and

secure way?" I asked. "And are we still thinking the same location?"

Angelo hugged me hard. "Yep, it has the landscape we need to keep this hidden. Don't worry about it, Bella. I promise that our plan will come to fruition soon. This will be dealt with by the end of the week."

I was shot through with fear and relief in the same instant—fear because so much could go wrong with this plan. But it was the only way to draw Wilson out into the open. It seemed I was still his only weak link, and it didn't bother me remotely to use that connection to take him down.

He killed my mom and daughter. He abandoned me, leaving behind a few million dollars and no fucking cares, like his dirty money could take away from everything he'd done to me. I'd known all along not to touch that shit; now I knew it was tainted with the blood of my family.

Whatever was coming Wilson's way, he deserved.

"Get dressed, Rose," Jace said to me. "Make it convincing."

No need to explain what he meant as I hurried to my room and dug out something drab and boring, loose enough in the abdomen to look like I was covering a bump. I also pulled my hair back in a messy bun, with no care taken, and I wore no makeup.

My current state would be photographed and posted everywhere, but I could live with that as long as my father fell for the charade.

That was literally all that mattered, and I wouldn't rest until his presence in our lives was done.

thirty-eight

JACE

Tears had been streaming down Billie's face as she drove away, and my entire body screamed at me to go after her. To bring her back and reassure her that we didn't need to do it like *that*. She didn't need to sacrifice her heart and her goodness to neutralize the threat of her father. Fucking hell... if anyone had asked me ten years ago if Bruce Bellerose was capable of murder, I'd have laughed in their face.

Nothing shocked me anymore, though.

Over the past week, we'd had some major changes with Angelo and Vee tightening their hold over Ricci Corp and the Siena Mafia, proving themselves to be a dynamic duo. Or trio, with Giana's assistance. For now, Angelo was maintaining the illusion that he was the one calling the shots, just until the transition was set in stone and he could be sure that his people wouldn't turn on Vee the first moment they could.

Billie had made several additional calls to Wilson—I couldn't think of him as Bruce anymore—to build the story that she was scared of Angelo and, by association, all of us. My heart broke a little when I overheard her on the phone to him yesterday, sobbing about how I was no longer the boy she'd loved as a child, that I was now cold, cruel, selfish... and she wasn't wrong.

She was lying, building a false narrative to suck Wilson into our trap, but the line between exaggeration and truth was at times very muddied, and it was creating an enormous amount of strain between us all. Add to that, Rhett wasn't with us to provide that softer perspective, to hold her and let her melt into his unconditional love in a way that only Rhett seemed able to do.

By the day we'd decided to enact our plan, we were all strung tighter than bow strings and snapping at each other over the dumbest shit.

That didn't diminish the love between us, though. If anything, it was a million times harder to watch her drive away with tears in her eyes, knowing how abrasive I'd been with her all week. Regrets were a venomous thing that could really poison the mind.

"I don't like this," Grayson barked, his fists balled like he was barely stopping himself from hitting a wall. "We could have come up with another plan."

"Do we even need a plan at all?" I asked, folding my arms to try and contain my own nervous energy. "He hasn't tried *anything* since that shootout at the docks. Maybe he's decided that he's satisfied now that Giovanni is dead and the whole structure has changed."

Angelo sighed, running a tired hand over his face as he brought up our GPS tracker on Billie. "He hasn't tried anything because he recognized that I was *also* trying to get rid of my father. Why expend your own resources when someone else is willing to do the job for you? Now that we've literally done all the dirty work, he thinks he can just eliminate Vee and I, then his mission to control this fucking town would be complete. And do you think he'd spare Billie if she were caught in the crossfire?" He arched a brow at me. "Need I remind you how close she came to being shot in Monaco? Or dying in the bomb at Big Noise? Or what would have happened if that baby belly had been real at the farmhouse? This *caring father* act is just that. An act. He's luring her in, just like we're luring him in. The second he gets his hands on Bella, he'll have a gun to her head and demands sent."

He was right. We all knew he was right, Billie included. But that didn't make this whole fucking thing any easier to swallow.

"Besides," Angelo continued with a grimace. "In the process of replacing management in Ricci Corp, I've uncovered several Wilson-planted moles. And they had active orders to be ready for another a strike against us all soon. What this strike was, I'm not clear on. But whatever the plan is, I have no doubt he wouldn't leave *any* loose ends to chase retribution. Bella included. We either act first, or we're dead."

I threw up my hands with frustration. "Well shit, with *those* options on the table... let's just get this over and done so we can all go into therapy afterward. Fuck knows we all need it."

Our plan to use Billie as *bait* was the part we were all sick with worry over. The rest of it I had confidence in, and I knew Angelo and Grayson agreed. Billie's role was the sore point for us all and the source of all our anxiety. She needed to pretend she'd gone on the run, taking nothing but her phone and a car. She'd call Wilson, hysterical, and ask him to meet her while she was *alone*.

"Let's go," Grayson said, already moving toward the

garage. Our vehicle was packed up and ready; we just needed to drive out to the rendezvous point and *wait*. That would be the hardest part of all: having no clue whether Billie was okay until she arrived.

The three of us were silent as we drove out of Siena and into the wide expanse of barren land bordering Lake Michigan, where we had agreed to deal with Wilson once and for all. There were basically no places to hide an ambush, which would lull Wilson into a false sense of security when Billie lured him here.

We parked our SUV a solid mile away in an old cattle shelter, then loaded up our weapons and camouflage blankets before approaching on foot. Grayson checked his watch and gave us a reminder to get in our designated hiding places quickly. This plan had been mapped down to the *minute* with the only variable being Wilson's response time when Billie begged him to come to *her*, not the other way around.

Waiting, in our trenches covered by camo blankets, was fucking torture. Billie's car arrived right on time, parking in the precise location we'd mapped out, but then she needed to feign a panic attack on a call to Wilson, telling him that she'd run out of gas and had no idea where she was.

Maybe Angelo was right, and Wilson truly wasn't

fooled by her act. But even if he knew she was setting him up, he wouldn't resist the opportunity to take such a valuable bargaining chip—especially if he was *confident* she hadn't driven to an ambush... hence the wide-open space with no *obvious* hiding places.

Come on...

It took all my self-control not to fidget, but Grayson had been crystal clear with us that we weren't to move. He'd put himself in Wilson's shoes and immediately dismissed the idea that Billie's GPS location and acting skills would be enough. He said the first thing *he* would do, in that position, would be to survey the area and check for things like other cars that might indicate an ambush. Whether it was done by satellite or drone or fucking binoculars, it'd be done.

Minutes ticked by, and my imagination ran wild with all the what-ifs of this plan, the worst of them being: *What if Billie got hurt?*

Almost as if the universe knew I'd reached my breaking point, the sound of a car engine cut through the silence, and a potent combination of anticipation and dread nearly choked me.

He was here.

But had Wilson himself come? Or had he sent a lackey to pick Billie up and bring her to him? That was one of the variables Billie had insisted she could handle. She said she knew him well enough to pull the right threads. I trusted her to know what she was doing.

After what felt like forever, the approaching vehicle came to a stop and car doors slammed.

"Billie Jean?" Bruce Bellerose called out, instantly transporting my mind back to those years of friendship when he'd call her home for dinner while we were in my treehouse. Fuck, that wasn't Bruce. Bruce was dead. *Wilson* had arrived.

Another car door slammed. "Daddy?" Billie's voice cut through the night, full of pain and fear. "You came for me; I knew you would." She sobbed, and my arms ached to hold her.

Boots crunched on the gravelly dirt. "Yes. You *did* know just what to say, didn't you?" The suspicion in his voice was undeniable. Angelo had been right. "Are you alone?"

Billie gasped. "Yes, of course I am; I told you that I—"

"I know what you told me, sweetheart, but I'm also no fool. Check her car." It made sense that he hadn't come alone, but I wondered how many men were with him. Grayson had been paranoid enough about remaining undetected that we didn't even have radio comms.

More car doors opened and closed while they searched her vehicle for stowaways or some shit, then one of Wilson's goons reported that it was clear. Not even a gun present.

Silence stretched after that, then my hearing barely picked up on a heavy sigh. "Billie, this was a foolish move, coming out here alone with no weapons. Do you know how many psychos there are in this area? How many opportunistic bastards would love to hurt you just to hurt Angelo?"

"Like you?" Billie replied, still somehow managing to keep her voice weak and sniffly.

Another pause, then a cold chuckle. "Yes, sweetheart. Like me. Take her; throw her in the trunk. I'll get a message to Ricci that we have his girl."

Billie shrieked, fighting back no doubt, and it took everything in me not to give away my position. I *had* to trust the plan. Sure enough, a moment later, the suppressed sound of gunfire popped through the otherwise quiet night, and bodies dropped.

"You *bitch!*" Wilson snarled, gravel crunching as he no doubt dove for cover. No other shots followed, though, and Billie's laugh told me that the targets had been hit. Whoever had been holding her must be dead. "Where are they? How many?"

"Like I'd fucking tell you, *Dad*," she snapped back. "I'd think *real* long and hard before putting your hands on me again, though. I'm not as *foolish* as you think."

Wilson gave a feral growl, then barked orders to his remaining men to *find the shooter and deal with it*. But how he thought they'd achieve that, I had no clue. The moment they stepped out from behind the car, they'd be sitting ducks.

Grayson gave a sharp whistle, Billie's cue, and I couldn't help but raise my head and watch as she took off running. My heart lodged firmly in my throat as I watched her sprint closer, zigging and zagging as instructed. In the distance, Wilson stood from his hiding place, gun raised to fire, but something stayed his trigger finger. Then a split second later, Billie was in the safe zone and leaping without a single hesitation into Grayson's camouflaged pit. Thank *fuck*. He would strap her into a Kevlar vest, offering a layer of safety in case shit went sideways.

"Billie!" Wilson shrieked. "Get back here! We're in the middle of nowhere; you can't outrun me forever and—"

"And nothing," Billie shouted back, reappearing beside Grayson's pit with her vest on. "You're smart enough to see you've been outplayed. You *lose*, Wilson. Cut the posturing bullshit because we both know you didn't prepare for this. You thought I was weak, sad, pathetic Billie Jean. Well, fuck you, old man, I'm Billie Bellerose, and I claim this name. It's mine, *Wilson*."

Wilson scowled, then waved his men forward. "I don't think you're as well set up as you're pretending, sweetheart. Your shooter seems to have run out of bullets, or I'd be dead already. In fact, this reeks of a haphazard, slapped-together ambush planned out by an amateur. A child. So where is he, then? Come out, Ricci!"

The response he got was Vee's people taking out each and every one of his goons with synchronized headshots. As the sound of those shots faded into the night air, Wilson just stood there, his jaw loose with shock, and the three of us—Grayson, Angelo, and I— tossed off our camo blankets to crawl from our trenches.

Wilson started a slow clap, taking a few steps forward. "Oh bravo, the three musketeers are here. Very dramatic. Jace, son, I didn't expect you to get your hands dirty in all of this. You used to be such a nice boy."

I bit my lip, refusing to rise to the bait. But my curiosity was choking me, desperate to know how the fuck he'd gone from *Bruce Bellerose* to this. How he could turn his back on his only child and leave her to die in that original fire while pregnant with his grandbaby.

Billie had made it abundantly clear she didn't want to

keep him alive for evil-villain monologues, though. So none of us bit back.

"Toss your weapons down, Wilson," Grayson ordered, positioning himself in front of Billie. If he could take a bullet before it touched her vest, he would. "Nice and easy, before our friends need to help you out."

Wilson took another step toward us, casual as anything, while slowly reaching for his gun. "I'll admit I underestimated you kids," he commented, walking forward another pace as he carefully pulled his weapon and held it out between his fingers to demonstrate he wasn't going to shoot. "Perhaps I've gone about this all the wrong way. There's no reason why you should pay for the sins of your father, Angelo. Maybe we could come to a mutually beneficial arrangement."

He directed the question to my best friend, but Angelo's face was a mask of ice. Not a single emotion reflected across his features.

Bruce—*fuck*, I meant *Wilson*—took another few steps. The sneaky bastard was going to try something, I was sure of it. My hand tightened on the butt of my gun, even though I knew how many of Vee's people had Wilson firmly within their sights from a distance. That was a nice thing about all this wide-open space; there were no obstructions for long-range rifles.

"Don't you want to know why I've done all of this?

Don't you want to know why I spent sixteen fucking years playing the role of *Bruce Bellerose*, mild-mannered neighbor? When all the while I was gaining Giovanni's trust as I slowly corrupted his businesses?" His voice was low and coaxing, trying to seduce Angelo's curiosity and desperate need for answers.

"And you would have succeeded too, if not for your wife's appetite for money laundering and making bad deals, huh?" Billie spoke up, her voice hardened with bitterness and resentment. "You are aware this isn't *Scooby Doo*? We don't give a fuck that your mommy didn't hug you enough as a child, *Wilson*; none of it will matter when you're dead."

Ouch. The ice in her tone even made me flinch. Billie had done a *lot* of soul searching in the past week, making her own peace with what boiled down to patricide. She hadn't shared her process with us, but the result was clear to see. She had decided.

Wilson scoffed a laugh. "Come on, Billie Jean, you want me to think you're cold enough for murder? Of your own dad? You don't have it—" *Boom.*

The landmine he'd just stepped on detonated, and Grayson grabbed our girl, shielding her with his body as falling debris set off several more. Billie might have played an irreplaceable part in this plan, but deep down, all we wanted was to protect her. Sometimes that meant lying to her... by omission.

"Go!" Angelo roared to Grayson, "Get her out of here!"

Grayson didn't need to be told twice, scooping our girl up and running with her back to Wilson's car. He deftly leapt over the line of buried explosives just like Billie had when she'd run toward him, lulling Wilson into a false sense of security so he never saw that strike coming.

She screamed at him, kicking and thrashing to be let down, but he was utterly immovable, tossing her into the car and accelerating away into the night before the doors had even closed. She'd make his life *hell* for this, and the rest of ours too. But it was unavoidable. She knew what needed to happen; she'd played her part. We could spare her the rest of the graphic details. Particularly because Angelo and I wanted Wilson to *hurt* for what he'd done to Billie.

Which he was right now, as he writhed on the ground, howling his agony into the night. Not that I blamed him, considering that landmine had exploded his left leg. We'd dialed the power of the explosives down to *maim painfully* not *kill instantly,* and a sick part of me was satisfied as fuck watching him squirm like a worm on a hook.

Angelo strolled over to where Wilson lay in the dirt and crouched down to take a better look at the bloody stump where his leg used to be. "Ouch, I bet that stings." He poked the shredded flesh with his gun, making Wilson scream. Then we noticed the grenade Wilson had been holding in his hand, which, thankfully, still had the pin attached. Wilson, that motherfucker, had been trying to get close enough to aim for ultimate impact. We knew the bastard had been up to something.

"All yours, Jace," my friend said, rising back to his feet. "But you might wanna be quick before he bleeds out."

I nodded, drawing my own gun as I approached the dying man. Fuck, it was hard to shake the memory of *Billie's dad* as I scowled down at him. But I had to because that man was dead. Hell, that man had never even existed, if I was correctly following that shred of info he'd just dropped.

"Bruce," I said in a calm, emotionless voice. "I hope you understand why it has to be like this." I fired a bullet into his hand, which was reaching for a small gun that must've been his backup plan if that grenade had missed the mark. My bullet turned his hand to mincemeat, and I silently thanked Gray for being such a dickhead teacher.

"Why?" Wilson howled. "What is it to you, Jace? Why do you care? The Riccis had this—"

"This isn't *about them!*" I roared, swinging my leg back and kicking him brutally hard in the gut. The steel cap of my boot sank deep, and he made a satisfying whooshing sound. "This is about you, Bruce. And your decision to *kill your daughter* all those years ago. Why'd you do it? I don't give a fuck about your marriage or the Riccis or any other criminal shit. Why hurt *Billie* when she was just an innocent girl? Why *kill my daughter?*"

Wilson took a few tries to get words out as he floated in and out of consciousness. "She wasn't supposed to be home that night. Everything was in place... I couldn't change it. She wasn't supposed to be home."

"Oh well, that makes it all okay, doesn't it?" I knelt down to get in his face, my hand balling in the front of his shirt. "You *murdered your grandchild*, Bruce, and never fucking looked back. You don't deserve mercy, but for the sake of Billie—because I know, deep down, she still loves the memory of you—I'm going to give you one chance. One. Chance. To save yourself."

I released him with a shove, then rose back to my feet.

"What do you want me to do?" he moaned, his blood already pooling around him. Surely, he knew he was fucked. We were nowhere near any hospitals out here, even if I were inclined to seek medical attention for him.

I nodded, walking back over to where Angelo waited some eight or nine yards away. "It's real simple, Bruce.

You get from there"—I pointed with my gun to where he lay—"to here"—I pointed to the dirt at my feet—"and I'll let you go. Hell, I'll even let you take Billie's car, which, by the way, has plenty of gas. You can drive off into the sunset for all I care. This is me... offering you the chance my unborn baby never got. A chance to save yourself."

Wilson moaned, then rolled onto his belly in a flop. I wondered for a moment if he'd just given up already, but no... not *Wilson*. Not the man who'd worked so fucking hard in the shadows for so fucking long to get revenge on the Ricci family for fuck only knew what insult. Nope, he was a fighter. So when he started dragging himself across the gravel and dirt, leaving a thick trail of blood behind, I almost had a flicker of respect.

Almost.

It took a long time. Painfully long, for Wilson to drag his maimed and bleeding body that short distance to freedom, but he did it. His fingers touched my boot, and the gasp he gave was of pure elation like he hadn't believed he would actually make it.

"I did it!" he rasped, rolling onto his back to look up at me and Angelo, side by side. "I did it! I did it! You thought I'd give up, and I didn't!" He started laughing, the sound wild and uncontrolled. Delirious. "Now you have to let me go!"

Angelo and I exchanged a glance, and I returned my

cold glare to the dying man at my feet. "I don't have to do shit, Wilson."

I aimed my gun at his head and pulled the trigger.

"I guess that makes me a liar," I murmured, feeling dead inside. "But the world is better off."

Not only the world, but Billie, and I'd kill anyone to ensure that was always true.

thirty-nine

BILLIE

I'd been angry with Grayson, Jace, and Angelo before. Furiously angry, borderline hatred, but as Grayson wrestled me into the car and tore off from the ambush, I'd never felt so much rage.

My screams were near deafening in the car, and I only just managed to hold onto enough self-control to not start whaling on Grayson physically, since I didn't really want to kill us both in a car crash.

He still got a front-row seat to my off-key screaming teamed with a multitude of curse words and hate-filled anger.

"Prickles, you need to calm down. There's no danger to your boys, okay. I would never have left, otherwise."

His words were barely registering, and I knew deep down this was all just a delayed reaction to the stress of what I'd just had to do. The stress and fear of knowing, despite pretending to care, Wilson still had planned to take us out. Knowing that I'd had to run away from him and his gun with just a dodge, duck, and weave maneuver to try and keep myself from getting shot.

Knowing that I'd looked into Bruce Bellerose's eyes and seen nothing but empty darkness. He was broken, his mind completely gone at this point, and that made him a scary and unstable opponent.

A scary and unstable opponent who was near Jace and Angelo. My hearts and souls. My best friends since I was a mere child, before I'd understood how irrevocably we would be tied together for eternity.

I couldn't live without them. Same as Grayson and Rhett. Hence why I hadn't punched this big asshole in the fucking face.

At some point I stopped screaming at him and sank into my chair, turning my body away from Grayson and staring sightlessly out the window. The tears had dried up, the panic softened to just a low-level hum, and when Gray's phone rang a few seconds later, I didn't even flinch.

He put it on speaker. "Yep."

"It's done," Angelo's low tone further calmed my panic. "Tell Bella to stop raging at you."

Grayson let out a low, strangled chuckle. "I think she's far from done, bro. Billie Bellerose will let you both know in no uncertain terms how she feels."

Fucker was right about that. Now that I knew everyone was safe, my fury was gone, but the low-simmering annoyance would stay for some time.

When Grayson hung up, he tried to talk to me again. "Baby, please. I'm sorry I had to haul you away like that, but we will *never* risk your safety more than absolutely necessary."

If I gritted my teeth any harder, I was likely to break them.

The silence extended, but it had never been my style to just stew away internally and not let my feelings out. Besides, unless I explained, he wouldn't truly understand why this had triggered me so hard.

"You four are the most important part of my life," I rasped, not even remotely disguising the pain I felt. "Every single time you hide me away while you face danger without me, it feels like you're stabbing me in the chest. I feel like you're putting me in a gilded cage, separate from you all, and I don't want that. Not now or ever." I sucked in a deep breath. "We're a team, right? I mean, we either are or we're not. Why don't you trust me in these situations? I'm not a fucking idiot who randomly throws myself into danger or anything like that. So... why do you treat me this way?"

It was a long speech, jumbled and messy, but since that was the norm for this relationship, I just went with it.

Grayson took a second to answer, such a long second that I wondered if he was even going to answer, and then he shocked me by taking a swift right turn, getting off the main road, and coming to a halt down a side street under a few large trees.

He turned in his seat, reaching over to unbuckle and haul me out of my seat and into his lap before I could take a surprised breath. He wrapped me up tightly, his arms briefly trembling before they stabilized around me.

Despite my lingering pain and anger, I melted into this hold, realizing that I needed this connection more than anything. A few hot tears escaped as I pressed my face into his chest, and he appeared to be breathing me in as his face buried against the side of my head.

"Baby, I'm sorry," he murmured. It was so odd to see Grayson vulnerable like this it knocked what remained of my anger loose. Knocked it loose so it could drift away until the pressure in my chest was gone.

Until I could finally breathe again.

"We don't put you in a gilded cage," he continued,

voice still muffled against me. "We protect you because you're our reason for existence. It's not that you're not capable. Fuck, we've all seen you shoot, and I have a feeling with a little more practice, you're going to outshoot every man I've ever known. Including myself. But we are your men. The boys of Bellerose. We were put on this fucking world to ensure that you were surrounded by love and protection. We can't stop doing that, not even for you."

Fucking hell. Now I just sounded like a petulant brat getting mad at them for loving me so much they had to protect me.

"It goes both ways," I told them. "A king is nothing without his queen, you know? We stand together, or we fall apart."

His hold grew even tighter, and despite the fact that I could barely breathe now, I would die like this before I told him to ease up. Poor dude was so worried about someone else breaking me that he'd forgotten he was the strongest person we all knew and could crush me in a heartbeat. Maybe that thought occurred to him in the same second because the pressure eased up. "Maybe we can both try and work on it," he finally suggested.

Grayson compromising on safety rules. Fuck. Second surprise of the day.

"I'd like that," I whispered. "If you had just let me in

462

on the plan, we would have fought about it before, but we'd have reached an agreement eventually. I don't like being kept in the dark because you all think I'm a girl and can't handle this shit." I mean, Vee and Giana more than proved that chicks could handle anything.

"We're all sorry for that. It was a last-minute decision made when we watched our fucking soul drive away in a car on her own. When we had to trust that Wilson wouldn't just walk up and put a bullet straight into your head. You have to understand how that felt, Prickles, for all of us—including Rhett, who has been blowing up every single one of our phones since you drove away."

"Fuck," I breathed. "I guess the fact that you did let me be the main distraction in this plan kind of negates my *keep me in a gilded cage* argument." My anger before had wiped out some of my reasoning skills. "And I love you all so much for loving me the way you do. I don't want to change your protective instincts—"

"Never," Grayson rumbled. "You can scream all day every day, Prickles. You're ours, and we protect what is ours."

That one hit me hard in the chest... and a little lower. Damn.

"I don't want to change you," I continued with a smile. "Just don't leave me in the dark again."

"Deal," Grayson said immediately, and before we

could utter another word, his mouth descended on mine. "Time for make-up sex."

My groan was low, and I had to start wiggling to try and ease some of the tension swirling in my gut. "Out here," I moaned, "in public?"

Grayson laughed, and it was finally carefree. "We can do whatever we want, baby girl, but I won't be sharing you with the world in that way. You're just going to have to wait until we get home."

I was back in my seat, belt in place, hands clenched in my lap as I fought the urge to touch myself. "Drive like we're in danger, big man," I said in a rush.

He laughed again, and fucking hell, I was growing addicted to the sound.

We made it back to Angelo's place in record time, and I was already figuring out how to ditch all my clothes before we'd even made it into the garage, only it seemed our plans were going to have to wait.

We had a visitor.

She was standing in front of the gates, two of our security on either side of her, not touching her but also not allowing her in. Grayson slowed to a halt, and when Fiorella Ricci, Angelo's completely absent-for-most-of-his life mother, approached my window, he shook his head and gestured for her to step around to his.

He hadn't been kidding about the protective thing

going nowhere, and I only felt love from his actions now. Fiorella didn't argue as she moved to where Grayson had lowered his window a fraction, his gun in his hand as he eyed her cooly. "What are you doing here?"

Grayson clearly knew who this was: the Ricci wife who was no mother to Angelo, since she'd spent most of her life overseas shopping or in a pill-induced stupor.

"I need to talk to Billie," she said softly, her expression blank. Giovanni had destroyed any life in her years ago. "Now that the players in this game are dead, I want closure too, and until I can get this off my chest, I won't find it. I know the reason for the Ricci-Bellerose feud. I know it all."

"Try fucking therapy," Grayson growled, before he started to raise the window again, but I stopped him by wrapping my hand around his forearm. He turned to me.

"I want to hear her out," I said with a nod. "Closure is important for everyone. I might have told Wilson I didn't care to hear his explanation, but a part of me still does want to know. I want the truth."

Grayson examined my features briefly, before he nodded. "Okay, Prickles. We will hear her out."

He gave the guards instructions to search her and then told them to bring her to the main living area on the first floor. He drove us into the garage after that, and then, keeping his gun in one hand, he handed me a second gun.

"You sweet talker," I teased, rubbing my thumb over the rough grip. "Always with the big gestures."

Grayson shook his head at me, the tough guy back in place again, but I saw his small smile. We entered the house together and arrived in the living area at the same time as Fiorella and the security. They deposited her on the couch. "She's clean. No weapons," the first one said to Grayson, and then Grayson dismissed them.

We didn't sit, choosing to stand over her, side by side and silent as we stared down at the petite woman, her dirty-blond hair perfectly styled, her pantsuit worth a few thousand bucks, and her soul dark and tarnished. My scowl grew.

Fiorella didn't give a shit, though; she'd grown up in the mafia world and was well used to being looked down upon by powerful people. I almost felt sorry for her. *Almost.* Because she'd had a child who needed his mother, and she'd never been there for him, choosing to escape and leave him in the clutches of that evil world.

"What do you need to tell me?" I asked shortly. Grayson and I had make-up sex to get to, and I really didn't want to waste time.

She cleared her throat, her joined hands fidgeting together. "I want to explain why your life turned out the way it did. Why my life turned out this way. And the reason you and Angelo have been and will always be tied together."

Jesus and fuck. If she told me that my dad was Angelo's dad too, I was going to shoot her on the couch. Then vomit.

"Calm, Prickles," Grayson said soothingly, clearly picking up on my distress. "Hear her out before you shoot her."

Bastard knew me so well. Fiorella went a little paler, but she didn't try and leave, so I had to give her some credit.

"Your father and I were childhood sweethearts," she said simply. "We grew up next door to each other, were best friends, and then lovers."

The panic I felt at this moment was second to none.

"I loved him with all my heart," she said with a choked sob. "And I believe he loved me."

I lifted the gun, and Grayson let out a laugh, holding my hand with the gun so I couldn't shut her the hell up. Not that I would, but *damn*.

"When I was sixteen, I crossed paths with Giovanni. He was a few years older and had recently inherited a new position in the family business. He had a fight with Bruce that night, and the next day, I was taken—stolen off the street as a punishment to the man who'd offended

Giovanni Ricci and forced to marry into the mafia family before the week was out."

I almost dropped the gun and didn't protest when Grayson took it from me. "You were kidnapped, and no one called the police?"

Her laugh was bitter. "The police are owned in this town. My fucking parents were owned. I'm fairly sure they were the ones who told the Riccis where to find me."

She shook her head, face screwed up as pain and anger took over. "I fought as hard as I could, but there was no hope. If I didn't go through with it, they would have killed Bruce. As it was, they beat him pretty badly."

"Then what happened?"

She swallowed hard, her throat moving as if she couldn't get the next words out. "I told Bruce I'd fallen in love with Giovanni. I told him that he had been just a stupid childhood crush and that he wasn't man enough for me. I told him whatever the fuck I had to tell him to keep him alive."

The parallels between our lives had my head spinning, and if Grayson hadn't been at my side holding me up, I would have fallen. "Why have you never mentioned this story to Angelo?" I breathed. "Why keep it to yourself for so long?"

She shrugged. "Giovanni is dead now. Bruce and Wilson are dead, and I hope to find some sort of peace with whatever years I have left, maybe even develop a relationship with Angelo since I don't have to panic that his father will use us against each other to get what he wants."

"Wilson literally *just* died," Grayson said roughly. "How do you know he's dead?"

She laughed. "I have my ways. I have survived by keeping up with all the underground news. You don't take out a player like Wilson without news of it spreading very fast. Surely, you didn't think you were alone out there?"

Great, at least that part of Vee's plan was coming to fruition. The scarier and faster this takeover happened, the securer their new reign would be.

Fiorella continued, clearly wanting to get it all out. "The reason that we lived next door to you all, when Giovanni could afford a much better house, was to taunt your father," she continued. "The reason he allowed Angelo to be friends with you was to torment your father, and the reason he took it all away in the end was to punish us all. I'm just sorry that you got caught up in the battle, that you ended up as collateral damage."

Giovanni was one petty bastard, but apparently, so was Bruce Bellerose.

The pieces were starting to fit together. "My father said he spent years trying to take down Giovanni, piece by piece. He faked an entire life with me and my mom all as part of his revenge plot."

Fiorella nodded. "Yes, after many years I admitted the truth to him, and he started trying to win me back. But I'd had Angelo by then, and I couldn't risk him. Not even for Bruce."

"What happened the night of the fire? Why did he lose what remained of his humanity then specifically?" Grayson asked, a question he'd clearly pondered over more than once.

She wore a look of pain. "Giovanni seduced your mom, Billie. They were having an affair, and Bruce found out. It was the last straw. I tried to talk him out of his plan, but he was a crazed man. From then on, he was Wilson. I'd never feared for myself around him before, but that night... what was left of my Bruce died. I went abroad the next day and have only returned when forced."

I honestly had no idea what to say. Not a fucking clue. I just stared at her and hated that she looked so much like my Angel. But there was a vast difference. She chose to run and hide, to take extended vacations while leaving her son to suffer at Giovanni's hands. Angelo would cut his own hands off before abandoning his loved ones.

"Get the fuck out of my house," I breathed, barely containing my anger. "You will find no peace or forgiveness here because your weakness cost all of us so much." I was being overly harsh, I could hear it in my every word, but I couldn't stop myself. She knew... all along, she knew about my dad. The suffering that she could have saved us all, had she spoken up sooner...

She didn't flinch. She didn't seem to care. Standing, she smoothed down her skirt. "All I needed to do was tell my side of the story. I don't care about your forgiveness."

"You never even apologized." I pointed out.

She hadn't. It had been an explanation, plain and simple. A way to relieve her own mental burden, but with very little accountability for her role in it all. Sure, she'd never asked to be kidnapped and have her life stolen like that, but fuck, if she didn't at least attempt to stab Giovanni while he slept, I'd never have an ounce of respect for her.

Logically, I knew I was holding an abused woman accountable for her own shitty situation and that wasn't fair. But I was so enraged I was shaking. Maybe one day when I cooled down, I could apologize. Today wasn't that day.

Once she was gone, I collapsed on the couch, and Grayson lifted me once more into his lap. "You okay, Prickles?"

I just shook my head. "Not even remotely."

It felt like my mind was fracturing, a cracking pane of

glass that continued to shatter as her story stirred in my mind. Thankfully, the door opened a few seconds later, and when Jace and Angelo entered the room, I took one look at them and burst into tears.

Jace hadn't been kidding about the therapy thing. I would be camping out at Dr. Candace's office until she could see me.

No fucking excuses.

Fiorella Ricci taught me one thing with her weak bullshit attempt at an explanation. It was time to wipe the slate clear and move forward from this.

As my boys surrounded me, I knew that unlike her, I had everything to live for now, and I planned on doing just that.

epilogue part one

BILLIE

EIGHT MONTHS LATER.

"Billie Bellerose," Dr. Candace said with a broad smile. "I've been waiting all morning to see you."

The doc had taken to using my full name when we started our session, mimicking the media's overuse of *Billie Bellerose* for the past eight months. The *boys of Bellerose* had been trending across all social media platforms for months, fueled by the marketing genius of Brenda, who remained the boys' publicist.

"Can I just start our last session by saying how proud

I am of you, Billie," she continued. "The woman who sits before me today would barely recognize the woman who sat on my couch a little over a year ago."

My smile was genuine because the doc was right. So much had changed over the past year that I wasn't remotely the same person. It was bittersweet to know that this would be my last session with Dr. Candace for a long time. The boys and I were about to set out on a worldwide tour for our new indie label, Bellerose Music, starting tonight in Madison Square Garden. Our plane was leaving in two hours, so this was my last chance for therapy and closure.

Not that I hadn't spent the last eight months ensuring that I could have the clean slate I'd always wanted.

"Let's just sum up the last eight months, Billie," Dr Candace said with her gentle smile, "so you can truly see how far you've come. I know we've covered all of this many times, but this is the moment you acknowledge your hard work and growth and enjoy the bright future you've fought so hard for."

"I can hardly believe it," I said with a sigh. "I've never known as much happiness as I do today, with all the dark clouds that had been hanging over us finally gone."

She just smiled, waiting patiently for me to continue. Dr. Candace had a real skill in knowing when someone needed her help to get words out and when they just needed an extra second to rearrange their thoughts.

"Okay, let's start with Rhett," I said, thinking of my sweet knight. "His family is dealt with, once and for all. Townsend Community is no longer, and the town of Townsend is now the number one refuge in America for women escaping abusive relationships. His kind heart somehow managed to turn a depraved, misogynistic, brainwashed cult into something truly good.

Dr. Candace nodded. "Rhett is one of the most genuinely kind souls I've ever known. I'm grateful that you have each other. And the rest of your band."

No one was more grateful for that than me.

"Jace's sister, Tess, has been so much help in Townsend. Her knowledge about trauma survival and recovery was instrumental in saving many of Jeremiah's victims. And surprisingly enough, now that Mary has had time to rest and recoup, she's turning into a real powerhouse in dealing with trauma victims. She and Rhett don't have a super close relationship, but their closure has really helped him move on."

"Outside of checking in on his mom, does Rhett have anything to do with Townsend these days?" Dr. Candace asked. "The last time we chatted, he was scaling back his duties there."

I smiled. "Not a lot. That city will always hold trauma

and bad memories for him. His focus is mostly on our new label."

Dr. Candace didn't appear shocked by this, since she knew Rhett pretty well by now, even if their therapy sessions were also coming to an end, at least for now.

"What about Angelo?" she continued. "Is everything still clear on that front for him?"

It wasn't like we'd shared the craziest parts of our lives, such as the planned murder of Wilson and such, but I had told her about Giovanni and the accident on the stairs, and she knew that there had been a lot of upheaval in our lives over the last few months. "Angel is perfect," I said with a smile. "He's all in with Bellerose, and their new album is the best music I have ever heard from any of them, full stop. I can't wait for the world to hear these songs."

"Starting tonight, right?" she said with a smile. "Lots of debut numbers, I'm guessing."

"Yep," I confirmed. "The fact that an indie band can sell out Madison Square Garden, and a full world tour, is mind-blowing. The boys are so happy, and fuck, that makes me so happy too. It's almost too much."

A broad smile flashed her perfect, white teeth. "You deserve it, Billie. This is the future that should have always been."

Most of the time in therapy, Dr. Candace was all

professional, but occasionally, she made a statement that told me she genuinely cared about me and my future, that she had been rooting for us all along.

She relaxed into her chair. "This is one of the happiest moments I've had in my many years doing this job. To know that you have made the choice to live an unconventional life with Jace, Angelo, Grayson, and Rhett and that you're all thriving and successful... I could ask for no other outcomes from our last session together. And I'll be buying *Beautiful Thorns* the moment it's available."

The next Bellerose album. The accumulation of the last year of work and pain and change and loss but, most of all, the last year of love.

"Thank you, Dr. Candace," I said, standing because we were done here.

She stood as well, and I was shocked when she stepped forward and wrapped her arms around me. "I know this is unprofessional," she whispered as she gave me a squeeze. "But let's keep it between us."

I hugged her back so hard, my eyes burning. This woman had been a lifeline many times as I traversed dangerous storms of emotions. She had given me tools to deal with my past and my future. I admired and respected her so much. "Thank you for everything," I choked out. "I'll never forget how you saved me."

"Oh, Billie. You saved yourself," she said as she pulled away. "And you always will."

I got out of there before I bawled all over her, and when I saw a familiar car in the parking lot, the swell of joy inside me couldn't be contained. I sprinted toward it, unsurprised when four gorgeous, talented, perfect—for me—men emerged to greet me.

Grayson reached me first, pressing a long kiss on my lips before he handed me off to Rhett, who cuddled me into his body, his eyes closed as he breathed me in. Jace and Angelo were last, the two of them hugging me together, as was their preferred way.

"We missed you, Bella," Angelo said pressing a kiss to my forehead. "Are you ready to leave?"

I nodded. "Oh yeah. I can't wait, actually."

Our bags were packed and in the car, the plane sitting on the runway just waiting for its band, and we were off to the city. New York City.

Fuck yeah.

The noise was deafening as the crowds erupted, screaming and stomping their feet. I'd been to a lot of Bellerose concerts by this point, but there had been nothing comparable to this. It wasn't the largest venue they'd played in, with the sold-out show only holding about twenty thousand, but there were at least a hundred thousand more in the streets around the arena, screaming for Bellerose.

My boys, the four rock-fucking-stars of my dreams, were the most famous band in the world once more, and they were doing it all on their own.

The opening acts had already finished up now, and Bellerose had just taken their spots on stage, hence the crowd losing their mind. Watching from a suite were Jace's parents and Tess, along with Vee and Giana, who refused to miss the opening leg of the Burning Bridges Tour.

Yeah, they weren't even remotely subtle about how they felt these days.

I'd decided for this part I wanted to be closer to them, so I was side stage where they could all see me and I could see them. I was part of Bellerose as well, even if I never stepped foot onstage.

"New York," Jace said into the mic, the low husky thrum of his voice sending the fans to heaven. And he hadn't even sung a song yet. "We're so fucking happy to be here tonight. I know it's been a long time since you saw us all live, and so much shit has gone down, but we are back, better than fucking ever. This is as authentic as you'll ever get our music. Strap the fuck in."

He strummed the first chord of their opening song, "Lead from the Heart." This was not one of their newer numbers, but it was the first single they'd released after leaving Big Noise, so it was well known.

They'd dropped half a dozen tracks in the lead-up to their new album, which had kept everyone desperate for the final release.

They played by no one's rules but their own, and it was working exactly as we'd hoped. Jace's voice cut through the noise as he began to sing, the music fading for real impact at the beginning of this song.

Through the sorrow and pain, across the lies and the shame, we broke through the chains.

The oceans may fade, and we bleed through the rain, but our heart will never change. Not through this or the fame.

Heeeere we stand. Together and stronger than ever before.

Heeere we stand. Saying no fucking more.

We lead from the heart, and we won't be torn apart.

We broke through the chains, we annihilated the pain, and we lead from the heart. No fucking chance for regret, no more loss or demands, we are stronger than ever before.

There was still no backing music, outside of a few chords from Rhett, and the crowd sang along so loudly that chills chased up and down my spine through the entire opening verse and chorus of the song.

Halfway through, the rest of the band joined in,

adding their instruments to the magic of Jace's voice, and I realized that tears were tracking down my cheeks. Everything about this moment was filled with pure emotion and happiness, filling every part of me, and I wondered if this would ever be topped.

Standing here, together, and finally free.

The rest of the concert was the most incredible experience of my life. I'd heard them all play and sing a million times now, but tonight they were next level, every single one of them a once-in-a-lifetime talent.

The new songs were met with the same frenzy as old favorites, and I had the sense that this new album would break records. Maybe all the records. As far as I was concerned, biased as I was, there was no limit to what Bellerose could achieve.

Not now that they were no longer restricted by stupid bigwigs who had no idea what true music lovers wanted.

"You have been fucking amazing tonight," Jace said, moving forward on the stage as he engaged twenty-plus thousand people with his fucking presence. Charismatic bastard. Fuck, I loved him. "And we can't say how grateful we all are for the support you've shown us. We only have two songs left for you tonight, but just know this is only the beginning for Bellerose. We'll never stop giving back to you all, and this one is for you."

This was one of their new songs, and it was a love

ballad to their fans. Once again, it was Jace's beautiful voice accompanied by only a few chords on his guitar, and then the chorus was all four members of Bellerose joining together to express their fucking love and gratitude to the people out there in the stands—the reason they got to make music and live this amazing life.

"They're amazing, right?"

I'd been mesmerized, standing on the edge of the stage, hand pressed to my heart as I sang along. I'd help write many of these songs, but it was their music and voices and presence that truly brought them to life.

The person who'd spoken was one of their new roadies, someone who probably had no idea who I was because the boys were overly protective of me still, to the point that when we walked, they stayed around me like a circle of bodyguards.

"They're beyond words," I breathed with a happy sigh. My bodyguard for tonight shuffled forward then, but I waved him off. "All good, Sam," I said shortly, before I went back to watching the band. The roadie shot me a curious look, then seemed to realize that they had a job to do and scurried off.

When Jace finished that number, the crowd screamed, and I was fairly sure there was a lot of crying too, since there was only one song left.

"Before we finish up tonight," Jace said as the crowd grew quiet once more, wanting to hear his words, "there's someone that we need to thank. Someone that you all know pretty well by now, thanks to the media's obsession with our lives. Someone who co-wrote every single one of these songs. I know you're all aware that Billie Bellerose is a fucking smokeshow. Girl absolutely slays me every single time she looks my way. But what you may not know is that she's the most talented songwriter in the world. I'll fucking take on anyone who wants to argue that fact. Can't sing for shit, but she will destroy you with her words. And there's no way we can finish up this concert without expressing our thanks to the person who saved our lives."

As I stood there in shock, blinking and wondering if my damn ears were malfunctioning, all four of my boys turned and held their hands out to me.

On the motherfucking stage.

I shook my head, desperately freaking out that I would throw up or do something embarrassing like fart the moment I went on stage. My stomach wasn't feeling the most stable, in all truth, so this wasn't even a weird intrusive thought.

"Baby, can you come out here," Jace said with a laugh. "Come on, Rose. We're all friends here."

The crowd was screaming and stomping their feet,

and I heard my name chanted over and over. *Billie Bellerose. Billie Bellerose. Billie Bellerose.*

Yeah, apparently, I was always going to be a full-name kind of chick from here on out.

This wouldn't end until I found my way onto the stage, so I forced my shaking legs to move, thankful I was wearing a fairly decent rock-star outfit in black, ripped-up jeans; black, heeled boots; and a cropped Bellerose tank that showed off a sliver of my tanned stomach. My blond hair was tied back in a high ponytail, and my makeup was all smoky eyes and nude lips, so I was as physically ready as I'd ever be.

The rest though... *just don't fart.*

"There you are," Jace said, that perfect smile in place, and I narrowed my eyes at him.

I'm going to kill you, I mouthed, and he just laughed.

Moving a little easier, I focused on Jace, ignoring the thousands of faces out there before us. When my hand landed in his, most of my nerves faded away, and I let myself relax and return his smile. "Hey," I said, my voice projecting through the mics out into the stands.

"Hey, love," he replied, and all I could hear was *awwwww*s.

Turning to the crowd, I shot them a cheeky smile. "Don't let him fool you; he's not always this sweet."

There was laughter, and when I turned back to Jace, I

gasped to see all of the band there. My boys surrounded me once more, and as I looked between them, I wondered what they were doing. "We have something to give you, Thorn," Rhett said, confirming to the world exactly why their next album had the name *Beautiful Thorns*. That and a play on the full circle they'd come since *Poison Roses*.

"Are you ready for this, little hedgehog?" Grayson rumbled, and fuck if the crowd didn't lose their minds a little.

Angelo leaned over and kissed my cheek. "This is for you, Bella."

He strummed a chord, and it wasn't the familiar opening to any of the songs I'd worked on with them.

"What's this called?" I whispered, though there was no real way to be quiet with this many mics.

"'It's our new title track on the upcoming album, Beautiful Thorns,'" Jace said, then leaned into the microphone to address the crowd, "available on Spotify next Thursday, you guys, don't forget to stream it."

Then his smile turned intimate as he leaned in and kissed me solidly on the lips. "This is for you, Billie Bellerose."

Every bad thing that had happened to me through my life had led me to being strong enough to make it to this moment. To be able to stand on stage with four rock stars, while they serenaded me with our love story.

Jace's smile was sexy and sweet as he started to sing.

It was the eyes that got me first, little girl of green,

As you stole my rock collection and my heart, as it may seem.

The one who challenged us through the years as we all fought against the fall.

But there's no way to fight fate. Billie Bellerose, you're our greatest love of all.

So much for not embarrassing myself as I started to literally sob on stage, looking between all four of them as they joined in, the softest melody I'd ever heard from them swelling around me.

With the help of the band, Jace wove our story into the most beautiful song I'd ever heard. Piece by piece, broken shards were made whole again, until the moment we stood here tonight, with thousands watching us.

And when all of my boys joined him for the last line, "Billie Bellerose, you're our greatest love of all," I wasn't the only one crying. The entire fucking stadium sang along, all of them bawling as hard as me, and now I knew this was the moment.

The best moment of my life.

Well, the best moment so far. Which was a fucking amazing thought.

It was only going to get better from here.

epilogue part two

BILLIE

The high of the flawless concert had us all buzzing as if we'd been doing lines of the best quality cocaine. I'd never fully grasped the concept of being *high on life* before, but the elation and satisfaction we all shared was something from another planet. Added to that, though, I was tingling with excitement over the surprise I'd planned for my guys tonight.

The whole drive from Madison Square Garden back to our new home in SoHo I could barely sit still, but I also wouldn't let the guys get too handsy in the back of the limo. I had an important question to ask and the perfect location all set up for the *big moment*. So I playfully batted their hands away when things got heated, telling them to be patient.

We'd moved into our new home six months ago, when Rhett started handing over the Townsend Community to the team he'd hired, spearhead by Tess. It was a five-story terrace, which gave us all our own bedrooms—allowing us each our privacy and individual space—as well as a top-level *fuck pad* for all the kinky sex fun a woman could get up to with her four *very* enthusiastic lovers.

We'd hired an incredible interior decorator named Hank, who'd absolutely nailed our vision, and the house had quickly become *home*. There had been no debate when it came to leaving Siena and Naples. Those cities held so much darkness for us, and that poisonous residue had no place in our happily ever after. We'd been unanimous on that.

But I'd been waiting for *this* night, *this* concert, which marked the first official moment of our futures, to take this next big step.

"Are you gonna tell us what's got you all squirrelly, Prickles?" Grayson drawled as we climbed out of our limo. "You look like you've got a secret."

I couldn't wipe the grin from my face. "I do."

"Well, we're dying to know..." Rhett prompted, but I just blew him a kiss and skipped up our front stairs. He caught up to me as I unlocked the door with the thumbprint scanner we'd had installed, and kissed my neck as I keyed in the alarm codes. We'd learned our lesson about securing our safe space.

"I'm nervous," I admitted in a whisper, leading the guys into the foyer of our cozy, beautiful home.

"Why?" Jace asked suspiciously, slipping out of his leather jacket and hanging it on a coat hook.

I shrugged. "Because... this is a big deal. And I feel weirdly like I'm flipping gender roles by asking..." Fuck, I'd already said too much. My face flaming, I hurried past the stairs to a door which *used* to lead to a storage cavity beneath the stairs.

"So..." I paused with my hand on the knob, turning to face the four of them. "I've been working on a surprise for you all."

"For us?" Angelo asked, tilting his head in question.

I nodded. "Well, for *us*. All of us. I thought..." I trailed off, blowing a long breath with nervous energy. "Screw it, I'll just show you."

Before I could pussy out, I twisted the doorhandle and pushed the door open. Instead of revealing a storage closet, it revealed a newly constructed set of stairs leading down. I flicked on the lights, then stood aside for them to enter.

"Why do I feel like Alice heading down the rabbit

hole?" Rhett teased, brushing a kiss over my lips as he passed. I took up the rear, watching for their reactions as they reached the bottom. There was another door they needed to pass through, then it opened up into a huge space.

"Holy shit," Jace breathed when I flipped the switch to light up the room. "*This* is what you've been so sneaky about these last few weeks?"

I grinned, casting my eyes around the newly completed recording studio. "Yup."

"This is so cool," Rhett enthused, running his finger over the neon *Bellerose Music* sign hanging on the wall, while Angelo and Grayson checked out all the sound mixing decks. "Are we next door right now?"

I nodded again. "Yup. I bought the building a couple of months ago. It's going to be the new *Bellerose Music* headquarters, but this was the first area we renovated." Filled with nervous excitement, I switched on the lights inside the recording booth and held my breath.

"Rose, baby," Jace purred in my ear, his hands gripping my hips from behind as we looked through the glass. "Is there something you wanted to say?"

I bit my lip, my cheeks hot. The inside of the recording booth was set up with a bed, decked out in lush pillows and bedding and scattered with rose petals. Fairy lights decorated the ceiling, making it seem like twinkling stars.

Taking his hand in mine, I pushed open the door from the sound booth and crossed over to the bed, where I pushed him to sit, then indicated for the other guys to join him on the bed. They all did as directed, watching me with varying degrees of confusion and curiosity.

My heart raced, and I drew a deep breath as I took it all in. It was perfect. *They* were perfect.

"Guys... I have something I've been wanting to ask you all for a really long time, but we've all been *so busy* lately that I just kept waiting for the perfect moment. But then I realized I needed to *make* our moment. And I don't think I could think of any more perfect one than this, after your MSG debut as the *new* Bellerose under our own record label, in our very own recording studio." I wet my lips, the excitement nearly bringing tears to my eyes. "I know it's something we've kind of joked about before, but I can't get it out of my head and... I just know I'm ready. We're ready."

Grayson leaned forward, his dark gaze intense. "Ready for what, Prickles?"

The unquestionable love and adoration in his gaze gave me the boost I needed, and I sank slowly to my knees on the carpeted floor in front of them. My boys.

"Will you..." *Oh shit, was I brave enough to really ask for what I wanted?* Yes. Yes, I was. "Guys. Will you... try triple penetration with me?"

The stunned looks on their faces said I'd taken them all by surprise, and a flash of panic zapped through me as I questioned if maybe I was taking it a step too far. But then Rhett whooped a laugh and scooped me up off the floor, dragging me onto the big bed with all of them.

"I thought you'd never fucking ask, Thorn! Yes. Fuck yes. Wait, are we talking double ass or double vag? Because I don't want you to get hurt, and if—"

"Not double ass," Angelo snapped, scowling. "That could damage her, and we have to be on a long-haul flight tomorrow."

"I'm cool with double in the pussy," Jace piped up, nodding enthusiastically. "Who do you want where, Rose? You look like you have it all planned out." His grin went sly as he tipped his head to the pump bottle of lube strategically placed beside the bed.

Happiness bubbled through my chest as they worked together to strip me naked, then shed their own clothes. These boys were *all in*; I couldn't believe I'd second-guessed whether they'd do this with me.

"Um, I think... I don't want Rhett and Angel getting their piercings caught against each other, so maybe can we try Angel and Jace in front and Rhett behind? Sorry, big man, I need you in my mouth for this one." I offered

Grayson an apologetic smile, but his answering smirk was pure fire.

"Fine by me," he rumbled, "so long as I can have my pick of positions when the three of them blow."

I nodded so hard my head nearly bobbled off my shoulders. Everyone was so excited to try this new combination that foreplay was rushed at best. Handfuls of lube were spread around, then Gray generously offered to get me warmed up on his cock.

He placed his back against the pillows, dragged me into his lap, and stuffed his massive equipment into me way faster than usual. I was so lubed up that it didn't hurt, but *by god* it felt amazing as he stretched my pussy out to take him all. A litany of curses fell from my lips as he gripped my hips, using his strength to lift and lower me on his monster, faster and faster until I was nearly ready to come. Then the bastard slammed me down hard and held me still.

"Bend forward, sweetheart," he told me in a deep purr. "Let Rhett prepare that tight little ass for his cock."

I moaned as Rhett did just that, squirting even more lube into me and starting with his fingers. I'd been putting in the work over the last few weeks, though, begging the boys to fuck my ass any time we had a spare moment in our schedules and wearing plugs when we were all too busy to mess around. I was totally ready, and

Rhett knew it because he soon swapped out fingers for a pierced dick head.

"That's it, Beautiful Thorn," he praised as I pushed back on his cock. "You're a fucking queen, you know that?"

"A dirty, filthy, sex-addicted queen," Jace agreed, standing beside the bed with his erection firmly in hand as he watched. "Hurry up, Gray, you're in our spot."

Grayson *did not* hurry up. In fact, he took his sweet fucking time as he and Rhett pounded a screaming climax out of me, but then he reluctantly lifted me off his dick when Rhett moved back.

"Fine," he huffed, fisting his throbbing shaft. "But I hope you all napped this afternoon because this is gonna go all night."

My breathing was too harsh for me to get words out, but they all knew I was totally on board.

Rhett took Grayson's position, lying on his back, then guided me to straddle him reverse-cowgirl style. Jace lifted my hips, his mouth closing over my clit while Rhett pushed his cock back into my asshole from beneath. Whimpers and moans escaped my throat at how *good* it felt, and Jace only prolonged that feeling as his tongue speared into my pussy.

"You good there, Thorn?" Rhett asked, sounding breathless.

"Uh-huh," I gasped, my hands gripping Jace's hair tight and demanding more. My thighs were already shaking; it wouldn't take much to make me come again.

"Patience, Bella," Angelo chuckled, peeling my fingers out of Jace's hair and tugging his face away from my cunt. Dammit. Not that they left me waiting long, though. A moment later, Jace was on his knees, his fist wrapped around his base as he fed the tip through my wet folds.

"Oh my god," I moaned, shuddering in ecstasy as he filled my pussy up with his cock, moving in countermotion to Rhett's slow, shallow thrusts in my ass. Fucking hell. Was I really ready for three?

Screw it. We'd come this far... why not try it?

The guys needed a bit of awkward shuffling to get their positioning right, but ultimately, we'd *all* watched enough porn to be well aware whose legs needed to go where in order for all three dicks to fit inside me at once. Months ago, when Rhett and I had started watching that kind of porn, I'd been in shock and disbelief that it was even possible. Now, though, I was much better educated about how stretchy the vagina could be. And more than ready to put it to the test.

"The things we do for love," Jace muttered as he held onto Angelo's naked hips, steadying his friend while their cocks smooshed together and Angelo pushed his way inside. "Christ, bro, those ladder rungs are an experience."

Angelo chuckled, pushing a little further into me. "That's what Bella tells me. You still with us, baby girl?"

"Uh-huh," I squeaked, keeping my legs spread as wide as physically possible while they filled me tighter than I'd even thought possible.

"Good," Grayson rumbled, kneeling on the bed. "Now, open that pretty mouth for me."

I did as ordered, flattening my tongue and holding eye contact as he inserted the tip of his huge cock into my mouth. I closed my lips around him, trying hard to focus on sucking cock, but it was impossible. How could anyone even remember their own name with that much dick inside at once?

Who the fuck needed marriage and babies to know their love was unbreakable? Not me, that was for sure. My guys showed me in a thousand different ways, every damn day, that they were in it for this lifetime and the next—that what we had was stronger than any fleeting liaison. It was a soul connection that no one could shake. We were made for each other, the five of us, and needed no *formality* to reinforce that fact.

I'd never known anyone could love this strongly, but I thanked all the stars that I now knew it. We all did, and we weren't afraid to show it.

Moaning, I gave myself over to the intense experience that I'd been dreaming about for months. My whole body radiated pleasure as the boys found their pace, fucking me together. All of them, all at once.

My Boys of Bellerose.

...and we all lived happily ever after.

The End.

also by tate james

Madison Kate

#1 HATE

#2 LIAR

#3 FAKE

#4 KATE

#4.5 VAULT (to be read after Hades series)

Hades

#1 7th Circle

#2 Anarchy

#3 Club 22

#4 Timber

The Guild

#1 Honey Trap

#2 Dead Drop

#3 Kill Order

Valenshek Legacy

#1 Heist

Dark Legacy

#1 Broken Wings

#2 Broken Trust

#3 Broken Legacy

#4 Dylan (standalone)

Royals of Arbon Academy

#1 Princess Ballot

#2 Playboy Princes

#3 Poison Throne

Hijinx Harem

#1 Elements of Mischief

#2 Elements of Ruin

#3 Elements of Desire

The Wild Hunt Motorcycle Club

#1 Dark Glitter

#2 Cruel Glamour (TBC)

#3 Torn Gossamer (TBC)

Foxfire Burning

#1 The Nine

#2 The Tail Game (TBC)

#3 TBC (TBC)

Undercover Sinners

also by jaymin eve

Boys of Bellerose (Dark, RH rock star romance 18+)

Book One: Poison Roses (Release Jan 2023)

Book Two: Dirty Truths (Release Feb 2023)

Book Three: Shattered Dreams (Release March 2023)

Book Four: Beautiful Thorns (Release April 2023)

Demon Pack (Complete PNR/Urban Fantasy 18+)

Book One: Demon Pack

Book Two: Demon Pack Elimination

Book Three: Demon Pack Eternal

Shadow Beast Shifters (Complete PNR/Urban Fantasy 18+)

Book One: Rejected

Book Two: Reclaimed

Book Three: Reborn

Book Four: Deserted

Book Five: Compelled

Book Six: Glamoured

Supernatural Prison Trilogy (Complete UF series 17+)

Book One: Dragon Marked

Book Two: Dragon Mystics

Book Three: Dragon Mated

Book Four: Broken Compass

Book Five: Magical Compass

Book Six: Louis

Book Seven: Elemental Compass

Supernatural Academy (Complete Urban Fantasy/PNR 18+)

Year One

Year Two

Year Three

Royals of Arbon Academy (Complete Dark Contemporary Romance 18+)

Book One: Princess Ballot

Book Two: Playboy Princes

Book Three: Poison Throne

Titan's Saga (Complete PNR/UF. Sexy and humorous 18+)

Book One: Releasing the Gods

Book Two: Wrath of the Gods

Book Three: Revenge of the Gods

Dark Legacy (Complete Dark Contemporary high school romance 18+)

Book One: Broken Wings

Book Two: Broken Trust

Book Three: Broken Legacy

Secret Keepers Series (Complete PNR/Urban Fantasy)

Book One: House of Darken

Book Two: House of Imperial

Book Three: House of Leights

Book Four: House of Royale

Storm Princess Saga (Complete High Fantasy)

Book One: The Princess Must Die

Book Two: The Princess Must Strike

Book Three: The Princess Must Reign

Curse of the Gods Series (Complete Reverse Harem Fantasy 18+)

Book One: Trickery

Book Two: Persuasion

Book Three: Seduction

Book Four: Strength

Novella: Neutral

Book Five: Pain

NYC Mecca Series (Complete - UF series)

Book One: Queen Heir

Book Two: Queen Alpha

Book Three: Queen Fae

Book Four: Queen Mecca

A Walker Saga (Complete - YA Fantasy)

Book One: First World

Book Two: Spurn

Book Three: Crais

Book Four: Regali

Book Five: Nephilius

Book Six: Dronish

Book Seven: Earth

Hive Trilogy (Complete UF/PNR series)

Book One: Ash

Book Two: Anarchy

Book Three: Annihilate

Sinclair Stories (Standalone Contemporary Romance)

Songbird

Printed in Great Britain
by Amazon

20738809R00294